Prairie Rose

Prairie Rose

SUSAN KIRBY

AVON BOOKS ⬙ NEW YORK

PRAIRIE ROSE is an original publication of Avon Books. This work has never before appeared in book form. This work is a novel. Any similarity to actual persons or events is purely coincidental.

AVON BOOKS
A division of
The Hearst Corporation
1350 Avenue of the Americas
New York, New York 10019

Copyright © 1997 by Susan Kirby
Published by arrangement with the author

ISBN: 0-380-78503-X

In loving memory of Aunt Rosemary

Prologue

May 1904

🏵 Elizabeth Watson hopped up on the steel train track at the edge of the small town called Thistle Down. The sunshine set her long copper curls aflame and highlighted a fistful of freckles across her fair cheeks. Blue-eyed and bubbling with energy, she had promised herself this rest throughout a day of cooking and washing and seeing to the needs of her father's household. Her sleeves were rolled up. Her shirtwaist was open at the throat, exposing a slim white neck. A capricious breeze molded her muslin apron and blue gingham dress to her small frame. The southern Illinois countryside, a profusion of spring color and fragrance, dipped and rolled and curved about her as she tripped nimbly down the train tracks, slim arms outstretched, singing with childlike abandon:

"Come Thou Fount of every blessing, tune my heart to sing Thy grace; streams of mercy, never ceasing, call for songs of loudest praise . . ." Her foot slipped from the rail. She laughed at herself and tried to tailor her stride to the irregularly spaced ties between the rails. The soles of her high-button shoes were thin from wear, and the rocks filling the space between ties jabbed her feet. She alternated from rails to ties to the weedy shoulder, and back again, all the while singing, "Teach me some melodious sonnet, sung by flaming tongues above; praise the Mount! I'm fixed upon it, Mount of Thy redeeming love."

1

Two section men came toward her in a handcar. Both were local men. She stepped off to the side as they bore down on her, their handcar gliding over the rail with the whisper of steel on steel.

" 'Lo, Miss Libby. Nice day for a stroll, ain't it?" one fellow called.

"So long as you watch where you put yer feet." The second fellow's eyes twinkled in a leathery face. "I seen a bull snake about a hundred yards back."

"Don't you worry about him. I'm feeling kindly toward reptiles today," countered Libby.

The men went on their way, their laughter trailing behind them.

A mile from town Libby paused, eye drawn to the tall wooden tank where the steam engines took on water. Once, on a dare, she'd followed her brother Jacob up there for a swim. Though it was only May, she was nearly hot enough to try it again. The whim was sufficient to curl her lips at the corners.

Feeling the tremor of a distant train, Libby left the tracks just beyond the Calkin switch. She skidded down the steep ditch, jumped the trickle of water running along the bottom, and clamored up the other bank to the chutes and corral.

Colonel Calkin had constructed the convenience for shipping cattle and horses and mules by rail. The fenced-in pasture and rocky woodlands beyond belonged to the golden-haired colonel too. A decorated Civil War veteran, he had retired to private life a dozen years ago to oversee the mining interests and the farm he'd inherited from his father. Stoutheaded, impervious to public opinion, he could not abide any hint of weakness in man, woman, or beast. In Libby's opinion, this streak of intolerance in his character accounted not only for his bachelorhood, but for the rapidity with which he fired miners and traded livestock.

Wary of being caught by the old warhorse, she climbed to the top fence board and took a good look around before whistling to the sorrel mare. Bootsie, the colonel's buggy horse, held the longest tenure in the pasture. She lifted her head and came trotting over to the fence.

"There's my Bootsie. Pretty lass, good old girl, too sweet for the likes of the old scoundrel colonel, aren't you. Yes!"

Libby held out an apple and chuckled at the warm damp sensation of the horse's soft muzzle tickling her hand. Jumping to the ground, she stroked the mare's neck and took another careful look around. No sign of the colonel or his hired men. Satisfied, she pulled a rope from her apron pocket and with quick, sure fingers fixed it to Bootsie's halter before climbing back up on the fence. After gathering her long skirts in one hand, she slipped from the paint-bare board onto the mare's broad back. She waved away a floating cloud of insects and let Bootsie enjoy her bribe before nudging her with her heels.

The rope was a mere formality. The mare knew the destination. She broke into an easy canter, the breeze rippling her mane and sifting Libby's long hair. The simple harmony of blue sky, green earth, and pounding hooves blew away the responsibilities of the day. Nearing the fence that enclosed and separated the pasture from the wooded hillside, the horse stopped of her own accord. Libby tangled her feet in her skirt as she dismounted, and fell in a heap.

She scrambled up and flung her arms wide to the world, improvising, "Praise the mount! I just slipped from it! Pick me up, and brush me off!"

Laughing out loud, she reclaimed her rope, pressed her cheek to Bootsie's neck, and petted her with soft-spoken praises until the rumble of a train on the rails that skirted the pasture sent the handsome sorrel racing away.

Someday. Someway when things were better, she would toss her head, too, and gallop away. Libby lifted her face to the sun, dreaming of new sights, new faces, new experiences far removed from this rough little mining town.

A cloud scuttled overhead, stealing the warmth from her face. Her heart jerked, torn for an instant between the tug of home and the tow of independence. But the shadow passed quickly. She was seventeen; her heart brimmed with dreams. Writing dreams. To come true, she must first *live*. Grab life with both fists. Taste it, touch it, smell it, hear it, feel it, until she was full and could spill it onto the page. Like the water tank back at the switch. Ninety-five-thousand gallon capacity, she'd read in the paper, but useless unless it was connected to the well beneath.

Pleased with the comparison, Libby started up the steep bluff where squirrels scampered over rocks and birds sang and the earth gave off its rich musky scent. From the top there was a breathtaking view of up and down country, with timbered hills and lush shadowy ravines. She sat down on the exposed root of a burly old oak and tucked her knees beneath her chin, gazing down on the meandering creek and a waving sea of bluebells. A fusion of blues and greens with textures of bark and limb and last year's moldering leaves carpeted the earth. Inspired, she withdrew a folded paper and a pencil from her pocket and tried for a moment to paint in words the scene before her.

Her attempt fell short. She wrinkled her nose, but wasn't discouraged. She'd been entrusted with a gift as a storyteller. She would not, like the faithless steward, drop it in a hole and throw dirt upon it. It'd take another year, maybe two, but she'd save her washing money for college. *If Father can get along without me. If Adam doesn't feel unfairly burdened. If David doesn't make too much of a fuss.*

All of the *ifs* were a reminder of just how fragile the plan was. Restless, Libby stirred to her feet and poked beneath a dead elm until she'd found enough mush-rooms, tasty morels, to fill her apron pocket. She started back beneath the canopy of trees just as the deep, melodic blast of another train whistle came floating through the woods.

Old Lonesome. Owned by a small local line that linked up with the busier lines running to the larger cities, the train would sidetrack to take on water at the Calkin switch. If she hurried, she could ride it back to town. But it wasn't the saved steps that excited her. And it wasn't the certain welcome of the aging engineer, endeared to her since early childhood. It was the whistle and the simple act of *going*.

"Let thy goodness, like a fetter, bind my wand'ring heart to thee. Prone to wander, Lord, I feel it . . ."

Snatches from the final verse of the song floated in her head as she raced to catch Old Lonesome.

1

➹ Libby awakened the next day with the same song in her head. The red glow of sunrise and the dew upon the lilacs crowded it out for a time. As the sun climbed into the azure sky, she wiped the clotheslines clean and began the wash, belting out the lighthearted lyrics to "In the Good Old Summertime" and the song on everyone's lips, "Meet Me in St. Louis Louis." But by midafternoon, the old hymn came floating back. Libby swung the wicker basket onto one slender hip and lugged the wet laundry out into the sunshine, once again singing, "Come Thou Fount of every blessing, tune my heart to sing Thy grace; teach me some melodious sonnet, sung by flaming tongues above."

The old blacksmith across the alley stepped out of his shop and thrust a red-hot plow shear into a wooden water barrel. "Hey you, caterwaulin' amongst the sheets. I hear yer brother Adam got set out alongst the road while drivin' his lady friend into town last Saturday night. Now, what do you suppose *that* was about?"

It was the first Libby had heard of it. But if Mr. Rhodes was speaking the truth and not just baiting her, as he was prone to do, she supposed it was about Abigail wanting to marry and Adam putting her off on account of Father's frail health. She admired Adam's sense of duty, for he was older than she by seven years. But by staying home,

7

he set a precedent, one that filled her with guilt at the very thought of breaking away.

"What'd Adam do to rile her so?" the old fellow prodded.

Pretending not to hear his sly insinuation, Libby tossed her head and sang the verse over, improvising for the second line, "Spiteful stories told by neighbors, spread by smithy's flaming tongue . . ." Basket empty, out of line and out of pegs, she ducked between sheets and stopped short.

"Why, Mr. Rhodes. I was just thinking of you."

He cackled at her feigned innocence, winked, and retorted, "Better not let on to Mrs. Rhodes, Blue Eyes. She's the jealous sort." The old man knocked the dust from his hat and limped back inside, tickled with himself.

Meddlesome old reprobate, Libby thought. A wonder Mrs. Rhodes tolerated him at all. Grinning, Libby strode back toward the washhouse Father and the boys had built two summers ago when she'd announced her plans to take in laundry. They'd bought a used stove for a song. She did much of the cooking and baking out there in warm weather, and the men, covered each day by the dust of the mines, bathed there. The scent of lye soap wafted on the steamy air, as familiar as the lilacs at the back gate. Water for baths simmered on the stove behind her, and a chicken pie was in the oven. Finding the crust nicely browned, she transferred it to the warmer and hung up her apron just as a train lumbered through town.

The clothesline, swagging from prop to prop with billowing sheets and shirts and trousers, blocked her view of the tracks, as did their house and another row of homes beyond. But Libby knew the train was loaded with coal. The weight of its passing strummed the earth like a bass fiddle. The whistle blew at the north crossing, a siren whisper of distant places. As always, it struck a responsive chord in her. She yearned for an hour to call her own, but there was no time today. Father and the boys would be home soon. She called across the garden to where her little brother and the neighbor girl were floating newspaper boats on the horse trough.

"I'm going to the store. Are you coming, David?"

He and his young playmate put their heads together. "Marta wants me to stay. All right?"

He was a bustling, busy lad of seven, a wellspring of ideas from morning to night, and yet uncommonly tender of other folks' feelings. Libby smiled her consent, then collected her flat straw hat and her shopping basket from the house and set out for the store. By the time she returned, the men were home. Father and Adam were in the washhouse. Jacob, still black from the mines, was sitting on the laundry bench, reading the paper while he waited his turn to bathe.

Libby greeted him on her way inside, then turned back to ask, "Did you hear anything about Adam and Abigail?"

He laughed, his teeth flashing straight and white in a face coated in coal dust. "Now, there's a lass with a fiery temper."

Libby shot a quick glance toward the washhouse and asked in a whisper, "Then she *did* set him out? Poor Adam!"

"It could be a favor she's done him, showing her stripes before Adam puts on the yoke." Jacob looked like a mischievous raccoon, eyes shining from his blackened face.

"They'll patch it up, they always do," said Libby, though Abigail had been waiting a long time. Maybe she had reached the end of her tether.

"Say, if you have your heart set on her for a sister, I could ask for her hand. Unlike Adam, I know a secret or two about toning down a temperamental miss."

"Hush, he'll hear you."

Laughing, Jacob fanned himself with the weekly newspaper and slipped effortlessly into Father's Scottish dialect, teasing, "Aye, she's a bonny lass, and a guid catch, but for that temper she takes too much from her brither."

Libby went on inside rather than encourage him in his nonsense. He was disgracefully sure of himself. Handsome and full of fun and laughter, he could have his pick of the Thistle Down lasses.

Libby set the table and was putting the finishing touches on the evening meal when the sound of coughing drew her back to the door. Standing at the screen, she looked out at the children, playing beneath the lilac bush. Jacob had stretched out on the bench, left knee bent, right foot on the ground. The paper was over his face, blocking out the light, but his left foot was tapping.

The deep bark of a cough sounded again. Libby caught her breath. "Is that Father?"

Jacob stirred from beneath the paper and nodded. His tapping foot betrayed an uneasiness that matched Libby's own.

"When did the coughing start?"

"I noticed it at lunch."

"Why didn't he come home?"

"Adam tried to get him to, but he said it was just a wee cough."

There was no such thing as "a wee cough" when years of mining had weakened a man's lungs. The colonel himself knew that. But despite the tension and occasional outbursts of violence brought on by long hours and meager pay and labor unrest, the colonel never had a problem finding replacements when a man proved too sickly for the job. Libby started across the yard the moment Father appeared on the washhouse threshold.

He fussed when she felt his forehead, and offered flowering trees and blooming bushes as an excuse for his itchy eyes and "thunderin' head." He would not go to bed early, nor would he stay home the next morning.

But by evening of the next day, he was too sick to bathe without the boys' help. Heart in her mouth, Libby summoned Dr. Dillman. And so the vigil began.

It had turned cool again. The moon had come up. The house was quiet, the windows open to the night air. Libby huddled in a chair by her father's bedside, a blanket over her shoulders. Her eyes drifted shut. Her harried thoughts began to gather and nest.

"Dinna run the cup over." Her father's weak voice penetrated her thin veil of rest.

She struggled free of the blanket and touched a match to the oil lamp on the bedside table. "Are you thirsty, Father?"

His feverish gaze wandered the cramped, dimly lit room. "Hear, lass? Aye, 'tis the whistle doon at the mines."

Crickets sang in the cool of the night and an owl hooted from a nearby tree. But the whistle calling his shift in wouldn't blow for hours.

"It's only the wind, Father. Closer now, just a sip." Libby held the cup to his mouth. He plucked at the covers, refusing to drink. She dipped a soft cloth in the cup and bathed his cracked lips. Heated bricks covered the oily red flannel rag on his chest. She moved them down to the foot of the bed, then tucked the covers in place again.

"Are you warm enough, Father?"

"Dinna be saucy wi' your poor husband, guid woman. Oot o' the way, now. What have ye done wi' my dinner pail?" His words came in short, shallow chuffs.

Tears stinging, Libby squeezed his hand and said, as her mother used to say, "I don't know what's become of it, Thomas. Shall I see if those two fellows came and took it away?"

It had been a small joke between her mother and him, a joke to do with his forgetful habits. "Aweel, sweet Annie. A bit o' a restie." A wan smile crossed his pallid features. He closed his eyes and spoke no more of going.

It had been a week now. Dr. Dillman had come and gone and come and gone, his face growing longer with each day that passed. The boys, when they were not working or at school, drifted in and out. Little David, his face worried and pinched. Jacob, at nineteen, with forced cheerfulness. And Adam, trying to prepare her for the worst. She would show him. She'd show them all. Stubbornly, tirelessly, she'd persisted in trying to bring healing with fresh air. With kerosene and hot camphorated oil poultices. With warm broth, as much as she could spoon down him.

Now she repented of her anger and weeded out her pride. She'd been wrong to think she could heal her father through sheer determination. Eyes filling afresh, Libby took his hand, pleading, *Please*. It was a rough-grained hand, palms callused, knuckles scarred by pick and shovel and falling chunks of coal. *Please, God.* It was a serving hand, a loving hand, a praying hand.

Please.

The tight knot between Libby's shoulders had grown into a boulder. Her back ached; her bottom was tender from sitting so long. She moved through the house to the kitchen and worked the hand pump until fresh water gushed into the basin, then returned to her father's side. His skin, a craggy map of lines and crevices, had a gray tinge to it. His eyes were sunken and darkly circled. A day ago, his coughing spasms had sounded like a ravaging tempest ripping away at his chest. Tonight they were weak and whispery and even more alarming. She feared he had wearied of fighting and dreamed now of going to his "sweet Annie." She blew out the lamp, kissed his forehead, and said with misting eyes, "Rest now."

The sound of plodding hooves drew Libby to the window. She watched as a riderless horse passed on the dirt street. The moon painted the beast in pale light. *And I looked, and behold a pale horse: and his name that sat on him was Death . . .* Her nerves reeled. With the lines came the faded memory of Uncle Willie Blue, his expressive blue eyes aglow as he mixed Scripture with spine-tingling Welsh tales of spirits and signs and premonitions.

Libby dragged her hands over her face to erase the memory and pulled her chair to the window. The damp night air stirred the curtains and cooled her burning eyes. She leaned forward, arms on the windowsill, chin resting on folded hands. She'd prayed until God's ears must have been numb. Too tired for fresh words, she lifted her gaze to the starry sky. *I will lift up mine eyes unto the hills, from whence cometh my help.*

Her father had taught her that verse the year her mother died. She had been too young to take much comfort in it, for the hills before her were hills of dishes, hills of washing, hills of baby tending, and hills of hurt. Her mother, her schooling, her childhood—all lost to her with the birth of her little brother. The acrid scent of the lamp freshly extinguished carried her back to the night when her mother had called her to her bedside. Her voice, with that proper Welsh lilt, rang in Libby's memory:

"Elizabeth. I have decided you shall name this wee one."

Libby looked with awe upon the wrinkled red face and tiny flailing fists of her infant brother as he lay curled up next to her mother. "Me?" she exclaimed, and Mother nodded. Not Father, not Adam, not Jacob, but her. In the glow of that honor, she stretched a finger to the baby and, as he clutched it, proclaimed, "I shall name him David."

The devotion that began with the naming of her baby brother had strengthened over the years. Though, in the beginning, there was a bit of resentment mixed in. Not over the workload, though that was difficult. Over the loss of school. How she had loved school! Looking back, Libby knew that it had grieved Father, too. He put high stock in education, and having suffered abuse over his peculiarities of diction, he insisted his children follow their mother's example and speak proper English. His solution to the dilemma was to fill one kitchen wall with a blackboard and become Libby's teacher. He wrote out her lessons each morning before going to the mines, and checked them each evening. When "class" was over, she filled the board with make-believe while her brothers taught the baby new tricks and Father fell asleep in the midst of their commotion. All at once he'd start up, eyes batting open, with a "Hum . . ." and "Aweel" and a "What is it ye're wantin'?" As if it were they, and not his own snoring, that had awakened him. Then he'd stir to his feet, smiling at their giggles, and pack them off to bed with a prayer and kiss for each forehead.

A dirty, backbreaking job, plus tending to four motherless children, and still he could smile. How had he kept his goodness? A lump formed in Libby's throat and she thought how only a week ago she'd been champing at the bit for her freedom. She lifted her father's hand to her face and held it against her cheek.

2

🌺 *Patience Corners.* Libby's fingers recognized the quilt with her eyes closed. But something was not right. The stillness. As she tried to shake off the dregs of a heavy sleep, she saw her father standing on the threshold of her bedroom. Puzzled, she rubbed her eyes and gazed at him. His form slowly changed and melted away until it wasn't Father at all, but Uncle Willie.

Libby jerked upright, and came awake to find herself in her own bed, beneath her own quilt, fully clothed right down to her shoes. There were people in the next room. Jacob and Dr. Dillman, and a third voice she didn't recognize. The nightmare had left its stamp of alarm. She swung her feet to the floor just as Adam appeared in the doorway.

His clothes were clean and he was bareheaded. She had heard the mine whistle yesterday afternoon, signifying there would be work today. Why wasn't he wearing his cap with the mining lamp strapped on? Where was his round dinner pail? His presence here when he should be at work confirmed her worst fear. *Dear God!* Her shrinking spirit could find no words. All the strength drained from her limbs. The faded flowers on the wallpaper blurred as an agonized wail rose within her. She slapped her hands over her ears as if she could stop the expected words from coming.

Adam strode toward her, splashing coffee in his haste.

"It's all right, Lib. It's not what you think. There was some shifting at the mine. The colonel shut down until the inspectors can have a look." He set the coffee down. "I'm sorry, I didn't mean to frighten you."

Libby crossed her arms, holding herself, trying to stop trembling. "I thought it was Father. I thought he had . . ."

"No, no. Dr. Dillman's with him."

The lump in her throat thickened. "Is he worse?"

"No, he's better. Go see for yourself."

Better? Adam's face swam before her eyes. She flung her arms around him and sobbed her relief. He was reserved, this blue-eyed, broad-shouldered, square-chinned brother of hers, not given to easy emotion. Yet he held her for a moment, and before pulling away, said, "You deserve some good news, Lib. You never give up, do you?"

Jacob strode in and flashed her a radiant smile, his dark eyes shining. "That's pretty good doctoring for a washerwoman."

Libby hugged him, too, laughter overtaking her tears. "It wasn't me, it was God who made him well."

"He isn't well, not by a long degree," Adam cautioned.

"Dr. Dillman is having a look now." Jacob started after her, protesting, "Wait a moment. This just came. You had better read it."

"A telegram?" Libby dried her eyes on her wrinkled apron.

"Seems Uncle Willie has died."

Her heart slammed against her rib cage at the remembrance of her dream. The telegram was addressed to Elizabeth Watson of Thistle Down, though it was apparent Jacob knew the contents. Yesterday she would have protested this invasion of her privacy. This morning it seemed trivial. Her eyes swept over the short message:

Mr. Willie Blue expired this night past. Funeral plans pending. With Condolences, Your Servant, Angus S. Cearlock, Attorney.

Cold fingers walked down her spine.

"Who would expect Uncle Willie to have an attorney?" mused Jacob.

Adam, reading over her shoulder, noted the return

address. "Edgewood. A hundred miles or more north of here. There's no mention of how he died."

"Drowned in a bottle, I'll wager."

"We don't know that, Jacob. He could have changed," said Adam.

The reprimand fell on deaf ears. Jacob rubbed his chin and speculated, "Or maybe he put a gun to his head. What a melancholy chap."

Libby flinched. Death had brushed too close last night to be so callous and cavalier. Her eyes raced over the message again. Willie Blue was Mother's uncle. They had not seen him in years, but her thoughts of his wild Welsh tales had no doubt precipitated the dream.

"I wonder why it's addressed just to me."

"That's easy. He liked you best."

Libby started to protest, but Adam was nodding in agreement. "It's true, Libby, he did."

"He laughed at all your far-fetched stories and songs and plays," Jacob said.

"He used to say to Mother, 'Where is it wee Redtop gets her imagination?'" Adam added.

"Why, whaur could it be but the company store—the verra same as her bonny freckles and fiery hair." Jacob tugged at a disheveled lock and laughed when Libby slapped his hand away. "Will you be going?"

"To his burial? How? I can't leave Father."

"If he continues to improve, you could," said Adam. "I'll pay your train fare."

Still grinning, Jacob bobbed his head to say he'd pitch in too.

Like Father, they worked too hard for their money at a job that would make them old too soon. Old and frail, with a cough that never went away. Fresh tears burned her throat.

She turned away, hiding from her brothers what had been simmering inside her for a long while. If they remained in the mines, their lives would be like a story in which the ending could be guessed from page one. Her gnawing frustration wasn't due to Father's illness alone. It was for her brothers, too, and for the harsh realities of life here in Thistle Down. And for herself.

Herself? Libby stopped short, ashamed. She had gotten her heart's request; Father was better. She had no right to ask for more. Further education, her writing, independence—it would all have to wait.

"You don't have to make up your mind right now. Talk it over with Father first," Adam said, following her into the kitchen.

The stove was still warm. Cooked oats congealed in a pan that the boys had neglected to remove from the stove. Libby put it to one side, added coal to the firebox, then measured camphorated oil into a pan. She'd need a fresh flannel cloth, too, and some kerosene to continue the treatments.

"Are you all right, Lib?" asked Adam.

Her tears under control, she reached into the oven to test the heat of the bricks she'd placed there last night. "I'm tired is all. And sad about Uncle Willie. But grateful. Very, very grateful."

"Well, you should be." Dr. Dillman shrugged into his jacket as he came to join them. He was a heavily built man, his hair and whiskers grizzled with age. Blunt of feature as well as manner, he added, "He's cheated the grim reaper. Just broth yet today, Elizabeth. Don't let him out of bed for several days, I don't care how loud the old Scot squeals. And he isn't to go back to the mines."

"For how long?" asked Jacob, joining them.

"He cannot go back at all. His lungs will not stand it."

"But what will he do?" Adam protested.

"Something aboveground." The doctor's piercing gaze shifted from Adam to Jacob to Libby.

"You told him?" asked Libby.

"Yes. Just like I've told so many others. Too few listen." The doctor snapped his black bag shut. At the door he turned back. "Mark my word, if Thomas returns to the mines, he won't be long for this world."

What else is there in Thistle Down?

"He knows how to darken a room, the old sawbones." Jacob strode back through the house, fighting his emotions with a rare flash of anger.

But Libby stood in the back door, looking on as Adam followed Dr. Dillman out to the alley where his buggy

waited. Voices carried well on the still morning air. It was
Adam's tone more than his words that caught her atten-
tion as he asked the doctor a question, something about
Abigail.

"She's fine," said the doctor. When Adam pressed for
more, the doctor climbed into the buggy, adding, "Won't
do you any good to drill me, young man. If there's one
thing deadlier than germs to a man in my trade, it's
peddling gossip."

3

"Ach! A wee cough keepin' me from goin' a-funeralin'," said Father when he learned of the telegram and Uncle Willie's death. "Go, lass. Annie would hae ye to go."

Reassured he could get along without her for the day, Libby boarded the train for Edgewood the next morning, fare paid from her laundry money. Seated next to the window, she enjoyed the ride north, watching miles and miles of trees and soil and new grain unfold like the petals of a flower warmed by the sun.

At Springfield she made the Springfield and Blooming-ton connection, and felt lucky to find an empty seat by a window. A lumpy-looking woman with eyes sunken into a face as pitted as a pickle dropped down beside her. They were scarcely under way when across the aisle a baby just big enough to stand on her own began to whine and kick to be let down. The woman to Libby's right gave the child a hard look.

"Young 'uns what cain't weather travel had ought be left at home," she announced in a voice as grating as a carpenter's rasp.

Studiously ignoring the older woman, the young woman stood the child up on her lap and did not resist the pudgy fingers that reached out to explore the white plume on her hat. "Mama's love. Such a good girl at the fair. Tess be nimble, Tess be quick. Tess jump over the

19

candlestick," she chimed, lifting the little girl high in the air on the last word, her face soft with laughter.

The squat, middle-aged woman took out her crocheting. The thread looped around her bowed fifth finger, over her leathery middle fingers, fed through her forefinger and thumb to the hook. From the hook, the fine ecru strand spilled onto the doily taking shape beneath her skilled hands. The sheen of the thread and the delicacy of the needlework seemed at odds with the woman's surly demeanor.

Libby edged closer to the window, thoughts turning to her early childhood days and Uncle Willie Blue's periodic visits. A handsome man of middle age, he came via the "Down and Out," Jacob's name for any freight train moving slowly enough for Uncle Willie to jump. He arrived at their gate dirty and ragged and so utterly defeated by drink that he was no good to himself, much less anyone else.

Her mother welcomed him with nourishing meals. Her father cleaned him up and provided him with a new suit of clothes, charged to his account at the company store. Uncle Willie would stay a few days, meekly submitting to her father's gentle reminders that "God is guid, His strength made perfect in weakness" and to Libby's little back-porch plays, orchestrated with the help of the neighbor children and the reluctant assistance of her brothers.

The love and laughter and cheery commotion of their household seemed to strengthen Uncle Willie's resolve for self-improvement, and he would leave, "a better man," as he put it, vowing not to stray along the wayward path again. But, of course, he did. Repeatedly. And back he would come when life had once more defeated him.

By and by, Libby's seatmate put her crocheting to one side and withdrew a sandwich from one of the bags at her feet. Libby had come prepared, too. She spread a napkin on her lap and unwrapped soda biscuits she had baked early that morning in hopes of tempting her father's appetite.

Thinking of the doctor's dire warning, Libby finished her bread, then reached into her valise for her writing tablet. The rocking of the train took a toll on her handwriting as she collected her thoughts in a note that began:

Dearest Mother:

I saw mama robin nudge her baby from the nest in the lilac bush this morning. His squawking and clumsy hopping and flapping were painful to watch, and still I envied him.

The words looked selfish on the page, and yet she was only being honest in what was in reality a journal of private thoughts. Some of her friends had married, little birds falling from one nest into another, some snug and weather-tight, some a good bit less cozy. But marriage was fearfully final, and if any fellow in Thistle Down measured up to her brothers, let alone her father, she had yet to meet him. No, she didn't want to marry. She wanted to write.

I was so sure the other day on the bluff that the time had nearly come for me to pursue my education, for what is my ambition to write without an education? Now, after Father's brush with death, I feel all the more bound to him. He is so fragile.

"Next stop, Edgewood!" The conductor made his way through the densely packed car.

The iron wheels clanked and creaked as Libby strained for her first look at the town. No, not quite a town. They hadn't cleared the woods yet. Limbs and leaves waved in passing. Lovely, towering old things, drenchingly green.

Bending over her tablet, Libby scribbled a final few words:

I see how this town came by its name. Oh, what lovely trees. I would love someday to live in the woods with my tablets and pencils and nothing but time.

She tucked away her writing tablet and scrutinized her murky reflection in the dust-mottled window. The sprig of lilacs pinned to the lapel of her black serge suit was wilting. Her freckles were showing. Her refurbished black velvet-brimmed toque, stretched out by too much wear and too much hair, was banking to the left upon a mass of loosely pinned strawberry curls. She straightened it, and lowered the black mourning veil that she had attached before leaving home.

The service was scheduled for two o'clock at a building Mr. Cearlock had, in his second telegram, referred to as "the Columbian." But the wake was being held at the store, which had apparently served as Uncle Willie's home.

Even Father had been surprised to learn Uncle Willie had acquired a store. "And him so hiltie-skiltie," he'd exclaimed.

Libby fingered the watch pinned to the jacket covering her dainty linen shirtwaist. Twelve noon. She dusted a few cinders and bread crumbs from her lap and tugged at her black gloves. On her left, the trees gave way to the back side of a lumberyard, a few businesses the nature of which she couldn't in so brief a glance determine, and a sprawling, prosperous-looking flour mill. Ahead loomed a grain elevator.

Her vision was partially obscured by passengers, but she caught a glimpse of the station on the right and a good-sized crowd. She leaned forward, looking past her seatmate, across the aisle and out the sun-washed window. Red, white, and blue bunting hung over the station door. The wooden awning built out over the platform was trimmed in bunting too.

"It's Decoration Day!" she blurted.

The woman uttered a monosyllabic grunt.

"Until this moment I had forgotten. My brothers and I took bouquets out to the cemetery last night." Though the woman betrayed not one whit of interest, once started, Libby couldn't seem to stop herself. "The irises were fairly well spent, but I can't remember the peonies ever being any prettier. We filled two bushel baskets for the graves. My youngest brother even found some late violets."

She did stop then, thinking of David's small hand clutching those violets as he squatted beside Mother's grave and traced the date of his own birth. *Seven years she's been gone.* Though officially set aside to memorialize the soldiers lost in battle, Decoration Day belonged, in Libby's heart, to her mother, too. She had placed her own bouquet of lilacs beside David's handful of violets.

There would be ceremonies at the cemetery in Thistle Down today. Had the crowd gathered here for a similar service? The train station seemed a peculiar choice. Hesitantly she ventured, "Quite a crowd for such a small town."

"Whistle-stop tomfoolery." Her seatmate glowered at the young mother and child as they stepped into the aisle, preparing to disembark. "Chester Gentry's doin'. He's thicker'n ever with the politicians now that his boy's runnin' fer the state legislature."

"Who is the speaker to be?"

The woman shrugged as she made a wide loop of her last single crochet. She extracted the hook and folded the doily she'd been crafting along with the hank of thread into the satchel between her feet, then leaned over Libby to pin a lethargic fly to the glass with her crochet hook. "He'll be a Republican, that much I know. Died-in-the-wool Republican, Mr. Gentry is. Gits the politicians passing through on their way from Springfield, and coaxes 'em into stepping out to shake hands and spew words."

"Then Edgewood is your home?"

"For the past twenty-seven years," said the woman.

"Did you know Willie Blue?"

"Yep." She spared Libby a glance.

"I'm his niece."

"Come for the funeral, then?"

Libby nodded.

Expressionless, the woman said, "There wasn't no meanness in him."

"No," murmured Libby. Willie Blue wasn't mean. That much, she knew.

"Heard tell it was Frankie McClure's doin'. Cavorting

out in the pasture, teasing his grandpa's old bull. It tossed him once and was makin' for him again when Mr. Blue happened along."

Gooseflesh rose on Libby's arms. "A bull killed Uncle Willie?"

The woman's gaze sharpened. "You didn't know?"

She shook her head. "We received two telegrams from his attorney, Mr. Cearlock, but neither one said how he'd died."

"Figures Angus Cearlock'd be stingy with words when they cost money. I'd allow he ain't nearly so sparing when he goes a-stumpin'."

Her thoughts still on Uncle Willie, Libby asked, "Was he killed instantly?"

"The way I heard it, he lingered long enough to suffer his heroics." She shook her head, and went over it in more detail, saying, "Willie parlayed with that bull jest long enough for Frankie's grandpa to pull the boy under the fence. Root tripped your uncle up, or he mighta got clear. Least, that's what they're sayin'."

"Was he conscious?" asked Libby, grappling with grisly crimson images.

"The way I heard it, he spoke some there at the last to Decatur and old Hascal Caton. Least that's what Hascal's sayin'. Wouldn't take it for gospel, though. Lies is that man's native tongue."

Libby was beginning to see why Mr. Cearlock hadn't tried to pass the information along by telegram. Poor Uncle Willie.

"Saw a man gored once," mused the woman. "It ain't a picture you soon forget."

Fearful the woman would paint a description, Libby turned her eyes toward the window again. An old man with a drum rested in the shade of the C. Gentry Flour Mill on the west side of the tracks.

Her seatmate changed the subject. "There'll be a parade about two o'clock. Then Spike Culbertson'll recite the Gettysburg Address. 'Lessen funeral proceedin's git in the way." Seeming in no hurry to disembark, she plowed the underneath side of a ragged fingernail with the crochet hook. "Old fool cain't find his way home most the time. But he's got the queerest head fer poems and sech as that."

The woman hauled herself to her feet and implemented the versatile crochet hook to snag the strings on the boxes she'd stowed on the shelf over Libby's head. She caught one. The other tumbled into Libby's lap, knocking her hat askew on the way down. As Libby hastened to repair the damage, the woman tunneled the crochet hook into the hair behind her ear, scooped up the fallen box, grabbed her wicker basket and satchel, and lumbered into the aisle.

Libby gripped her valise tightly and followed.

"Watch your step, ma'am." The conductor reached up from his place by the step to guide Libby's seatmate down. Vision obscured by her burden of belongings, the woman dangled her foot in midair, feeling for the step.

It was a man's shoe she was wearing. The run-down heel and cowhide patch aroused Libby's conscience. "Would you like some help?" she offered.

The woman thrust her satchel at her. Once down, she retrieved her belongings and, with an unintelligible grunt, opened a path across the crowded platform, the crochet hook gleaming like a feather from her scraggly nest of ginger-colored hair.

Libby scanned faces, wishing she'd thought to ask her seatmate for a description of Mr. Cearlock. Her valise grew heavy as she waited, but no one came toward her.

The smell of coal dust, hot oil, and dissipating steam assailed Libby's nostrils as the train rolled ahead and stopped again on the side track, still hissing. The door opened and two men stepped out on the platform at the back of the car, subduing for the moment the restless stir of the crowd. The elder of the two men hooked his thumbs beneath the lapels of his suit and introduced the statesman.

"Ladies and gentlemen, friends and neighbors, it is my privilege and honor to present to you Senator Simon Rawlings. He has come up here from Springfield to say some words of remembrance for those honorable men who fought on various battlefields for the just cause of this great nation of ours."

A broad-shouldered fellow in overalls and a weather-stained hat pulled down low on his forehead crowded in front of Libby just as the senator launched into his speech:

"Since 1868, following the North-South Conflict, this day has been set aside to commemorate the memory of brave men across our land who have suffered and bled and died to preserve this great United States of America."

The big-shouldered man in front of Libby worked the wad in his jaw and remarked to the farmer beside him, "Puny specimen, ain't he?"

"I got taller chickens. Squawk louder, too," the farmer retorted.

"Who don't?"

The farmer chuckled. He tipped his wide-brimmed straw hat back, scratched his head, and remarked, "Hear they're buryin' Willie Blue today."

"That's right."

"You come to town for the funeral, Decatur?"

"Reckon I'll stop by and pay my respects."

"Frightful way for poor Willie to go. How's your boy takin' it?" asked the farmer.

"Cain't say as I've noticed he's takin' it any way atall."

The farmer averted his gaze. He rocked back on his heels, looking this way and that, but spoke no more of Uncle Willie. Directly he tugged at his hat and excused himself, saying, "Good seeing you, Decatur."

"So long." The first man's tone was mild enough. But once the farmer had walked away, he muttered an expletive so raw, Libby backed hastily out of his path. But not before catching the sharp, tangy scent of alcohol on his breath.

Mr. Cearlock had obviously been delayed. Further waiting seemed pointless. Libby squeezed through the crowd and set off to find Uncle Willie's store on her own. She followed the street from the station to the crossing half a block to the north and was making her way across when the chatter of children drew her attention. Looking south, she saw a boy and a girl balance a bicycle on one rail of the sidetrack that skirted the back side of the flour mill Libby had noticed earlier. The boy had a bruised cheek and a gash on his chin. He held the bicycle in place while the girl, who wasn't much bigger than David, straddled the seat.

"Hang on! Don't let go of me till I'm balanced good," the girl said.

"I won't." The boy gripped the back of the seat with one hand, the right handlebar with the other.

"Pretend I'm Mrs. Bee, ridin' a tightrope in the circus."

"I cain't hold ya forever. Start pedalin'," he ordered in that imperial manner of an older brother.

Unable to reach both pedals from the seat, the little girl gripped the handlebars and stood up to pedal. The boy let go of the handlebars. The front wheel wobbled and nearly skidded off the rail.

"Yikes!" screeched the girl, correcting the wobble with a light touch on the handlebar.

"I gotcha." Holding on to the seat, the boy continued to trot alongside her, shouting orders. "Hold 'er steady! Pedal faster. Ya gotta go fast to hold steady. Are ya steady?"

A look of fierce concentration wrinkled the girl's brow. "Okay. I got it now."

"Yer steady?" asked her red-haired brother, running to keep alongside.

"I got it. Let go jest for a second."

"Give her plenty of speed," he warned, gave her a push for good measure, and let go.

"Whee!" squealed the girl. "See! I told you I could . . ."

It all happened so fast, Libby had no chance to intervene. Just as she stepped back out of the path of the rail-riding girl, the front wheel bounced off the track and threw the child headlong over the handlebars.

The little girl whimpered as Libby and the boy raced to her aid. A bump was rising on her forehead and her nose was bleeding. Lifting a hand to her face and coming away with blood scared her. She let out a squall to reach the heavens.

"Are you hurt? Where does it hurt?" cried Libby.

"She ain't hurt, she's scared is all. Hush, Opal. A real circus lady don't bawl," chided the boy. He mopped at her face with his shirttail. "Quit yer squallin' so's we can git a look. Can ya git yer legs under ya?"

A long shadow fell over them before the girl could rise. Libby lifted her face to trade glances with the same whiskey-soured man who had cursed the farmer only moments ago. The girl's bawling tapered to a whimper.

"Daddy, I'm bleedin'."

"She fell off the bicycle, trying to ride the rail," Libby explained.

The man plucked his daughter up with one large hand and shoved the boy with the other. "What'd ya go and push her for? I declare, if you ain't a menace."

The boy jutted out his chin. "I didn't push her, she fell."

"Don't lie to me, boy. I saw ya give her a push."

"He did push the bicycle, sir," said Libby, troubled by the look in the boy's eyes as he dropped his gaze. "But only so she could get enough momentum to ride the rail."

"Who the devil are you?"

"Libby Watson."

The father's gaze, a deeper blue than his son's, bored into her. "Ain't seen you around here b'fore."

"I'm Willie Blue's niece. Perhaps you know hi . . . knew him."

"I reckon I did."

He hadn't raised his voice, but something in his tone made Libby's pulse quicken. His eyes were cold and the veins seemed to stand in bold relief against his sun-weathered temples. The little girl was too distracted by her injuries to notice. She sniffed and wiped her bleeding nose with the back of her hand.

"I ain't gonna die like Willie, am I, Daddy?"

"Not this minute, anyways. Though ain't no tellin' what'll become of ya if ya keep goin' along with sech flea-brained stunts."

"It was a circus stunt, Daddy. Frankie was helpin'."

"Oh yeah. Frankie's a heap of help, ain't he?"

Frankie. Libby's eyes lingered on the boy's bruised cheeks and gashed chin. Was this the boy? The one Uncle Willie had given his life to save?

"My nose hurts," complained Opal.

"Ain't no good makin' a fuss," said the man, trying to still her whimpering. "Hold yer face steady so's I can get a look."

His big raw-boned hands were gentle enough as he held a rag to the little girl's nose. No longer needed, Libby picked up her valise and was edging away when a fashionably dressed woman darted up to the accident scene.

"I thought that was you, Opal!" She stooped for a closer look. "What happened? No, no. Don't try to talk when your nose is bleeding. What happened, Decatur?"

"Frankie pushed her."

"No, he didn't," said Opal. "Tell her, Frankie."

Relieved the boy had been vindicated by his sister, Libby tarried a moment longer, wondering if the woman was the children's mother. She had an attractive way of cocking her head to one side as she listened to Frankie's brief explanation. Pleasant, even features were framed by the fringe of soft dark hair curling from beneath a stylish hat. One distinctive white tress curled from her center part to her left temple. It was hard to guess her age. Fortyish, perhaps, though on the young side of it. She tipped up the girl's chin and clucked her tongue.

"So the station agent's bicycle threw you. Dear me, you're bleeding like a stuck pig. Dr. Harding is in his office if you think she needs attention, Decatur."

"Ya want I should git him?" asked the boy.

"What you'd best do is stay out from underfoot. I ain't in no mood for yer shennanigans," growled the man.

The boy righted the bicycle, dusted it off, and darted a glance to meet the man's dark, glowering face. "Reckon I'll jest put this back where we got it."

"That's a good lad." The woman patted the boy's shoulder as he started away with the bicycle. She shifted her basket and offered, "Why don't I take Opal to Baker's and clean her up a bit?"

Looking uncomfortable, the man said, "I cain't put ya out."

"You're not. I was on my way there."

"Please, Daddy?" pleaded the little girl. "I wanna go with Mrs. Bee. Can I, Daddy?"

"Hush then, and go," he muttered brusquely. "I got business to tend to."

"Certainly. We'll run along and let you get to it."

Once the man had strode away, the woman discarded the bloody rag and retrieved a handkerchief from her pocket. "Hold your head back, Opal. Now pinch your nose."

"Excuse me," said Libby, noting the confidence in the woman's hands as she administered first aid. "I'm looking for Willie Blue's store."

She spared Libby a curious glance. "Far side of the square, middle of the block. But I'm afraid it's closed for business today."

"Yes, I know." Libby thanked her, then smiled at the little girl. "Feeling better now?"

"Keep pinching, that's the way," urged the woman. "See there, it's nearly stopped." To Libby she added, "If you don't mind a little detour, I'll show you the way."

"Would you? I'd appreciate it," Libby said, and introduced herself as they resumed walking. "I'm Elizabeth Watson, Willie Blue's niece. I've come for his funeral."

"I declare! Hear that, Opal? This is Mr. Blue's niece." The dainty lady smiled warmly and reached for Libby's gloved hand. "We've been expecting you. We're all so sorry about your uncle. I'm Sarah Jane Brignadello."

"She's a circus lady," said Opal, pinching fingers lending her voice a nasal tone.

"Yes, well, that was a long time ago. And a questionable distinction at that. Though you're a dear heart for thinking it noteworthy. That's it. You keep pinching." Mrs. Brignadello turned to Libby again. "Are you just coming from the station?"

"Yes. I thought I'd be met by Uncle Willie's attorney. But if he was at the station, we missed one another."

"Angus Cearlock? He's my nephew. He's usually quite punctual." Mrs. Brignadello's brow puckered momentarily. "Something must have kept him. Ah well, it's a little town. He'll find you soon enough. Mr. Lamb will be relieved to hear you've arrived. This warm weather makes holding a body over a worry. He's uncommonly fretful for an undertaker, Mr. Lamb is." Mrs. Brignadello sighed. "Poor Mr. Blue. This town won't be the same without him. He made that store his life. For the past seven years, anyway. Since he . . ."

Discretion shuttered the woman's eyes. Libby wondered if she should come straight out and ask what had transpired in Uncle Willie's life since her mother's funeral seven years past. That was how long it had been since he had been to their home in Thistle Down. But it was awkward, particularly with the child along. She'd save her questions for Mr. Cearlock.

Mrs.Brignadello ushered them past the flour mill to the structure adjoining it. A two-story brick building with its back door facing the alley and railroad tracks, and its front facing the town square, it was shaded by a handsome canvas awning. The wide glass window was lettered *Baker's Restaurant & Boarding House.*

"This won't take but a minute."

"That's fine. I'll wait here."

Libby drew impressions, as she waited, of the town that had been Uncle Willie's home. A concrete curbing and a handsome wrought-iron fence encircled the park at the center of the town square. The lush green grass was shaded by sturdy hardwoods and several kinds of conifers. There was a bandstand, painted white and decorated in filigree. A man and two women with parasols lingered beneath its shadowy shade while several children splashed one another at the public pump. Libby smiled, vicariously enjoying their fun, then looked over her shoulder into the restaurant.

On the other side of the glass, Mrs. Brignadello was pressing something to the knot on Opal's head. To look at her, one would not think immediately of the circus. Yet there was a vestige of showmanship that clung to her, just as the gold-embroidered silk braid clung to her exquisitely fitted blue-black dress. She had tiny feet, expensively shod. The plumage adorning her hat fluttered at her lively nods as she chatted with a second woman Libby presumed to be Mrs. Baker. Libby quickly averted her gaze as the little woman exited the restaurant alone.

"Opal's going to be fine. But that Decatur McClure! I declare, I could shake him for being so gruff with poor Frankie."

Relieved by her forthrightness, Libby said, "I tried to tell him it wasn't the boy's fault."

"Decatur and Mr. Blue were close. He's bound to be upset. Rumor has it he started drinking shortly after Willie died and hasn't let up since." She sighed and added, "Still, that's no excuse for taking it out on Frankie. I've got a feeling the lad's feeling badly enough about Willie without Decatur being hard on him."

"He *is* the boy Uncle Willie saved, then? I wondered."

"Yes, he's the one," said Mrs. Brignadello. "Frankie's always been a bit of a daredevil. It's just like him to take chances with a bull. Of course, if he could have foreseen what a tragedy . . ." She clucked her tongue and added, "It has him in a real stir. He can't seem to settle down and just let the grief out."

"He lives here in town?"

"No. Three miles from here, up at Old Kentucky. That's what they call the grove north of town. Beautiful spot, though kind of isolated. Decatur was raised in the woods, and so was Naomi. That's his wife. She doesn't get to town often. Doesn't need to, I guess. She and Decatur grow a big garden, plus enough grain for their stock. Decatur hunts and fishes and traps, too. Living off the land is passing in these parts, but you still find a few doing it up at Old Kentucky."

"The little girl seems fond of you," ventured Libby.

Mrs. Brignadello chuckled. "I don't have any children of my own, so I enjoy making a fuss over Opal. She and Frankie come to town quite a lot with their grandpa Caton. I have to say, though, Mrs. Baker's giving me some competition. She took Opal right under her wing." She laughed and added, "I tried to give her some muffins, but she said to give them to you. 'She's sure to be hungry after a morning on the train, Mrs. Bee.'" With a tremulous smile Mrs. Brignadello added, "It was Mr. Blue who started the 'Mrs. Bee' business. He always was one for nicknames."

Libby smiled, remembering he'd had a nickname for her, too.

"Verna Baker's husband ran a hatchery for many years," Mrs. Brignadello was saying as they made their way through the park. "But after his death, Verna had it made over into a business she could run. We get a lot of drummers here. Salesmen, not the musical kind. They get off the train here, rent a rig at Woodmancy's Livery, and set out on their routes. Folks coming and going to the big fair down in St. Louis hasn't hurt her trade any." She continued her chatter as they walked along. "Gram Steadman—Verna's mother—was always such a help to her until her memory failed. Now she follows Verna about like a little lost pup. She hasn't forgotten my muffins, though. I insisted on leaving a couple for her."

Mrs. Brignadello peeled back the corner of the linen napkin covering the basket to give Libby a peek. "The secret is in the spices. It's my own special recipe. Ladies all over the countryside have pleaded with my husband to share it with them. He hints, of course, but just enough to keep them picking through the spices."

"He's a huckster?" asked Libby.

"No, dear. A rural merchandising agent."

Unsure what that meant, Libby refrained from revealing her ignorance. Her gaze swept the entire block as Mrs. Brignadello led her toward the north side of the square. The bank at the west end of the block was of brick with a tile roof identical to the railway station's. A canvas awning similar to the one at Baker's jutted out over the wooden walk. The rest of the buildings were of wood frame with wooden awnings.

"That's Willie Blue's there in the middle."

The two-story structure was wedged between the freshly whitewashed *Gazette* office and a butcher shop. The foundation was crumbling. The roof sagged. A broken windowpane on the second story had been replaced by boards, and moss grew like green whiskers beneath a wide front window lettered *Willie Blue's*. In smaller letters at the corner of the window was the notation *United States Post Office*.

Mrs. Brignadello led her to the door, saying in a hush, "Mr. Caton's been here ever since Mr. Lamb laid out the body. He's Frankie and Opal's grandpa. Naomi's father. He lives up at Old Kentucky, too. Though you'd hardly guess it is a three-mile trek, for all the time he spends here in town."

The black crape on the door and covered windows sent a shiver up the back of Libby's knees. She'd never attended a wake or a funeral without Father and the boys. She lifted her chin, trying not to betray her trepidation.

"Generally, Mr. Caton's not one to be beholden," Mrs. Brignadello continued. "But the whole affair rattled him badly. He declared he wouldn't leave Mr. Blue's side until he's in the ground." She leaned closer and added, "Mr. Caton has some queer ideas. He's strong-willed as they come, even for Old Kentucky. He's haranguing Mr. Lamb."

"Haranguing?" echoed Libby.

"He wants him to hold off a day on the funeral, being of the opinion a quick tuck under the sod is disrespectful. Particularly considering your uncle's heroics."

"Mr. Cearlock surely told him my father's just recovering from a lung ailment and is unable to come. Uncle Willie has no other relatives to speak of."

"Don't be timid about speaking up if his arrangements don't suit you." Mrs. Brignadello caught a quick breath. "Would you like me to take you in and introduce you around?"

Libby's hair was by now testing the holding power of her hatpin. She hadn't slept well last night, and the handle of the valise was cutting into her fingers. Uncertain she was up to "queer ideas" from a strong-willed man hailing from someplace called "Old Kentucky," she accepted Mrs. Brignadello's offer.

4

It was a substantial door, weighted by the heavy glass window. Libby followed Mrs. Brignadello into the gloom of covered windows and unlit lamps. Spices, oiled leather, wilting flowers, and dust assailed her nostrils as she waited for her eyes to adjust.

"Don't trip over the umbrella display. Watch the case, there. Mercy, it's dark in here. Mr. Blue had just ordered gas lighting. Pity it wasn't installed."

They wove their way among wooden cases, boxes, and barrels. Merchandise spilled into the aisle from every nook and cranny. Libby kept her valise close to her body so as not to brush by and start an avalanche. They turned past a wall banked in postal boxes.

A group of men had gathered around a cold stove. They sat on crates and nail kegs and straight-back chairs. Smoke curled from cigars and pipes and swirled in ever-changing patterns above their heads. An oil lamp cast eerie shadows as it swung from a nail in the passageway between the wall of postal boxes and a long counter behind the men. A candelabrum burned at one end of the counter, the flickering flames contributing to the heat that was wilting the flowers banked against the counter.

"Mr. Blue never threw anything away. He hadn't a tidy bone in his body, God rest his soul. Mr. Lamb has done the best he can to make room," said Mrs. Brignadello.

Her words prepared Libby, and still her heart lurched

35

at the sight of Uncle Willie's corpse stretched out on the counter. Quickly she looked away.

"Gentlemen, this is Mr. Blue's niece, Miss Elizabeth Watson."

An old fellow with hands the size of hams drew to his full height and greeted her in a deep, low voice, saying, "Captain Benjamin Boyd, at your service, Miss Willie."

Libby blinked, even as Mrs. Brignadello gently corrected, "Miss Watson, Captain. Captain Boyd is one of our rural mail carriers here in Edgewood," she told Libby.

"How do you do?"

Captain Boyd took her hand and bowed over it, saying, "It's a sad day, I'm afraid. Willie was a good friend, Miss Willie."

"Miss Watson," she reminded him.

"Beggin' yer pardon, miss, but you'll have to excuse our poor captain. He's plum prostrate with grief," whispered a burly old fellow with grizzly jowls.

Uncertain what to say, Libby murmured awkwardly, "I'm grateful Uncle Willie had such a close friend."

"Oh, he had lots of friends. More friends than you could shake a stick at, ain't that right, boys?" attested the same burly old fellow who'd whispered excuses for the captain.

"Elizabeth, I'd like you to meet Mr. Hascal Caton," introduced Mrs. Brignadello as the circle of men voiced unanimous agreement to Uncle Willie's many friendships.

"Proud to make your acquaintance, miss." The bearded gent had a nose as flat as an old fence board. He peered down the length of it from dagger-sharp eyes. "Cain't tell ya how it grieves me to see sech a one as yer uncle snatched away. Abominable way to die, jest abominable."

The man sitting next to him came to his feet and offered his hand. He had a gaunt face and snow white hair that stood out from his head like a dandelion gone to seed. But his voice was strong, as was his grip. "Willie was a caring soul. A master at drawing others out, but he never had that much to say about himself. It wasn't until I tried to write his obituary that I realized how little I actually knew about Willie."

"Mr. Gruben is editor of *The Gazette*," explained Mrs. Brignadello.

"It's a pleasure to meet you, sir." He was the first writer Libby had ever met in person. A little in awe of him, she flushed and added, "I'm sure whatever you've written will be just fine."

"Major Minor," Mrs. Brignadello introduced the next fellow.

White muttonchops hugged a jaundiced face like bookends as the spry fellow pumped her hand. "Jest call me Minor, little lady. Wish we was meetin' under happier circumstances."

And so it went, down the row of crates and kegs until each man had spoken his condolences. Eight men in all. All up in years and all wearing black armbands.

Mr. Caton turned a chair so it was facing the corpse and gestured for Libby to take the seat. She declined and stood instead, hugging her valise. She had not expected to feel such a jolt at the sight of Uncle Willie. Or the odd turning of her heart at the spoken kindnesses of his friends. The veil on her hat was a welcome buffer now, for she could feel the watchful gaze of Mrs. Brignadello, multiplied by eight.

"Could I help you with that, miss?" The fellow with the unhealthy yellow complexion stepped forward and relieved her of the valise.

"Take it on upstairs for her, Minor," said Mr. Caton.

Libby's gaze followed the man to the open staircase hugging the east wall. The steep stairs popped and creaked as he climbed.

"See here, miss, what a fine job Mr. Lamb done." Mr. Caton took her arm and turned her to face Uncle Willie. His body, from the chin down, was draped in a blanket. His hands were folded over his chest, fingers laced. "Not a mark on his face."

The face was older than she remembered. Unnaturally still, but handsome yet. With a bit of leakage from the eyes and the nose she was trying hard not to notice. And a fly crawling over his clean-shaven chin. Libby flinched, her detachment of the past two days falling away. To hear he had died was one thing. To view him laid out, his eyes unseeing, his voice silenced, his heart forever stilled, was quite another. The choking smoke and stifling, odor-laden air burned her eyes and throat.

"Meaning no disrespect, miss." Mr. Caton's voice made her jump. "But it perturbs me some, Willie's services being so rushed-like on account of the mail."

"The mail?" asked Libby.

A sandpaper voice volunteered from the shadows, "The post office operates out of the store here. Mail can't be gone over so long as we're keeping vigil on Willie."

"Nor can any go out."

Mr. Caton thrust out his grizzled jaw. "It don't bother me nary a bit that Willie's holding up the mail. Nor Minor. Nor Benjamin. You hain't troubled over it, aire ya, Benjamin?"

"No, but Mrs. Payne will be vexed," said Captain Boyd.

"To blazes with Zerilda. No woman of any account would cart the mail about the countryside anyways." Mr. Caton's judgment came as flat and uncompromising as his nose. "The mail can wait."

Mrs. Brignadello spoke up. "Now, Mr. Caton, Mr. Lamb's been all over that. Mr. Cearlock, too. Under the circumstances, there's no shame attached to getting a body in the ground in a timely fashion."

Mr. Caton's eyes flashed. "Well, I fer one don't cotton to hurry-up funerals."

Mrs. Brignadello squeezed Libby's hand in silent warning. Libby's fear of this ordeal being drawn out another day and keeping her from Father's bedside contributed the needed ounce of courage. Tactfully she offered, "Thank you for your devotion, Mr. Caton. However, Uncle Willie was in the military himself once. I can't help thinking he would be pleased to have his services on Decoration Day."

"Then yer mind's set on it?" asked Mr. Caton.

"Yes, I suppose it is."

Seeing disapproval in the stiff set of his shoulders and his outthrust lip, Libby caught her breath, expecting further argument. But he gave none, rather turned to his peers and sighed heavily.

"Iffen it's to be today, then let's see he's properly honored, men."

Relief in her voice, Mrs. Brignadello said, "It's settled, then. I'll be leaving now, unless there's something more I can do. Captain Boyd, you look after her, you hear?"

"Be pleased to, Mrs. Bee," said the silver-haired soft-spoken old mail carrier in the polished boots and military cap.

Mrs. Brignadello murmured words of comfort, thrust the basket into Libby's hands, and departed with a rustle of skirts.

Mr. Caton offered his chair with a sweep of his gnarled hand. "Set yerself down."

Libby settled the basket of muffins in her lap.

Mr. Caton waved away the fly that was making an excursion of Uncle Willie's ear, then joined his friends in the smoky shadows. A respectful silence fell upon them, broken only by a thin creaking and the soft pat-a-pat of one old fellow's fidgety feet. Catching herself rocking, Libby stopped and the creaking stopped too. They seemed to be waiting for something. When the lull grew heavy, she swallowed hard and offered, "I regret the rest of my family couldn't come."

No one spoke.

A pulsing began behind her eyes and spread to the base of her neck. "I guess you know Mr. Blue was my mother's uncle. "

Again nothing. And still she sensed expectancy.

"She'd be grateful for your loyal watch, Mr. Caton. And your friendship to Uncle Willie. All of your friendships. As am I." Libby flushed at the halting ineptness of her words.

No one moved.

"We'd lost touch with Uncle Willie after my mother died," she tried once more, then paused, nerves leaping as the sandpaper voice spoke from the row of watchers.

"Willie said something about your mother's death just a few days ago. I'd come in for some bootblack, and he made mention of it. Seemed to be on his mind."

Another fellow nodded knowingly. "A premonition, most likely."

"Reckon so?" chimed in a third.

"He told me once how with his family, the grim reaper comes collectin' in twos."

"Hear tell how his parents went just hours of one another? And two of his uncles just a day apart."

Mr. Caton peered at her from squinted eyes. "Yer father still ailin', miss?"

"He's much better now." Heart jumping, Libby was reminded again of Uncle Willie's superstitions. He'd been a grand storyteller, frightening her so with stories of spirits he called "tokens" that Mother had asked him to please not repeat those barbaric tales in front of the children.

"No cause to worry, miss. What'll be will be."

"Could be a cousin in a far-off place you don't even know about'll be taken."

"That'd fill the bill."

"Sure it would."

The light was too dim to clearly distinguish their faces. But there was a patronizing, pitying timbre to their voices. They had dismissed her as young and naive. It stirred a stubborn resistance in her. It was superstition, born of coincidence and overactive imaginations. Like her dream of Uncle Willie standing in the doorway yesterday morning. She spoke up, saying, "There was no other death in the family when my mother passed away."

"Now, there's where yer wrong, miss," Mr. Caton's raspy voice intruded. "Willie's wife was took sudden-like while he was off, attending your mum's funeral."

"His wife? Uncle Willie was married?"

"Yes, ma'am. That's how he come to have the store."

"Married a gal by the name of Addie Linegar. The store'd been her father's before her. Mercy, she was a worker," added Mr. Caton in a tone that indicated grudging respect. "Always a-hurryin' from this to that."

"Hurried out in front of old engine No. Forty-eight on the day Willie left for his niece's funeral," said Minor.

"That's right. She was headed across town when the Bloomington and Springfield Accommodation pulled up and shut off the crossing ahead of her."

"She waited a few feet from the siding until the train

pulled out, then shot out on the tracks, never noticing the sudden approach of a freight engine."

"It was hidden from view by the elevator," another voice chimed in.

"Engineer blew the whistle."

"Reckon she thought the sound came from No. Forty-eight. She never even knew what hit her."

"Willie always reasoned, somehow or another, it was his fault."

Stunned to learn more of Uncle Willie in a few short minutes than she'd known all of her life, Libby asked, "Because he was gone?"

"No, ma'am." Mr. Caton struck a match on the sole of his shoe, touched it to his pipe, and blew it out again. "On account he'd got a premonition he was the one chosen to go after yer mum. The curse of twos. Scairt him so, he begged and pleaded, jest like that thar feller in the Good Book . . . What was his name?"

"Hezekiah?"

"That's it. Willie made a bargain with God. Said he'd lay off drinking and try to live right iffen He was to take the curse off of him."

"I wouldn't call it a curse, exactly," mused Captain Boyd.

"Whatever you call it, it landed on Addie 'stead of Willie. He hadn't bargained on that. Piled on the guilt right smart."

"Kept his word, though, didn't he? Leastways, I cain't recollect Willie gettin' crocked even once since Addie died."

"He ain't," Mr. Caton said, and none of the men contradicted him.

"I reckon it's been nigh on to seven years since Addie died."

Libby's head was swimming with the smoke and the tales and the heavy-laden air. She got to her feet, clutching the basket. "If you'll excuse me, I'll just take these upstairs." She picked her way toward the stairs. But the veil hampered her vision, and her foot collided with a copper boiler, ringing out a resonant note.

Captain Boyd sprang to his feet and plucked a single

candle from the candelabrum, saying, "I'll light your way, Miss Willie."

"Miss Watson," murmured several of the men in unison.

"I beg your pardon," said the old mail carrier.

"It's quite all right, I don't mind," murmured Libby.

"Right this way." Captain Boyd motioned for her to follow.

The hand holding the candle was unsteady. His cheeks were flushed, his eyes a bit glassy. And the stairs, Libby noted, were steep.

"After you, miss," he said with a sweeping gesture and a courtly bow that nearly set his fine silver hair on fire.

"You needn't follow me up," Libby said quickly. "If you'll just hold the candle right here at the bottom, that will be plenty of light."

"No, no. I don't mind at all, miss," he insisted.

Concerned for his safety, Libby lifted her veil, dashed up the stairs, and dropped the basket on a lampstand on the landing. She was halfway down the steps again when she met Captain Boyd still making his way up.

"Willie didn't tell me you were so quick on your feet. I'm dizzy just watching. Perhaps I should . . . sit down."

Libby took the candle as he sank down on the step. "There now, you just rest a moment."

"I'd be pleased if you'd join me," he said.

Libby settled on a step just below him. The veil had fallen over her face again. She pushed it back, the better to see him as she asked, "How is it you and Uncle Willie came to be friends?"

"My wife was sitting on the back porch, doing some mending one summer evening, when a fellow climbed down off a boxcar to ask if he could borrow a needle and some thread to do his mending. The train left before he could finish the job, but he called to my wife, promising he'd return what he'd borrowed the next time he passed through. A year went by and here comes a fellow to the door. He introduced himself as Willie Blue and asked for the lady of the household, saying he'd come to return her needle and thread."

"Was she surprised to get them back?" asked Libby.

His slow smile was tinged with sorrow. He linked his hands around one knee and said, "Actually, she'd passed on, miss. I was having a hard time of it. Willie invited me to do some traveling with him. So I sold the house and went with him, and never once have I regretted it. He had friends all across the country. It didn't matter where we stopped, we could get a hot meal and, more often than not, a place to sleep."

"That's the Uncle Willie I remember," said Libby quietly.

"When I came back to Edgewood, he came with me," Captain Boyd continued. "He bought some ground out there at Old Kentucky, though the wanderlust still came over him now and then. He'd get to feeling blue and the next thing you'd know, he'd be climbing aboard a freight train."

"Melancholy," said Libby, nodding. "That's what my brothers remembered about him."

The stairs creaked as the captain got to his feet and offered Libby a hand up. The reflection of the candle flames illuminated the tears standing in his eyes. Was it Uncle Willie he was mourning? Or did the memory of his dead wife account for the tears? Feeling bad for him, Libby averted her gaze, and waited for him to collect his composure before they rejoined the others.

It wasn't long before the door opened at the front of the store and folks filed in for a final viewing of Uncle Willie Blue. Libby recognized Chester Gentry, who'd introduced the statesman at the train station. She wanted to ask about Mr. Cearlock. But Mr. Gentry, with his silk hat, blackened mustache, and silver-headed cane, had a detached manner that discouraged her from doing so. He was the exception in coming alone, for in most cases, entire families came, right down to the wee ones.

Libby recognized Frankie McClure from the bicycle accident. He didn't look her way, so intent was he on Uncle Willie's corpse. His bruised cheek and the cut on his chin were not so noticeable in the dim light. His head was up, his thin shoulders squared, his hands locked behind his back. His blue eyes, while arresting, were unfathomable. There was something about his features, something that flitted just beyond the grasp of conscious thought. Decatur McClure strode behind him and stood looking at Uncle Willie, his jaw working.

Alarm flickered in Mr. Caton's eyes. He sidled up next to the big man. Libby heard him say, "He saved our boy, Decatur."

The man's eyes were hard and hot. The odor of whiskey was stronger now. Libby could smell it from several feet away.

"You and him was friends fer some years," said Mr. Caton.

"Hesh up, old man," said Decatur.

Mr. Caton "heshed," but there was a worrisome quality to his silence. Was it McClure's drinking that was troubling him? If so, he had company in his concern. The room had gone silent, throbbing with tension not unlike that which stirred through Thistle Down when some normally reasonable, law-abiding fellow got crazy drunk and went looking for a quarrel. McClure was big enough to do some damage. Was it just the drinking? Or was it something more?

Opal slipped up on soundless feet and tugged at her brother's hand. "Let's go out, Frankie."

"Scairty-girl." He reached up, tapped Uncle Willie's forehead, and with a fleeting glance at his father, taunted his sister, saying, "See, Opal? Hard as a melon. Want I should boost you up for a feel?"

The little girl shrank from him. Mr. Caton circled the counter and swept down on the boy like an eagle, talons extended. A shaft of sunlight poured in as the old man tossed the lad out the back door. Giving Mr. Caton a wide berth, the little girl scampered out after him. The burst of light and air was all too brief.

Mr. McClure paid no heed to his father-in-law's method of dealing with his children. Rather, he turned his burning gaze on Libby. "Yer his kin, all right. Got the same hair and eyes."

Conscious of Captain Boyd moving a little closer, Libby said, for want of better words, "I appreciate your coming, Mr. McClure."

There was no warmth in his monosyllabic response. Libby sensed hostility, yet could think of no rational reason for it. Unless he thought she and her family had in some way been neglectful of Uncle Willie. Or was it just the alcohol? The silence stretched to a fine, thin strand.

"My wife's grateful for what Willie done," Mr. McClure said finally, and darted a glance to the stairway before turning to go.

Libby heard every footfall as he strode to the front door. Shoulders aching from holding herself so tense, she lifted her gaze to Captain Boyd. "I don't understand. He seems . . . angry."

"Don't take it to heart, miss. Decatur isn't himself lately," he replied.

"Some folks cry it out when the grim reaper takes a loved one," ventured Mr. Gruben from his cracker barrel. "A few get angry. Decatur appears to be one of the latter."

"He's takin' Willie's death hard," Mr. Minor offered, and spit a stream of tobacco juice into the coal bucket as the volley of opinions settled into a natural rhythm.

"Been on a binge ever since it happened."

"Have you tried talking to him, Hack?"

"He's a stout-headed cuss, he ain't gonna listen to me," said McClure's father-in-law.

"He might if he'd get off the sauce."

"They was awful close, him and Willie."

"Drinkin' ain't gonna bring Willie back."

"It can't be good for the children, either. What got into Frankie, misbehaving like that?"

"I swan, I nearly dropped my teeth, seein' him knockin' on poor Willie's noggin. Jest like he'd forgot it was Willie what saved his skinny little hide."

"Now, hold on there, that's my grandson yer meddlin' with!" Hascal Caton scowled at the lot of them, stanching the flow of public discussion as to what ailed the McClure father and son.

"I didn't aim to criticize. Jest pointin' out maybe the boy's got a hurt ain't bein' attended." Minor backed hastily down.

Hascal snapped his suspenders, but offered no explanation.

The funeral hour was nearly upon them when Captain Boyd introduced a latecomer as Mrs. Payne, the carrier for Rural Route Number Two. Libby saw with surprise that it was her seatmate from the train. Mrs. Payne had donned a tattered black hat and veil, but she wore the same boots and had the same terse manner.

"Best throw open the doors and windows once this is over and done, Mr. Caton," said she, dispensing with expressions of sympathy. "I got a finicky nose, and I can't be sortin' mail in air heavy enough to cave yer knees."

"You won't be sortin' none today, so don't trouble yerself about it, Miz Payne," snapped Mr. Caton.

The dour woman took one last look at Uncle Willie and shuffled out again.

A mustached man in a black, long-tailed suit coat introduced himself as the undertaker, Mr. Lamb. His left eye twitched intermittently as he offered his condolences. Respectfully he said, "The hearse is waiting. I'm not rushing, mind you. But whenever you are ready, we'll transport the body to the Columbian for services."

Libby wondered again about her uncle's attorney, Mr. Cearlock. It seemed odd that he hadn't made an appearance. Reluctant to delay any longer, she said, "I'm ready."

Mr. Lamb said, "The Columbian's on the next block, if you'd care to wait there. Left, as you leave the store."

Light once again swept the back of the store as a rear door was opened. Libby swung around to see two husky fellows roll a casket toward the counter. Anxious to be gone before they lifted Uncle Willie into the casket, she made her way to the front of the store and out into the street.

The Columbian was a handsome brick building with a patterned brick sidewalk in front and a wide staircase leading up to the door. There was a landing inside the door, with a modest set of steps leading down and more substantial stairs leading up to the main floor. The room was spacious and light, with seating for a large crowd and a balcony above to accommodate any overflow. The breeze circulating between east and west windows cooled

Libby's neck and face as she was ushered to a chair on the front row.

The casket was brought in and the flowers arranged around it. By the time the funeral began, the hall was filled all the way back to the doors. Uncle Willie had seemed to her young mind a private man. And yet, judging by the outpouring of sympathy, he was held warmly in the hearts of these people.

Scriptures were read. Songs were sung and the funeral discourse preached. Something to do with God's tender watch over the death of his saints. As the hall emptied out, the word "saints" lingered in Libby's ears. It wasn't a word she'd expected to hear applied to Uncle Willie.

When only the pallbearers remained, Mr. Lamb escorted her from the hall into the foyer where people tarried, exchanging hushed greetings. "There's a buggy waiting in front to drive you to the graveyard."

Libby descended the wide staircase, glad for the sunshine.

Opal was balanced on the hitching post just in front of the Columbian. Undaunted by the knot on her forehead and the bloodstains on her dress, she struck a pose with her arms outstretched and called to her brother, who was splashing in the horse trough nearby. "Look at me, Frankie. I'm walking the tightrope, just like Mrs. Bee. See?"

Libby breathed in the clean fresh air as in her head another voice sang, *Swing me, Uncle Willie. Watch me stand on my head. Listen, Uncle Willie, I know all the words to the song.*

She closed her eyes and pictured him at the gate of her childhood home. Cheeks ruddy. Eyes shining brightly blue. And a tumble of curls, as red as her own. She recalled how pleased she'd feel when he would call her Redtop, and Mother would laugh and say, "She has your coloring, Uncle Willie."

The memories rolled over Libby in gently lapping puddles, and with them, the realization that she had once loved Uncle Willie. And that the song was life and she didn't know all the words. No more than she'd known Uncle Willie.

5

𝕾 The funeral-goers clustered in front of the Columbian. Some on the brick walk, some on the stairs, some spilling over onto the weed-infested lawn of the jailhouse next door. Standing by herself, overhearing them chat of Mr. Minor's liver ailment, Squire Palmer's eighty-second birthday reunion, and the fruit butters stolen from the station agent's cellar, Libby felt the isolation of being a stranger where everyone else was intimately familiar. Their covert glances, while not unkind, made her lonesome for home. A black buggy and a glass-walled funeral carriage were parked along the street. She emptied her lungs of the bottled-up odors of death and sweat and rosewater, and angled for the buggy.

"Miss Watson?"

Libby paused and lifted her face. The driver put aside his whittling and swung down out of the seat. He wore a long-tailed black coat over khaki trousers with yellow cavalry trim, and a hat that was a duplicate of the undertaker's. As he swept it off his head with a work-roughened hand, a shower of unruly brown curls spilled across his high forehead.

"Isaac Galloway, ma'am. Mr. Lamb asked me to drive you."

With a sweep of her lashes Libby noted his firm clean-shaven chin, strong sunbrowned features, and a badly scarred left ear. His coat was tight across the shoulders,

48

and his shirt, though clean and neatly pressed, showed considerable wear. He carried himself well, his head up and his shoulders back.

"Watch your step, miss." He offered his arm for the remaining feet to the buggy.

Libby gathered her skirts, avoiding the mud surrounding the horse trough, and let him hand her into the rig. A dark mare stood in the traces, tail lashing at the rabble of hungry flies. She quivered and stamped a hind leg, setting the black fringe on the buggy top to dancing.

"Easy, Babe, easy," soothed Mr. Galloway. He shooed the flies and patted the horse's flank before circling behind the buggy and climbing up beside Libby. "Regular epidemic of green flies. Drivin' every critter in the county wild."

"They're bad at home, too." Libby blinked as he flicked the buggy whip and snagged a fly right off the horse's croup. The mare stood fast, unscathed by the whip.

"Sorry about your uncle. I'm goin' to miss him."

"You and Uncle Willie were friends?"

"Yes, ma'am. I've got a little ground I'm farming north of here at Old Kentucky. But there's no house there, so I've been staying with Willie over at the store."

Libby didn't remember seeing Mr. Galloway at the wake or the funeral. She estimated him to be near in years to her brother Adam. Discerning a hint of the West in his twang, she asked, "I take it you knew him well?"

"I'm not so sure anyone *really* knew Willie."

She waved away a sweat bee. "Here I thought it was just me."

"No, ma'am." The straight line of his mouth relaxed a little. "It was a complicated business, pickin' through the layers."

She admitted, "We hadn't seen him in seven years."

"Back when he wasn't worth shootin'."

"I wouldn't go quite that far," she said, vaguely discomfited by how openly he watched her.

"Willie would. He wasn't proud of his drinkin' days. But he wouldn't back away from owning up to them, either."

"I was beginning to think I was the only one who remembered."

"Get pretty flowery in there at the funeral, did it?" Gentle humor flickered in his deep-set gray eyes. Shallow lines fanned out from the corners, crinkling upward at her smile of affirmation. "Company manners. Their memories will sharpen, once the shock scabs over."

Thistle Down was no different. The meanest of tongues wagged more gently in the shadow of tragedy. Finding Mr. Galloway's honesty refreshing after an afternoon of extolled virtues and sugary praises, she confided, "I didn't even know he'd been married. He never mentioned the store, either. Or that he was prospering here in Edgewood."

"Reckon it wasn't important to Willie."

"But he should have been proud of the change in his life," she protested.

"That wasn't his way. He wasn't a prideful man."

She shot him a quick glance. "Perhaps you aren't giving yourself enough credit. It seems to me you understood him fairly well."

Mr. Galloway brushed a curled shaving off his knee, but his eyes never left her face. "Ma'am, if that was the case, I'd of been in there with the rest of 'em, eulogizing." He went back to picking off flies, his aim as sure as a swallow skimming supper over the meadow.

Libby slipped her wrist through the strings of her reticule and folded her gloved hands in her lap. A distant fife and the slow, somber beat of a drum sent a group of children racing past the Columbian and around the corner out of sight. Remembering the day and the parade that was to honor it, she glanced toward the door of the Columbian, then planted her feet wider and gripped the arm of the seat as the mare took a nervous step, rocking the buggy.

"Steady there, Babe." Mr. Galloway spoke to the mare in his rich voice. "A little marchin' music, is all. Where's your military bearin'?"

A moment later, the Decoration Day parade came around the corner and on toward the Columbian. Folks spread out along the walk, eyes fixed on the street.

Behind their buggy, Frankie McClure ceased splashing in the horse trough and watched the parade's approach. Libby saw him pick up a stone. The ribs of a slingshot protruded from his back pocket.

Opal scrambled under the hitching rail, panting, "You'd best not, Frankie. Paw-Paw hears, he'll wear you out."

"Not with *him* in town, he won't. Besides, I ain't doin' nothing. Quit following me now, you hear?"

"Don't have to."

"Best, if you know what's good fer ya."

The girl poked out her lip and tossed her mane of pale hair. "You ain't my boss."

"Am, when you tag after me."

"Are not."

"Am too, 'cause you ain't nothin' but a no-account piddlin' girl." Frankie jumped up and gave her a shove. She shoved back. They were about to lay into one another in earnest when one of the funeral-goers got between them. Sizing up the man's considerable height and breadth, the children ceased their pushing match. But Frankie brazenly shrugged the fellow's hand off his shoulders. The man stooped low, gripped Frankie by the ear, and spoke directly into it before ambling back to join his family on the steps. Mutiny smoldered in the boy's blue eyes as he watched the man retreat. His full lips moved in an unmistakable curse. He kicked up dust, crossing the street to the grain elevator, and flung himself down in the weeds.

Libby turned her gaze to the top of the steps where Mr. Lamb was propping open the doors of the Columbian. The pallbearers made their way out and started down the steps, straining beneath the weight of Uncle Willie's casket. Mr. Caton followed close behind them. He stood by as the casket was loaded into the glassed-in funeral carriage. Mr. Caton mounted the seat. Mr. Lamb climbed up beside him, took the lines, and waited as the parade came on.

Resigned to waiting until the parade had passed, Libby turned and faced forward again. Captain Boyd led the march, carrying the flag. He held his liquor well, never missing a step. A fife-and-drum trio of ancient vintage followed. Then came half a dozen old soldiers.

"Civil War veterans," Mr. Galloway explained. He blew the shavings from the stick he'd hollowed out and used it to point out a short-legged barrel-chested old fellow with a tremor in his step. "That's Spike Culbertson on the left. He fought at Gettysburg. Knows Lincoln's speech word for word."

A point of pride here in Edgewood, apparently, Libby thought. Men waved their hats, and women their hand-kerchiefs, as the old soldiers passed, while the children strained closer, the better to see the horse-drawn cannon rolling behind the old men. Spontaneous applause arose from the crowd, a heartfelt gesture of esteem and affection. The uniformed young man who marched behind the cannon answered the spectators' patriotic fervor with a smart salute in Mr. Galloway's direction.

Isaac Galloway returned the salute and said for Libby's benefit, "Billy Young."

There was a fellow in Thistle Down who'd been a part of the Spanish-American conflict. He'd come home in a uniform just like Mr. Young's. Libby spared the yellow stripe on Mr. Galloway's trousers a second glance and wondered if he, too, had played a part in liberating the Cubans from Spanish domination. She was about to ask when, from behind them, the funeral carriage pulled out into the street behind the cannon. Sudden alarm pushed aside her idle curiosity. Peering over her shoulder, she asked, "What are they doing?"

"Beg yer pardon, ma'am?"

"I said what are they doing?"

"Fallin' in line."

"But why?"

"Makin' a funeral parade. You didn't know?" At her denial, he looked from her to the hearse and back again. "Must be Hascal's doin's. He's pretty set on Willie bein' properly honored."

Heat rushed to Libby's cheeks. She should have heeded more closely Mrs. Brignadello's warning, but how was she to know Mr. Caton would intrude upon a parade meant as a tribute to those who'd served their country?

What would the townfolk, so proud of their war heroes, make of the intrusion? Perspiration stung her eyes and turned her gloved hands clammy as the funeral carriage rolled past them and on toward the town square, where the townspeople had gathered. She couldn't bring herself to look at their faces.

On the seat beside the undertaker, Mr. Caton motioned to Mr. Galloway. The young man gathered the lines and spoke to the horse.

"Wait!" cried Libby as the horse ambled away from the curb.

Mr. Galloway's head was turned toward the street. He did not reply. Nor did he halt the buggy. Panic rising, Libby prepared to climb down. One foot was reaching for the ground when, without warning, the horse bolted. Libby teetered between the buggy and the street, every nerve screaming as the churning wheels chewed up the dirt street. Squeaking, squealing, rushing to pull her under.

The buggy rocked as Mr. Galloway lunged and caught her by the skirt. He jerked so hard, she fell back against him, knocking the reins from his hand and causing the buggy to list precariously to the left. Just as it began to right itself, the wheel dropped into a rut so deep, it heaved the conveyance onto one side and over, spilling both Libby and the driver onto the fringed top. A scream filled Libby's throat as the frightened horse pounded the dust. Thundering hooves flashed close, sunlight glinting off iron shoes.

Blue sky, green trees, gaping bystanders, and buildings melded into whipped-up dust as Libby struggled to dislodge her foot from beneath Mr. Galloway. If she could pull herself up, up and over the side of the inverted buggy top, she'd be free. She struggled in vain. Mr. Galloway, flat on his back, cradled his hand and shouted words she could not make sense of. Something about a knife.

A farmer dashed into the street, darting close, trying to stop the horse. But the terrified mare raced on, dragging Libby, Mr. Galloway, and the upside-down buggy past the funeral carriage. Past Billy Young and the cannon. Past the old soldiers, Captain Boyd, and the flag.

In a tangle of petticoats and limbs, over ruts and stones and down a muddy alley, Libby fought to extricate herself from the pliant top, until finally, mercifully, the crossbar snapped. It let the horse forward enough of the buggy to tighten the lines, which had caught on the springs.

Mr. Galloway scrambled to his feet. Hatless, dust-coated, and blood-smeared, he leaned over her, still holding his hand. "Are you hurt?" he asked.

Libby swept her skirts down, rose to her elbows, rolled up to her knees, and waited for the world to stop spinning.

"Can you get up?"

"I think so." She coughed the dust from her lungs and sucked in her breath at the sight of his heavily bleeding hand.

"Gouged with my own knife," he said tersely. "Careless trick, leavin' it open on the seat."

Libby cast a wild glance for her reticule, only to find it still looped to her wrist. She took the handkerchief from it, stumbled to her feet, ripped off her gloves, and used them to pad her linen handkerchief before pressing it to his wounded palm.

"Harder," he said.

She increased the pressure, so hard she could feel the pulse throbbing in his palm. She lifted her face. "Is it deep?"

"Feels like it. You're sure you're all right?"

Her heart was still pounding and her limbs were wobbly, but she nodded, and in so doing, eased the pressure on his hand.

"That's right, leave go. I've got it."

His callused fingertips brushed the top of her hand as she pulled back and left him holding the makeshift bandage to the wound. His blood was on her jacket and skirt and heaven only knew where else, the way they'd been tossed about.

Mr. Galloway was taking stock, less concerned with the improprieties of being dragged through town in the lid of a buggy, tumbling and colliding like beans in a coffee grinder, than he was with the physical damage done. He eased up on the mare, soothed her with his voice, and looked for signs of injury.

"Is she hurt?" Libby asked.

"Doesn't appear to be." He kept his voice low, adding darkly, "Lucky for Frankie."

As she remembered the slingshot, Libby's gaze met his livid gray eyes. "You mean he . . ."

"Had to be him and his stones. Why else would the horse leap like that?"

Libby looked on in silence as he straddled the broken crossbar and surveyed the wreckage.

"I'd like ta take that slingshot of his and fling him clear to Old Kentucky." Already the handkerchief and gloves were saturated with his blood. Keeping the pressure on his hand, he swung around, adding, "Didn't help any, you starting down with the buggy still movin'. "

His directness seemed suddenly less refreshing. "I asked you to stop."

A look of consternation came and went so quickly on his face, Libby reasoned she had imagined it. "You might give a fella a little more time. What was your hurry, anyway?"

"I didn't want to be in the parade."

"So you were aimin' to what . . . *walk* to the cemetery?"

Though she refrained from saying so, Libby hadn't gotten that far in her thinking.

"It's three miles."

"More fitting, you'll have to agree, than a parade through the streets," she replied, her temper getting the best of her.

"Fittin'?" He crooked an eyebrow and looked from her to the wreckage to the trembling mare and back again.

Bumped and bruised, her limbs still as flimsy as matchsticks, Libby swept her hair out of her face and resisted a quick retort. He was upset, too. And rightfully so. His horsemanship—or lack thereof—had been on display. She had not lived with three men and a boy without knowing something about pride. She swallowed hers and said, "I'm sorry. It wasn't your fault."

The glint in his eye cooled only marginally. He leaned over and let go of the wound long enough to extract her hat from the wreckage. He gestured with it, saying, "You're bleeding."

Libby drew her hand across her cheek and saw that he was right. She took her crumpled hat. The veil was in tatters. She was a bloody mess, with no place to hide, and half a dozen long-legged men were rushing down the alley toward them.

One stood out from the rest, as he loped along with his neck thrust forward. His cap flew off. He squealed, clumsily trying to retrieve it, and Libby saw with a pang the eyes of a child peering out of a man's face.

Fleet of foot for one so short of leg, Mrs. Brignadello was among those racing to their rescue. "Would you look at that rig!" she cried, as the men rushed to Mr. Galloway's assistance. "I swan to goodness, it's a blessing you aren't both a pile of broken bones." Mrs. Brignadello rose on tiptoe and touched Libby's face. "I don't know what you hit, but it must have laid your cheek open. My, my! First Opal gushing blood, and now you."

"Sorry, ma'am. Musta been my knife," Mr. Galloway called over his shoulder.

"Oughta be here in this mess someplace." A second fellow kicked through the wreckage as a third man attempted to free the mare.

"I swan to goodness, Ike, you've struck a bleeder, too. Never mind the knife," ordered Mrs. Brignadello. "Leave it to Teddy, he's got good eyes. Teddy? Teddy Baker! See if you can find Ike's knife. He needs medical attention."

The fellow with the loping gait and childlike expression bobbed his head.

"I gotta take Mr. Lamb's horse home first," protested Mr. Galloway.

"Nonsense!" exclaimed Mrs. Brignadello. "Mr. Woodmancy's tending the horse. You come along with me."

Mr. Galloway looped a proffered bandana around the blood-soaked pad on his palm, and trailed along after Mrs. Brignadello. Libby nearly overran his heels when he stopped to call back, "Appreciate you lookin', Teddy. Bring my knife to Doc Harding's if you should find it."

"Forget the knife, would you?" Mrs. Brignadello chided. "We've got to get that bleeding stopped. You're not weakening, are you?"

"Only when I think of telling Mr. Lamb I wrecked his rig."

Libby shot him a quick glance as he fell in beside her. His color had faded, whether from loss of blood or concern over being held responsible by the undertaker, she wasn't certain.

"How about you, dear? Feeling light-headed?" Mrs. Brignadello turned a concerned eye Libby's way.

"No, not at all." Libby hesitated, weighing her need to see a doctor. Her cheek ached, as did her battered knees, but she hadn't much money in her reticule and she could not pay here, as she did back home, in laundered shirts and trousers. As she paused, debating the wisest course, the rest of the onlookers were catching up.

"It isn't far," Mrs. Brignadello was saying. Realizing Libby had fallen behind, she looked back. "Come along, dear."

Her need to escape the probing eyes of a town full of strangers was the deciding factor. Libby overcame monetary concerns and hurried to catch up.

6

🐞 Mrs. Brignadello held open the rear door leading into the doctor's office. Libby followed Mr. Galloway into the cluttered back room. The smell of ether and pig manure nearly drove her back out again.

Mrs. Brignadello clamped a hand over her nose and called, "Land of mercy, Melville, what have you done?"

A voice as dry as parchment echoed back, "Be with you in a minute, Sarah Jane. And don't touch my desk."

"As if there were danger of my finding it." Mrs. Brignadello's brisk step carried her to the window. She flung it open, then whipped through the room like a fresh breeze, picking up a shriveled apple core, a cold pipe, a scattered newspaper.

Thinking of her valise and that she could not be more than a block from Uncle Willie's, Libby wavered once more. "Perhaps I'll go back to the store."

"That cut needs attention. Doctor's a fair man. He won't overcharge you."

Feeling transparent, Libby flushed, and explained what now seemed a fortuitous last-minute decision. "I brought along a change of clothes in case I should run late and miss my train home. They're in my valise back at the store."

"I'll send someone over, or go myself, once the doctor's had a look at you." Mrs. Brignadello tied on an apron, drew water from the stove reservoir, then set the shallow basin on the washstand. She returned a small brown bottle to a cabinet where powders and pills and liquid medicines vied for space behind painted doors, and returned with a cotton cloth.

Sweeping a pile of books off the chairs flanking the washstand, she said, "Sit down, Miss Watson, and I'll wash your wound. You too, Ike. You're dripping on Doctor's floor."

Mr. Galloway did as he was told, but his gaze was uneasy as it came to rest on the medical utensils strung across the table. "Don't go threadin' any needles just yet, Mrs. Bee. See here, it's nearly stopped bleeding."

"You relax and leave the diagnosing to Doctor." Mrs. Brignadello squeezed the water from the rag and stretched to her full height to dab gently at Libby's face. "What was your knife doing in the buggy seat, anyway?"

"Hollowin' out spiles while I waited, ma'am."

"Spiles?"

"Yes, ma'am. For tapping trees."

"Ah, yes. Your maple sugar camp. Next time fold the blade back into your pocket." She clucked her tongue and announced crisply, "You don't want to be like Doctor, never putting anything away properly."

Mr. Galloway had nothing to say in his own defense, but there was reproach in the glance he sent Libby. Or was she being too sensitive? She winced as the damp rag skimmed over her tender cheek.

"There now, we're almost done. The bleeding has stopped, but it's left a bit of a gap. We'll see what Doctor thinks." Mrs. Brignadello marched to the door with the basin, flung the water into the alley, then crossed to the horsehair sofa and began folding bedding and stray articles of clothing strewn across it.

"You didn't go home last night, did you, Melville?" she called to the doctor.

His voice answered, "My wife was holding auditions for that musical group she's been planning ever since Angus announced his candidacy for the legislature. My services weren't required."

A balding gentleman with a long face and hunched

shoulders strode into the room from the back. His all-encompassing glance took in Mr. Galloway, Libby, and Mrs. Brignadello. "What have we here?"

"That mare of Mr. Lamb's flipped the buggy and ran away with Ike and Miss Watson." Mrs. Brignadello brushed the lock of white hair back into place amongst her sleek, raven-dark tresses and patted her shining face dry. "Miss Watson is Willie Blue's niece. Miss Watson, this is my brother, Dr. Harding. "

Libby held out her hand. "I'm pleased to meet you, sir."

"Likewise," said the doctor. His cold fingers pressed her warm ones briefly. He leaned closer, eyeing her cheek. "Is this the extent of your wounds?"

Reluctant to speak of her stinging knees with Mr. Galloway looking on, Libby said, "It's the worst of it, anyway."

"Surface cut?" queried Mrs. Brignadello, looking over his shoulder.

The doctor grunted something unintelligible to his sister before saying to Libby, "If you can wait a few minutes, I'll have a look at Ike's hand, then we'll see about a suture or two for you."

Libby stepped out of his way, Mr. Galloway's wound being of a more serious nature. Mrs. Brignadello filled the silence, expanding upon her abbreviated account of their freak ride through the streets of Edgewood.

The doctor's spectacles slid down his nose as he examined Ike Galloway's hand. Standing straight again, he nudged them back to the thin bridge of his nose and met Mr. Galloway's uneasy gaze. "The puncture wound is deep, Ike. Have to be careful of infection. The swelling in your wrist concerns me, too."

Galloway set his jaw. "Do what you have to, Doc."

The doctor turned his head to one side in an attitude of listening. "See if Angus is stirring out from under the ether, Sarah Jane, would you?"

"Angus?" Abruptly Mrs. Brignadello stopped tidying the forbidden desk. "What happened to him?"

"The best I can piece it together, he had an accident on his way back from Old Kentucky where he'd gone on business. Dislocated shoulder and a broken ankle. I'm a bit unclear on the details, but it seems he awoke to find himself in a pig wallow. His surrey gone."

"Dear Lord!" cried Mrs. Brignadello, as Libby stood wondering if the Angus they were speaking of and Angus Cearlock, her uncle's attorney, were one and the same.

"His clothes are on the floor in there," the doctor called as his sister hastened down the corridor. "Hang them in the alley to let them air out."

"How'd he get back to town?" asked Mr. Galloway.

"Mrs. McClure came along in her springboard and gave him a lift."

"Excuse me, but . . . the fellow who was hurt . . . he isn't by chance my uncle's attorney?" Libby asked.

The doctor nodded, then said on a dismissive note, "There's an alcove to your left, just outside the door, Miss Watson. Or wait up in the front room if you wish. Sarah Jane?"

His sister hurried past Libby with a purposeful stride. "He's just beginning to stir. Melville, he looks terrible! His mother's going to take one look and faint dead away. And Chester, with all his plans for the upcoming campaign . . ."

"Let's not worry about that just yet," interrupted the doctor. Brusquely he added, "How about some water here?"

Mrs. Brignadello clamped her jaw shut tight and did as he asked. But her thoughts must have been scurrying, for all at once she looked at Libby as if seeing her for the first time. "My goodness. Angus was supposed to meet your train!"

"So you're the one." The doctor stretched his neck out like a turtle, squinting into her face. "He kept insisting I send someone to meet the noon train. Something to do with an inheritance. But I couldn't make sense of who, what, or why."

"Inheritance?" echoed Libby.

"It's Mr. Blue's—" Stopped short by her brother's severe expression, Mrs. Brignadello amended, "I gather he hasn't had a chance to—"

The doctor's tone sharpened without lifting in volume.

"Whatever business Angus has to discuss, he can do without any help from us, once the ether wears off."

"Yes, of course," said Mrs. Brignadello, coloring. "I'll go sit with him awhile, if you have no further need of me."

Libby wished the doctor hadn't shut off the tap of information quite so abruptly.

"Find a seat, Miss Watson. I'll be with you directly," the doctor said, dismissing her.

A few steps down the central corridor was the alcove he'd indicated. There was no door. Libby could hear water splashing in the basin as the doctor cleaned Mr. Galloway's hand, and Mr. Galloway's hiss of indrawn breath. Affording the doctor and patient more privacy, she continued on toward the front of the building and passed a second alcove on the way. Beyond the cot and sheeted patient was Mrs. Brignadello, holding the offending articles of clothing at arm's length as she crossed to the open window.

The front office was a surprising contrast to what she'd just left. A clear case of putting one's best foot forward, it gleamed with cleanliness, from the wide glass window to the pine floor to the whitewashed beams overhead. Even the brass spittoon was brightly polished. Mrs. Brignadello's touch, Libby supposed. She took a chair at a right angle to the window, and promptly found herself being peered at through the glass by the same uniformed young man who'd marched behind the cannon in the parade.

Libby had forgotten his name, but he was a tall fellow, very wide at the shoulders and chest, then tapering at the waist and through the hips. He had arms like fence posts and large, long-fingered hands. Cheeks flushed, eyes dark and thickly lashed, he called something to her through the window. She cupped a hand to her ear, and a second later he strode through the door.

"You're Willie Blue's niece, aren't you? Mr. Caton sent me to see about your injuries."

"A few scrapes. It's nothing serious, Mr. . . . "

"Young. Billy Young, ma'am. Do you want him to delay the burial while Doc patches you up?"

"No, no. Thank Mr. Caton for the consideration," she

added hastily. "But it would be best if they went ahead without me."

"All right then, miss. I'll deliver the message." He turned in the door and asked, "How's Ike faring?"

"He's being cared for now."

"That's good. If he should start to leave, would you tell him for me I'll be right back?"

"Certainly." On impulse Libby called after him, "Mr. Young, if I might ask a favor? I've left a valise upstairs at the store. Would you mind stopping by and bringing it to me when you return?"

"Be happy to, miss." He let himself out with a careless bang of the door.

Foot traffic was brisk on the sidewalk in front of the doctor's office. Conscious of her bedraggled state, Libby retraced her steps to the narrow alcove. There was no door to close. She backed into the corner that afforded the most privacy, swept her skirts out of the way with one hand, peeled back a cotton stocking with the other, and assessed the damage to her knees.

On the other side of the wall Dr. Harding was suturing Mr. Galloway's hand. She gleaned from the conversation that the patient wasn't to do any heavy lifting until his injuries had healed. She had fared much better. The injuries to her knees were no worse than she'd suffered on a regular basis as a child, tagging along after her brothers. Not even worth mentioning, she decided, smoothing her bloodstained stockings into place.

Libby was adjusting her skirts when the stick Mr. Galloway had been whittling fell out of her petticoats. She picked it up and saw that it was four or five inches in length, hollowed out, the rest cut in a trench. A spile, he had said. For tapping sugar maples. She tucked the spile into her reticule until she could return it.

As she waited for the doctor to finish with Mr. Galloway, indications of Mr. Cearlock stirring from beneath the ether cloud issued from the other alcove. Mewings and mumblings gave way to the unmistakable sound of disgorging, and Mrs. Brignadello's soothing reassurances. A moment later, Libby heard the doctor leave Mr. Galloway to check on Mr. Cearlock. He was still with him when Billy Young returned, the door slamming behind him.

He made a straight line for the back room, striding past the alcove without noticing her. Libby heard Mr. Galloway's cheerless greeting and the young veteran's whispered "Did the girl leave?"

"I don't know," said Mr. Galloway. "Why? What've you got there?"

"Her valise."

"She sent you for it? And you went?"

"Course I did. Why? Were you plannin' on beatin' me to it?"

Galloway growled something inaudible, then ordered, "Hand me my shirt, would you?"

"Reckon I would have seen her if she was headed back to the store. I don't think she should be there alone, Ike."

"Why? What's the matter?" Galloway's tone shifted.

"I'd never been up over the store before. I know Willie Blue wasn't tidy, but . . ."

"But *what*, Billy?"

"It's wall-to-wall furniture up there."

"I know."

"There's a chair all busted up and papers strung to kingdom come. The door's standing open, and down toward the bottom, looks like somebody kicked a hole through."

"That's jest dandy," growled Galloway. "Somebody's broke in and messed up the place. Doc? I gotta go. I'll stop by later and settle up."

Hurried footsteps were followed by yet another slamming door.

Who would break into Uncle Willie's store? And why? Libby rushed out of the alcove into the deserted back room. Mr. Galloway's funeral jacket lay abandoned on the table. Unfortunately, there was no sign of her valise. Afraid Mr. Young had taken it with him, Libby jerked open the door and stepped out into the alley just in time to see the men disappear between two buildings, Mr. Galloway pulling up his suspenders, her valise beating against Billy Young's leg.

"Mr. Young! My valise!" she cried, but too late. She hovered indecisively in the open door.

Mrs. Brignadello bustled in and stopped short. "I thought I saw Billy Young."

"He left with Mr. Galloway." Libby closed the door and related what little she knew.

Mrs. Brignadello's startled expression shifted to one of indignation. "Who would do such a shameful thing? And Mr. Blue not even in his grave yet."

Libby thought back to those last moments before leaving the store. "The door may have been unlocked."

"Mr. Lamb would have been preoccupied with the business of getting Mr. Blue to the Columbian, it's true. But I assure you, if that is the case, it was an innocent oversight. He's an honest man, is Mr. Lamb."

Libby hadn't intended to suggest otherwise. "I'm sure he is. I was puzzling out loud how the intruder may have gained entrance."

"Were items stolen? Was there damage, too?"

"I have no idea. Mr. Young didn't say."

"You aren't to worry, dear. Sheriff Conklin will get to the bottom of this matter, I'll warrant. You needn't think your rights of property will be trod upon any more than if it were Mr. Blue himself who'd—"

"Wait a minute," Libby interrupted, head humming. The faint idea planted by the earlier mention of the word "inheritance" was suddenly looming large. "My rights of . . . Mrs. Brignadello, what are you saying?"

A guarded expression brought the color back to Mrs. Brignadello's cheeks. Crossing on soundless feet, she peeked down the corridor and came back again, saying quietly, "Doctor doesn't want any hint of suspicion that he's been meddling in Angus's business."

Libby's heart was beating so hard, she could only nod. Mrs. Brignadello took her by the arm and led her over to the sofa. Her rich skirts rustled as she sat down next to Libby. One eye on the door, she kept her voice low:

"It hardly seems fair that everyone in Edgewood knows but you. And I'm not telling anything you wouldn't already know if Angus hadn't been delayed on his way to meet your train." Convinced by her own whispered rationale, she said, "Mr. Blue left you his store."

Libby jerked as if brushed by an unseen hand. She sank to the little stool in the corner. Thoughts rushing, spilling one over another. *A store! Above the ground, far away from the mines.*

"You're pleased?"

"Oh yes! Very! The timing couldn't be better." In a tumble of words, Libby explained Dr. Dillman's warning to her father. Scarcely able to contain her excitement, she added, "I'm going right over."

"But your face!" Mrs. Brignadello protested.

"The bleeding has stopped." Anxious to get to the store, *their* store, Libby flung open the door, crying, "I'll be fine. Really. Thank you, Mrs. Brignadello. You've been wonderful."

7

$\mathfrak{S2}$ The front door was locked. Libby circled around to the back of Willie Blue's where young hollyhocks grew along a woodshed and a whitewashed privy, and a bur oak spread lofty branches. The wide wooden door whined on rusty hinges. Late afternoon sunlight flooded the rear of the store, glancing off the silver-plated ornately etched cash register and spilling onto the counter where Uncle Willie's corpse had so recently lain. Scattered leaves, crushed blooms, and the smoke-tainted odor of death lingered from the wake.

Earlier, the lighting had been so poor within these walls and the space so crowded, Libby had overlooked the mail cases with their sectioned cubbyholes. Likewise the safe against the back wall, the scales, the spool of string and brown paper and sundry other items common to storekeeping. The overcrowded shelves and cases and counters exhibited no signs of wanton destruction.

Our store. Libby could scarcely take it in.

Hearing voices overhead, she closed the back door and picked her way through the gloom to the stairs.

Mrs. Brignadello's basket of muffins remained undisturbed upon a lampstand at the top of the steps. There were two doors off the landing. The one straight ahead was closed, her valise discarded in front of it. The door to the left stood open, its lower panel ragged with splinters

67

and ruptured wood. Beyond the threshold was a large, unpartitioned room running the length of the building, with windows on three sides and bare rafters overhead. Sunshine filtered through the unwashed, curtainless windows, heating the room and shining on a proliferation of furnishings. There were tables of various sizes, uses, and descriptions. Ladder-back chairs and rocking chairs and chairs with woven seats. Lampstands and washstands, blanket chests and hall trees. A dry sink, an armoire, a library table, a pie safe, a jelly cabinet, and much more. There were no curlicues or carvings or etchings or fancy inlays in any of the pieces. Rather, they were plain solid pieces, crafted from enduring hardwoods, beautiful in their simplicity. She expelled a breathless "Good faith!"

Conversation among the three men in the room ceased so abruptly, her face burned. A short, small-framed, wiry-looking fellow with a pencil-thin mustache and a tense jaw turned away from Isaac Galloway and Billy Young, his scrutiny swift and thorough.

Libby smoothed ineffectually at her wrinkled and bloodied attire. "I came for my valise. I hope I'm not intruding."

"Quite a collection of furniture, isn't it?" Billy Young was the first to speak.

Libby stepped over the threshold. "Mr. Galloway."

"Miss Watson." He doffed his hat, though his tone was cool.

Billy Young's lively gaze and enigmatic grin heightened her suspicion that she'd been the subject under discussion. "This is Sheriff Conklin. Sheriff, I'd like you to meet Willie Blue's niece, Miss Watson."

"I'm pleased to make your acquaintance, sir."

"Likewise." The Sheriff acknowledged her with a perfunctory nod. "You'd be the one got banged up in the wreck that's left Ike in such a glad mood."

"I was in the accident, yes. Though it would be presumptuous of me to take credit for Mr. Galloway's disposition."

Billy Young chortled. Galloway's expression remained unchanged, but for the tightening of his jaw.

"I'm going to confiscate that slingshot of Frankie's. Have half a mind to put him behind bars while I'm at it. He'd just as well learn right now this isn't Old Kentucky, and we don't take stone throwing lightly," droned the sheriff.

Billy Young was still grinning. "Aw, Sheriff, you can't throw a boy that age in jail. Anyway, it isn't like he's a habitual troublemaker. He's had a rough couple of days, that's all."

"Excuse me, Sheriff," said Libby, "but did anyone actually *see* Frankie throw a stone? It could have been the flies that startled the horse. They were tormenting her something terrible, as Mr. Galloway will recall."

Isaac Galloway's pained gaze flickered over her. He beckoned toward the doorway. "Your valise is on the landing."

"Thank you, I saw it." Libby stepped deeper into the room, her gaze on the sheriff.

Grudgingly Sheriff Conklin asked, "You see the boy fling a rock, Ike?"

"Nope. But I know he done it."

"Probably aimin' at his grandpa and missed. Heard old Hack got riled at the wake and put the boy out on his ear," said the sheriff. Abruptly he changed the subject. "I understand Willie left you his store, Miss Watson."

"I only just learned of it. It seems Mr. Cearlock was involved in a mishap on his way to the station to meet me."

"It was no mishap," the sheriff was quick to correct her. "He was ambushed by Decatur McClure."

"Ambushed?" Her heart bumped.

Sheriff Conklin nodded. "Seems Decatur got a little too much juice in him. Headed up the road on foot, and Naomi followed."

"That's Mrs. McClure," said Billy, for her benefit. "Reckon she knew he wasn't holding his liquor too well."

"Durn amateur drinkers are always the ones to up and catch a man off guard. At least with the habitual drunks, you know what to expect," groused the sheriff.

"So what happened?" asked Libby.

"According to Naomi, Decatur flagged Angus Cearlock down as he was leaving Old Kentucky and heading into town," the sheriff said. "They fell to arguing. Naomi claims she wasn't close enough to know what it was about. Could be Decatur just wanted a ride. Whatever the case, they came to blows. Decatur flung Angus over the fence into a mud wallow as slick as you please, then took off in his rig."

"Mrs. McClure brought Angus in to Doc Harding's," Billy inserted.

Sheriff Conklin tapped his hat against his leg. "She came to my office from Doc Harding's and told me what had happened. Decatur'd been down at the train station earlier. Heard he was at the wake, too. Reckon he was at the funeral, too?"

"I don't think so. At least I didn't see him," said Billy.

"Probably spotted Naomi's wagon in front of your office and realized he'd gone too far, walloping an attorney and taking his ride." Billy glanced around the room and added, "You don't suppose he broke in here, too?"

Libby paused in running her hand over an oaken table. There was a deep gouge in the otherwise smooth surface. The seat of a chair lay beneath a window a dozen feet away. Splintered spindles and rungs were scattered on the floor like matchsticks. She stooped to pick one up. "I thought he and Uncle Willie were friends."

"Yes, ma'am," said Galloway. But there was something in his expression that made her heart jerk.

"Had they quarreled?" At Galloway's silence, she looked to Billy Young for confirmation. "They had, hadn't they!"

"I've heard rumors the last couple of days," he began, only to be stopped by a cautionary glance from Galloway.

"About Naomi?" The sheriff picked up where Billy Young had been cut off.

"What rumor?" asked Libby.

The sheriff must have gotten a look from Galloway too, for he averted his gaze and smoothed his skimpy mustache.

"Nothing for you to concern yourself with at this point, miss. Thing to do now is find Decatur, see what the blazes he thought he was doing, roughing Angus up and taking his rig. I'll see if he knows anything about this mess while I'm at it."

Libby looked back at the fractured door. Kicked not on the way in, as if to gain entry, but on the way out. Her fingers curled around the broken spindle. The memory of Decatur McClure's harshness to his son at the railroad tracks and the pall his presence had cast upon the room earlier were like a cold hand on her neck.

"Be a job finding him if he doesn't want to be found," warned Billy. "Timber up at Old Kentucky rambles on and on."

"Yes, and he knows every square foot of it, and how to stay hid," said the sheriff. "I'll save me some time and check with Naomi, see if she has some idea where to look."

"I wouldn't drag her in any deeper, going against Decatur," cautioned Galloway. "Once he's sober, he may come in on his own."

"Can't bank on it, Ike."

"Maybe we could be of some help," offered Billy.

"You've got a pretty fair knowledge of Old Kentucky, Ike. Any idea where I should start looking?" asked the sheriff.

"Can't say as I do." Nor did he echo Billy's offer to help.

"I'd keep an eye on the house if I was you. He's liable to slip back," said Billy.

The sheriff turned to Libby. "You're staying over, Miss Watson?"

"I hadn't planned on it. My family is expecting me home tonight."

"Seeing how this property is yours now, maybe you'd like to stick around until we've sorted this out. You could stay here at Willie Blue's."

Before Libby could reply, Mr. Galloway cut in, saying, "Do you think that's a good idea, Sheriff?"

"Ike's right," said Billy. "By the look of this place,

somebody was looking for something. Smart enough, too, to do it when most everyone in town was at the funeral."

"With a wake going on, he didn't have much choice. Been somebody here ever since they laid Willie out. Course, if he didn't find what he was looking for, he might try again," said Galloway.

"Can't puzzle out what he could possibly have wanted," mused the sheriff. "Cash box downstairs wasn't even touched."

Libby ended the discussion by explaining about her father's illness, and the necessity of returning home immediately.

"If you want any action taken over the busted door and chair and those scattered papers, stop by my office and sign some papers before you leave town," said the sheriff.

Libby surveyed the cluttered room. "What scattered papers?"

"Those over there on the far table. Billy stacked them up for you. In the meantime, I'll see if Cearlock's in any shape to shed light on his scrape with Decatur."

Libby nodded, thinking she'd like a word with Mr. Cearlock too.

Sheriff Conklin tipped his hat. His boots rang across the landing and down the stairs. Galloway started down after him, calling back to Billy, "I'll ride out to the tile factory, if you're still of a mind to make that delivery this evening."

"Let it go, Ike. You won't be much help, anyway, with that hand." Getting no reply, Billy smiled at Libby and said in parting, "It's been nice meeting you, Miss Watson. I'm sorry it wasn't happier circumstances. "

"Thank you, Mr. Young. That's kind of you."

"Guess you realize I ain't gonna be much use with this hand," Ike Galloway called from the bottom of the stairs. "But if ya hurry, may still be a man or two around to help load that tile."

"I said I'd find somebody else." Billy motioned from the top of the landing to indicate he'd be right down and lowered his voice, adding, "He can't hardly hear out of his right ear. You gotta speak up."

His *right* ear? Libby blinked, the seconds before the accident flashing in her mind. She'd been seated to Mr. Galloway's right when she'd asked him to stop the buggy. He hadn't heard her! Why hadn't he just said so?

"You come back real soon, Miss Watson," Billy Young was saying.

Libby followed him down, secured the door behind the men, then returned upstairs to sift through the papers Billy had gathered. They were business invoices and inventory sheets, nothing of much interest. She fetched her valise, shook the wrinkles out of the dark blue silk dress she'd brought along, and opened a window. The dress, with its pleated bodice, cinched waist, and floating skirt, caught the breeze as she turned her attention to cleaning herself up.

For all the lovely pieces of furniture, Uncle Willie's home was sorely lacking in amenities. There was a battered old stove, but no wood in the woodbox and no water in the reservoir. Nor was there a scrap of food to be found, though the shelves were stocked downstairs. Remembering a pump out the back door, Libby found a bucket and returned with enough water to sponge herself off, clean the dust from her shoes, tidy her hair, and wash down three of Mrs. Brignadello's muffins. She opened a second window and looked out over the town square as she rested for a moment.

A handful of lads played marbles in the dirt while a couple of old fellows lounged on a nearby bench and young ladies strolled through the park. The wooden canopy blocked her view of the sidewalk below, but the restaurant where Mrs. Brignadello had left Opal earlier in the day appeared to be doing a good business. The fellow loitering near the entrance looked familiar. Watching a passing buggy, he stood as still as a totem pole, one arm at his side, left hand snaked behind his back gripping his right elbow. At length his attention skipped to the old men on the bench, then flitted past the ladies and on to the children playing marbles. But it was only when he looked up at her window that Libby recognized him as the gangly fellow who'd come racing to the accident scene with Mrs. Brignadello and the others. The one who'd promised to look for Isaac Galloway's knife. He seemed to be staring right at her. Remembering his childlike eyes, she lifted her hand, but instead of acknowledging it, he gave his cap a jerk and stooped to pet the dog at his feet.

Turning from the window, Libby wandered the narrow paths between furnishings and wondered if Uncle Willie had planned to turn the upstairs into a furniture store. Or had he crafted the pieces himself? The questions brought to mind again how little she knew of him. Trying out a rocker and finding it comfortable, Libby closed her eyes. What a strange day it had been!

The afternoon sun was waning thin. She hoped to talk to Mr. Cearlock before she caught her train home. Her pulse quickened at the thought of telling Father and the boys about the store. After wrapping the last of the muffins and packing her soiled clothing, Libby carried both her valise and the empty muffin basket downstairs. It took only a moment to write a note thanking Mrs. Brignadello for her kindness. She slipped it into the basket and took it along with her to Dr. Harding's office on the next block.

Mrs. Brignadello was not there. Libby left the basket in Dr. Harding's back room where he heard out her request to visit Mr. Cearlock.

He diverted her attention by examining the wound on her cheek, grunting to himself and insisting she needed a couple of sutures. Concerned the wound would scar if she didn't comply, Libby bore the discomfort as best she could, paid his modest fee, and asked once more for permission to visit her uncle's attorney.

"It's rather important that I talk with him, or I wouldn't ask," Libby pressed in the face of his reluctance.

The doctor laid his glasses aside, stroked the bridge of his nose, and sighed.

"I won't stay but a minute."

Dr. Harding didn't look happy about it, but he led the way to Mr. Cearlock's alcove. She understood the doctor's hesitation. The poor fellow was ashen-faced.

"Angus?" The doctor touched his shoulder. The young man's hazel eyes fluttered open. "This is Miss Watson,

Willie Blue's niece. Are you up to talking with her a moment?"

"Miss Watson?" The attorney's manner was vague, his intonation confused. He stared at her from bewildered eyes.

His bruised cheek and split lip made Libby wince. She stirred uncomfortably. "I'm sorry, Mr. Cearlock. If you aren't up to talking, I'll get in touch with you after I return home."

"And where might that be?"

"Thistle Down," said Libby.

The confusion cleared from his expression. Squinting, he exclaimed, "Miss Watson. Of course. Forgive me. I'm having difficulty shaking off the haze. I was waylaid on my way to meet your train."

"Yes, I heard." Libby moved away from the door to let Dr. Harding pass.

"Then you probably heard as well that your uncle chose you as his heir. I'm afraid I've lost my glasses. I understand you were in a buggy accident. Are you injured?"

He was staring at her sutured cheek. Libby flushed and assured him. "It's nothing serious. Mr. Galloway got the worst of it."

"Sheriff told me about his hand. I must confess, I'm a bit disappointed. I'd expect better of one of Mr. Roosevelt's boys." Seeing her puzzlement, he amended, "Mr. Galloway was with the Volunteer Cavalry under Colonel Wood and Mr. Roosevelt. Better known as the Rough Riders."

"Truly?" Libby exclaimed, for the special regiment was highly publicized during the campaign in Cuba, both for their courage and their riding skills. No wonder he was disgruntled about the accident. He'd been defamed by a docile buggy horse.

Mr. Cearlock smiled gravely. " 'Rough Rider Takes a Rough Ride'—I can envision Mr. Gruben over at *The Gazette* having fun with headlines as we speak. I'm almost sorrier for Galloway than I am for myself."

"Have you any idea why Mr. McClure accosted you?" asked Libby.

"He was under the impression I had some papers of interest to him."

"What sort of papers?"

Mr. Cearlock patted down the windowsill in the absentminded way of one accustomed to searching for his glasses and replied, "I'm not at liberty to say. I'm pressing charges. It's a legal matter now, you understand."

"Someone was in Uncle Willie's store this afternoon and did a bit of damage. Papers were involved there, too. "

"Nothing of value was taken, I trust."

"I have no idea," said Libby. "The possibility was raised that Mr. McClure might be responsible."

"The sheriff mentioned as much. Infernal glasses, I keep forgetting." His hands came to rest across his chest. Fingers interlaced, he regarded her with the squint to which she was quickly growing accustomed and said, "Have you had time to consider what you wish to do with the store?"

The wonder still fresh, Libby shared with him just how timely Uncle Willie's bequest was in the scheme of things, and her eagerness to return just as soon as Father was well enough to withstand the move.

"I think that would please Mr. Blue." Mr. Cearlock winced as he tried to shift upon the cot.

"I should go and let you rest," said Libby, stirring to do so.

"One more thing," he said, forestalling her. "If I might offer a suggestion—Mr. Galloway is a capable fellow. He's been staying nights over the store, and knows as much as anyone about running it. You might impose on his friendship with Mr. Blue. Ask him to serve as proprietor until you return."

Libby rather doubted Isaac Galloway would be willing. Hedging, she asked, "What is Mr. Galloway's vocation, exactly?"

"He's establishing a maple syrup camp on a piece of timber north of town at a place the locals call Old Kentucky. I hear he's also saving up to buy some adjacent ground he has been cash renting."

"So he farms and was working for Uncle Willie, too?"

Mr. Cearlock nodded. "And Mr. Lamb, and some other folks too. Edgewood's a progressive little town. There's plenty of work for the man who's looking to better himself."

"We can't move until Father's stronger. I guess you're right. I should at least ask Mr. Galloway." She checked her watch. Her train was due within the next quarter hour. "Where would I find him?"

"Try Baker's on the south side of the square. He often eats supper there." It was Dr. Harding who answered her question. She turned to find him in the doorway, glowering as he looked from her to his patient. "Bid Angus good-bye now. He needs his rest."

Libby did so quickly, wishing the young attorney a speedy recovery. He, in turn, promised to be in touch.

Libby set a brisk pace, and was about to cross the railroad tracks when she spotted Billy Young and Ike Galloway coming across them in a wagon loaded with what looked to be the sort of tile used to drain fields. She lifted her hand as they drew closer.

Billy flashed his open smile and stopped the team on the street between the flour mill and the elevator. "On your way home, Miss Watson?"

Libby nodded. "I was hoping for a word with Mr. Galloway before I go." Trying not to bristle at the wariness creeping into Mr. Galloway's expression, she continued, "I'm sorry for the accident, Mr. Galloway, and the difficulty it has caused you. We seem to have gotten off on the wrong foot. I'm sorry for that too."

He lifted one eyebrow, and waited.

Words were her gift, but he wasn't making it easy. Flushing, she lifted her chin and plowed ahead. "You mentioned earlier that you'd been staying at the store with Uncle Willie?"

"I'll be moving my things out before nightfall," he said. "Would have done it sooner, except I was uneasy about leavin' the place deserted."

"Exactly," said Libby, seizing the opening. "I was hoping you'd stay."

Holding the reins loosely, Billy grinned his approval. "There you go, Ike."

"And do what?" Ike ignored the interruption.

"Run the store until I can return."

His surprise quickly gave way to a guarded expression. "Don't know as I'd want to be tied down to it just now. Got a lot of work to do."

Billy frowned. "You can't split wood with that hand, or farm, or work on your sugarhouse, either."

Her memory jogged, Libby reached into her reticule and withdrew the spile. "I believe this belongs to you." Ike accepted it without comment. Resolutely she tried to get the conversation back on track. "Regardless of what you think, Mr. Galloway, I *do* feel partially to blame for your circumstances. It would relieve my conscience considerably, and be a service too, if you'd see to the store until I can return."

Billy opened his mouth as if to urge him to accept, then seemed to think better of it. Ike, for his part, seemed to struggle between pride and common sense. At length he tapped the spile against his knee and said, "What kind of wages are we talking?"

Billy was grinning, an indication that this had more to do with pride than money. Libby peered into Ike Galloway's face. "I don't know, Mr. Galloway. What do you think you're worth?"

He considered his bandaged hand. "Not near what I was worth when I pulled my boots on this mornin'."

"Make out a bill then, for your time, and I'll pay you when I return."

"When will that be?"

"It depends on my father's recovery. I'll wire you in advance of our arrival. Fair enough?" Libby held out her hand.

He hesitated a brief moment, then reached out with his good hand to seal the deal.

The arrangement appeared to please Billy. He beamed like Edgewood's official goodwill ambassador and offered to turn the wagon around, saying, "We'd be happy to see you to the station, miss."

Libby smiled. "That's kind of you, and I appreciate the offer, but I believe I'll walk."

"Can't say as I blame you." With a bold wink Billy

added, "I had second thoughts myself about climbing into a buggy with Ike after that exhibition he gave this afternoon."

Ike tipped his hat back, a spark kindling in his eye. "Is that true, miss? You afraid to ride with me?"

"Not at all, Mr. Galloway. So long as the horse is bolted down to a carousel."

Taking it in the spirit intended, he grinned and nudged a chortling Billy. "Guess nobody told her, once yer thrown, ya gotta climb right back up."

"The fellow dispensing *that* sage advice is missing some teeth, walks with a limp, and has his arm sewn on backwards," retorted Libby.

Billy gave a shout of laughter and slapped his knee. "Give it up, Ike. You've shot your wad with her."

"Now, there you go, makin' a challenge of it." A set of dimples came out of hiding as Ike smiled and confided to Libby, "Ain't nothing I enjoy so well as provin' Billy wrong. How about when you come back, I hire a buggy from over at Woodmancy's Livery and see if I can't redeem myself, showin' ya a bit of countryside?"

"You gonna keep it right side up this time?" quipped Billy.

Libby laughed, enjoying their easy bantering after a day of jostling, crowding emotions. But when her eyes met Ike's, the invitation lingered in the gray depths. A discomfiting heat swept up her cheeks.

"You take good care of my store, Mr. Galloway, and who knows? I just may take you up on that offer," she said, and turned quickly away.

"I'll take that as a yes," he called after her.

Libby pretended not to hear. But halfway to the station, a smile had stolen to her lips.

8

It was two weeks before Libby's father was well enough to travel to Edgewood to see the store. Libby had wired Ike Galloway of their scheduled arrival time. She'd sent a second wire to Mr. Cearlock, who promptly wired her back, and arranged for a meeting at the Gentry homestead where he was recuperating from his injuries.

Libby was relieved to find the sallow-faced fellow from the wake waiting to take them by buggy from the station to the store, for Father was weary from the trip.

"Cecil Minor," he said, when Libby faltered in attempting to introduce him. "Most folks just call me Minor. All but Willie, and he always called me Major Minor. Don't know why exactly, 'cept I never whooped him for it."

Father chuckled. "Sich a one for nicknames. Elizabeth, he called 'Redtop.'"

The old gentleman slid her a scanty-toothed grin. "That 'un's not too hard to figger."

Father laughed. He gripped the man's hand and finished the introduction Libby had begun. "Thomas Watson. 'Tis a pleasure meetin' ye, Mr. Minor."

"Jest plain 'Minor.'" Minor stirred the horses into an easy amble, chatting amiably. "I'll wait right here, iffen yer wantin' ta go on out to Erstwood," he said as the buggy came to rest in front of Willie Blue's.

Libby thanked him as she helped Father out of the

buggy. "I'll just say hello to Mr. Galloway. I won't be long."

The floors of heartwood pine had been swept, the doors and windows propped open, and the gas lighting that Mrs. Brignadello had mentioned Uncle Willie ordering had been installed. But it was pure sunlight spilling over dusty shelves and cluttered cases and murky smoke-stained walls. A sad-eyed dog wandered in on their heels, her toenails tapping against the floor. As Libby glanced back, the dog sat down and lifted a white paw flecked in blue tick.

"Ah, a bonny lass, ye." Father smiled and stooped to grip the dog's front paw.

Libby found Ike Galloway with his boots propped on the cold stove, an open ledger in his lap, unaware of her approach. He was hatless, drawing her eye to his right ear, scarred white and misshapen, half-hidden beneath unruly brown curls. But the loss of hearing, now that she was aware of it, was apparent. She was almost upon him before he lifted his head.

Swift recognition flashed in his deep-set slate eyes as his feet came down. A drooping left lid and deep dimples lent his face character as he smiled a welcome.

"Miss Watson. Just bringin' the accounts up-to-date. How was yer trip?"

"Fine, thank you." Libby looked back at Father, who was still making friends with the dog.

Ike followed her glance. He closed the pencil into the ledger and came to his feet. "That's Sugar moppin' yer shoes. Willie's hound. She's used to coming and goin'. Hope you don't mind."

Father petted the dog's soft patchwork coat of brown, black, and ivory. "Has she a guid nose?"

"Fair to middlin'. But rheumatism's set in and her legs won't keep up. Most of her goin' these days is at the heels of Teddy Baker. She doesn't know what to make of Willie's passin'. Do you, girl?" A sigh lingered in his rich deep voice as he hunkered down beside Father and fondled the dog's velvet ears.

Her tail brushed the floor with a flagging thump. She closed woeful eyes and whined, relishing their attention.

"Ever wonder what a dog's thinkin'?" Ike's faint western twang wàs more pronounced in the stillness.

"Aye, lad."

"This is my father, Thomas Watson. Father, Mr. Galloway," Libby inserted.

"Most folks call me Ike."

"And it's pleased I would be if ye'd call me Thomas, laddie."

As they shook hands Libby saw that Ike's bandage was gone.

"Healing nicely. The wrist, too," he said, when she remarked upon it. He drew closer and studied her cheek, that lazy left lid softening his face. "How're you comin' along?"

"There's nothing left but a scratch."

"Reckon it'll fade away till it ain't even noticeable." He circled behind the counter to put the ledger away, his attempt at tact leaving Libby all the more aware of the blemish.

She clutched her hands through the loop of her reticule and asked, "Has anything been done about Mr. Lamb's buggy?"

"It's bein' fixed. Mr. Lamb's supposed to be taking it out of Frankie in labor."

Libby was relieved, for it seemed a fair solution. "And Frankie?"

He grimaced, one corner of his mouth tilting. "Undertaker collared him once, made him muck out the livery where he keeps Babe and the gelding. He hasn't been to town since."

"And Frankie's father? Was his altercation with Mr. Cearlock sorted out?"

"After a fashion. Decatur heard the sheriff was lookin' for him and came and turned himself in."

"What was his explanation for manhandling poor Mr. Cearlock?"

"From what I hear, Decatur stopped to ask him a few questions about Willie—he knew Cearlock was Willie's attorney. Cearlock said some things he probably wishes he hadn't. Decatur had enough liquor in him not to give too much thought to the consequences of wallerin' Angus about in the mud and takin' his rig to town."

"What was it Mr. Cearlock said?" asked Libby.

"Beggin' your pardon, ma'am, but I won't be repeatin' it."

Libby chewed the inside of her lip, more curious than ever. "And the monkey business upstairs? Was that Mr. McClure's doing too?"

"You'd have to ask the sheriff about that. He's holding Decatur over at the jail."

" 'Tis no place for a family man, caged up so unnatural-like," said Libby's father.

"Bail's been set, but either he can't raise it, or Naomi hasn't seen fit. Either way, I reckon Decatur's stuck there till the circuit judge comes to town." Ike changed the subject, saying, "Your timin' couldn't be better. A friend of mine is needin' help cutting oats, the sugarhouse is beggin' for a roof, and Minor quit this morning."

"Quit what?" asked Libby.

"He was filling in for Willie as postmaster."

"Now he's driving our buggy."

"He is, is he?" said Ike.

"Is it a problem ye're havin' with Mr. Minor?" asked Libby's father.

"Him and Miz Payne wasn't gettin' along. Said either she would have to leave or he would. But that's a postal decision. Wasn't up to me to make it. Miz Payne declared she wasn't goin' anywhere, so Minor quit."

"It's something that needs immediate attention, then?" Libby asked.

"Either a replacement, or you'll have to sort mail yerself till the powers that be appoint somebody. Have a seat, why don't you, and we'll go over some business." Ike indicated the abandoned chairs scattered about the stove.

Libby pulled one up for her father, wondering at the identity of said "powers" and how she was to contact them. Of equal concern was the growing impression that Ike thought they were here to stay.

"We haven't come to take over just yet, Mr. Galloway.

Father wanted to see the store and get some idea of what we're getting ourselves into."

"Lass, ye're keeping Mr. Minor waitin'," Thomas Watson intervened. He turned to Ike. "How is it ye first came to know Willie?"

Excusing herself, Libby left them talking and hurried to the buggy to keep her appointment with Angus Cearlock.

"Ain't no rush on my account. I get paid whether I'm sittin' or drivin'," said Minor when she apologized for keeping him waiting.

An amiable grin lit his sallow features as they left the town square, angling north. The forms were still on the new hard-surface sidewalk on the right side of the street. Libby commented upon them.

"Portland cement," Minor said with pride. "Town council's been workin' hard on improvements this past year."

"There are no cement walks in my hometown."

Minor looked pleased at the admission. "Wouldn't it be somethin' if they was to do the streets thataway? Lift us plum out of the mud."

Libby, who detested mud, could not have agreed more.

Children romped on the sloping lawn of a handsome two-story residence set amidst oaks and elms and maples. "Lester Morefield's place," said Minor, as she admired the well-kept home and grounds. "Lots of Morefields here'bouts. Lester's branch runs the tile factory east of town. They make the tile what drains the farm ground in these parts. And bricks, too, like what his home's made of there. Purty, ain't it?"

Two large but less elegant homes with spacious yards, and a low-slung house tucked close to the sidewalk, followed. Minor identified each by family and occupation. Libby appreciated his efforts, though she'd never remember the names. The new cement sidewalk gave out as the dwellings grew more modest, all with porches, and painted and trimmed in different colors. Several yards were fenced in wire, with clotheslines, vegetable gardens, a fruit tree or two, and sometimes flowers. Chicken houses, buggy sheds, even small barns, were common. One dismal cottage reminded Libby of the bachelor

shanties back home. There was a leaning privy, a tumbledown woodpile, and a trash heap out back. Two barefoot
children frolicked on ground trod bare, skillfully dodging
tin cans, rusty wire, and brush spilling into the weed-
choked alley.

"Village board wrote an ordinance aimed at gettin'
messes such as that cleaned up. And they're threatenin'
to fine folks when their critters get loose." He indicated a
pig wallowing in a mudhole right at the edge of the street
and said with a sniff, "Bound to be a big squabble if they
do."

They bore right at the corner and slowed for two girls
racing along, rolling hoops. Farther on, Libby recognized
the fellow who'd searched for Ike's knife at the accident
scene two weeks earlier. He was scooping manure out of
the street and trundling it away in a wheelbarrow when
two lads dashed up behind him.

"Hey, Teddy! What's your mama serving for dinner—
well-done horse dung?" teased the first boy.

"Dinner at Baker's, a dime a dip," called his companion.

The boys giggled and chimed in unison, "Dime-a-dip
horse dung, pipin' hot at Baker's. Dime-a-dip horse
dung."

Teddy ignored his tormentors. But Mr. Minor could
not.

"Young scalawags!" he growled, and pulled the buggy
up short. "Teddy? Wanna ride out to Erstwood with us?"

The lads flew down the alley and disappeared through
a space in a whitewashed board fence as Teddy tugged at
his cap and strode over to the buggy.

"I was out there just yesterday. Yeah, wel-l-l, a telegram
came for you-know-who, so I took it out."

He shot Libby a skittish glance, leading her to wonder
if he knew it was she who'd sent the wire.

"Angus pay you for your trouble?" asked Minor.

Pink gums and large white teeth flashed in his tanned
face. "Now-w-w." He dragged the word out. "What do
you think?"

Minor chuckled. "All right, then. Don't ya work too
hard, ya hear?"

"Aw-w-w," he said in acknowledgment.

Libby glanced back as they continued on. Teddy's hand was in the air, but his gaze fell away when he saw her looking at him.

"Is that Mrs. Baker's son?" she asked, and Minor nodded. "Did Mr. Cearlock pay him?"

"Durn tootin'." Minor slid her a sidelong glance and grinned. "He wouldn't go out there again if he didn't. Don't you worry none about Teddy."

"Does he work as a street sweeper?"

"Not officially, but he's clever about opportunities. You and me see horse droppin's and sidestep it? He sees coins lying in the street. Scoops it up, pedals it about door to door."

"People actually pay him for manure?"

"Them that don't have a supply of their own often do. Fer their gardens and orchards and such. Besides, if they was to turn him away, they'd be payin' a street tax in no time. It's the same with bottles and cans and jars and crates left lying about. Teddy picks 'em up and sells 'em back to them what fill 'em."

Overall, Minor seemed a cordial sort. Libby was sorry he'd quit as interim postmaster, and not just because of the immediate need of finding a replacement. Hoping she could coax him into returning, Libby disregarded Ike Galloway's prediction and phrased her request in such a way as to let Minor know she'd consider it a favor.

Minor shot tobacco juice over the side of the buggy and wiped his mouth on a tattered cuff. "No offense, miss, but they wasn't payin' me enough for the aggravation."

"The problem, as I understand it, was with another employee," she persisted. "Perhaps we could sit down together and work something out."

"Not with Zerilda Payne, you cain't," he said shortly. "That was her at the wake, got so snippy with Hascal. Her husband's sickly. Cain't work, or won't. Their girl's married to a fella running a concession along the Pike down at the big world's fair in St. Louis. Sent her young 'uns up here for the duration of the fair, and that ain't helpin' Zerilda's disposition none. Why, with Willie gone, there ain't a man alive who could work alongside her.

'Cept maybe Benjamin Boyd. He's got a steady wick, Benjamin does."

They headed north out of town beneath a blue sky. The sun's slanting rays crept beneath the canvas cover of the buggy. Libby shaded her face with her hand, hoping to discourage a host of new freckles. She drew a cleansing breath as they bumped and creaked along the dirt road. Ripening grain grew in the field to the west; to the east was corn and undulating meadow. "Is it far, Mr. Minor?"

"Jest Minor," he reminded. "No more'n a mile." Minor sent another stream of tobacco juice flying. "Erstwood, they call it. Mr. Gentry's pride and joy. That's the tower sticking up over the trees way up yonder. See it there, miss?" He pointed with the buggy whip and went on to describe all twelve rooms of the house.

Libby listened with interest as he went on to share what he knew of the family. Mr. Gentry's father, along with the Morefields and the Dorrances, were among the earliest settlers in the township. Each family had amassed sizable landholdings. Agriculture, he told her, was the bedrock upon which they'd built their fortunes.

"Angus Cearlock's runnin' fer the state legislature— he's Miz Gentry's boy from her first husband, Earl Cearlock. Earl made a bundle off railroad parcels. Miz Gentry got a grown gal by old Earl too—Miss Catherine. You jest might bump into her out here visitin' her mama. She's married to a feller travels about selling what they call insurance."

Minor coaxed the balky team onto a bridge spanning a tree-shrouded creek and picked up where he'd left off. "Closest I can tell, you pay this feller jest in case lightning strikes. Say, for instance, yer house burns. Now, iffen it burns, then he gives ya back yer money, and some more with it so's you can rebuild. But iffen it don't burn, then he's got yer money, and you with nothin' to show. Why, I'd jest leave take my chances. Cain't for the life of me imagine how folks'd fall for such a fiddle-headed deal. But I hear tell they do, and enuf of 'em to keep Miss Catherine's husband a-humpin' all over the Midwest. You ever hear the like?"

A team was approaching from the other direction. As it

drew closer, Libby saw that it pulled a tinker's wagon. K. *Brignadello Traveling Store* was emblazoned in bright paint along the body of the wagon.

"Brignadello. The rural merchandising agent?" said Libby.

Minor's muttonchops twitched. "Kersey's a tinker, and that's the plain truth. Though you won't hear it from Miz Brignadello. Always tryin' to keep up with her sister, Ida Gentry. A body less determined woulda seen the futility of that years ago. Shootfire, can't nobody match Gentry's mill and his elevator and his bank and his finger in every pie in town, not even with a smart-soundin' title like 'rural merchandizin'' whatever." Minor cackled and shook his head. As they drew even with the tinker's wagon, he raised his voice and called, "'Lo, Kersey. Yer headed in kinda early, ain't ya?"

The dapper fellow in a dark suit and string tie grimaced. "Three days early, to be exact. I broke a line. Fixed it after a fashion, but not to suit Bob and Bess. They won't turn. Not unless I climb down and get hold of them."

"Woodmancy'll fix ya right up."

"I thought as much." Mr. Brignadello's button-bright eyes flicked over Libby and back to Minor. Censure in his glance, he said with mock severity, "Now, that's about what I'd expect of a bachelor such as yourself, driving a lady out to the country without a side curtain to shade her fair skin." He tipped his hat to Libby and smiled warmly. "Good afternoon, ma'am. Could I interest you in a parasol? I have a blue one, the very shade of your lovely eyes."

Minor snorted. "Watch out fer this 'un. He could sell a set of pearl teeth to a shark."

The tinker's full cheeks glowed like ripened peaches. "Why, Minor. You flatter me." He smiled inquiringly at Libby.

"Thank you, Mr. Kersey. Perhaps another time," said Libby.

"My pleasure, ma'am."

"Giddup, there," Minor called to the team. "So long, Kersey. Don't you take no wooden nickels."

Mr. Brignadello doffed his hat and went on his way.

"Now, about Miz Gentry's first husband, Earl Cearlock, the one what sold the railroad land," Minor said,
resuming his gossip. "He up and died of gallopin' con-
sumption. Ida was a fine-looking woman, and it sure
didn't take Chester Gentry long to appreciate that fact. He
married her right quick and raised her young 'uns jest like
they were his own."

Minor gathered the reins close and spoke a soothing
word to the team as a rabbit zipped out of the tall grass
and across the road. "Course, Miz Bee's no slouch in the
looks department, neither. A worker, too. Don't let no
daylight grow under her feet. No, sirree. She's the work-
ingest woman. Doc'd be lost without her. Lord knows
that woman he married ain't no help. She's got her nose
stuck in garden parties and the Women's Christian Temperance League and the Thespians down at the Columbian. Now they say she's puttin' together some singin'
group to provide entertainment when Angus goes
stumpin' for votes."

By the time they passed through the gates of the
Gentry estate, little mystery remained as to Uncle Willie's
choice of a nickname for Mr. Minor—the man was
indeed a *major* source of *minor* information.

9

The lawns of Erstwood sloped uphill from the road. Flowering shrubs and young trees lined the driveway. There were endless beds of cannas and lilies and other bright flowers abuzz with butterflies and bees. It was an extraordinary house with its gingerbread trim and deep verandas and tower reaching for the sky. Mr. Minor stopped the buggy next to the mounting block. Libby climbed down unassisted, let her head fall back, and admired the eyebrow windows and small white-railed catwalk adorning the slate roof.

"I'll pull around to the back and wait in the shade."

Intimidated by the grandeur of the place, Libby hesitated three steps up the stone walk, turned back, and called to her driver, "You're sure this is the right entrance?"

"A door's a door, ain't it? Giddup there." Minor urged the team ahead.

In Thistle Down a door was a door. Libby wasn't so sure that was the case here.

A sturdy green-eyed girl stepped out on the veranda with a broom, sparing her further indecision. Her face was shiny with perspiration and the starch had wilted from her bibbed apron and high-collared cotton dress. Wholesome in a plain sort of way, her features quickened with interest as Libby climbed the steps and stated her business.

90

"You're Mr. Blue's niece then? I'm Chloe Berry. I work for the Gentrys. Come along and I'll show you up to Mr. Angus's room."

Leaving the broom, she led Libby through the spacious vestibule, past a large reception room where palms flanked a granite fireplace and a heavy gilt mirror threw back the reflection of handsome statuettes. A fragrant bouquet of roses adorned a marble-top table at the foot of an open staircase. The carpet on the stairs muffled the girl's steps, but not her voice.

"Mr. Angus has his own place in town, but Mrs. Gentry, his mother, insisted he come here to recover from his injuries. Decatur McClure deserves a good thrashing for acting up like that." Chloe whistled tunelessly as she climbed, then said with a glint of humor, "Lost count how many times I've traipsed up these stairs. Why, if Mrs. Gentry had only thought of it, she could have settled him up in the tower room and given me a real workout."

Libby paused on the polished landing at the top of the stairs. From where she stood she could see four bedchambers. Sunlight and fresh air poured from the chamber windows through the open doors and onto the landing.

Chloe knocked on the darkly stained casing framing the open door. "Mr. Angus? Your guest is here."

"Client, Chloe. That is the proper term." Across the room, a softly rounded woman of interminable age finished adjusting a gauzy window curtain. Other than her diminutive stature and small features, her resemblance to her sister, Mrs. Brignadello, was minimal. A fading beauty with a heart-shaped face, a tiny waist, and delicately shod feet, she came to Libby with a rustle of rich skirts and a sweetly puckered mouth, her small white hands outstretched.

"You must be Elizabeth Watson. Welcome to Erstwood. I'm Mr. Cearlock's mother."

"Mrs. Gentry," said Chloe helpfully.

Distracted, Mrs. Gentry turned to the girl. "What is it, Chloe?"

"I was telling her your name."

"For goodness' sake. Aren't you supposed to be sweeping the veranda?"

Unruffled, Chloe said, "You told me to bring Mr. Cearlock's gu . . . client up when she came. I didn't know you'd changed your mind."

There was nothing surly or impudent in the girl's manner, just a matter-of-factness that elicited soft laughter from the anteroom beyond.

Mrs. Gentry sighed and beckoned for Libby to follow. "I'll be down in a moment to see about that sweeping, Chloe. Right this way, Elizabeth. You don't mind if I call you Elizabeth, do you?"

Libby gave her consent as Mrs. Gentry led her into what looked to be a sewing niche turned into a convalescing room and a makeshift office. The tasseled linen cloth topping the library table was wrinkled and stained with ink and overrun with books and papers, a cigar humidor, a deck of cards, and sundry other items.

Mr. Cearlock lounged on a green and white striped fainting couch with pillows beneath his injured ankle and embroidered cushions at his back. Dapper in white flannels, starched cuffs, and a bright cravat, he was a pleasing complement to the young woman seated on a low stool beside him. Dressed in yellow, she reminded Libby of the little caged canary Father took into the mines to give them fair warning in case of poison gas. There was a familiarity about her, but before Libby could track it down, Mr. Cearlock was reaching for her hand.

"Miss Watson! A delight to see you again. I apologize for the dreadful dusty ride out, but it will be a few days yet before I'll be back in my office in town," he explained, releasing her fingers.

"It's quite all right, Mr. Cearlock. I'm enjoying the countryside."

"And have swallowed an acre or two of dust, I'd imagine. Catherine was just complaining of the dusty roads."

Libby demurred that it was no hardship at all. His smile, amiable and charming, completed the transformation from the pale pain-ridden gent of recent memory to the debonair young attorney.

"You've met my mother. This is my sister, Catherine

Morefield, come to cheer me up. Catherine, I'd like you to meet Willie Blue's niece, Miss Elizabeth Watson."

The woman came to her feet, a younger version of her mother, with her heart-shaped face and thick-lashed violet eyes. She cocked her golden head with quick, bright interest, recognition swift.

"I remember you! You were on the train the day Tess and I returned from the world's fair."

"Of course!" cried Libby, smiling. "I was trying to place you."

"Angus, be kind to this girl. She's an angel come to earth. She shared a seat with Zerilda Payne all the way from Springfield and never once attempted to throttle her."

Angus laughed, while Mrs. Gentry reproved, "Catherine, really!"

"You have no idea, Mother!" Catherine insisted in her animated fashion. "You should have heard the woman. She was a perfect witch to poor Tess. Wasn't she, Miss Watson?"

"Enough! I won't have you dragging my client into your attempts to justify your wicked grudge against the fair Zerilda."

"Angus, don't encourage her," pleaded Mrs. Gentry. "With your laughter and goading, she'll soon be as fresh as Chloe."

"Leave Catherine to Charlie. She's his problem now."

"Charlie doesn't find me a problem at all. Quite the contrary," his sister responded sweetly.

Hazel eyes twinkling, Mr. Cearlock gestured, saying, "Draw up a chair, Miss Watson. Mother and Catherine were just leaving."

"It was lovely meeting you, Elizabeth." To her son Mrs. Gentry said, "I'll send Chloe up with some refreshments."

"You told her to sweep the veranda," Catherine reminded her, to which her mother sighed and said as she followed her out, "Didn't you bring your tatting?"

"It's in knots, Mother."

"See what practice will do? Which brings us to your French."

"Tess will be up from her nap soon."

"Chloe can occupy Tess."

"Chloe's sweeping the veranda."

"Why *don't* you practice your French? Charles will be so proud when you go abroad next year."

"I'll sweep the veranda, let Chloe untangle the French."

"Catherine, really! Sometimes I worry it was a waste of Chester's hard-earned money, sending you off to Wells College."

Angus chuckled as the door closed behind them. "Mother's meeting formidable resistance—instructing Chloe, on the one hand, to be useful, and Catherine, on the other, to be idle."

Libby relaxed in the warmth of his gentle humor. Perching on the upholstered sewing stool his sister had vacated, she let him guide the small talk, and gathered in unobtrusive glances details that had escaped her notice upon their first meeting. The yellow lights in his hazel eyes, easily missed behind his spectacles. The small scar dissecting his right eyebrow. The center part of his sandy hair. Slender, artistic hands that lifted and fell as he talked. He was a good conversationalist, and equally adept at listening in a way that left Libby feeling he was genuinely interested in Father and the boys and Thistle Down and even the colonel's buggy horse, Bootsie.

"Let me guess—she has four white feet?"

Libby laughed and admitted, "Bootsie is my name for her. I couldn't say whether Colonel Calkin has named her at all."

"If he hasn't, he should. Or relinquish her to someone who cares enough to do the thing properly." Angus smiled warmly.

Chloe brought iced tea and sliced pound cake drizzled in strawberry glaze. Over this repast Angus turned the conversation to business.

"Mr. McClure has hired himself an attorney. A Mr. Randolph Sparks from Bloomington. I regret to tell you that he has filed papers with the court, contesting your uncle's will."

"Contesting it?" cried Libby, catching her breath. "But why?"

"Decatur McClure believes that Willie Blue fathered Frankie, and that therefore Frankie is entitled to the possessions Mr. Blue has left behind. Namely, the store."

Good faith! First a wife and now an illegitimate son. Flushing, Libby managed to ask if there was any basis to his claim.

"At this point, I really couldn't say. I was hoping, being family, you might have some knowledge . . . No?"

"None whatsoever." Libby went on to explain how little they knew of Uncle Willie's life.

"Frankly, I'm surprised by Mr. McClure's legal maneuverings." Mr. Cearlock took off his glasses and rubbed at the lenses, all the while looking at her in a vague nearsighted way. "He's in his element up there in the woods, hunting and fishing and trapping game. A store in town would be of little interest to him, I should think." He fitted his spectacles to his face again and mused, "I can only conclude he sees this as an opportunity to better himself through his boy, and at your expense. The burden of proof, of course, is on him. Which will be difficult."

"Is Mrs. McClure . . . Is she in agreement with him in this?" asked Libby.

"I have yet to ascertain that. These blasted injuries have kept me from calling on Naomi. I do know that her name was not on the petition. Though perhaps Decatur plans to bully her into going along." He sighed and reached for the silver letter seal off the bedside table. "Even then, I'm blessed if I can figure out how the man thinks he can get the court to rule in his favor. Unless he has a more recent will in his possession. But if that were the case, I believe his attorney would have filed it."

"And he hasn't?"

He shook his head, and returned the seal to the table. "Not that I'm aware. So you see, it's more of a nuisance than a threat to your inheritance. But I did want you to be aware of it. I suggest as well that you press charges against him for the damage he did at the store."

"Is there proof it was him?"

"Sheriff Conklin asked him about it. He didn't deny it."

"Did he say why he did it?"

"No. He has somehow gotten the idea he doesn't have to answer to the sheriff, the court or anyone else. You need to make a firm stand against him, Miss Watson. He's a rugged fellow, and restless as a panther, pacing that jail cell."

"Do you really think that's necessary?" asked Libby. "The damage was fairly minor. And as you just pointed out, he's already behind bars."

"It's a matter of strategy, actually. Hear me out, now, before you make up your mind."

"I'm listening," said Libby, when he paused.

"Your charges, if McClure's found guilty, may add to his sentence. Knowing as much, he might be willing to drop this nonsense about contesting the will if you drop your complaint. A bargaining tool, you see? And one more thing—I advise you to take up occupation of the store immediately."

Libby looked at him in surprise. "Can we do that?"

"You can and you should in accordance with your uncle's will." Holding her gaze, he added, "And if the need arises, I'd be pleased to represent you against this suit of McClure's."

"Thank you," said Libby, relieved. "I'll certainly keep it in mind."

10

🌿 Mr. Cearlock's summation of what Mr. McClure hoped to accomplish raised Libby's righteous indignation. *Who does he think he is?* Not that Uncle Willie's character was so exemplary as to exclude his having sired an illegitimate child. Libby recalled Uncle Willie, ten years past. He could have been a philanderer as well as a drunkard, and she'd be none the wiser. Though Father might know something of it.

Good-byes said, Libby found her own way downstairs, and waited by the mounting block as Chloe sped off to fetch Mr. Minor. What of Naomi McClure, Hascal Caton's daughter? What sort of woman was she?

Libby was certain Minor had a good idea of the news she'd received. His curiosity, as he pulled the buggy up to the mounting block, was as pungent as the dampness gluing his shirt to his rounded torso. Was Uncle Willie guilty as charged? Or was McClure, as Angus Cearlock intimated, out to take advantage, whatever the toll to his family?

It seemed ill advised to put such a delicate matter before a man of so loquacious a nature. So Libby kept quiet, and with exemplary courtesy, Minor limited his conversation to observations about the dry weather, the crops, and the level of water in Mr. Gentry's cistern.

They were almost back to town when they came across Spike Culbertson headed in the opposite direction. To

Libby's untrained eye, the white-haired gentleman with his short waist and long sticklike legs walked with the purpose of one who knew where he was headed. But Minor thought not.

"Spike made his home out this way fer fifty-odd years. These days he lives in town with his daughter. But he gits queer notions now and agin, and when Cordelia—that's his daughter, Cordelia Robins—ain't payin' him much mind, he gits away from her and wanders about the countryside, lookin' for the old homeplace. He lights where he wearies, and deceives himself into thinkin' he's home."

Minor stopped to pick up the old veteran. "Spike Culbertson, this here's Willie Blue's niece, Miss Watson."

The pale-haired gent's nod and vacant smile tugged at Libby's heart. His fingers drummed his knees and his feet tapped the buggy floor as his gaze wandered out over the sunny field.

"Why don't ya recite somethin' for the lady? Say, Lincoln's Gettysburg Address? You know, 'Fourscore,'" Minor prompted.

It was as if the sun had come out behind the old man's face, clearing away the fog. Libby caught her breath as he bolted to his feet in the buggy. One hand over his heart, the other stretched out as if to still the crowd, he flung his head back and let the words roll like thunder:

"'Fourscore and seven years ago our fathers brought forth on this continent a new nation, conceived in liberty, and dedicated to the proposition that all men are created equal.'"

Libby sat taller, surprised at such power and such pitch from his seemingly frail frame.

"'Now we are engaged in a great Civil War, testing whether that nation or any nation, so conceived and so dedicated, can long endure. We are met on a great battlefield of that war.'"

Even the team pricked up their ears as the words poured forth, carrying with each ensuing phrase the stark, bloody reminder of war.

"'We have come to dedicate a portion of that field as a

final resting place for those who here gave their lives that that nation might live.' "

His hands, thin and blue-veined and age-spotted, moved with the sure strokes of a skilled conductor leading his orchestra through a dark stormy chorus.

" 'But, in a larger sense, we cannot dedicate—we cannot consecrate—we cannot hallow—this ground. The brave men, living and dead, who struggled here have consecrated it, far above our poor power to add or detract. The world will little note, nor long remember, what we say here, but it can never forget what they did here.' "

Like a callused finger touching the string that made a note ring, his voice carried hoofbeats and cannon shots and the cries of wounded men. His fine old voice marched on, the aftermath of battle spilling from him like the haunting strain of a flute, conjuring bloodstained soil freshly turned, and white crosses. The words slowed, then built again like the great rush of a runner reaching deep inside himself as he stretches for the finish line.

" '. . . and that government of the people, by the people, for the people, shall not perish from the earth.' "

The plodding of hooves raising little puffs of dust, the rocking of the buggy, and Minor's solemn "Amen" punctuated Libby's awed silence. The smoke cleared and the guns stilled and the horror of men killing and being killed receded. Libby's eyes filled as the old man sat down and clutched his dented hat to his breast.

Marveling at the mystery of such a flawless recitation from a man who could not remember where he lived, Libby shook his hand and thanked him for the performance, saying, "That was beautiful, Mr. Culbertson."

It struck her as he averted his gaze to the tranquil countryside that it was for this—this field of wheat, this patch of corn, this sun-washed meadow—that he and his comrades had paid such a high toll. And kept on paying as they wandered old battlefields of the mind.

Facing Father across a corner table at Baker's, Libby thought fleetingly of Mr. Culbertson and hoped that she was not deceiving herself, that she knew where *she* was headed. Dinner ended with a tasty salad. There was an hour remaining until the southbound train was due. She folded her napkin in her lap and announced her intention of staying on in Edgewood.

Father looked up from his plate, his gaze suddenly keen. "Tonight, lass?"

"If you're able to travel home alone, yes." Libby braced herself, hoping he would not feel she was abandoning him or her family duties.

"Aye, I can get home well enough." Peering into her eyes, he added quietly, "But I canna feel easy about ye stayin' behind."

"It's the best solution, Father." Libby went on to remind him of Mr. Minor's untimely resignation as temporary postmaster and of Ike Galloway's eagerness to be relieved of the responsibility of storekeeping now that his hand had healed. Both were weighty considerations. As was the attorney's advice to claim what was hers, and claim it swiftly. She gestured with a slight nod to the ginger-haired, apron-swathed lady briskly serving a table of men toward the front of the restaurant. "I've already spoken to Mrs. Baker about getting a room for the night."

Father set his coffee cup down and eyed her with dawning suspicion. "And ye with valise in hand as we boarded the train. I've a strong notion ye had it in mind to stay from the moment ye left home."

"After what happened last time, a change of clothes seemed a good idea," said Libby.

"Hum!" he said mildly. "I dinna know it was a 'new woman' I had raised of me own dear bairnie."

"Oh, Father! It isn't like that at all." Still, Libby couldn't help feeling a little pleased, for she admired those head-strong moderns with their educations and their independent ideas. She sandwiched his frail, thin hand between her two small, work-roughened ones. "We didn't go looking for this opportunity. But now that it's before us, I'm anxious to put my hand to the plow and not look back."

Father acknowledged her biblical application with a little smile. "'Tis wiser still, lass, to seek discernment before ye go tearin' up the earth with ye plow."

"Oh, but I have, Father." Stung, Libby withdrew her hands. "And now, are we to drag our feet simply because of Mr. McClure's unsubstantiated claim?"

Father gave her a long, hard look. He'd been as surprised as she to learn of Mr. McClure's assertion that the boy he'd raised as his son was not his son at all, rather Uncle Willie's.

Uncertain what path his thoughts had taken, Libby shook the crumbs from her napkin and reasoned, "Mr. Cearlock doesn't view the suit as a serious threat. He called it a nuisance, nothing more."

"If there be validity to the fellow's assertion . . ."

"Would Uncle Willie have left the store to me if he had a son?" Libby countered.

"Aye, ye've hit upon the rub, now haena ye?"

Flushing, Libby took aim at Mr. McClure. "He isn't a nice man. His treatment of Mr. Cearlock was deplorable. He unfairly took sides between his children, and was rude to me when I tried to explain he was jumping to conclusions. Why, there fell such a hush when he walked into Uncle Willie's wake, you could hear the lamps hiss."

"A dandy-doodle of a fellow, 'tis no doubt. Accusin' a leddy of fornication—his verra own wife and in the public eye, too. Verra troubled, he is, and verra angry, I'm guessin'."

"And greedy."

Father's smile was gentle and patient. Though he was not arguing against her plans, Libby knew him too well to deceive herself into believing their thoughts were running parallel. "I feel very strongly about the store, Father. This is a fine opportunity and I'm eager to work at making it a success. But it can't be done from a distance."

"Ye're a restless lass. But right about the distance factor."

He acquiesced too easily. Cautiously Libby asked, "You agree then that I should stay?"

"I dinna say that. Though 'tis true we be unfairly monopolizin' Mr. Galloway's time. We canna keep the lad from bringin' the oat crop in. Nor from the sugarhouse he delights so in buildin'."

"Then you *do* understand the urgency of it?"

"Aye, lass. I settled accounts with the laddie while ye were gallopin' about the countryside. Mr. Galloway will be movin' his belongin's out to Old Kentucky tomorrow."

Surprised, she cried, "You'd already made plans!"

"'Twas in my mind to stay myself and have a wee visit with Mr. McClure." He sipped the last of his coffee and moved the cup to the corner of the table.

All the concerns of a new business venture, and what was in his head? A visit to Mr. McClure's jail cell. *The adversary*. Now, wasn't that just like him? "And do you think Mr. McClure will make you welcome? Or thank you for coming?"

"'Tis verra plain ye're hopin' he won't. Is he so mortal dangerous to the plans strutting' aboot in that bonny noggin of yers that ye'd turn me from havin' a look for myself?"

His twinkling eyes brought heat to Libby's cheeks. Nevertheless, she defended herself, saying, "It was you, Father, who gave me a thirst for knowledge. And now you fault me for seeing the chance to make my dreams a reality?"

"Ye're misunderstandin' me, lass," he said quietly.

But Libby, fired by her own plans, talked right over him. "If the income from the store is sufficient, college can be a reality. I'll study writing and follow my dreams, all because of Uncle Willie's bequest!" Trying to smooth the pucker from his brow, she added playfully, "And when I'm rich and famous, we'll go back to Thistle Down and buy out Colonel Calkin. You and the boys can raise everyone's wages, and still have enough to live like kings!"

He wagged his head, and gently admonished her about setting her affections on things of this earth. "Nevertheless, ye are right about one thing. 'Tis the time for decision makin'. Is it home to the boys and the packin' with ye, or are ye to stay here, doin' the work of three men and a lad?"

"Mr. Galloway handled it quite nicely. How hard can it be?"

"Merciful patience, 'tis a new woman with all the monkeyshines!" he exclaimed.

Mrs. Baker came and refilled their cups and left them to bandy back and forth until Father agreed to see it Libby's way. A short while later, as the conductor called, "All aboard!" Libby issued last-minute warnings to her father not to overexert himself. Whether they were coming or staying behind, the boys could do the necessary packing. A hug and she backed beneath the Western Union Telegraph sign, the engine popping off steam as Father boarded.

A moment later, he waved from a window. Cheered by his good spirits, Libby blew him a kiss. The train hissed and rolled forward, bell clanging. Libby waved as the cars clacked and chuffed out of the station, watching until the thundercloud curling down the train's back shrank to a misty speck on the southern horizon.

Behind her, the stationmaster, with the help of two husky men, was carrying the heating stove out of the station. There wasn't a lot of room in the station. With summer around the corner, they no doubt were willing to go to the trouble of making a little more space by removing the stove. Libby stepped out of their way as, with a good deal of exertion, they loaded it onto a baggage cart, rolled the cart to a storage building, unloaded the stove, and came back, shirts dark with perspiration.

A moment later, Libby was alone on the empty platform, the scent of cinders and airborne steam lingering on the still evening air. She was truly on her own for the first time in her life. A store and the daily mail, under her charge. Undaunted by the fact that she had no more business knowledge than it took to jog miners' trousers from the washwater to the line, she felt like jumping into the air and kicking her heels together. Indeed, she might have given in to the temptation, but Teddy Baker was coming over the crossing, trundling the wheelbarrow in front of him. The aging beagle Sugar weaved along beside him, her nose to the ground, her brown ears dragging in the dust. The dog stopped at Libby's feet and lifted her face to be petted. But Teddy passed within two feet of her without looking up or returning her greeting.

She didn't press a conversation, simply watched as he

emptied a load of corncobs into a bin and disappeared inside.

"Fill 'er up, did you, Teddy?" The stationmaster's hearty voice drifted out the door on the evening air.

"We-l-l-l, the cobs were just lying there in the way."

Libby listened to the amiable exchange. When Teddy came past her again, his head was down, the bill of his cap hiding his deeply tanned face as he counted the change in his fist. He had sold corncobs on a warm summer day to a station manager who had just moved his stove out of the depot. There were kind people in this town. It strengthened her sense of well-being and made her feel like throwing her arms wide and racing to meet her future here in Edgewood.

Instead, Libby retraced her steps to Baker's and watched from her second-story room as the sun set over the town. She could hear Mrs. Baker and Teddy on the walk below, exchanging tidbits of the day. It made her think of their backyard in Thistle Down: the screen door closing behind her after dishes were done; sitting for a while with Father and the boys; watching the fireflies rise from the grass and smiling as David gave chase.

Later, sitting up in bed with the lamp burning, Libby opened her Memorandum book. A page had turned in her life. Her exhilaration in newfound freedom had waned to a more realistic level. Yet still, it seemed important to capture some of the day's experiences.

Dearest Mother,

The room is plain, but neat and clean and quiet, like Mrs. Baker herself. The quality of dinner was excellent, and the sheets on the bed smell of sunshine. And still Mrs. Baker found time to sit on the bench in front of her establishment, Teddy at her side. Their voices drifted up to me through the open window of my hot little room. I'm impressed that she does not hover over her son. When I saw the boys teasing him today, I wanted to leap down and scold them soundly. It isn't until now, as I think of it, that I realize how deftly Minor handled the matter and how often my hasty impulses lead me astray.

I like the newness of this progressive town, and at the same time suddenly realize how comforting it is to know people and be known. The streets and houses and faces, I can learn readily enough. But the geography of friendships and affiliations will require more than amiable intentions. They will take time.

11

Libby awakened to the wafting aroma of fresh coffee, baking bread, and frying meat. She retrieved her clothes from before the window, where she'd hung them the previous evening, pulled up the shade, and lighted a lamp. She poured cold water from a rose-colored pitcher into the matching basin and splashed her face. The room was dim. A mirror hung on the wall over the stand, the glass dark and wavy. Her reflection was little more than a shadow as she made a single braid of her hair, wound it into a neat coil at the back of her head, and fastened it in place with tortoiseshell pins. Her bangs, with the skillful tease of the comb, fell in loose curls on her forehead.

Some of the wrinkles had fallen from the lawn shirt-waist and dark broadcloth skirt. Libby pulled them on over bleached muslin petticoats and her corset cover. The wide band of the skirt came to a V in the front. Gathers spilled from the fitted band, giving her the needed fullness to move freely. Many washings had shrunk her skirt to "walking" length, though her high-top shoes prohibited any risk of flashing ankles. She propped first one foot, then the other, on the only chair in the room and buttoned her shoes up with the button hook, then poked the hook into her dark cloth reticule with the mother-of-pearl sides.

She donned her black sailor hat. The hat had once belonged to her mother. But she'd given it a new look with a red ribbon around the crown and a jaunty white feather. She drew a deep breath to calm her nerves, asked God's blessing on the day, and was on her way.

The tables had been pushed together in the restaurant downstairs, with breakfast served family-style. Libby saw at a glance that there wasn't another woman in the room. The men hunched over their plates, their hats pegged to the beaded board behind them. She could not possibly join them. It was not done that way, not even in Thistle Down. Her step had been light and quick, but it had stopped the rumble of voices and the clank of cutlery. The men turned her way of one accord. With her nose to the wafting odors and an instinctive squaring of her shoulders, she turned and headed for the door.

As in Thistle Down, the railroad made mail deliveries throughout the day. Ike Galloway had told Father the mail drop was made just south of the station. Beside the tracks was a post with a hook on it. It was here she would hang the outgoing mail later in the day. The incoming mail, flung from the Chicago and Alton limited, had bounced into a weedy ditch. The canvas bag was heavy. Libby shifted the mailbag over one shoulder and picked up the valise with her free hand. She stopped north of the station to change shoulders and hands, and even that didn't help much. The sun was just beginning to rise as she dragged the mailbag the rest of the way to Willie Blue's. She reached for the brass handle, but the door would not open. It was locked, and she still had no key.

There was nothing to do but beat on the door until Ike Galloway appeared, his face half-shaven, the lather on the other half drying on his chin. His shirt was open at the throat and buttoned crooked the rest of the way down. She bid him good morning and apologized for having neglected to secure the key.

He passed a set into her care and said from the open door, "Heard yer father went home. Take sick again, did he?"

"No, not at all. The visit lifted his spirits."

"Last we talked, he was plannin' on stayin'."

"Yes, Father was thinking he'd stay and I'd go home to pack. But he tires easily. At home he can go at his own pace. My brothers are there to help." When Ike did not move out of the doorway, Libby adopted the comfortable plural and added primly, "We apologize for imposing on your friendship with Uncle Willie, but we're awfully grateful you filled the gap."

"You'll keep shop till he comes?" His deep voice rolled in that understated western twang. There was no mistaking his disapproval now.

Her chin came up. "That's right, Mr. Galloway."

He sighed and shifted to the other boot, hands on his hips. "Teddy had it straight, then."

"He's been here already this morning?"

"Last night. He walked the dog home."

As if summoned, the beagle came on tapping toenails and wagged her tail in a doleful brown-eyed welcome. The *only* welcome she was getting.

Libby stooped to fondle the dog's ears. Her hat, secured by a single pin, toppled forward like the lid on a hinged teakettle. She grabbed the neck of the mailbag and turned, preparing to back through the door, dragging the mail in behind her. She glanced over her shoulder and met Ike's gray gaze. "Excuse me, please."

He twisted his mouth to one side, scratched his scarred ear, and stepped out of her way, remarking, "Yer gonna have trouble handling it all."

The bluntness of his prediction chafed, but Libby curbed a quick retort and said with all the pleasantness she could muster, "I'm praying you're wrong, Mr. Galloway."

"You don't always get what ya pray for."

"No, Mr. Galloway. Sometimes you get better."

"Looky where yer goin'," he warned as, with much aplomb, she plowed backward into the umbrella display.

Fumbling to catch the rack, Libby succeeded only in scattering the umbrellas further. One crashed into a display of enamel cookware, another into a pyramid of small jars. A third flew over a case of ribbons, hatpins, and pompadour combs and knocked a perfume atomizer off the shelf. It hit the floor, not breaking, but releasing a cloud of flowery sweet fragrance.

"Jest as leave give it to me b'fore you bring the store down about our ears." He swung the mailbag effortlessly over his shoulder.

"Thank you, Mr. Galloway." Libby removed her bobbing hat. She placed the atomizer back on the shelf and scanned a label as she restacked the pyramid of jars. *La Dores Bust Food. For developing the bust and making it firm and round.* Good faith! And fifteen jars of it, too. Hearing Ike's returning footsteps, she finished stacking the jars in haste.

Mr. Galloway wiped his face on a towel and waited until her hands were free to show her how to light the gasoline jets that had been so recently installed. His satisfaction in the lighting system was such that Libby didn't share her disappointment at the cold blue light they gave off. He passed her the mantle stick, followed her to the next light, and straightaway began dispensing information.

"The first thing you want to do is get the mail counted and presorted. Before Miz Payne and Captain Boyd get here. You met the captain at the wake, didn't ya?" At her nod he added, "He's a good man. He can answer any question comes up and he'll help if you fall behind."

"I have to count the mail?" asked Libby.

"Every letter, postcard, paper, magazine. Sort it first, to the two separate rural routes and the box section here in the store. Those are all town folks. Willie was in the habit of unlockin' at eight. That's when you can expect 'em to start filin' in. There, you've got the hang of it," he added, as she successfully lighted the last of the gas lights. "You can turn 'em off once the sun's fully up."

If the store didn't open until eight, she wondered at the necessity of lighting up the front at all. She passed back the mantle stick without comment and followed him to the rear of the store where he emptied the mailbag onto a table and began sorting. Observing the separate piles, Libby asked, "How do you know what's in town and what's rural route?"

He pointed out a long sheet of brown paper he'd hung by a string from the ceiling. "I wrote them all out last night. Should help until you get them memorized."

"Thank you, Mr. Galloway. That was thoughtful."

He was stuffing his shirttails in when the misaligned buttons came to his attention. Libby averted her gaze as he righted the matter, acutely aware that she was alone with him.

Woodmancy. Her gaze moved down the alphabetical listing. Town.

Palmer. Again she consulted the brown paper. Route One.

Brignadello. That one she knew. At least she thought she knew. Quickly she looked. Town.

Lamb. She scanned the list. The undertaker with the sleepy eye. In town, of course.

Morefield. Abner, Erick, Lester, Maudie . . . The place was overrun with Morefields. She checked the first name, *Miss Maudie.* Route Two. Hum. This was going to take some time.

Young. Billy Young.

"Your friend got a letter."

"Billy?" Ike reached for it.

"In town?" she guessed.

"I'll take it. I'm goin' right past."

Libby hesitated in handing it over. "Is that allowed?"

His mouth changed shape upon his half-shaven face. "Reckon I was too hasty in worryin' 'bout you and Miz Payne."

Uncertain of his meaning, but sensing it did not bode well, Libby protested, "I only meant . . . aren't there privacy rules?"

"Bound to be. Though Willie was too busy gettin' the mail out to worry much with proper procedure. Miz Payne, now, *she's* read the book."

"There's a book?" echoed Libby, and he grinned for real. Exasperated, she protested, "Mr. Galloway, I've a great deal to learn and very little time."

"On the shelf, back of the counter. But I haven't looked up nothin' yet that I could catch the gist of what it was sayin'."

"I'll look into it," said Libby, certain she'd have no such problem. "Here's one for you, too," she added, noting that the return address was identical to the one Billy Young had received.

Ike stuffed them unopened into his pocket and began sorting again. His hands flew over the letters, a dozen or more to every one Libby placed. The piles grew until only the papers and a handful of magazines remained to be broken into sections.

Ike pulled out his pocket watch.

Feeling obligated, Libby said, "I appreciate your help, but if you're in a rush to be off, I won't impose further."

"I'll stay until Captain Boyd gets here. You can muddle through most anything with him helpin'. Besides, it don't seem sportin', leavin' you at the mercy of Zerilda Payne."

"We've met," said Libby, surprised he'd warn her a second time. "First on the train, and then at Uncle Willie's wake. I've given her a lot of thought."

"Yes, and you'll be givin' her some more, shortly."

"Has anyone tried to be her friend?"

The corners of his mouth lifted again. "You got that much spunk, reckon I'll jest go on back upstairs and finish shavin'. If there's anything left of ya when I git back, I'll bring yah some breakfast from Baker's."

"What makes you think I haven't eaten?"

"If ya did, ya swallowed it fast. Saw yer light go out upstairs."

She didn't give him the satisfaction of asking how he'd identified it as her room. It was a little town, after all. It didn't take a Pinkerton detective to piece it together. Though a gentleman wouldn't have brought it to her attention.

A moment later he was moving around upstairs. Ravenous, Libby grabbed an orange, peeled it fast, and ate it even faster. Not much of a breakfast, but it would have to do.

12

Zerilda Payne banged the door shut behind her and wheeled to face Libby. For a fleeting moment there was a whisper of familiarity in the rough topography of her face. Arms folded across her front porch of a bosom, she rasped like a saw on wet wood. "It's true, then. Yer gonna stay put and stand up to Decatur McClure."

Back in Thistle Down, folks who meddled in other folks' business had the courtesy to do it behind their backs. Assuming it was a consideration unfamiliar to Zerilda, Libby overlooked the intrusion.

"Good morning, Mrs. Payne. Mr. Galloway is anxious to get back to his own business affairs. But he was kind enough to help me get started this morning." Libby's word's were as carefully chosen as last night's journal entry.

"Humph." Zerilda picked up the pile for Route Two. "These been counted?"

"Yes."

"And writ down?"

Libby nodded and tried out her planned strategy, saying, "I appreciate your asking, though. It'll take me a while to get it all straight. This letter, for instance." She picked up a letter Ike had set aside without comment. "It's marked with numbers. What's that about?"

Already sorting, Zerilda finished casing her first handful before turning her head to look at the letter. "It's a registered letter for Mr. Gentry."

"He's on your route, isn't he?"

"No, he's Captain's Boyd's. But ya hafta record it b'fore passin' it on."

"I see. Where do I record it?"

She showed her, though not without a long-suffering sigh.

Libby finished her stack of papers and asked, "What do I do now?"

Open annoyance took shape on Zerilda's pitted face. "Well, you put up yer town mail, of course."

"Of course," Libby murmured, and set about doing so, matching the names on the letters to the names on the back side of the mailboxes. Her smile felt like a flower dried between the pages of a heavy book. At length she said, "I understand more mail will come in later."

"Five times a day, it comes, and five times a day, you fetch it." The woman looked at the watch pinned to her dingy gray shirtwaist.

"Will Captain Boyd be along soon?"

Out of patience, Zerilda snapped, "I got no idea 'bout Captain Boyd. Now, quit jawin', and let me be about my sortin'."

Ike picked that ignoble moment to reappear at the bottom of the stairs. Libby presented her back to him, methodically stuffing letters into slots. He greeted Zerilda, got a hostile grunt in reply, and fell without invitation to helping Libby. By the time the town mail was up, Zerilda had finished, too. Libby watched out of the corner of her eye as the dour woman pulled two cords from a cigar box. Her full skirt, she saw now, was divided like a pair of trousers. Zerilda tied each leg at the ankles, straightened, and slapped a pith helmet over her bird's nest of a coiffure.

"Oranges came in late yesterday," Ike called after her as she started away.

She turned back. "Any good?"

"I'm not so partial to them as to be discriminatory. Test 'em out, if you care to."

The woman retraced her steps, shaking the floor with

her rough-shod man-sized feet. She circled the counter that divided the work space from the store, plucked an orange from the display Libby had so briefly visited, clumped past them again and out the back door.

"Sunshine may burn off some of the vinegar," Ike ventured.

Libby recognized it as a peace offering and bent her pride enough to meet him halfway. "An orange would be a small enough price."

"Willie always said it helps if you pretend she likes you."

"It taxes the imagination. I know. I tried."

"You did, sure enough." Ike picked up a letter she dropped and handed it back. "I had no business discouragin' you."

She glanced at him in surprise. Had he had an attack of conscience? Tucking the letter into the corresponding slot, she said, "I'm not discouraged, Mr. Galloway."

"Struck me you were takin' it well."

That, she deduced, was the closest to a compliment she would get from him. He left shortly thereafter, though his belongings from the room upstairs were still at the foot of the steps. He must be getting breakfast, she decided, and took the stamp drawer from the safe Ike had opened. As she was familiarizing herself with it, Zerilda pushed a bicycle in the back door. She loaded her mail into the basket and tied it down in so fastidious a fashion, Libby found herself recalling the woman's skill with a crochet hook.

"Good-bye," Libby called, as Zerilda rolled her bike toward the door.

Zerilda turned back. "About the mail drops—next one's at nine. Ya got to pick it up yerself. Cain't send nobody else for it, not unless they got a contract to do it regular. That's what it says in the book."

"Thank you, Mrs. Payne. I appreciate your telling me. Anything else I should know?"

"More'n any one body kin tell ya in a day. You'd best get young Galloway to stick around through the end of the week."

"He's pretty set on going."

"Jest so ya know. I got a route to run, no time to stand around jabberin' and dishin' up mollycoddle."

"I understand," said Libby. "I'll read the book at the first opportunity."

Zerilda lumbered out, making a clatter with the door. The woman wasn't the sweetest flower in God's garden, but then neither was Mr. Rhodes, the blacksmith back in Thistle Down, and she'd managed to get along with him.

With the mail up, she was free to familiarize herself with the store. It was crowded and poorly organized, the space badly utilized. Shelves sagging. Displays hodge-podge and unappealing. And some of the merchandise, she was certain, had been around longer than Uncle Willie's old dog. Libby circled like a gardener on freshly turned soil. Charting it out. Envisioning how it could be. A face at the window startled her until she recognized it as Teddy Baker. His hand went into his pocket. Out came a pocket watch.

Libby checked her own timepiece. Eight o'clock. She flew to the door, hung the *Open* sign, and stepped out to greet Teddy, only to find the walk empty. Sugar, the old beagle, slipped past her and raced for the corner, ears flapping. It was a gorgeous morning. She filled her lungs, and thought of home. The boys would be at the mines by now. David would be crawling out of bed. And here she was, beginning her own grand adventure. Bursting with optimism, she grinned and just barely refrained from warbling a song right there on the sidewalk.

Minor passed on the street in a hack with Woodmancy Livery emblazoned on a board. He tipped his hat and called a good-morning. "Got to hump it on over to Doc's. He busted an axle on his buggy, and him with rounds to make."

"Minor to the rescue," she called back with a smile, and retraced her steps inside, feeling a small part of things simply because he had shared that bit of news.

Ike returned shortly thereafter, and still no Captain Boyd. Ike didn't comment, but the next time Libby looked, he was casing the mail for Captain Boyd's route.

Villagers trickled in, got the mail from their boxes, and trickled out again. By and by the pace grew to a steady drumming of feet and a drone of voices.

Libby greeted by name the folks she had previously met. She'd sold half a dozen oranges, a money order for a rug beater from Sears, Roebuck, and two stamps when Mrs. Brignadello breezed in for her mail and expressed interest in the fabric. Libby led her to the front of the store. The rumble of voices drew her eye to the window. The chairs that had been around the cold stove a short while ago were now lined up out front on the walk, and filled with lounging men.

"Rich fabric and some needle skill—that's the secret to a fashionable wardrobe," she confided. They enjoyed a brief visit, Libby mentioning that she'd had the pleasure of meeting her sister, Mrs. Gentry.

"She has a lovely home," Libby added.

"Owns her. Absolutely owns her body and soul," declared Mrs. Brignadello. She went on to invite Libby to attend the Wednesday evening Ladies Aid in her home. The group, she said, was comprised of ladies within the newly chartered New Hope Church. Libby readily accepted.

By nine, transactions had escalated to a steady pace. Ike lingered in the background, unobtrusive yet ready with an answer each time Libby hit a snag. By ten o'clock the place was empty. Even the chairs out front were deserted. Belatedly Libby remembered the second drop.

"Be a piddlin' amount this time. Go on and get it, I'll spell yah," Mr. Galloway offered.

By this time, apologizing for keeping him had grown redundant. Libby grabbed her hat and set off across the square.

There was no mailbag waiting at the drop sight. Had someone snatched it? Her heart hit her shoes. She conjured other possibilities. Maybe they'd missed their mark. Maybe it was hidden in the grass. She walked ten yards, turned and walked twenty, and still no mailbag. Hungry just minutes ago, Libby now felt too tied up in knots to even think of eating. She climbed up on the tracks and looked down. But it wasn't a mailbag that caught her eye:

rather, Teddy Baker, half a block away, with the beagle
snapping at gnats beside him. Libby turned her palms up
and shrugged. He motioned toward the station, tugged
his cap down, and walked away, the dog at his heels.

The station? With nothing to lose, Libby set off for the
depot. The sun was hot. Regretting having come away
without a handkerchief, she dried her face on her sleeve
and let herself in to the depot. The stationmaster was a
thin-shouldered, gray-haired fellow with a green eyeshade hiding his brows. He looked up from serving a
customer at the ticket window, and with a knowing
glance, waved her back out the door.

"By the milk cans there."

The mailbag was between the cans. She grabbed it up
quick. It was as light as a feather. Couldn't be more than a
dozen letters. But for all of her relief, it might have been
gold. Libby walked back inside, waited until the fellow
was free, and introduced herself.

"Saw you here last night, didn't I?" he asked.

"Yes. You were busy removing the stove and doing
business with Teddy." Libby smiled.

"Takes up too much room, that stove," he said. The
telegraph began to clack. He turned away, calling hurriedly over his shoulder, "Sometimes the mail'll be on the
ground by the hook, sometimes here at the station.
Depends on which train and if it's stopping."

Libby returned to the store with a train schedule and an
only slightly clearer understanding of the procedure.

Captain Boyd had arrived in her absence, collected the
mail Mr. Galloway had sorted, and was about to leave.

"Miss Willie! It's good to see you again," he greeted her
warmly.

"Watson, Captain," said Ike. "The lady's name is Miss
Watson."

Captain Boyd ran a hand through his silver hair. "I
know, Ike. But every time I look at those blue eyes and
red hair, I think of Willie. Anyway, the young lady
doesn't mind. Do you, miss?"

"I think I prefer it to 'Redtop,'" said Libby, smiling.

Captain Boyd chuckled and nudged Ike, explaining,
"That was Willie's name for her."

Ike's puzzled expression shifted to a grin. His gaze lingered on Libby's red hair. "Sounds like him."

Captain Boyd leaned against the threshold of the back door and crossed his arms over his chest. "Willie thought quite a lot of the little miss and her brothers."

"Me?" Libby lifted her face.

Smiling, he nodded. "He'd say he'd been down to see Little Redtop and the boys. It tickled him, how you liked to sing. I remember him telling me one time how you'd confused the words in 'My Country 'Tis of Thee.' Said you did fine until the last verse, then you belted out, 'Our fathers' God, to Thee, Arthur of liberty, to Thee we sing . . .'"

"Long may our lambs be bright," Libby chimed in, for it was a favorite family story. "I thought it was a song about a man named Arthur washing sheep." Egged on by their chuckles, she added, "Looking back on it, I worry I was destined from the start to be a washerwoman."

"You? A washerwoman?" Ike laughed and shook his head as if he couldn't picture that. "Be a waste, with an imagination like that."

Libby grinned and said with all due modesty, "Oh yes, well! You should see what I can do to a song when I'm *really* trying."

The old mail carrier pushed away from the door. "You were good tonic for Willie. Your family, too." His smile waned, and his chin quivered. Averting his gaze, he added, "He had a place to go when the loneliness got to him."

Never before had it occurred to Libby that Uncle Willie might have come to their house for reasons beyond simple physical needs. Being here in his store made her aware of how seldom he'd crossed her mind at all as the years passed. She wasn't proud of that. Still, she appreciated the captain sharing his memories. Though it hadn't escaped her notice that he offered no explanation for his tardiness. Nor did she miss the flush on his cheeks or the brightness in his eyes as he tipped his hat and bid her good day in his velvet-soft voice.

Libby lingered in the open back door as he climbed into his handsome red mail cart and sat down. Unaware that she was watching, he reached into his pocket for a silver flask. Seeing him tip it to his mouth, Libby sighed and turned back into the room to find Ike studiously counting the pieces of mail he'd shaken out of the sack.

Concerned for the captain, she felt her way around the subject, saying, "That's a handsome mail cart. It would be a shame if the contents of his flask make him careless."

"He got the cart free from *Popular Mechanics.*" Ike did not look up from his work. "A premium fer selling magazine subscriptions. He didn't twist any arms, mind you. Folks on his route heard he was goin' for it, they jest naturally wanted to help."

Libby wondered if that was his subtle way of telling her that folks liked the captain, and that she'd be borrowing trouble if she were to make too much of that flask. She dropped the subject and went over the train schedule Mr. Noonan had given her. Ike indicated when she'd need to pick up at the station, when at the hook, and how she was to hang the outgoing mail.

Libby mentioned Zerilda's comments concerning having to do the pickup and delivery in person, and learned that it was one of the issues that had caused trouble with Minor.

"He'd been sending Teddy after it. Mrs. Payne said it went against the book."

"She mentioned something about contracting the job out on a regular basis. Do you know anything about that?" asked Libby.

Ike shook his head.

"I'll look into it. Maybe there's a way to give Teddy the chore after all," she said.

"Don't know as I would."

Libby looked at him in surprise.

"He does all right, Teddy does, but he isn't one fer bein' tied down."

"I see," said Libby.

Ike didn't elaborate, and a customer came in before she could question him further. When she was free again, he was gone. This time he'd taken his bedroll and saddlebags with him. The full weight of the job was squarely on her shoulders now. Not to be intimidated, she walked out the back door, crossed to the buggy shed, and gathered a bouquet of lilacs off the bush that was blooming there.

"Mmm," she murmured, burying her nose in their fragrance and inhaling the sweet joy of life.

13

The heat of the second story sucked the air from Libby's lungs as she trudged up the stairs at the end of the day, the store ledger and "the book," as Zerilda called it, tucked under her arm.

All of that furniture, and only one soft chair. She collapsed into its frayed cushions, unlaced her shoes, and peeled off her stockings. Top buttons opened, skirt hiked, Libby propped her throbbing feet on the sill of the boarded window and fanned herself with a *Lamb's Mortuary* fan she'd found downstairs. Tired, but in good spirits, she was busy mentally rearranging the store. Not just a removal of outdated items and a reorganization of shelves, no. She wanted to bring the store into the twentieth century. Eye-catching fashions. Progressive displays that captured the town's optimistic mood. And a spirit of youth. Plus some glass to replace this broken window. Good faith, it was bleak, looking at a boarded window! Libby got up and picked her way through the warehouse of furniture to the next window, this one open to the twitter of birds, the chatter of children, the clatter of traffic on the street below.

Libby drew up a wooden chair, parked her elbows on the windowsill, and cupped her chin in one hand. The air stirred the bangs upon her moist brow as she glanced across the park to see Teddy talk to the old beagle, pat her on the head, then slip inside his mother's establishment

121

on the heels of Mr. Noonan, the stationmaster. The dog found a scrap of shade and lay down, facing the door.

The wooden canopy obscured Libby's view of the walk below, but the pleasant aroma of a pipe and the easy conversation of men settling in for a chat served as a reminder of the chairs left out on the walk. She recognized the granular voice of Hascal Caton. The other man's labored wheeze wasn't one she recognized. The conversation seesawed in lazy familiarity, a lullaby of weather, crops, and green-fly complaints. Libby rested her head on her arms, her thoughts drifting back to her plans, when a familiar name snapped open her eyes.

"Hear tell young Galloway packed up and moved out this morning."

"Woman-shy, I reckon," wagered Hascal Caton.

"Likely as not. Though I don't like sayin' it 'bout one of Mr. Roosevelt's boys. Charge a hill, but there he is, scairt off by a slip of a gal."

"Don't matter if it's a big hornet or a little one, Squire. A sting is a sting."

"They oughta horsewhip that Dr. Daniels fer stealin' Ike's sweetheart."

"Doctor of quackery. Play actor, that's all he be," snorted Mr. Caton. "And that raven-haired Dorrance demon. She weren't no account anyways."

"Tarnation, Hascal!" said his friend in exasperation. "You say that 'bout all the wimin, and you with daughters and granddaughters, too."

"Ain't like I got to handpick 'em," said Mr. Caton. "My grandson Frankie is the only man-child in the bunch. I been cursed, Squire. Cursed."

"Heard the sheriff had Decatur in the jailhouse."

"Yeah, fer borrowin' Cearlock's buggy."

"Cain't hardly blame Cearlock for bein' peeved, seeing how he was drivin' it at the time."

"Sorehead, that Cearlock. Got a tart tongue in his head, too," groused Hascal.

"Decatur didn't deserve jailin', is that what yer saying?"

"Well, it ain't like he took it fer keeps. He parked it right on the square, once ta town. Politics, and that's a fact. Been anybody but Gentry's son, wouldn'a been no big ta-do."

Libby caught her breath, striving to follow as the other fellow said: "The way I heard it, Decatur weren't too gentle in his dealin's with Angus."

"You takin' his side?"

"It ain't a question of sides. The question is, what the devil was that son-in-law of yers thinkin'? Why, it weren't nothin' short of crazy, roughin' up Angus like that. Any idea what got into him?"

"For one thing, that young whippersnapper lawyer insulted Naomi's honor on account of her bein' in the family way when Decatur married her," said Hascal.

"That's reaching back a few years," said his comrade. Sounding doubtful, he added, "Don't even sound like Angus. You sure ya got yer facts straight?"

"That's how Decatur remembered it, anyways. There he was, feelin' bad over Willie dyin', and Angus, blast his eyes, brings Naomi into it. No call fer him insultin' Naomi, no call at all," fumed Hascal.

"Shoot, Hascal, even if Angus did get careless and run his trap when he shoulda kept it shut, there ain't nobody any harder on Naomi than you," said the squire. He talked right over Hascal's sputtering protest. "Anyways, ain't nobody knows fer shore what was said but Angus and Decatur, and how reliable is Decatur's memory when his head was all fuzzed up from drinkin'?"

"Now, hold on there, Squire. Willie was more of a father to Decatur than Decatur's own old man. Losing a friend like that comes as a mortal shock to any man."

"We was all friends to the man, Hascal. But ya don't see the rest of us crawlin' into a bottle and drinkin' our way out."

"What about Captain Boyd?" retorted Hascal. "Tarnation, if he don't turn rural mail delivery into a hide-and-seek game. You'd think the addresses was writ in a foreign language, all the mail swappin' been goin' on out our way."

"I reckon the captain does hit the wrong box now and again."

"Why, folks is growin' old waitin' on their mail whilst

Boyd pulls up under a tree and sleeps one off," declared Hascal. "If he weren't such a likable feller, people'd be havin' a fit."

"He's a good sort. Most folks ain't anxious to make trouble for him."

"Me neither. Though I been thinkin' about gettin' me a box in town jest so's I can be assured my mail don't go astray," said Hascal.

"Ya may as well, ya spend most yer time in town anyways."

"Feller lives to be as old as me, he got a right to do what he wants with his free time, ain't he, Squire?" demanded Hascal. "Besides, how's a man gonna keep up on the news if he don't come to town?"

By and by the old men went on their way, leaving Libby to wonder about Captain Boyd, for it sounded as if his drinking was affecting his ability to do his job. He was such a nice man, she couldn't help but feel concerned. Was his drinking directly related to Uncle Willie's death? If so, perhaps the problem would go away once he came to terms with the loss.

Fervently hoping so, Libby drew water from the reservoir in the cold stove and washed with rose-scented soap, then laundered her soiled cotton waist and her small things in the same water. She donned yesterday's finely embroidered linen waist, tucked it into her dark skirt, smoothed the placket, then moved to the twin windows overlooking the alley. An oak tree partially curtained her view. One branch was so close to the building, she could reach out the window and touch it. It would shield her small wash from the back doors on the other side of the alley. Libby was hanging her undergarments to dry when a melodious "Hello, the store!" rang out from below.

She looked out on the back lot just as Angus Cearlock's sister, Catherine Morefield, lifted a small gloved fist to the back door. Her pale pink dress was stitched in layers so light that the skirt fairly floated about her trim figure. Her frothy picture hat was equally stunning. Libby jerked her head back, praying the young Mrs. Morefield hadn't seen her. For how could she invite her in and up these stairs to this hot, dusty, disheveled warehouse of a room where wet laundry hung from the windows? She snatched her chemise, stockings, and bloomers out of the window, inadvertently catching the string of the shade in the process. The shade snapped to the top of the window with a clatter.

"Miss Watson!" Catherine held on to her hat as she craned her slim white neck, smiling up at Libby there in the window. "It's ladies night at the Columbian, and I thought perhaps you'd care to go roller-skating."

"I don't have any skates."

Catherine's throaty laughter put Libby in mind of playful fingers chasing over the middle keys of the piano. "Of course you don't, neither do I. But we can rent a pair for fifteen cents."

Libby was tired. She'd never skated before and she had nothing to wear but the clothes on her back, which in no way compared to the loveliness of Mrs. Morefield's dress.

"I hope you don't think it presumptuous of me to drop by unannounced. Mama coaxed Tess into staying the night with her. I could have stayed, too, but Angus had a meeting and Mama was anxious about him coming to town alone. His injured ankle, you know." Catherine Morefield ended her breathless rush of words with a self-deprecating laugh. "Charlie won't be home until the weekend, and I'm lonesome. Can you come out and play?"

There was something so winsome about her, so open and unaffected, Libby hadn't the heart to decline her invitation. "I'd be delighted, Mrs. Morefield."

"Splendid! You can start by calling me Catherine. And I'll call you Elizabeth, if I may."

"Libby would be even better." Catherine's answering smile was like a tonic, relieving her physical weariness. She poked her key into her reticule, grabbed her hat, and hurried downstairs.

"I left the buggy at the Columbian, thinking the walk would do me good." She flashed her bright smile and added, "You have to eat like a farmhand out at Mama's or Chloe gets her feelings hurt."

Libby made the mistake of confessing she hadn't had supper yet. Nothing would do but that they stop by

Baker's before skating. The supper crowd had thinned to a few lingering customers. Catherine marched Libby past them and into the kitchen.

Mrs. Baker, Teddy, and a hired girl were cleaning up while an old woman sat in a corner rocking chair with an ear horn in her lap. She wore her hair in a thin bun with a large intricate comb that fanned out like peacock feathers. Her long black dress was buttoned up to her chin, and her petticoats were so numerous and stiff, her withered torso seemed in danger of being devoured by the voluminous skirt.

Catherine asked without preamble, "Have you any scraps left, Mrs. Baker? Libby hasn't eaten, and here we are on our way to skate."

Mrs. Baker moved away from the stove and welcomed them both with unhurried grace. "Look, Mother. Company." She patted her mother's shoulder and spoke into her ear horn. "This is Elizabeth Watson, Willie Blue's niece. And you remember Catherine."

The old lady's wintery gaze swept over Catherine. "The tinker's daughter."

Teddy turned from the sink and corrected her, saying, "No-o-o. He doesn't have a daughter."

"It's all right, Teddy." Catherine stooped and kissed the old woman's cheek. "You're looking pert this evening, Gram Steadman. Shall I help you with your towels?"

Gram wiped the kiss from her cheek with one of the muslin dish towels Catherine had so artfully slipped into her lap.

"Teddy, go out there and clear off those tables like you're supposed to." Barely reaching his shoulder, the hired girl wagged a wooden spoon under Teddy's nose and added with mock severity, "Move onto the sidetrack, you're in my way."

Teddy grinned and shuffled his feet, knowing it was a teasing more than a scolding. But in the end he did her bidding. The girl, Libby soon learned, was Chloe Berry's younger sister, Dorene. She had a similar wholesome look about her and was every bit as plainspoken as Chloe as she whipped about, filling a plate of chicken and noodles for Libby, cutting Catherine a piece of pie, pouring Mrs. Baker a cup of coffee.

"Sit yourself down, Missus Baker. I'll get to that stove once the dishes are done," Dorie urged.

"You take such good care of us, Dorie." Mrs. Baker pressed her cheek to Dorene's, a spontaneous caress that left the girl blushing.

"Bother!" Dorene hitched her apron. "Now, what've I done with my rag?"

Mrs. Baker led the way to the dining room just as the last diner left. Libby and Catherine joined her at a small table near the front of the room.

"I'm glad you stopped by, Catherine." A smile lifted the lines of a face beautified more by expression than feature. "I've got a recipe for a remedy that takes the ache right out of a broken bone. Why don't I write it out for Angus?"

"If it isn't too much trouble. His ankle *is* tender yet."

Mrs. Baker pushed a strand of ginger hair away from her brow and said with a sigh, "Decatur sure caused a lot of pain, drowning his own. It's odd, isn't it, his acting up that way?"

"He caught Angus off guard, that's for sure," said Catherine. "He said when Mr. McClure flagged him down, he could tell right away he'd had too much to drink. He seemed to be under the impression Angus was carrying legal papers that were of interest to him."

"What sort of papers?" asked Mrs. Baker.

"I don't know. Angus was irritatingly vague about the whole thing. His pride's still a little bruised, I suspect."

A dish clattered to the floor behind them.

Mrs. Baker turned. "I'll do that, Teddy, if you're wanting to get back to the station. There's some scraps by the sink for Sugar."

Teddy collected the scraps and left by the front door. As it swung closed behind him, Mrs. Baker said, "Mr. Noonan is lighting the Chicago and Alton platform with new lamps."

Afraid she'd failed to meet her obligations to Uncle Willie's dog, Libby said, "I'm not used to thinking about a dog. If Sugar's a bother, I can take her over and close her in the store right now."

"You couldn't possibly," said Catherine. "Sugar's a free spirit. Just like Teddy. Isn't that right, Mrs. Baker?"

"Mr. Blue did spoil her, letting her come and go as she pleased," conceded Mrs. Baker.

"If Teddy would like to keep her . . ."

"That's kind of you, but Teddy doesn't have to own Sugar to enjoy her company. Let's just keep sharing her, if that's all right with you."

Pleased with the arrangement, Libby agreed.

"You be sure and close her in with you at night," said Catherine. "With Charlie gone so much, many's the night I've wished I had a dog."

"How is Charles, anyway?" asked Mrs. Baker. "I haven't seen much of him lately."

"Nor have I!" complained Catherine. "But he promised me he wouldn't be traveling quite as often, once he's appointed branch manager in the St. Louis office."

"A promotion, then? That will be wonderful, Catherine. Charlie always was a bright boy."

"He's already begun looking at houses in St. Louis. We haven't mentioned it to Mama yet. You know how attached she is to Tess."

"Of course she is, dear. But Charlie must miss you and Tess terribly."

"Yes. However, he's very busy, which makes the days go quickly for him. I, on the other hand, feel as if I'm watching the clock and twiddling my thumbs, just waiting for him to be home again."

"Perhaps you should be down there with him, looking for a house."

"It's a dreadful time to be looking, what with the city swelled by the exposition. Men are better equipped for that sort of business. I wouldn't know where to begin."

"You could learn," said Mrs. Baker.

Doubtfully Catherine asked, "Do you really think so?"

"But of course!" assured Mrs. Baker. "Why, the Lord gave you all sorts of capabilities. Or do you think He intended you and Charlie to endure these separations indefinitely?"

"I should hope not!"

"Why, of course He didn't. You're young. You haven't learned yet just how eager He is to help. If you don't get down on your knees and ask, you've no one to blame but yourself for the miles keeping you and Charlie apart."

Catherine covered her ears, saying with mock severity, "You're incorrigible, Mrs. Baker. I'll be on the next train, and Mama'll be reaching for her fainting salts."

Libby joined in the laughter. The dinner was delicious, the conversation relaxed and amiable. As they were preparing to go, Mrs. Baker, who was also a member of the recently established New Hope Church, repeated Mrs. Brignadello's invitation to attend tomorrow night's ladies' meeting.

"I heard about Pastor Shaw's memory contest. Mama's talked to Chester about donating a prize for incentive," Catherine said.

"Oh, dear. Mr. Gentry's already been so generous. I hope he doesn't think he has to—"

"He *does* have to, if he's going to have peace with Mama." Catherine dimpled.

Libby shot Catherine a questioning glance. "Will you be at the meeting?"

"No. Charlie's family is Methodist. He won't hear of me changing."

"Good for Charlie. It isn't our intention to draw folks out of the other churches. Though if it were, you'd be high on my list." Mrs. Baker patted Catherine's hand.

"Still, there's something exciting about a church coming together. Mama makes me jealous with all her talk of the building program and fund-raisers and Sunday sings with dinner on the grounds."

"Ground is all we have. Where else would we have a dinner?"

Catherine chuckled at Mrs. Baker's practicality and conceded there were a few advantages to membership in a church where a building was a reality rather than a goal. Libby suspected that Catherine was perfectly content in her husband's church, that her feigned complaints were just her congenial way of sharing Mrs. Baker's anticipation in regard to the new church.

She made a good point, though. It was rather exciting to think of a new church springing like a blade from the ground. It coincided so well with her own fresh start here in Edgewood.

14

ℜ "There's something so familiar about Mrs. Baker," said Libby as they strolled toward the Columbian.

Catherine stepped around a wheelbarrow on the walk. "Should be. You work with her sister."

"Her sister?"

"Zerilda Payne is Mrs. Baker's sister."

"Their features are similar, now that I think of it," said Libby as they crossed the street.

"Edgewood's full of family connections. 'If you can't be kind, best be quiet.' That's what Chloe always says." Catherine shot her an impish grin.

Libby chuckled. "I'll remember that."

"Oh, yes. Well! Chloe's top drawer at dispensing sage advice."

When she spotted all the conveyances drawn up around the Columbian, Libby's trepidations crept back. It looked as if half the town had turned out to skate. "You did say it was ladies' night, didn't you?"

Catherine smiled. "You needn't worry. There will be plenty of room on the floor. It's the meeting upstairs that's drawing the crowd. The Republican Club." With an exaggerated sigh she added, "It isn't enough that Chester salts every conversation with politics. Now he's dragged Angus into it too. The election is months away, and I'm weary of it already."

"Mr. Gentry rode in with you and Mr. Cearlock?"

Catherine's hat caught the breeze as she shook her head. "He stays after work and has dinner in town on the days the Club meets."

Admittance was free at the Columbian. Libby noted the enclosed staircase leading to the second floor as she paid for her skates and followed Catherine into the open auditorium, where a dozen or more skaters sailed clockwise about the room.

The curtains were open on the stage up front, and the balconies, which had been full on the day of Uncle Willie's funeral, were empty. A few chairs remained against the back wall. Following Catherine's lead, Libby sat down to don her skates, then rose again before her courage could fail her. Why, it was like walking on marbles! She moved back to the wall and inched along, admiring Catherine's effortless glide out onto the floor.

"You make it look so easy!" she wailed, as her new friend returned from her first graceful sweep of the room.

"You've not skated before?"

"Never. It's like having ice underfoot!"

"It isn't so hard, once you get onto it. Move away from the wall."

Libby laughed. "I'm trying! But my feet have a mind of their own."

"Oh, my. We shall have to do something about that," exclaimed Catherine.

The "something" they did was fall. Rather, Libby fell and, in trying to save herself, pulled Catherine down too. Her nervous apology was drowned out by Catherine's giggles. Getting up without the aid of the wall was difficult. Nor was staying up easy. Libby flailed her arms like a windmill, which tickled Catherine so, she could scarcely offer support for laughing.

"We're like poor Minor and Captain Boyd going down the street, each claiming he's holding the other fellow up!"

"Minor, too?"

"Oh my yes! Hadn't you noticed? Why, he's as yellow as a—ouch! That's my . . . pumpkin."

They both got so tickled, they fell again, Catherine rubbing the toes Libby had just mashed, with Libby babbling apologies between gales of laughter. Skaters, like migrating geese, made a V and went around them as a voice called down from above: "Squeal 'uncle,' Miss Watson, and she'll let you up. It always worked for me, anyway."

Libby lifted her face to find Angus Cearlock leaning on the balcony railing, his suit coat over his arm and a pair of crutches beside him. Heat rushed to the very roots of her hair.

Catherine retorted in mock severity, "Pay no attention to Angus. I didn't give him a single thrashing he didn't deserve."

Angus laughed. "And what, prey tell, has *Miss Watson* done to deserve such a mauling?"

"Angus, you wretched thing! Go back to your meeting or I shall complain to the chairman that his membership is ducking meetings to abuse innocent skaters."

"Uncle!" cried Angus, holding up his hands as if to ward off a blow.

"Oh no! I'm not letting you off so easily as that. Go ahead and rest your foot while I think of a fitting punishment."

Libby used their light banter as a shield as she gathered her awkward feet beneath her and got them pointing in the same direction just as Catherine announced, "I know, you can fill in for Aunt Sarah Jane! Come down on the stage and play some skating music."

"I'd be honored, if it weren't for the stairs," Angus graciously declined.

"You climbed up to the Republican Club, didn't you?"

"Only with the help of a couple of good-hearted chaps."

"Libby and I are good hearts," claimed Catherine. "You wait right there while we get out of these skates."

Angus protested in vain that he would have to return to the meeting in short order. By now they had attracted the attention of the other skaters. It was a young crowd, some mere girls. They began calling out requests from the floor.

"Can you play 'Sweet Adeline'?"

"How about 'Don't Throw Snowballs at the Soda-Water Man'?"

Catherine was out of her skates in a twinkling. Libby hung back, venturing, "We hadn't ought to force him down the stairs, had we?"

"Oh, pooh! He's milked enough sympathy with those crutches. No procrastinating, now. I'll need your help."

There was a back staircase leading up from the stage to the twin balconies that skirted the east and west walls. Left with little choice, Libby went along with Catherine to help Angus down. Sensing her reluctance, he relieved her discomfort, saying, "Between Catherine and the stair railing, I can make it, if you'd be so good as to bring my coat and crutches."

It was close quarters on the staircase. The warm air enhanced the faint scent of tobacco and shaving lotion. Libby followed them down, aware of the straight part of his hair and the whiteness of his collar and cuffs, and the slender length of his fingers on Catherine's shoulder as he braced himself for each step. Once to the stage, where the piano awaited, their hands tangled in the exchange of the crutches.

"Thank you, Miss Watson." Angus's smile was as warm as the queer stirrings in Libby's stomach. She averted her gaze and retreated as he got the crutches beneath him, but not without noticing the healing gash on his chin, a memento of his unfortunate meeting with Mr. McClure.

From the floor, the girls were still calling requests. Once seated on the piano stool, he looked to Libby, his hazel eyes large and luminous behind his glasses lenses. Hands poised over the keys, he waited. "The choice is yours, Miss Watson."

"'Ta-ra-ra *Boom* De-ay.' " Libby blurted the first tune to dance through her head. Or was it her heart, with its booming, that brought the song so swiftly to mind?

Angus's nimble fingers glided over the keys. The girls on the floor skated away, singing along and hitting the *booms* with great gusto. Angus finished with a flourish and was leading into the familiar strains of "Meet Me in

St. Louis, Louis" when heavy footsteps rang out on the balcony overhead.

"Sarah Jane, it sounds like cannon fire down here!"

Angus swung around on the bench and lifted a sheepish face. "I'm sorry, sir. I'm your culprit."

"Angus!" Mr. Gentry fairly bristled with indignation as he leaned over the railing. "We only sent you out until the vote could be taken. What are you doing down there?"

"I asked him to play, sir." Unruffled, Catherine added, "Aunt Sarah Jane usually plays for us, but Uncle Kersey came back to town early, so I guess she couldn't come."

"Kersey had nothing to do with it, Catherine. I asked her if she would kindly refrain. The fellows have an abominable amount of planning to accomplish if the Fourth of July rally is to be a success."

"A pity no one told us. Had I known, I wouldn't have asked Angus to stand in."

Mr. Gentry grimaced, the heat of his impatience seeping away. "Catherine, I must say you're making uphill work of your brother's campaign."

"I'm sorry, sir. It wasn't intentional. Shall we boost Angus up the stairs again?"

Mr. Gentry sighed from the very depths of his rotund frame. Gamely he capitulated, saying, "That won't be necessary. I wouldn't want it bandied about that I'd deprived you ladies of your piano man. Carry on. But in moderation, if you please, Angus. And when you're through, kindly join the meeting again."

"You heard him, Angus. Carry on!" urged Catherine, as the upstairs door closed behind her stepfather.

Once again Angus launched "Meet Me in St. Louis, Louis." "Sing, ladies. But in moderation, if you please!"

He winked at Catherine, his good-natured parody so perfect, Libby suspected the pair of them made a private joke of miming their stepfather.

Angus played with a rollicking rhythm that inspired the skaters. From "Annie Carroll" through "In the Good Old Summertime" to the close harmony of "Sweet Adeline," he led them along until they were all breathless. He took his bow from the piano stool, and answered their applause with a modest "Thank you, ladies. Thank you. It has been a privilege to fill in for my nimble-fingered aunt."

With Libby as crutch bearer, the dapper young attorney made his exit up the treacherous stairs.

"How's your ankle holding up? If you're suffering, I'll make your excuses to Chester. We can cut the evening short and go home," Catherine offered.

"And deprive Miss Watson of her skating lesson? I wouldn't hear of it," he replied, getting his crutches under his arms again and starting toward the closed door of the Republican Club. "Oh, and Miss Watson?"

As she turned back, Libby saw the flash of his smile. "Yes, Mr. Cearlock?"

"When she takes you down, what is the word?"

" 'Uncle,' " said Libby, smiling.

Though Catherine was an encourager, patient and unfailingly good-natured, it seemed to Libby that the skates and the hardwood floor had contrived to steal every ounce of grace she possessed. She spent more time on her derriere than on her feet. It was disconcerting, hearing her name pass from lip to lip. Still, there were sympathetic smiles with the passing, and as the evening wound to a close, Libby had put some names to the faces even if she hadn't quite mastered the skates.

Angus was waiting in the trap when they came out. A high-stepping horse strained at the traces, anxious to head for home. Angus kept a firm grip on the lines as Libby disembarked at the front door of Willie Blue's.

"Thank you, Catherine, for a lovely evening. And you, Mr. Cearlock, for the music," said Libby from the walk.

"The pleasure was mine."

"I'll step in while you make a light." Catherine stepped down after her.

"Careful getting past Uncle Willie's diligent watchdog." Laughing, Libby indicated Sugar, stretched out on the threshold. Her fur was damp. "By the look of her, she's worn herself out, swimming in the mill pond."

"As I was saying earlier, good company when you're home alone." Catherine nudged the dog with her foot, adding in a loud whisper, "Get up and wag now, Sugar, before you make a liar of me."

"Watch your step, everything is hiltie-skiltie," Libby said, borrowing one of Father's expressions. She made a light with the wick stick, adding, "I'm going to compartmentalize a bit, as soon as I have time."

"Like a city department store?"

"Exactly! A niche for the ladies and a niche for the gentlemen." Libby indicated with a sweep of her hand the front west corner. "I thought perhaps a wardrobe against the wall with fashions hanging up instead of folded away where the gentlemen have to dig to find them. And over here," Libby said, gesturing, "a hall tree for hats. A bureau would help, too. And a washstand."

"With a razor strop hung from it," Catherine said, grasping the idea at once. "And a good array of lotions that smell nice."

"Instead of overripe fruits and wet dogs." Libby laughed and wrinkled her nose.

Eyes aglow in the cold blue light, Catherine cried, "Please say you'll let me help."

"I couldn't! It will be pure drudgery. Just look! The corner must be cleared out. And once that is done . . ." Libby stopped, for Catherine's face had fallen. "What is it?"

"Nothing."

Libby's heart banged against her chest. Catherine's swiftly shuttered lids were concealing the sheen of tears. The pleasure of the evening went suddenly flat. "Catherine? Have I injured you in some way?"

"No, no. I was envying you, that's all. All this . . ."

Libby could only gape.

"It isn't the store. It's having an objective," Catherine struggled to explain. She wiped her eyes, half-weepy, half-laughing. "Forgive me. You must think me terribly foolish. You've had a long day. You'll have another tomorrow. I'd best take my pony and skip."

Miserably aware she had hurt her, Libby caught her hand and confessed, "I'm sorry. I haven't had much practice at being a friend. Of course I want your help. But you have a husband and child and a home to care for. It would be thoughtless of me to impose."

"Then be thoughtless, I beg you!" Color stained Catherine's cheeks, but at least her chin was in the air again. "It's wicked of me to complain. Mama means well, trying to make things easy for me, but between her good intentions and Charlie being gone, I sometimes fear I shall lose my mind if I don't find something to fill my time."

"I see. Well, I thought I'd begin by clearing the corner. So if you want to stop by . . ."

"When?"

"It will be a week, anyway, before I can get to it. Maybe more."

"A week from Friday, then?" asked Catherine.

"Once the mail is up. You might want to wear something old. I don't think Uncle Willie ever stirred the dust in here."

"To tell you the truth, Libby, I haven't had much practice lately either."

"It's tedious, I know."

"Dusting?" Catherine's lightsome laughter rang out. "No, no. I was speaking of friendship. I've had no one since Maddie Dorrance eloped." She grinned and added, "Remind me to tell you about Maddie before the town gossips beat me to it."

15

🐾 The small room at the head of the stairs was swept clean, leaving nothing but a low cot and an empty, upended crate. There was no window and the air was stale and muggy. How had Ike endured it? Uncle Willie's bedchamber was a similar windowless cloakroom sort of space, this one long and narrow with a curtain closing it off from the rest of the cluttered second story.

A wooden settee in front of a window, well padded with blankets and draped in clean linens, became Libby's bed. She settled down with her journal, her thoughts wheeling over the events of the day.

Catherine has a lovely, vivacious spirit that kindles a good bit of fun.

Libby paused, thinking of Catherine's brother. There was a lighthearted, dashing side to his nature as well. A side she'd like to know better. She put her tablet away, unwilling to trust what was an altogether new feeling to the glare of words on paper.

Captain Boyd was late again on Tuesday. He smelled faintly of whiskey, but he was helpful and unfailingly patient with her questions. This in sharp contrast to monosyllabic Zerilda, who cased her mail, strapped it into her bicycle basket, and left as if she couldn't get away fast enough.

In the afternoon a postal agent dropped by unannounced. He introduced himself as Mr. Albert Tyson and alarmed Libby with his vigorous inspection of matters. Upon finishing his examination of the premises and having thoroughly drilled her, he went across the park to the telephone company and used one of their boxes to call his office. Libby was certain he'd return with the news that she'd been replaced. Instead, he informed her upon his return that he'd been authorized to appoint her clerk of the Edgewood post office.

"Repeat after me," he said.

Dazed by his swift efficiency, Libby took the oath of office, and under his watchful eye, completed all the papers pertaining to her appointment.

"We'll forward these to the Postal Department in Washington, D.C.," he said, and promptly did so.

An exacting sort of gentleman, Mr. Tyson stayed the night at Baker's, and was on hand the next morning when a farmer came in with a letter that had been left in his box by mistake. Learning that he was on Captain Boyd's route, Libby apologized on the captain's behalf.

"No harm done. I was coming in anyway," said the farmer. "Been wondering, though, if the mail has been heavy. Can't help noticing the mail has been late a couple of times over the last few weeks."

Libby admitted she was too new at the job to know whether the volume of mail had been heavier than usual. She was relieved that Mr. Tyson, who had heard the exchange, did not comment on the misrouted piece of mail or the customer's comment concerning late deliveries.

Putting aside her concerns for Captain Boyd for the moment, Libby listened carefully as Mr. Tyson resumed arming her with a more thorough understanding of what was expected of her until a postmaster could be appointed. When the opportunity presented itself, she summoned her courage and mentioned that her father would make a good postmaster. Mr. Tyson expressed doubt that her father's mining experience qualified him for the position.

"Oh, but he's very capable at whatever he does," Libby insisted. She went into detail concerning Father's sterling character, his quickness of mind, his leadership qualities. When Mr. Tyson departed, he carried with him her father's letter of application. He even looked the other way as she signed it, *Thomas C. Watson.*

Catherine, who'd collected her small daughter from Erstwood that morning, stopped by for a chat. When Libby confided how she'd applied on her father's behalf, Catherine praised her initiative.

A bit ruefully Libby mused, "I suppose Father will accuse me of being a 'modern' again, and overstepping my boundaries. Perhaps I won't tell him just yet. If nothing comes of it, he won't have chided me over nothing."

"Absolutely!" chimed Catherine as she rocked Tess in her wicker buggy.

It was comforting, just how thoroughly her new friend understood her rationale. In the conversation that followed, Libby learned that Angus had ridden into town with Catherine to keep an appointment with their uncle, Dr. Harding.

Libby averted her face lest her expression betray her quickened interest.

"He's made up his mind to return to his own home, with or without Uncle Melville's approval. Mama's nursing is wearing thin on his sunny disposition." Catherine chuckled and added, "I told him I'd pick up his mail."

"He lives nearby?" asked Libby.

"He lives across town. But his office is just kitty-corner across the alley from you on Pearl Street."

They visited awhile longer. Then, taking her brother's mail, Catherine left Tess with Libby just long enough to dash down the alley past the shed where Uncle Willie's buggy was kept, and enter by the side door a snug little brick building just a stone's throw away. So that was Angus's law office. Libby stood in the sunshine with little blue-eyed Tess in her arms, relishing her warmth and her baby gibberish and the realization that she and Angus were neighbors.

* * *

A trunk from home came on Wednesday, with a note from her father. He bid her be patient, that it would be at least a week before he and David could join her. Her older brothers, however, intended to stay in Thistle Down. It was no more than what she'd expected, and still, Libby was disappointed. The hazards of the work itself were bad enough, without the friction of recent years between mine owners like Colonel Calkin, and workers who were wanting to unionize. She would continue to pray for her brothers' safekeeping, and that a solution would come to Thistle Down without the violence that erupted sporadically in some of the neighboring mining communities.

Libby locked the front door at five and went upstairs to unpack. The truck contained all of her clothing, her hats, her books, her tablets, her trinkets, even her picture of Mother. She rode out a wave of homesickness as she ate a can of soup and heated water for bathing. Her white lawn dress would do well for tonight's meeting, but it needed pressing. She borrowed both iron and board from the store stock. The full sleeves, which puffed at the shoulder and cuffed just below the elbow, required special care, as did the sheer inset and blue satin sash.

By the time Libby was ready to go, the sky had clouded up and the flies were biting. Hoping the rain would hold off, Libby left the upstairs windows open in an effort to let out the combined heat of the day and of the cookstove. She folded a fan into her reticule, pinned on her hat with the blue ribbons, and pulled on her white gloves. Uncle Willie's shaving mirror reflected her blue-eyed freckle-dusted face, but told no tales of the butterflies stirring in her midriff.

Libby pinched some color into her cheeks and found a black umbrella among Uncle Willie's belongings. She locked the front door just as Mrs. Baker came across the park. Together they set off for the New Hope Ladies Aid Society at Mrs. Brignadello's home.

They passed Zerilda's house on the way. She sat in a chair on the porch, her crocheting in her lap.

"If you'll excuse me just a moment." Mindless of the weeds, Mrs. Baker dashed across the yard and up the porch steps to press her cheek to her sister's in greeting.

To Libby's surprise, Zerilda did not draw away. Though Libby couldn't make out their words, there was no mistaking the ease between them. It was odd, two sisters so different. A pair of barefoot children came around the house and flung themselves at Mrs. Baker. She hugged them both close and smiled as she responded to their animated chatter. Their disappointment at the brevity of her visit was evident as, with a parting word and a pat on their heads, she turned back to join Libby.

"Zerilda and her grandchildren are going to look in on Mother. Teddy's there, but he doesn't always understand her needs. It's sweet of Zerilda to go. She and Mother never did see eye to eye." Mrs. Baker sighed and said no more.

Mrs. Brignadello's white clapboard house with its forest green shutters was modest in size, the lawn neatly kept. A wooden walkway curved past beds of blooming flowers on its way to the door.

Mrs. Brignadello welcomed them warmly. She led them through the dining room into the parlor. It was a light, airy chamber, easily accommodating the fifteen ladies convened there. Dorene and Chloe Berry made room for Libby on the Turkish leather couch, while Mrs. Baker took the matching leather rocker nearby. A glass bordeau lamp graced a round oak table. A matching lamp spread soft light over the crystal collection adorning the top of the organ. An amiable atmosphere prevailed as the ladies greeted one another, laughing and talking and exchanging bits of news.

The meeting opened with prayer. A song service followed, with Sarah Jane accompanying on the organ. The harmony of voices and spirited clapping filled the parlor and set the delicate crystal collection to dancing. A lesson taken from a letter to the Corinthians on the subject of charity was given by Chloe and Dorene Berry's mother. Having finished, she slid her Bible onto a small pedestal table, inadvertently nudging a crystal cruet dangerously close to the edge of the table. With a quiet gasp, she closed her work-weathered hand over the handle of the cruet. Ever so gently she moved it out of harm's way while Mrs. Shaw began the business meeting.

In the course of things, Mrs. Madeline Dorrance asked if she might address the group on what she termed "the recent increase in public drunkenness." Her black gown was simple in style, her dark eyes and full firm mouth uncompromising, even in repose. Her alabaster neck was long and her carriage so correct, Libby wondered that the twin cords of muscle didn't snap from the strain as she read aloud from the letter she intended to send to Mr. Gruben at *The Gazette*. In it she urged the town council, Sheriff Conklin, and all individuals in positions of authority to do their duty and end this blight on their fair town. She circulated the letter for signatures and, with queenly composure, sat down.

Mrs. Lamb, the undertaker's wife, inquired about an ice cream social on the Fourth of July. Mrs. Baker offered the use of her restaurant kitchen for mixing and freezing the ice cream, and everyone agreed it was an ideal location, with its close proximity to the park where there would be baseball in the afternoon, a parade, and a band concert.

"Mrs. Gentry, would you care to collect receipts that day?" asked Mrs. Lamb.

"I'm sorry, but the Republican Club is having a barbecue and a rally on the Fourth. Mr. Gentry and I will be out at Spring Lake all day." She smiled and added, "But I would like to mention Pastor Shaw's proposed memory verse contest, if I may."

"Certainly."

It had been such a long day, Libby was fighting a yawn as Mrs. Gentry came to her feet, entreating, "Ladies, we need to support and encourage this contest in such a way that sends every man, woman, and child flying for their Bibles."

"If you'll excuse me, I'll be seeing to refreshments." Sarah Jane's taffeta skirt rustled as she brushed past her sister, Ida Gentry. There was no door into the dining room, rather an open archway between the two rooms.

"For incentive Mr. Gentry has agreed to pay both train fare and gate admittance to the Louisiana Purchase Exposition in St. Louis for the winner." Mrs. Gentry smiled benignly at the group's soft murmurs.

"Generous, Ida, but not very practical," called Sarah Jane from the next room. "Suppose a child wins?"

"Perhaps we should offer an alternate prize more suited to a child," suggested Mrs. Woodmancy. "Though it seems unlikely a child would win."

"Absolutely not," declared Mrs. Gentry. "That would detract from the excitement. If a child wins, then Mr. Gentry and I shall accompany him. With the parents' permission, of course. We plan to attend the exposition anyway."

"And do you plan to see the fair all in a day?" asked her sister.

"Oh my, no. Catherine says it would take at least three days, and even then, a visitor would be rushed to see the entire exhibition. Five, it seems to me, would be ideal."

"Then there would be the expense of four nights' lodging for the contest winner as well," said Sarah Jane.

"I shouldn't view that as an insurmountable obstacle. It is, after all, a worthy cause." Mrs. Gentry tipped a glance Mrs. Dorrance's way. She was scanning the signatures at the bottom of her letter and seemed not to notice.

There was an expectancy to the silence that Libby found uncomfortable. Mrs. Shaw must have found it so too, for she cleared her throat and said, "Could we have some discussion as to how we might fund the expense?"

Sarah Jane Brignadello lifted her chin. "That won't be necessary. Mr. Brignadello would be happy to donate the price of lodging."

Gently Mrs. Baker suggested, "Wouldn't you like to speak to him about it first, Sarah Jane?"

Sarah Jane flushed and tilted her nose. "That won't be necessary. He's always generous in worthy causes."

"Thank you, Sarah Jane. It's settled, then." Mrs. Gentry beamed.

"What about a date?" asked Mrs. Berry, as Sarah Jane busied herself once more dishing up desserts at the sideboard in the dining room.

"When had you and Mr. Gentry planned to go?"

"We'd like to be there for Illinois Day in mid-September."

"Ladies, the refreshments are ready, if you'd care to file past," Sarah Jane announced from the doorway.

The business portion of the meeting was adjourned. The ladies ambled toward the sideboard in the next room, chatting of gardens, children, and the C & A's reduced rates for weekend excursions to the fair.

Chloe prepared to follow, but Dorene caught her arm, teasing, "You've always been good at Bible verses. This should really inspire you."

"Am I missing something?" asked Libby.

Dorene whispered, "Billy Young got a letter inviting him down to the fair to parade with the Rough Riders on Illinois Day. Why, if Chloe learns enough verses, she could be in the crowd, waving her handkerchief at him. Afterwards, maybe he'd take her for a ride on the observation wheel. They say you can see the entire grounds from up there."

Chloe said stoutly, "She's talkin' foolishness. Don't pay her any mind."

Overhearing, Mrs. Baker asked, "Will Ike be parading, too?"

"He never does." Not to be distracted from her teasing, Dorene poked her sister. "Here's a verse for you, Chloe: 'Let him kiss me with the kisses of his mouth: for thy love is better than wine.'"

Libby hid a smile as Mrs. Baker gently chided, "Dorene."

"I'm only trying to help."

"It's all right, Mrs. Baker. I'm used to her playin' the fool," claimed Chloe.

"'But whosoever shall say Thou fool shall be in danger of hellfire,'" Dorene replied, rattling off another verse.

"It seems to me you're pretty fair at this yourself," said Libby, smiling.

Chloe laughed and echoed, "Yes, Dorie. You're pretty fair. You go wave *your* handkerchief at Billy Young."

They were lively company, the Berry girls, almost as much fun as skating with Catherine. Off in a corner, over dishes of strawberries and cream, they regaled Libby with family stories.

"There's seven of you?" asked Libby, trying to keep count of the Berry siblings.

"Plus three married sisters, makes ten," said Chloe, eyes smiling at Libby over the rim of her cup.

Libby laughed. "How will I ever sort you all out?"

Dorene listed the names with the speed of *Mississippi* in a spelling bee.

Nearby, Mrs. Gentry was confiding to Mrs. Baker her concern for Mr. Culbertson and his wandering, saying, "I took Tess out to the barn to see the kittens, and there was the old dear, sitting on a milking stool just as if he'd come home."

"Poor soul," murmured Mrs. Baker.

Mrs. Dorrance, moving her chair closer, interrupted the conversation, saying, "Excuse me, Verna, but I seem to be missing your signature on my letter." She indicated the varied endorsements at the bottom.

"I see how hard you're working, and I thank you for caring so deeply. But I'm afraid I can't sign," Mrs. Baker replied quietly.

"Come now, Mrs. Baker. If we fail to demand a high standard, what sort of society will we have?"

Mrs. Baker sipped her coffee, attentive but silent.

"Mr. Boyd was quite late with the mail again on Tuesday," Mrs. Dorrance went on. "Mr. Minor, I notice, has changed jobs once more. That's never a good sign."

"They're mourning Mr. Blue. He loved them."

"Ah, Mr. Blue. He set an example I'd like to see them follow."

"They're trying, Mrs. Dorrance." Softly Mrs. Baker added, "The spirit is willing."

"Which is exactly why it will take strong measures to rid our community of this vile abomination," insisted Mrs. Dorrance.

Mrs. Baker didn't argue. Nor did she sign the letter. Rather, she changed the subject. Libby was admiring Mrs. Baker's skill when, without preamble, Mrs. Dorrance turned to her. "I understand, Miss Watson, that you've replaced your uncle as postmaster now."

"I was appointed clerk until a postmaster can be hired," Libby explained.

"As I told Mr. Minor in his brief stint at the counter, I won't hesitate to write a letter to the postal authorities, should Captain Boyd's drinking continue to interfere with his duties." Her black gaze drilling Libby, she added, "You are aware of the problem, aren't you?"

Nerves jumping, Libby avoided a direct answer. "I've only been on the job for three days."

"I understand that. Nevertheless, you must have realized by now that he's often tardy. He naps on the route. And lately he's grown increasingly careless about getting letters into the right boxes. His infractions should not go undisciplined. I trust you'll make yourself plain to him, Miss Watson." Without another word, Mrs. Dorrance excused herself and moved across the room, leaving Libby feeling as if she'd been punched hard in the stomach.

Thunder growled off in the distance. Mrs. Baker's eye was on the changing weather as well. In mutual agreement, they finished their refreshments and prepared to go.

Sarah Jane Brignadello walked them to the door. She leaned her dark head close to Mrs. Baker's. "That was wicked of Madeline to put you on the spot that way, Verna. I'm sorry I signed her letter myself."

"Don't be. Not if it spoke your thoughts."

Sarah Jane turned to Libby. "What does she expect you to do—put poor Captain Boyd out on the street? And him a decorated veteran. I never heard the like!"

"She doesn't want that any more than we do," said Mrs. Baker soothingly. "She'd like to stop his backsliding."

Sarah Jane sniffed. "She has a strange way of showing it."

Mrs. Baker patted their hostess's hand and ended the matter, saying, "Thank you for a wonderful evening, Sarah Jane. Coming to your home is always a treat."

It had seemed so to Libby for a time. But after being cornered by Mrs. Dorrance, the joy had gone out of it. She followed Mrs. Baker out with a heavy heart, wishing she'd stayed home. For now, added to all the other responsibilities of the store was this new concern: What was she to do about Captain Boyd and his drinking?

16

$\mathcal{L}$ Lightning flashed and the heavens rumbled as Libby and Mrs. Baker turned homeward. The sun had slipped over the horizon, its dying rays gilding the ragged edges of angry black clouds. A gust of wind chased through the grass and down the street, kicking dust in Libby's eyes and whipping her skirt like a flag. Jarred from anxious thoughts of Mrs. Dorrance's demands, she lifted her gaze to the brewing sky.

"And me without an umbrella." Mrs. Baker wiped her eye as the dusky sky spit its first drops.

Hastily Libby spread her own umbrella and made room as the light peppering began. "Tuck your head under, Mrs. Baker."

A leaf-rattling gust tried to take the umbrella as Mrs. Baker joined her beneath the wide black arc. Lightning intensified its dance with thunder. Nerves leaping, Libby clutched her hat with her free hand and struggled against the wind.

A surrey pulled up beside them, the wheels churning dust. Mrs. Gentry beckoned from the front seat and cupped a hand to her mouth. "You can't walk in this. Climb up. Quickly!"

As she closed her umbrella, Libby saw that it was Angus handling the reins. She gathered her billowing skirt, scrambled up, and turned to give Mrs. Baker a hand before seating herself behind him.

149

"Good evening, Mrs. Baker, Miss Watson," Angus said.
"Hold on to your hats. Prince is a dry-weather horse!"

"Be careful, Angus," cried Mrs. Gentry as he strained
forward and whipped up the horse. "You shouldn't even
be out in this. I told Chester when he dropped me off to
watch the weather and—" The rest of her admonition
was left to the imagination, for a sudden blow snatched
her words.

The conveyance had a fringed top, but no side curtains.
They'd gone only a block when the heavens opened in
earnest. The whooshing onslaught of rain rattled on the
canvas lid. The dress Libby had taken such care pressing
swiftly succumbed to the wind-driven torrent as the horse
sped down the street. She clung to the seat, the memory
of her recent spill looming large, but Angus delivered her
safely. As she scrambled down unaided, he shouted an
apology for his inability to see her to the door.

"Hurry! The lightning's close!" cried Libby, as Sugar
crowded against her, whining to be let in. From the
covered boardwalk in front of the store, she saw the
surrey race around the square. Angus let Mrs. Baker off at
her door, bore right at the Columbian, and sped out of
sight. She tipped her reticule, searching for her key in the
stormy dusk, when a chair scraped in the shadows.

Her hand flew to her heart. "Mr. Galloway! Good faith,
you gave me a start. Where'd you come from?"

"Been sittin' here waitin' on you to come home." Ike
tapped his hat against his leg and stooped to calm Sugar's
anxious whimpers. "Didn't mean to scare you."

"What brings you out in this weather?"

"I'm lookin' for Frankie."

"Frankie McClure?" Libby had overheard Mr. Caton
asking his cronies if they'd seen his grandson, but that
had been early in the morning. "He hasn't turned up
yet?"

"Nope. And I'm purty near out of ideas. Would you
mind lookin' inside?"

Libby nudged the dog to one side with a gentle foot
and put the key in the lock. "Has he deliberately misplaced himself?"

"Be my guess. Though his mother, Naomi, ain't so

sure. The boy's brush with that bull is still fresh in her mind, I reckon."

The door swung open. Sugar was in such a hurry to be out of the weather, she tripped Libby getting in. Ike caught her arm and steadied her, but seemed disinclined to follow her inside. He continued his account from the other side of the threshold, raising his voice to be heard over the storm.

"Naomi came over to my place late this afternoon. Said Frankie'd been gone since yesterday mornin'."

"I doubt Frankie would come here. Anyway, how would he get in?"

"He could have shinnied up the tree out back and crawled in."

"The upstairs windows!" Reminded of all that furniture at the mercy of wind-driven rains, Libby left Ike standing on the threshold.

Misunderstanding, he called after her, "You're gonna have a look, then?"

"Come in and look yourself. I'll be right back." She hiked her wet skirts and scurried up the dark stairs.

Hastily Libby sped from window to window. When they were all down, she lighted a lamp and found some rags. The main deluge had come through the window facing the square. The settee had caught the worst of it. She pulled off the wet sheets and the padding of blankets, and found it dry beneath. Thankful for once that the second window facing the street was boarded, Libby mopped up the floor and had just found some toweling to finish the job when the light of the lamp fell across the stove. She stopped short. She'd eaten dinner hastily, leaving half the soup in the pan on the stove. It was empty. Gooseflesh prickled her arms.

"Mr. Galloway?"

There was no answer.

Libby walked to the head of the step and called his name again.

"Best come on down," he said without raising his voice.

The acrid scent of the lamp oil burned her nose as she made her way down. A match flared. Ike lighted the wick stick and touched it to the gas jet overhead. He crouched down behind the counter, pushed his hat back, and rested his forearms on his knees. His seeking glance and a silent gesture directed Libby's gaze to the bottom shelf. She sank down beside him. Her lamp dispelled the darkness of the shelf and illuminated a sleeping Frankie McClure.

She caught her breath. "Why would he come here?"

"Boy stays out all night, he gets a little worried about goin' home. The longer he stays, the harder it gets."

Ike's words brought to mind Mrs. Dorrance and a similar remark concerning Captain Boyd's drinking. Chilled, Libby muttered, "Sometimes I'd like to run away myself."

His mouth curled at the corner. "Train run over the mailbag again?"

"Nothing like that." Remembering his prediction of trouble, she watched the cold blue light overhead carve hollows in his stubbled cheeks. His lips were chapped by wind and sun, his eyes deep and dark and calm. Finding nothing there to suggest he'd relish having been right at her expense, she drew a swift breath and told him about Mrs. Dorrance confronting her at the meeting.

"Can't say I'm surprised," he said when she fell silent. "She was in here last week, layin' it out to Minor."

"About Captain Boyd's drinking? What'd Minor do about it?"

"Invited her to leave."

Libby guessed by his inflection that there'd been no warmth to the invitation. "Did he warn Captain Boyd she'd threatened to write a letter?"

"To the postal authorities?" He nodded and tugged his hat down again. "Him and Benjamin went out to the woodshed and studied the problem, a bottle between 'em."

"And you didn't stop them?"

"Didn't know how without offending them." Looking abashed, he added, "Willie would have, but I didn't."

She wondered why he hadn't told her before. She wanted to ask, but didn't, for indignation had yielded to empathy. It bothered him that he hadn't stopped them.

She was no more equal to the task than he had been. "How long did that go on?"

"Too long. Zerilda came in off her route to find Teddy dropping the afternoon mailbag on the counter, and Benjamin hadn't even run his route yet. She went out to the woodshed and gave the pair of 'em such a tongue-lashin', liked to skin the hide off. Captain Boyd got weepy and apologized. But Minor flew off the handle."

Libby had a clearer understanding now as to why Minor had quit. She winced at the image of Captain Boyd weeping. If she did try to talk to him, and he turned to tears . . . Dear Lord, dealing with *that* was beyond her imagination. She sighed. "Maybe I should take a page from Minor's book."

"And quit?" His gray gaze settled on her face before his lashes swept down from that droopy left lid. "I reckon you could. But somehow, I don't think you will."

He hadn't moved, yet he seemed closer all of a sudden. Libby was conscious of the dampness of her lawn dress. Of the scent of rain and the scent of him and the lamp's flickering light as it caught a draft. Struggling, she admitted, "I don't know what to do."

His head was down, and he did not hear. Or perhaps he did, and simply had no advice.

Sugar wormed her way between them, her damp rank-smelling hide breaking the spell. Libby wrinkled her nose and rose to her feet.

Ike patted Sugar between the ears, then stretched a hand toward Frankie. "Best shake him awake and see him down to the station."

"You're taking him home tonight?"

"We'll catch a train to the Old Kentucky crossing. It ain't far."

"But it's pouring down rain."

"I'll throw a blanket around him."

Impulsively she said, "Just leave him. He's not going to be any trouble asleep."

"You're sure?"

Libby nodded. "His mother can come for him in the morning. I'd like to meet her anyway."

A subtle shift in his expression broke the spell of shadows, soft voices, and shelter against the storm. "What for?"

"So we can get acquainted. Maybe she can shed light on some things that are puzzling me."

"What sort of things?" he asked.

"For one, I'd like to know what's going on with Frankie."

Carefully he said, "He's got some things on his mind, though under the circumstances, I'm not so sure you're the best person to meddle in it."

"Has his father mistreated him?" Libby went straight to the point.

"Decatur? He's in jail."

Impatient with his deftness at dodging her questions, she said, "I don't mean this moment. I mean has he made a habit of being hard on Frankie?"

"He ain't knocked him around, if that's what you're askin'."

"Words can hurt, too. Or feeling unwanted. Unappreciated. Out of favor."

He tugged on his good ear and observed, "You been givin' this some thought."

"Yes." Libby's cheeks warmed beneath his pewter gaze. She searched for a way to ask if there was any truth to McClure's charge that Frankie was Uncle Willie's son. With the family relationship, it would be indelicate enough to put the question to Catherine or Mrs. Baker or Sarah Jane Brignadello. But to a man? And with the boy lying right there? She eased into it gently, asking, "Is there anything you can tell me that would shed some light?"

He shifted to his feet and moved away from the counter. When he'd put enough distance between himself and Frankie not to risk being overheard should the boy awaken, he ceased dodging the issue and said quietly, "Decatur thought he was doing the decent thing, raising Frankie as his own."

Libby's heart dropped. Heat rushed to her face. "Then Frankie isn't his?"

Ike shook his head. "I reckon he and Naomi should have told the boy the truth a long time ago."

"You mean he just now found out? How is that?"

"Decatur started drinkin' after Willie died. Picked a quarrel with Naomi. Both of them said some things they wouldn't have said, if they'd known he was awake and listenin'."

"Who does he belong to?"

"That ain't for me to say."

"You must know," she pressed, having come this far.

"Don't know why you'd think that," he countered. "Seems to me there's only two people who know for sure, and I ain't one of 'em."

Libby flushed at his bluntness, and at the same time felt frustrated at having her quest for a more complete understanding thwarted. *If he doesn't know for sure, he can at least share his suspicions.* His deliberate silence on the subject perplexed her nearly as much as the McClures themselves did.

"If yer mind's set on keepin' him here, I guess I'll be going."

"You can stay until the rain stops if you'd like." Libby tried to buy some time in which to win Ike's confidence and get him to open up.

"Thanks, but I'll go on over to the station and catch the next train through. Sooner I get back, sooner Naomi can quit worryin'."

Libby followed him to the front of the store, Sugar clicking along at her heels. Rain sheeted off the roof and spilled into the street. He buttoned his coat, tugged his hat down snug, then turned at the edge of the boardwalk. "That door Decatur kicked in? I'll fix it for ya next time I come to town. Anything else he damaged, too."

Surprised, she asked above the pelting rain, "Are you pouring oil on troubled waters, Mr. Galloway?"

"Savin' some trouble, that's all. Just for the record, it ain't often Decatur sets in drinkin' like that."

What was he saying? That the McClures were just an ordinary family, trying to get over some rough water? Certain he knew Mr. McClure had filed a suit, claiming that Frankie was Uncle Willie's son, and therefore the rightful heir of his estate, she said, "Is it often he sues people, trying to take what has been bequeathed to them?"

"No, that's a first." Looking uncomfortable, and anxious to get away, he added, "I wouldn't lose any sleep over it just yet."

Libby watched him turn up his coat collar and step off the board walkway into the rain. *Easy for him to say.* He wasn't in danger of losing not only sleep, but a store. An education. A dream. A future. She shivered in the damp air, closed and bolted the door, then retraced her steps to the back of the store where Frankie lay sleeping.

Wondering if she could carry him up to the cot in the little room at the top of the stairs, Libby stooped to get her arms beneath him and saw with a pang that tears had made a crooked path along his dirty cheeks. The blanket he'd curled up in was the same one used to cover Uncle Willie at the wake. A good piece of it was bunched between his arms. Reminded of David and a tattered old quilt that gave him comfort, she felt her heart quicken. It gave her a queer feeling. He might be Uncle Willie's boy. And if he was, what was her obligation to him? The question was pain-filled, taking her places she had no wish to go.

A loud knock brought her to her feet with a start. It was at the back door, not the front. Cautiously she crossed to the door. "Who is it?"

"Angus Cearlock."

Surprised, Libby slid the bolt free. He was leaning on crutches, mud splattered halfway to his knees.

"I'm sorry, Miss Watson. I don't mean to disturb you. But Mother noticed Mr. Galloway in the shadows earlier." Looking uncomfortable, he asked, "Thought I'd see—is everything all right?"

Surprised, Libby explained that Mr. Galloway had been looking for Frankie.

"He's gone now?" He glanced past her in a way that rendered his concern somewhat less flattering.

"Yes, Mr. Cearlock. Though I wish you hadn't troubled

yourself, splashing from the surrey to my door on those crutches," Libby added evenly.

He had the good grace to flush. "I'm sorry. I'm being overprotective, aren't I? It comes from looking after Catherine, I suppose."

"I'm fine, Mr. Cearlock. Thank you for your neighborliness."

"I'll be going, then. Mother's waiting at my house while I collect Chester from his meeting. They'll be spending the night in town, unless the rain stops soon. What was it you said about Frankie?"

"He's been gone from home two days and a night, and his mother's worried. Mr. Galloway came to town looking for him."

"And he thought you might be able to help?"

"The search ended here."

His eyebrows climbed to the band of his hat. "The boy was here?"

"Fast asleep behind the counter."

"Cut from the same bolt as Decatur, eh? Breaking into your store," he explained in response to her blank expression. "I'd imagine in weather like this, the rascal was glad enough to be found and taken home."

"Actually . . ." Libby faltered, knowing instinctively he wouldn't approve of her decision.

"He's still here?" he guessed. At Libby's nod, Angus's smile dimmed. "Mr. McClure is your adversary, Miss Watson. If you don't take care, your kind heart will weaken your position."

"I hated to see Frankie dragged out in this weather," she protested. "I have a brother very nearly the same age, you see, and I really didn't think there'd be any harm in it."

"Of course you didn't. If it had been anyone but Ike Galloway put in charge of finding him . . ." Angus paused. A raindrop slid off his hat and trailed down his well-tailored jacket. "They stick together out at Old Kentucky."

In all fairness, she said, "Mr. Galloway isn't at fault. He intended to take him. It was my idea to let him stay."

"Your uncle engaged me to see to the settling of his estate, and I'll do it to the best of my ability so that you will receive all he intended." Another droplet spilled free of his hat as he picked his words with care: "You, in turn, must remember what I told you about Decatur. You never did go to the Sheriff and file charges for the damage he did here, did you?"

Libby admitted that she had not. Angus appeared about to take her to task for the omission, when the rain freshened in intensity and he went on his way, leaving her to grapple with the range of emotions he had stirred.

Wearied by the day and the trouble it had brought, Libby tried to lift Frankie and found him too heavy. She made him as comfortable as she could, tucking the blanket around him more thoroughly, then climbed the stairs. As she made her own bed with fresh linen and fell upon it, her thoughts skipped from the boy to Angus to Captain Boyd, and of her responsibility as laid forth by Mrs. Dorrance, and back to Frankie again.

Had he seemed a gentle, sensitive child like David, his tears would not have seemed remarkable. But he'd put on such a tough front. Had he cried because he was hungry and tired and afraid to go home? Had he cried for his father, locked up in jail? Had he cried for Uncle Willie?

Of all the places he could have sheltered, why did he come here?

17

S Sleep, when it came, was fitful. Libby lit her way downstairs before daybreak, and saw with a pang that Frankie McClure was gone. Apparently Sugar had slipped out with him. She was scratching at the door, wanting in again.

Libby fed the dog and caught herself worrying over the boy as she folded the blanket. She tried to shelve her concerns, reasoning that neither his tears nor his troubles were of her making. Nor was he the only one with problems.

Good faith! She could make a list of her own, not the least of which was what to do about Captain Boyd. He knew of Mrs. Dorrance's campaign to purge the town of alcohol, and so knowing, was aware he was putting his job in jeopardy each time he tipped the bottle. If that had not stopped him, what hope had she? Like a doodling pencil, Libby worked away at the problem as she collected the mailbag in the rain, hurried back to the store, and began sorting. If only Father were here!

A quiet reminder turned within. It came not in words, or as sound: it was heart knowledge of a Heavenly Father assuring her that her concerns, when entrusted to Him, did not go untended. *What am I going to do? What would You have me do?*

The question had no more poured from Libby's soul than Captain Boyd arrived. He greeted her and hung up his jacket. "Mite damp in here. A small fire'd take the chill off. Be all right with you, Miss Willie?"

Libby assured him it would. *I should take a firm line. Tell him right now he has to stop drinking on the job.* The pet name, accentuating the gentleness in the man, made the chore all the more difficult. Her heart was thumping, her head, too, as she studied him surreptitiously. Zerilda would be here soon. *I should speak out right now while we have some privacy.* Libby searched, but found no words. Nothing but a tangle of nerves in the pit of her stomach.

"Farmers were glad enough for the rain. Muddied up the roads, though. Maybe the sun will come out later." He shook the grate on the stove, spilling ashes into the ash pan below. He wadded up last week's newspaper, laid it on the grate, and piled a bit of kindling on top.

His hand was steady. Could it be his mourning was spent? That a better day had dawned? Optimist that she was, Libby took hold of the thought and prayed with renewed fervor.

"Pop the door open, would you, miss?"

Captain Boyd carried out the pan of cold ashes. He was gone so long, suspicions sprang up like weeds. Libby was about to see what was keeping him when he returned with several short chunks of wood and poked them into the belly of the stove on top of the paper and kindling. He struck a match with his thumbnail. The paper and dry kindling caught with a whoosh. He waited until he was satisfied it had got a good start, adjusted the flue, then ambled around the counter to his sorting case.

"Found anyone to fetch the mailbags from the station yet?"

"Not yet," said Libby, setting a registered letter to one side.

"I saw you'd put a notice about it in the front window. Maybe that will help."

"I hope so. It would take a load off me, not having to go after it."

"What does it take—ten minutes a trip? Five times a day?"

"About an hour's work, total. I'm afraid most folks

won't think that's worth interrupting their day," worried Libby.

Nodding agreement, Captain Boyd said, "Why don't you have Mr. Gruben announce the opening in *The Gazette?*"

"Would he do that?"

"Sure he would. News is his business, and that's news."

"That's a good idea. I'll do it right away."

"Another thing," said the captain in the same conversational tone. "I heard you talking to Mrs. Bee yesterday about all the clutter upstairs making it hard to set up housekeeping. Willie never was one for throwing anything away."

"It isn't just the clutter, it's the volume of furniture. I'd like to make it more homelike, but I hardly know where to begin," admitted Libby.

"Why don't you store the furniture you aren't using in the loft over the buggy shed? It'd come to no harm up there, and it'd give you some floor space."

"That's a wonderful idea," said Libby, touched by his consideration. "Why, there's hardly room to cook or clean or do my wash without stubbing my toes and banging my elbows."

"I'd imagine it gets pretty miserable up there in the summer, without you heating up the place, doing wash."

"Nevetheless, it has to be done."

Captain Boyd smiled. "You'd have got on well with my wife. She was murder on keeping that wash done up. 'Long may our lambs be bright,'" he sang to the tune of "My Country, 'Tis of Thee."

Libby chuckled, for the little story she'd told him had become something of joke between them. He had been kind from day one, answering her many questions concering all she needed to know to fulfill her postal responsibilities. But it was friendship, exhibited in a listening ear and an interest in her comfort, that Libby treasured the most. Reciprocating his kindness, she asked, "How many years has it been since you lost your wife, Captain?"

"Nearly twenty-five."

Surprised, she said, "And you met Uncle Willie about the same time. He must have been fairly young then."

"I guess he was, at that. Though even then, there was an ageless quality about Willie. He took an interest in folks, didn't matter if it was a child or someone's granny." Captain Boyd fit a letter to the correct slot. "Take Decatur, for instance. He was just a boy when Willie stopped wandering long enough to build a cabin out at Old Kentucky. Decatur's father worked sunup to sundown as a hired hand, never had much time for his children. It wasn't long, Decatur was tagging after Willie. Most of what he knows today, Willie taught him."

"You aren't the first person to mention their friendship. I certainly wouldn't have guessed it, based on Mr. McClure's behavior," said Libby.

"Don't you let him worry you, miss. Decatur's having some family troubles. I reckon he'll work it through, one way or another."

Libby told him of finding Frankie McClure on the shelf the previous night. But either he didn't know the facts concerning Frankie's illegitimacy, or he was dodging the subject, for he smiled and said, "That boy's a caution. Kind of reminds me of Ike when he was a young sprout. Sharp as a tack and quick to devilment."

Zerilda tramped in, banging the door behind her. She returned Libby's and Captain Boyd's greetings with a terse nod, hung her cape from one corner of her sorting case, and went to work.

Libby counted a stack of letters, then said, "Ike told Father he came here from Missouri."

Captain Boyd nodded and tossed back a letter for a town patron. "His father grew up here in Edgewood, half brother to Chester Gentry. Mrs. Galloway had never met Chester," he explained. "But after Ike's father died, and she was left with two children to raise and no means of supporting them, she came here hoping Chester would save them from the poorhouse."

Surprised, Libby said, "Mr. Galloway never mentioned he was related to Chester Gentry."

Zerilda sniffed. "Man who won't take in his kin when they's needy don't deserve claimin'."

Captain Boyd sidetracked her by asking, "How are the grandchildren, Mrs. Payne?"

"Troublesome. But I aim to see they don't starve whilst their mama and that shiftless good-fer-nothin' she hitched herself to hawk their wares on the Pike."

"Walt's a good salesman, and from what I read in the paper, the Exposition's drawing fine crowds. Might prove profitable for them," said Captain Boyd.

"Doubt it. Nothin' ever does," replied Zerilda.

Libby counted a pile of newspapers and gave them to Captain Boyd, curious about Mrs. Galloway's predicament. "Did Mr. Gentry offer any explanation as to why he wouldn't help?"

"Mr. Gentry isn't the sort to go around explaining himself. But I always figured he was afraid of being misunderstood," said Captain Boyd.

"How do you mean?"

Memories stirred in Captain Boyd's eyes. "Ida'd been the only one for Chester since he was in short pants. He took it pretty hard when she married Cearlock. Then Cearlock died, and left her with two small children. Chester was courting Ida in earnest when Ike's mother showed up with Ike and his little sister, needing a roof over their heads. Mrs. Galloway was a pretty little gal, kind of singsong like her name, Nona Kay. I think Chester was afraid Ida would misunderstand if he was to take her and the children in."

"Ida is vain as a peacock," inserted Zerilda. "Competitive, too. Just ask her sister, Miz Bee. She'll tell ya Ida likes havin' the most and the best."

Gently Captain Boyd inserted, "Ida has a kind heart."

Zerilda snorted. "Malarkey! Ida Gentry puts on airs about helpin' folk, but only so long as they ain't in danger of catchin' up to her socially. And Chester, he's jest fool enough to cater to her whims."

Libby's impression of Ida Gentry was more in line with the captain's. But Zerilda, she'd learned, cut very little slack. "So what did Mrs. Galloway do when Mr. Gentry turned her and the children away?"

"Somehow or other, Nona Kay got acquainted with Willie," said the captain.

"Them were the worst of Willie's drinkin' days, and he still come off lookin' better'n Chester," claimed Zerilda.

"Willie moved into an old boxcar the C and A had abandoned, and let her have his cabin. Told her to help herself to his vegetable patch, his cellar, the meat from his smokehouse, and anything else she needed."

"Was he in love with Mrs. Galloway?"

"I really couldn't say." Captain Boyd's hesitation was nearly imperceptible, but Libby noted the way his eyes slid away, and she drew her own conclusions. She thought once more of all that Uncle Willie had stored inside him, and never revealed a clue about on all his visits.

"What happened then?"

"Nothing much, for a year or more. Then an evangelist came along and pitched up a tent not far from where Ike's building his sugarhouse. Clifton Jericho, that was his name. He held the longest revival in the history of Old Kentucky—eight weeks and a few days. That's how long it took him to talk Nona Kay into marrying him."

"So they moved away?" asked Libby, her heart twisting for Uncle Willie.

He nodded. "Ike didn't take to having a preacher for a stepdaddy. He turned up in Edgewood now and again over the next couple of years. Willie and Addie would put him up awhile, then send him home to his mama."

"How long ago was all of this?"

"Oh, I don't know." Captain Boyd did some calculations in his head and ventured, "Nine, ten years, I reckon. Decatur and Naomi were courting, but they weren't married yet. I remember because Naomi kept going to hear Clifton Jericho every night. Hascal teased and said she was sweet on the preacher. Made Decatur so itchy, couldn't keep his mind off her long enough to tree a coon. Left his dogs under the porch, and walked her to meeting and back home every night. He'd hover right outside the tent, but he wouldn't sit in on the preaching."

"Decatur ain't got no use fer religion," put in Zerilda.

"The preacher moved on, taking his new family with him. And it wasn't long before Decatur and Naomi married and settled into the boxcar he'd vacated. Naomi's pretty handy with wood. She's made a nice little place of it."

Questions stirring, Libby gazed at a letter until her eyes lost focus. If Uncle Willie had been in love with Mrs. Galloway, why would he have become involved with Naomi? And what of Naomi? If she'd been sweet on the preacher . . . though maybe that was just Hascal's ornery teasing. Maybe she'd been in love with Decatur all along. Maybe Decatur had it all wrong about Uncle Willie.

"How long was it, then, before Uncle Willie married Addie Linegar?" she asked at length.

"Seems to me it wasn't much more'n a week or two after the preacher and Nona Kay and the kids cleared out."

"Before Naomi and Mr. McClure?" asked Libby, and he nodded. "He didn't pine away long, did he?"

"Yes, well, it isn't always romance brings two people together. Miss Addie needed help with the store, and Willie needed help of a different sort. They got on after a fashion."

"Same with Decatur and Naomi," said Zerilda. "Though here lately, a body'd wonder. Ain't like Decatur to get hisself in sech a mess. Anybody ought to know better'n poke a lawyer in the nose and steal his rig. Shootfire, I can remember the time they'd hang ya for takin' a man's horse."

"I don't think there's any danger of that," soothed Captain Boyd. "Though I reckon the sheriff must be going by the letter of the law on this thing, or he wouldn't still be holding Decatur over at the jail."

"Politics," scoffed Zerilda. "Ain't often I side with Hascal, but he's right on this one. If it was anybody but Angus, Decatur would've been fined and released. Instead, the sheriff's waiting on the circuit judge to try the case. Crazy, if ya ask me."

Prickly as she felt over Angus's checking up on her, Libby found herself biting her tongue to keep from defending him. As far as she was concerned, the horse was not the issue. The issue was Decatur McClure causing another human being bodily injury. Decatur ought to suffer the consequences of his rash behavior.

At eight Libby opened the front door to watery sunlight and a slow trickle of customers. She was making steady progress, getting the town mail up, when it clouded over again and distant thunder drove the bench brigade inside. Glad to see Mr. Caton among those gathered around the stove, she overlooked the mud he'd tracked across her freshly swept floor, and asked from her side of the counter, "Did Frankie make it home?"

"He was wolfing down eggs and grits and redeye gravy at Naomi's table less'n an hour ago." Droplets sizzled on the stove as Hascal slung his coat over the back of his chair, shook the rain from his hat, and sat down.

"Did he say why he ran away?"

Hascal scratched his grizzled jaw. "'Tweren't that he ran away, exactly. He was jest wearied of Naomi yappin' at him, so he gived himself a vacation."

Minor used a coal bucket for a spittoon while Mr. Torreyson and Squire Palmer brushed off rusty memories of folks who'd been struck by lightning under conditions such as this. Mr. Lamb, who could recount in gory detail the corpses of many he'd buried over the years, knew of several men who'd gone to the grave with blackened appendages. He was giving a blow-by-blow description when Mr. Gentry stopped by to see if Captain Boyd had already taken his mail on the route.

"Captain Boyd? Could Mr. Gentry have his mail?"

Libby saw portly Mr. Gentry tweak his jet black mustache and jitter his foot while he waited. Affluent, self-confident, civic-minded Mr. Gentry. He didn't look as if he had an ounce of romance in his soul. But he must, if Captain Boyd had his facts straight and Mr. Gentry had indeed turned his own half brother's wife and children away rather than risk inciting the jealousy of his betrothed.

Mr. Gentry reached into his inside pocket as the old mail carrier passed his mail over the counter. "Good morning, Captain. Here's one you left in my box by mistake yesterday."

The captain scanned the address and apologized, saying, "Guess it isn't yours, is it? Sorry for the inconvience, Chester. Thanks for bringing it in."

Mr. Gentry smiled pleasantly, tipped his hat to Libby, and passed a pleasantry or two with the men. They reciprocated, with the exception of Mr. Caton, who gave him a black look. Mr. Gentry soon continued on his way.

Teddy wandered in and pulled up a crate next to the coffee grinder. Sugar lifted her head at the sound of his voice. Tail thumping, she picked her way over the circle of damp boots and planted her paws on Teddy's knee.

"W-e-ll looky, looky. Missed you this morning. Missed the good doggy." Teddy stroked Sugar's ears and got her tail to wagging, then reached over and gave the brass handle on the coffee grinder a spin. Libby saw him catch the sprinkling of grounds, hold them to his nose, and breath deeply. Quiet ways, had Teddy Baker.

Lucius Gruben, editor of the local paper, tramped in, shook the rain off his long black ulster, and collected his mail, Mrs. Dorrance's letter among it. Libby took Captain Boyd's advice and wrote out a few lines, saying that as interim clerk at the post office, she was looking to hire someone to bring the mail from the station at each delivery. She had read some back issues of *The Gazette*, which came out on Fridays, and was impressed with the quality of the writing. Her admiration of the editor's skill made her a little shy about approaching him. Scrap of paper in hand, she made her way around the counter just as Mr. Gruben hoisted himself onto a barrel of pickled pork and put a fresh slant on the conversation with mention of a cow that had been killed by lightning out at the dairy. Not wanting to interrupt, Libby waited until he'd fallen silent again.

"Mr. Gruben? Captain Boyd suggested I ask you about printing a small notice concerning a job that needs to be filled for the post office."

A thin man with a head of white hair, Mr. Gruben reached into his pocket for a tablet, saying, "Certainly, miss. If you'll give me the details, I'll see it gets in the paper."

"Actually, I've already written it. Though you can

change it, if need be." As if he needed her permission. Flushing, Libby gave him the brief piece she'd written and amended, "That is, what I meant to say is, if it isn't written quite to your specifications . . ."

"It's just fine," he said, having scanned the few lines while she was stammering an explanation. "Clear and to the point."

Libby flushed again, this time with pleasure. "Thank you, sir."

Mr. Gruben smiled and tucked the paper into his pocket, then turned his attention to Hascal Caton, who was knocking the ashes from his pipe, and adding his own contribution to foul-weather tales.

"Lightning come down and singed a wing plumb off one of my hens about a month ago. Bird's still thrivin', that's the wonder of it."

Mr. Lamb tugged at his chin whiskers. "First time I ever heard tell of lightning striking a chicken."

Hascal paused in packing a new pipe as Libby made her way around to the other side of the counter again. "You don't believe it? You come on out and have a look. If it ain't an oddity, I'll throw in with ya."

"An oddity of nature." Minor scratched his mutton-chops. "'Tain't often ya get one hatched out thataway."

"Young Frankie stole your thunder, Hack," called Captain Boyd from his side of the counter. Between heavy mail and the rain, he was in no hurry to start the route. "He had a regular sideshow going behind the Methodist Church a couple of months back. Getting pennies meant for the Sunday school basket in exchange for a peek at the chicken."

"Beggin' yer pardon, Benjamin, but that wasn't my wingless bird he was showing off. No, sir. That'd be the one-legged pullet yer thinkin' of," Hascal said smoothly.

"It occurs to me, Mr. Caton, that it would make a better meal if you were to raise some poultry with no missing parts," said Mr. Gruben.

Hascal lit his pipe and retorted, "We give it a try once. But the gimpy ones is easier to ketch."

The men all hooted.

Zerilda glared at the lot of them and muttered, "Ain't no danger none of them gettin' lightning-struck, humped up around the stove where it's safe and dry. Not unless the Almighty sends a bolt to purge Hascal's lyin' tongue."

The old gents ran out of stories and drifted homeward a short while later. Intermittent showers proved bad for business, but good for accomplishing some much-needed cleaning. The morning was nearly spent when Angus came in for his mail. He tipped his hat to Mrs. Shaw, who was leaving with a few purchases, and wished her a good day before approaching the counter, swinging gracefully along on his crutches.

"Good morning, Miss Watson. You've been cleaning, I see."

"Making haste slowly."

Libby put her bucket of scrub water behind the counter out of the way of his crutches and injured foot. His collar and cuffs were crisp with starch and his face all but glistened, so clean was his shave. Feeling disheveled, she slipped out of her soiled apron and pulled off the faded cloth holding her hair back from her face.

"I received notice the circuit judge will be in town early in July. Mr. McClure will face charges then for his Memorial Day spree."

"I got a copy of the petition for probate sent out by the court clerk," said Libby.

Angus nodded, looking mildly uncomfortable. "I wanted to speak to you about that. I'm afraid it's going to be a little more involved than I first thought."

"Oh?"

"Yes, well, it seems I was premature, assuming Willie had left but one will."

The wind left her lungs as he went on to say that a more recent will had been filed.

"Naming Frankie as heir?"

He nodded. "Mr. Sparks, Decatur's lawyer, was told that Mr. Blue dictated it upon his deathbed. Hascal Caton and Decatur McClure witnessed it."

Libby could tell by his tone that he didn't believe for a moment that the will was authentic. Yet even as he explained what was required to make such a document legal, Libby wavered, wondering *What if Uncle Willie had changed his mind?*

Angus seemed to guess her thoughts; a grimness settled over his expression. "Hascal Caton's a wily old fox. This whole business has his mark all over it."

"How do you mean?"

"He's looking out for Frankie, of course."

"He'd lie about the will?"

Angus gave her a pitying look. "For his one and only grandson? He'd look the judge straight in the eye, put his hand on the Bible, and lie just as earnestly as he'd speak the truth."

"And Mr. McClure?"

"Oh, Decatur's involved, that's certain. Though I still can't figure what he has to gain even if Frankie *should* inherit. If the store were liquidated, the funds would be put in trust until the boy comes of age."

"What about Frankie's mother?"

"Naomi has a reputation for being an honest, hardworking individual. But that isn't to say she won't bend if, at the hearing, the judge asks for an admission that Willie was indeed Frankie's father."

"Would he do that?" asked Libby.

"Under the circumstances, he'd be remiss if he didn't."

Court was a man's domain. How wretched to face all those men, her husband among them, and be asked such a question. Libby wasn't surprised at the displeasure in Angus's expression. After all, he had warned her about being perceived a weak adversary in the eyes of Decatur McClure. "So let me get this straight. If this so-called 'more recent will' is recognized by the judge, I've lost my claim to the store?"

"Exactly. You're now facing a formal suit against you."

"I don't know how this works, but it sounds as if I had better hire a lawyer. Are your services available, Mr. Cearlock?"

"Of course. I'd be pleased to represent you. Eager to do so, in fact. Perhaps you could come to my office tomorrow morning, and discuss the case in greater detail."

"Yes, of course," Libby said, and made a mental note to find someone to mind the store while she met with him.

Leaning one crutch against the counter, he tucked his letters into an inside pocket. "I should mention, too, that it's not too late to file those charges against Mr. McClure for the damage he did upstairs."

"I've never been to court in my life, Mr. Cearlock, and I don't think I'm going to like it well enough to make a habit of it."

"So you're saying it's all right if Decatur breaks down your door and prowls through your things?"

"I'm saying I don't have the disposition for petty skirmishes."

"I think you underestimate the ferocity of Mr. McClure's temper."

Libby flushed, for his crutches bore witness that he knew whereof he spoke. Nonetheless, she stood by her decision. "Mr. Galloway offered to fix the door and any other damage Mr. McClure did."

"And you accepted?"

"No." She lifted her chin. "But I'm going to."

"I see. Well, you're clearly a woman who knows her own mind. I hope you won't regret your decision."

Angus's tone suggested otherwise. Was he simply annoyed because she hadn't heeded his advice? Or was there more to it? Straightaway she countered, "You don't like Mr. Galloway much, do you?"

A well-shaped brow lifted. "Are you leading the witness, Miss Watson?"

His choice of words, though spoken in that droll way of his, exposed a nerve, for hadn't she just pleaded her ignorance concerning everything to do with court meetings? She thrust out her chin. "Tell me, does Mr. Galloway have a reputation for being dangerous?"

"No, not that I know of."

"Then why should I be wary of accepting his offer to do repairs upstairs?"

"Again you misunderstand."

"On the contrary, I understand perfectly. I also understand why you came to my door on crutches in a raging storm, claiming it was out of concern for my safety when, in fact, you knew Mr. Galloway was no threat to it."

"All right, then, I was curious what had brought him to see you," he amended.

"And if he lurked in the corner just out of sight?"

Angus had the good grace to flush. He drew his hand over his face. "I hadn't thought . . ." Chagrined, he muttered, "That's it exactly. I'm a blundering fool, it would seem. I've insulted you, haven't I?"

Arms linked across her bosom, head tilted to one side, she further goaded his conscience with her silence.

His color deepened. "It's obvious that you're a woman of noble character."

"Thank you, Mr. Cearlock. I can't tell you how that relieves me."

Her tone took the starch out of him. "I'm sorry, Miss Watson. Truly I am. Is it too late to admit I was jealous and throw myself on the mercy of the court?"

She feigned cool composure, squared her shoulders, and said crisply, "Thank you, Mr. Cearlock. I accept your apology. Now, if you'll excuse me, I have to get back to work."

He started away, slim and straight and fluid on his crutches. But he'd gone only a few feet when he turned back and caught her watching him. His maddening confidence settled back over him like a cloak. "I was wondering, would you like to join me for dinner at Catherine's house on Saturday night? We could sign a peace treaty, sing a few tunes, and get the latest news of the fair from her husband, Charlie."

Stiffly she said, "I'm sorry. I'll be working here at the store."

"Of course. Saturday's your busy night. Though you could hire someone to stand in." He stroked his upper lip and shot her a speculative glance. "No? Then what about church on Sunday? I'm not sure exactly where the New Hope congregation will be meeting this week, but I'd be pleased if you'd let me drive you."

"I'll be going to the Methodist church."

"With Catherine, I suppose. She isn't helping my case much."

Libby's rebellious heart bumped to think he was making a case. She didn't tell him her choice of churches was based on the hope of avoiding Mrs. Dorrance.

"Well, I'm flexible," he said at length. "The Methodist church, it is."

"Another time, Mr. Cearlock."

"Then you do plan to forgive me eventually?"

It was hard to hang on to her resentment with his hazel eyes so entreating. Bending, she said, "Perhaps."

A smile spread over his face like thick, rich frosting. "Ah, a crumb of hope. You're much too good to me, Miss Watson."

Libby corralled a smile before it got loose and bid him good day.

She would have enjoyed dinner at Catherine's house. As well as an escort to church. But if her relationship with Angus Cearlock was to be a social one, then they had best get the business of Uncle Willie's will settled first. And he need not think she was looking for another "brother" to try her patience with a watchful eye. Or that she was impressed with his courtroom jargon or that imperturbable way he had of asserting himself.

No, it was the piano-man part of him that brought a glow to her heart. The fellow who stroked the keys and winked and sang. And humored his mother and teased his sister and conceded with a self-deprecating smile that he wasn't all he pretended to be. The fellow behind the public face of young Angus Cearlock, attorney-at-law, candidate for the legislature. That was the fellow she'd like to see more of. Yes, that was the fellow.

18

Libby hired Mrs. Brignadello to mind the store for her the next morning. Once the mail had gone out and business slowed, she flung her apron aside, tucked her hair under her hat, and trekked down the alley to keep her appointment with Angus.

Seated across the desk from her, Angus was polite, though brief and to the point, as he told her that he had met with Decatur's lawyer, Randolph Sparks, while in Bloomington the previous afternoon.

"At my request, Mr. Sparks showed me a copy of the deathbed will which Willie Blue supposedly authorized and signed. It is written in Decatur's handwriting, which in itself is legal, though suspicious, under the circumstances. The signature looks like Mr. Blue's. But, as I pointed out to Mr. Sparks, anyone who had a scrap of paper with Mr. Blue's signature on it could manage a close facsimile."

"What did Mr. Sparks say?" asked Libby, her heart sinking a little at Angus's professional, impersonal demeanor.

"What his client hired him to say—that he believes the will in his possession is genuine. I intend to prove him wrong."

"How?" asked Libby.

Angus rested his hands on his desk, fingers laced. "In part, by retracing the chain of events leading up to the

174

surfacing of this fraudulent will, beginning with Decatur accosting me the day of Mr. Blue's funeral. I don't wish to be indelicate, or in any way offend your sensibilities. But Decatur's purpose in stopping me that day was to learn if Mr. Blue was Frankie's father. I had no knowledge of it, and I told him as much. But McClure was convinced I was protecting my client's right to confidentiality. Somehow he got it in his head that I had proof to the contrary among my papers. An altercation followed, and you know the rest."

"What sort of papers did he think you'd be carrying that would prove such a thing?" asked Libby.

"I really couldn't say. Keep in mind, he'd been drinking heavily." Angus shifted in his seat and winced as if his foot was causing him pain. "As you know, Decatur was at the wake, but no one remembers seeing him at the funeral. It's obvious that, with Willie laid out downstairs and a handful of men taking turns sitting with the body, Decatur's first opportunity to search Mr. Blue's living quarters would have been during the funeral."

Libby nodded. "But what was he *looking* for?"

"I can only speculate he was seeking to prove what he had come to suspect at Mr. Blue's deathbed. The fact that he was searching, that he seemed not to be quite sure, speaks volumes."

"How do you mean?"

"If Mr. Blue had in truth changed his will on his deathbed, naming Frankie as beneficiary, there would have been no doubt in Decatur's mind but that he had fathered Frankie. There'd have been no need to waylay me on the road or rip through Mr. Blue's living quarters looking for proof which might or might not exist. The fact that Mr. Blue hadn't left anything to Frankie was, in effect, the only grain of doubt left in Decatur's mind."

What Angus was saying seemed to coincide with what Ike had told Libby about that night. She asked, "Do you think Mr. McClure found his proof?"

"I'm not sure about that. It does seem likely that he found the will naming you as beneficiary."

"He already knew that, didn't he?" asked Libby.

"Yes. By the day of the funeral it was common knowledge Mr. Blue had left the store to his niece. The reason I think Decatur found the will is the striking similarity in language between this will and the fraudulent one."

Libby listened as he went on to say that Uncle Willie's relationship to Frankie was a moot point, that his job as her uncle's attorney, and as her representative in countering Decatur's suit against her, was to see that Mr. Blue's wishes were carried out.

"Do you think it was finding the will that gave Mr. McClure the idea to make up his own version?" asked Libby.

"I suspect that was Hascal Caton's idea. He's a conniver and quite devoted to Frankie."

"Even if that's the case, it doesn't excuse Mr. McClure's going along with it."

"No, of course not. But don't underestimate Hascal Caton. He would know to play on Decatur's thirst for revenge."

"Revenge?" echoed Libby.

"I think that's a fair guess as to what Decatur may be feeling. All these years he has counted Mr. Blue as his best friend, and now he suddenly has strong evidence that the man had sexual contact with his wife."

A rush of heat swept over Libby. Finding it hard to look at Angus, she said, "Naomi wasn't his wife at the time."

"She *was* his sweetheart, though."

"Still, you could be mistaken. There's no proof."

"No, but there is such a preponderance of evidence that Decatur apparently believes it to be true. Wouldn't you agree?" At her silence Angus added, "And so believing, he's motivated to get even. How is he to get even with a dead man? Thwarting Mr. Blue's final wishes is about the best he can hope for."

Angus made a very strong, logical case. Strong enough that Libby was keenly embarrassed over the bad light it shone on her uncle. She found it difficult to process the swift flow of information that followed as Angus explained how Decatur's suit against her affected the probate process and what steps he would be taking to protect

Uncle Willie's final wishes, and her interests, which amounted to one and the same thing.

While Angus's bearing inspired her trust in his capabilities, Libby couldn't help feeling a little deflated and, quite frankly, hurt by his totally impersonal demeanor. It was as if she'd dreamed his wooing of her the previous night! Had he thought over the whole matter? Found her too temperamental? Undergone a change of heart?

Libby mulled it over awhile, and finally came to the conclusion that if he had, it was just as well. The legal entanglements were worrisome enough without concerning herself with the shifting winds of romance.

Her midmorning trek to the station to collect the mail drop strengthened that conclusion, for amongst the small packet of mail was a letter from her father, a fresh reminder of how her family's future rested upon Angus's legal skills. She sat in the sunshine and read with a chuckle that Jacob had accompanied a handsome lass berry picking and that chiggers had since made a meal of him. Her smile faded at the news of Abigail Emery's brother, Porter. He'd caught his leg in the wheel while working a span of mules out at Colonel Calkin's farm. Abigail had raced to town for the doctor while the men got Porter back to the house. Adam was on his way home from the mines when she came along. She'd been so upset, she'd flung herself into his coal-blackened arms and had scarcely left them since. The leg was pretty badly mangled, but Doc Dillman had saved it, and Porter was starting to mend. As for David, Father wrote that he and Marta, the little neighbor girl, were amusing themselves making mud houses for ants beneath the lilac bush.

Libby's eyes misted as they moved down the page, for her father's voice and the richness of home flowed in each curve of the pen. He closed with an admonition for patience, saying he and David would come as soon as they could. She dried her eyes and worked off her lonesomeness, mentally planning how to arrange the upstairs for her family. Maybe she could hire Billy Young to move the extra furnishings into the loft of the buggy shed. Once that was done, she could work in earnest at making the place into a real home.

Saturday was the busiest day yet at the store. Evening
came. Buggies and wagons encircled the town square.
Children flocked to the peanut vender, who'd set up his
wagon on the fringe of the park, then took turns at the
park pump, quenching their thirst. Farmwives came in
with cream and eggs and butter to sell, and strawberries
fresh from their gardens. Libby reached time and again
for the scissors as work-worn hands picked through the
ginghams, the cottons, the corduroys and wools, and
mothers studied aloud the math of how many dresses per
daughter and how many yards per dress. Their menfolk
looked over the tools in the shadow of the stovepipe that
crawled half the width of the store to the chimney. They
talked of ripening oats, of politics and baseball and a
grass fire sparked by a passing freight engine. The
children had eyes for the candy jars and the roller skates.
Sugar consoled with tongue and wagging tail those who
got their way about neither. It was a long night. A very
long night, and by the time the last light went out on the
square, Libby was wondering if Ike Galloway could be
coaxed into clerking Saturday nights, as he had for Uncle
Willie. She made up her mind to ask should he come to
fix her door.

To Libby's chagrin, Sunday morning was half-over
before the old beagle's whines awakened her. She
dressed and ate a bite of lunch, all the while thinking
about Decatur McClure's suit against her. The fact that
Naomi was not named in the suit against Libby indicated,
to Angus anyway, that Naomi knew the will her husband's attorney had filed was counterfeit and that she
wanted no part of seeking ill-gotten gains on her son's
behalf. Knowing Angus planned to question Naomi
about the alleged deathbed will, Libby reasoned she
ought to leave the whole matter in his capable hands.
And yet some internal instinct urged her to ride out and
meet the woman. She had no clear idea what she'd say, or
even if Naomi would talk to her. But she needed to draw
her own impressions.

After lunch, having fetched Uncle Willie's horse, Proctor, from Woodmancy's Livery, and hitched up the buggy

in the shed across the alley, Libby set out for Old
Kentucky. Using a map she'd found in the drawer of
Captain Boyd's mail case, she traveled north, then east.

She sipped from the water jar she'd brought along,
jogged the buggy south, then east again, over a bridge
and into the trees of Old Kentucky. Proctor plodded past
a cemetery, a church, and a school yard. The grounds
skirting the school were beaten to dust by the traffic of
children. Birds twittered unseen from the trees, and a
squirrel sat back on its red-bush tail as the buggy ambled
past. The road curled north and east and crossed the same
creek a second time. Libby gripped the reins and continued east to a jog in the road. North, then east again. The
C & A tracks, a freight depot, the switch, and the Old
Kentucky grain dump were fifty yards ahead as she
stopped for a wide spot in the road. There was a cabin to
the right and several mailboxes off to the left at the
opening of a lane that wandered up through the trees and
out of sight. One of the mailboxes belonged to Decatur
McClure's family.

She remembered Captain Boyd's talk of a boxcar
serving as the family home. Supposing she'd find it along
the wagon tracks leading through the woods, she turned
Proctor up the lane. Trees crowded the path, a green
sheen glazing all the eye touched. How much farther?
Libby peered into sun-dappled trees, watching for a
boxcar home, concerned she might pass by it unnoticed.
Why hadn't she asked someone for directions? At length
the trees opened up and there was the boxcar home with
a clearing behind it and a couple of outbuildings. A porch
had been built onto the front, with ferns and black-eyed
Susans and other shade-loving plants growing around it.
Though primitive, the place had a cared-for look.

Just as Libby was wondering what sort of explanation
she might give for having come, a woman stepped around
the home, carrying a bucket of water. Tall, big-boned, and
broad-shouldered, she acknowledged Libby with a nod
that rippled her waist-length auburn hair.

"Afternoon, miss."

"Good afternoon." As the woman set the bucket down,

Libby saw that her hands were as large as a man's. They were brown and weathered and callused, scarred from years of service.

The woman returned Libby's scrutiny from eyes as green and vivid as the trees enfolding her home. "It's a steamer, ain't it?"

"Yes, ma'am. Are you Mrs. McClure?" At her nod, Libby quickly introduced herself. "I'm Libby Watson, Willie Blue's niece. I hope you don't mind my dropping by."

A look of surprise gave way to swift pleasure. "Not at all, miss. Fact is, I'm ashamed I ain't been in ta make yer acquaintance, and tell ya in person jest how sorry I am about Willie. And how grateful to him for savin' my boy. Light awhile, won't ya?"

"If it's not an inconvenience," said Libby.

"Land sakes, no! Why, I'm mortal pleased fer the company. It ain't no small jaunt from town. And on sech a hot day. Come around to the pump and getcha a drink."

As they circled to the backyard, a little girl came out of the garden, cradling a cat. Libby recognized her immediately as Opal, the girl who'd taken a spill off the bicycle while trying to ride it on the railroad tracks.

"Hello!" Libby greeted her with a smile.

Recognition came slower to the child. She stopped short, looking puzzled. Naomi drew her in with an outstretched arm.

"This here's Miss Watson, Opal. Say howdy."

"We met at the train station a couple of weeks ago," Libby reminded her. "Your brother was helping you with your circus act."

A light came on in the child's eyes. "I remember you. You and Miz Bee walked me over to Baker's."

"Exactly. Your wounds have healed, I see."

"Shucks, that weren't nothin'," said Opal, grinning. Hugging the cat close, she added, "This here's Mother Cat."

"She has kittens?" Libby reached out to stroke the soft gray head.

Naomi chuckled. "Don't she *always*?"

"That's how we come to name her Mother. These 'uns

is gray, jest like her, with white stockings." Opal stroked the patch of white on the cat's throat. "They's jest been weaned. Ya want one ta take home?"

"I'd be tempted, except for my dog, Sugar. I'm not sure she'd want to share her home."

Her mention of Uncle Willie's dog brought a second memory. Expression dimming, Opal said, "I saw you at the funeral, too."

"Yes."

Resentment quickened in the little girl's eyes. "My brother got that store a-comin' to him."

"Hush, Opal, that ain't true," said Naomi.

"That's what Paw-Paw said."

"Yes, and it's a wunderment how Paw-Paw tangles matters. You run see if Frankie's there."

"Is he in trouble?"

"That's betwixt him and me. You go fetch him."

"Yep, he's in trouble." Opal picked up her bare feet and disappeared around the side of the house, taking the cat with her.

"The boy's been findin' his share of it lately," Naomi muttered, then added with a shake of her head, "I ort to say straightaway I'm railly sorry for his monkeyshines the day of Willie's funeral. Opal spoke of it, tho giner'lly, to all intents, she ain't so quick to tattle. Jest so ya know, it ketched up with Frankie, him throwin' a stone at yer buggy. Ike's set him to working off his debt."

Silently Libby credited Ike for his sense of justice. She drank the water Naomi pumped and settled beside her on the laundry bench, eye drawn to the clearing behind the house. It was like a hole in the woods, the sunlight pouring through, gilding the cornfield, garden, flowers, and pasture.

"Only fittin' Frankie works out Ike's doctor bill and clears his debt toward the buggy damage," Naomi continued. "Ike and Woodmancy studied it out betwixt 'em, onct Frankie locked horns with Woodmancy, refusin' ta turn a hand at the livery." She sighed. "He ort to know by now mischief don't pay. Though Pa's a detriment and that's a fact. Spoils him somethin' awful, and laughs at his pranks, so long as he's not caught up in 'em."

Her gaze darkened momentarily. "I'm beholdin' to you for letting the boy stay over the night he run off. Didn't want to let on to Opal I was scairt. But I *was* scairt. Scairt, and worried too, what with the storm."

Libby's murmured response passed unnoticed as Naomi talked on. There was an eloquence of hands and expression as she spoke of her children, her garden, her flowers, the corn crop there in the clearing, and the dryness of the pasture. Each gesture, each glimmer, bespoke a loneliness deeper than isolation, two children, and little adult conversation could account for.

At length she got around to her husband. "Circuit judge be comin' around sometime after the Independence holiday. I reckon he'll fine Decatur and send him on home. I'm plumb ashamed of him treatin' Mr. Cearlock thataway."

Seizing the opening, Libby said, "People say he isn't normally a violent person. What happened, do you know?"

Naomi sighed and said in lieu of answer, "There was a poet come to the Columbian last year. Mr. James Whitcomb Riley was his name. Knowin' from our school days jest how partial I be ta Mr. Riley's rhymes, Decatur took me ta hear him and he bought me a book of his rhymes. They's delicious words, full of wit and wisdom and melancholy and merriment. Listen at this 'un here."

Naomi withdrew the small volume of poems from her apron pocket and, with a sure touch, thumbed to a dog-eared page. She read:

"I would sing of love that lives,
On the errors it forgives;
And the world would better grow
If I knew what poets know."

Naomi's fingers on the closed book made Libby think of winter grapevines, brown and hard and enduring. Was she saying it'd take a poet to figure out her husband's behavior? Or was the poem a wish for the kind of love that was built on forgiveness? Ashamed of her prying,

Libby said, "Those are beautiful words. It'd be nice to write like that, wouldn't it?"

"Oh my yes! Snaggin' thoughts out of the air and puttin' them into sech words. It's a wonderment, ain't it?"

"Exactly!" exclaimed Libby. "Have you written any poetry yourself?"

Naomi's color deepened as she confessed, "They's thoughts come to mind of a sudden, I'd like to set 'em down in pencil. But I ain't got the learnin' fer it. Pa needed me at home after Mama died."

Startled, Libby blurted, "The same thing happened to me."

"Railly, miss? Don't stick out on ya none."

"I plan to go back to school. Maybe not right away, but sometime. I'd like to be a writer."

"My! That'd be somethin'," exclaimed Naomi.

The wistful note in her voice made Libby feel privileged, somehow, for the luxury of thinking her dream could come true. At the same time, she could not shake the sense of having found a kindred spirit in an unexpected place. "Perhaps when the children are grown . . ." she began.

"It's too late fer me. Best I can do is see to it Frankie and Opal git the kind of learnin' they need."

Uncertain why she persisted, Libby said, "Still, there's always someday."

"Maybe," said Naomi, though with no real conviction. A muscle jerked in her face. She sighed and rose to her feet. "Beggin' yer pardon, miss, but I need to get at them peas. Would ya mind if we was to move the bench out to the edge of the garden? We can talk while I pick."

Libby jumped up. "Oh, no. I'll go on my way. Forgive me for keeping you from your work."

"I wasn't aimin' to chase ya off. It'd do my heart good if you'd take some vegetables home fer yer supper."

"It does sound good," Libby weakened. "But only if you'll let me help pick them."

Seeming pleased, Naomi led the way. It was a well-kept garden with scarcely a weed in sight. A variety of flowers grew there, too, many of which had yet to bloom.

Naomi pinched some of the smaller buds on the flowers, explaining as she did so that the sacrifice of those discarded buds would strengthen the ones that remained.

Later, when Libby had said her good-byes and started home with a sack of peas on the seat beside her, she found herself drawing similarities between people and flower buds and how some got "pinched back" for the strengthening of others. Was that what had happened to Naomi McClure upon the death of her mother? Libby applied the same standard of measure to herself, and recoiled at the thought, for she in no way felt she had been sacrificed; rather, she'd been strengthened and encouraged and challenged to flower. If her dreams were never realized, it wouldn't be because they'd been "pinched off" by fate or hard circumstance. The responsibility of fulfilling her dreams seemed instead to rest on her willingness to trust her dream to God. If it was to be, He would open the doors. Wasn't that what He'd done with Uncle Willie's bequest?

Despite her empathy for Naomi McClure, she would heed Angus Cearlock's counsel and claim what God had already given, for the store was the key. She would do whatever Angus thought was necessary to keep it.

19

ℒ The days thereafter fell into a pattern of sorting and clerking and cleaning and ordering and stocking. Captain Boyd was on time some mornings and tardy others. His drinking, she suspected, had not abated, but he'd become more clever about concealing the odor with mint. Which made it easier to vacillate and postpone and look the other way.

When Libby opened the door at eight o'clock on Friday, there stood Mr. Galloway's friend, Billy Young, wanting the job of fetching the mail from the train station. He needed the income to supplement his newly begun dray service, he told her. Libby hired him on the spot and asked if he might also be available for moving furniture.

"I want to use some of the pieces downstairs. But the bulk of them, I'd like to store up over the buggy shed," she explained.

Billy took out his pocket watch. "I've got some deliveries today, but if I can get someone to help me, I'll see if I can't move the pieces over the weekend."

Having little choice, Libby resigned herself to waiting.

Mrs. Brignadello came in as Billy was leaving, and sold Libby some green onions, rhubarb, and asparagus from her garden. Seeming preoccupied, she breezed halfheartedly over the names of the injured and ailing who'd visited Dr. Harding over the past few days, Angus among them.

185

Libby had seen nothing of Angus over the past week. Chagrined that her pulse should leap at such a skimpy scrap of news, she lifted her chin as Mrs. Brignadello went on her way, and told herself she didn't care a whit that he'd been sending Catherine for his mail. Nor would she mention his name this afternoon, when his sister came to help her with the west corner. So vowing, Libby went back to rearranging and dusting and scrubbing, stopping only long enough for a light lunch of crackers and cheese.

The sun picked its way through the clouds just as Catherine arrived.

"Where's Tess?" asked Libby, seeing the baby carriage on the walk.

"Mama came into town with Chester so she could watch her this afternoon." She wrinkled her nose and added, "She's not taking the news of Charlie's promotion very well."

"I'd think she'd be happy for you," said Libby, though she, too, was dreading the impending separation from her newfound friend.

"Oh, she's happy he's gotten a raise and that I'll have a fine house. She isn't happy that it will be in St. Louis." Surveying the bare corner, Catherine planted her hands on her hips and accused, "You've cleared it without me."

"Yes, and all you missed was a lot of dust and a few sneezes."

Catherine tied an apron over her stylish black and white striped walking-length skirt, then pushed the carriage inside and parked it in the opposite corner.

Libby arched her neck, curious again as to why she'd brought the wicker baby buggy. "What've you got in there?"

"It's a surprise. You'll see soon enough. So where do we start?"

"There are some pieces of furniture I want brought down. I asked Billy Young, but he didn't have time, and we certainly can't do it without help."

Catherine walked to the door and looked down the street, then smiled back at her. "Leave it to me."

In no time at all, she'd coaxed two cousins off the street

and up the stairs. The young men expended a good deal of muscle lugging a bureau and a wardrobe down the steps, through the store, and into the corner, then went on their way. Libby and Catherine handled the much smaller washstand and a hall tree.

Catherine thought the arrangement should face the window so that those passing by would be drawn in by the view. She strewed samplings of gentlemen's merchandise and blended it all together as artfully as one might drape flags and bunting on the Fourth of July. A coat and vest hung from the yawning door of the wardrobe. Flannel trousers and a shirt with an ascot tie. And for "glad rags," a black dinner coat, a "fancy" suit, and a tall silk hat on a chair. Woolen hose draped over an open drawer with suspenders and long-handle underwear peeking out.

Libby hung the hall tree in hats, some for work, some for dress, some, like the baseball cap, for play. Linen collars and cuffs and a cigar humidor found a home on a bureau top.

"Something's missing." Libby stood back, trying to remember the clutter that had slowed her up each time she'd poured kerosene on a rag and dusted her brothers' room.

Dimples creased Catherine's smudged cheeks. "Close your eyes!" Her hurried steps sounded to and from the baby carriage. A curious whisper, clink, scrape, and thump of this on that, and she sang out, "All right, you can open them now."

On the washstand was a crumpled linen towel, a razor, a brush, and a shaving mug; on the shelf, an array of tonics and lotions in colored bottles with stoppers removed, emitting masculine fragrances that tantalized the nostrils. Playing cards spilled from a deck on the dresser. There were dice, a shoe horn, and a photograph of a pretty girl with her hair piled high and a cameo at her throat. A coin, a rabbit's foot, a tobacco can, a knife, a watch, a well-spent candle waxed to the brass holder. With a few well-placed objects, she had completed the picture of a gentleman's retreat.

Libby caught her breath and let it out slowly. "You have an eye for this, Catherine."

"It's not too fussy?"

"Not at all. It's perfect!"

Catherine tilted her head to one side and ventured with aplomb, "It does look rather nice, doesn't it?"

Delighted, Libby laughed. "Where did you find all these things?"

"Tidying up after Charlie. Oh, relax! He'll never miss them, and the hired girl will thank me for getting this old clutter out of her way."

Libby beamed. "I can hardly wait to begin the ladies' corner."

"But we're not finished yet. I thought we could drape the back of the furniture in dark cloth and display some more clothing."

Knowing she had to make the most of her limited storage space, Libby chimed in, "We'll have to fill the drawers, and the shelves and the wardrobe."

And so it went for the rest of the afternoon, right up to closing time when Catherine suggested they get a bite to eat over at Baker's. Libby washed the day's dirt from her hands and face, then donned her hat and paused in the open door, basking in the glow of what they had accomplished. It was only a start, but already she felt the pride of ownership.

Catherine pushed the baby carriage over to Mrs. Baker's and left it out front as they went inside to eat. It was the end of the dinner hour. They could have had their choice of tables, but Catherine sailed past Dorene, singing out, "Don't bother setting places for us, Dorie. We'll save you some steps and eat in the kitchen."

Mrs. Baker welcomed them warmly. Her gaze followed Catherine across the kitchen to where Gram Steadman dozed in her rocking chair. *The Gazette* lay crumpled at her feet.

"Mr. Gruben's editorial must have been a little dry today. She's sleeping like a baby." Catherine held her voice to a whisper.

Mrs. Baker chuckled. "It was the children who scattered the paper. Zerilda brought them by earlier. They were good medicine for Mother."

"I can count on the same sleeping tonic from Tess," said Catherine knowingly.

Mrs. Baker's features seemed less plain when she smiled. She filled three plates and joined them at the table. Roast beef and potatoes all but spilled over the edges. Pearl onions swam in the gravy, with a side dish of asparagus. "Fresh out of Sarah Jane's garden," she said.

Libby pierced one of the glistening onions with her fork and relished its tenderness and sweet flavor. "She came by the store, too."

"Aunt Sarah Jane's selling garden produce? That's funny. She never said a word about it to Mama or me."

Mrs. Baker reached for the salt shaker and changed the subject, saying, "Zerilda tells me you hired Billy Young today."

"Yes, for the mail pickup and delivery." Libby glanced over her shoulder as Dorene swept in, arms piled high with dirty dishes.

"Billy's working for you?" Dorene frowned as she slid the dishes into the sink. "But I saw in the paper where he's opened his own dray service."

When Libby explained that Billy was doing both, Dorene's expression shifted. Mischief danced in her eyes.

"A man who owns his own business. Wait'll I tell Chloe."

"Don't you start, Dorie," scolded Catherine. "Every time you get her dander up, she drags Mama's hall carpet out to the clothesline and wails the daylights out of it. The next thing you know, Mama will have to pester Chester for a new carpet. Isn't that right, Teddy?" She turned and smiled at Teddy, who'd just slipped in the back door.

"Pester Chester." He scooped up *The Gazette*, his lips moving as he tried out the words again.

Libby watched how painstakingly he folded the newspaper. He'd no more than accomplished it to his satisfaction when Dorene jerked it out of his hands.

"Did you see Mrs. Dorrance's open letter?"

"Dorene!" exclaimed Catherine. "Teddy was looking at that."

"He was just folding it, weren't you, Teddy?" She creased the paper to the inside front page and shoved it at Catherine. "We all signed it. See there, there's my name right at the bottom."

Catherine skimmed the first couple of lines, then began reading aloud: "'There has been an alarming increase of drunkenness and rowdy behavior on the streets of Edgewood lately due to liquor coming by COD express. We, the undersigned, urge the sheriff, the town council, and anyone else in authority to investigate the matter and work aggressively toward a solution by upholding the laws of our fair town through stiff fines and whatever other measures are deemed necessary.' "

"Heaven help us, Mrs. Dorrance is on the rampage. Why, you'd think Maddie had sneaked off for a dip in the lake with Ike all over again. Oh yes," Catherine said, at Libby's uplifted glance. "There was a time when your Mr. Galloway was quite the reckless swain. Then he went off to war and along came Dr. Daniels."

"He isn't *my* Mr. Galloway," disclaimed Libby, flushing.

"Dr. Daniels? Is he a friend of Dr. Harding's?" asked Dorene.

Catherine's laugh was light and melodious. "Goodness no. He's a handsome fellow with eyes like a tiger. Don't you remember? He came through Edgewood with his medicine show a few years ago. Why, he could cure anything, to hear him talk—and give old Mr. Culbertson a run for his money at recitations while he was at it! I never saw so many jars and bottles and potions and salves nor heard such silver-tongued talk! He sold Maddie an elixir to clear her complexion. Nothing more than dyed liquor, that's what Mrs. Dorrance said, and that it addled Maddie's brain. Brain, ha! It was her heart that man addled. His wagon left town a fortnight later, and Maddie with it."

"Have you wiped down the tables?" asked Mrs. Baker of wide-eyed Dorene, who was hanging on to Catherine's every word.

Catherine turned back to the paper as Dorene made her reluctant departure. "You signed it too, I see."

Libby flushed, but was spared a response by Mrs. Baker, who, with a thoughtful glance, perceived her discomfort and shifted the conversation, saying, "Bless Mr. Gruben. He gave our Fourth of July ice cream social a nice plug."

"The Republican Club's picnic got a good piece, too." Catherine went on to say she was torn between the town's holiday activities and those of the Republican Club out at Spring Lake. The railroad passed close to the lake, with a switch provided for the tile factory, which was on the east side of the tracks. People would come from a good distance away.

"Chester's set on Angus introducing the guest speaker he's trying to line up. With any luck, he'll be off his crutches by then." In a hurry to relieve her mother of Tess's care, Catherine ate quickly and soon departed.

"We missed you in church on Sunday," said Mrs. Baker, when they were alone.

Libby admitted she'd overslept.

"You've taken on quite a load." Mrs. Baker smiled and added, "I hope you can make it this week."

Seeing no way around it, Libby conceded, "I thought I might try the Methodist Church."

"Because of Mrs. Dorrance? I see." Mrs. Baker's gaze was steady. "And have you spoken to Captain Boyd?"

"No." Resenting Mrs. Dorrance all over again, Libby pointed out, "He's old enough to be my grandfather. He's been kind to me. I don't know what to say."

"What troubles you most?" asked Mrs. Baker. "The thought of Captain Boyd losing his job? Or the very real possibility that he could live out the rest of his days never learning what it is to be free of his own private demons?"

Libby flinched. "I don't think Mrs. Dorrance is concerned about any of those things."

"I wasn't asking Mrs. Dorrance."

Slow heat crawled up Libby's neck. "I can't see how losing his job will help matters."

"He hasn't lost it yet."

"But he will, if she persists. And I'll be the one to have to tell him."

Mrs. Baker's work-worn hand covered her fingers and

squeezed. "There are worse things than losing a job. Anyway, you can't make this go away. You've prayed?" At Libby's nod, she asked, "For Mrs. Dorrance, too?"

Mrs. Dorrance?

"God's not one for holding a grudge. If He doesn't hold one, what right have we?"

Libby tucked her chin and did not reply. If it weren't for Mrs. Dorrance, she wouldn't be in this mess.

"It's hard to nurse a grudge, once you start praying for a body. You're investing something of yourself in them," Mrs. Baker was saying. "Course, it means making a choice whether you want to work this out your own way, or listen to that still small voice inside. The one God put there."

Gentle though it was, the reprimand seemed unwarranted. Libby followed her natural inclination and nursed her hurt as she carried her dishes to the sink, paid for her meal, and went home.

The days had been long, the evenings wearing, with far too little time for household chores, much less daydreams and jots in her Memorandum book. Open notebook in her lap, Libby sat in the window overlooking the square and took up her pencil. But words were elusive tonight. She'd prayed a good deal for Captain Boyd and how she could approach him on the subject of his drinking without wounding his dignity. Mrs. Baker's words concerning Mrs. Dorrance came to mind, but she couldn't put her heart into praying for somebody who was making things harder than they had to be.

A surrey passing on the street below drew her eye. Libby couldn't see the driver for the fringed top, but she recognized the horse as belonging to Angus. She watched him circle the park beneath the purple sky, then cross the railroad tracks and head south. She let her breath go slowly and pulled the shade on the window before crossing to the stove to pour heated water into a basin for bathing.

Soon thereafter, Libby lay with the lamp burning, perusing the book of mail regulations. She was not long in agreeing with Ike Galloway—the manual was poorly written and difficult to understand. Wondering that

Zerilda had bothered reading it at all, she blew out the lamp and closed her eyes.

Somewhere in the breeze, a windmill whined for oil. A pigeon cooed and a train shook the ground. Just like the coal trains back home. She was homesick. Lonesome for her father. Lonesome for the boys. Just lonesome.

20

🏵 On Saturday morning Mr. Gruben came in on on the heels of Billy Young. He smiled at Libby from the other side of the counter and said, "Good morning, Miss Watson. I see you've hired yourself a helper."

"Yes, sir," said Libby. She smiled at the editor and then at Billy Young as he dropped the midmorning mail on the counter.

"The article in the paper was helpful, I take it," said Mr. Gruben.

"It would have been," said Billy, before Libby could answer. "Except Dorene over at Baker's told me over breakfast yesterday that Miss Libby was looking for help."

The editor winced. "Ach! And here I was all set to climb up on my soapbox and proclaim the power of the written word."

"Oh, there's power in it, all right," replied Billy with a wink for Hascal Caton, Mr. Lamb, and Mr. Noonan, who had gathered by the cold stove. "Take Mrs. Dorrance's letter in yesterday's paper. She sure is riled over liquor being shipped into town via the express office."

The editor said, "She has a point. It does circumvent the law."

"Buried a man once, drowned in his own vomit," said Mr. Lamb. "Put an end to his drinking once and for all."

"You're in a gruesome business, Mr. Lamb," observed Billy.

The mortician shrugged and allowed, "It isn't for everybody."

Testily Hascal Caton remarked, "I'd like to know since when is it Miz Dorrance's business what's shipped into your station, Mr. Noonan?"

"Kind of wonderin' myself if she expects me to poke a hole in every COD package, make sure nothing runs out," said Mr. Noonan. His eyeshade cast a green hue on his face as he sprang to his feet to greet Chester Gentry, who had just strode in for his mail.

"Good mornin', Mr. Gentry. That's what I call good timing. I've a telegram for you. Came in just a bit ago from Springfield."

"Thank you, Mr. Noonan." Mr. Gentry poked the telegram into his pocket unread, retrieved mail from his box, and departed.

Mr. Noonan pointedly ignored the nail keggers' inquisitive glances and stepped up to the counter to buy some cheese.

Libby wrapped it and gave him his change. "Thank you, Mr. Noonan."

He flung a hand in the air, boots ringing as he made for the door.

Minor spat tobacco juice into the coal bucket and observed, "Mrs. Dorrance's wasn't the only signature on that letter."

"Here, here! If you're referring to Miss Willy, she's got a right to her opinion," Captain Boyd called from his sorting case on the other side of the counter.

"Just like we folks on yer route got a right to expect the right mail in the right box at a right and reasonable time," muttered Hascal in tones too low for the captain to hear.

Mr. Lamb talked right over him, saying, "Mrs. Lamb signed that letter, and with my approval, too. 'Liquor has no defense.' It was true when Mr. Lincoln said it, and it's true enough today."

Hascal clutched his pipe and said with narrowed eye, "Well. I fer one don't hold with wimminfolk signin' letters to the public newspaper."

"Oh, come now, Mr. Caton. Signatures aren't the issue," said Mr. Gruben. "Whether the town is wet or dry is a matter of local option. You know that."

"Reason it out any way you like, I still say there ain't no harm in a man takin' a drink now and then."

Sheriff Conklin sauntered up to the counter just in time to catch the tail end of the conversation. "There is if they take it on the streets of Edgewood, Mr. Caton. I'm sorry, but that's the law."

"Maybe the law needs changin'."

"If you feel that way, write your own letter to the paper." Mr. Gruben offered a pencil. "Here you are, Mr. Caton. Miss Libby? Have you a piece of paper to spare?"

"Who you think yer foolin', Gruben? Even if I wrote it, you wouldn't print it. Yer a prohibitionist yerself."

"You're only half-right, friend. I'll print it, provided it isn't slanderous and you keep your language clean."

Hascal turned a blistering glare on the mild-mannered editor. "Don't I always?"

Minor slapped his knee, his muttonchops twitching. "Shoot-fire, that *is* a good 'un."

"Well, by cracky, somebody had better stand up b'fore the prohibitionists take over this country. It's the wimmin behind it, ya know."

His tone unvarying, Mr. Gruben challenged a second time, "Put it down on paper, Mr. Caton."

"My cipherin' ain't up to purr, or I would."

"Maybe one of your daughters could pen it." Mr. Lamb smiled so benignly, the jab was lost on Mr. Caton.

Thinking Mrs. Dorrance's letter had sown more than enough contention, Libby tossed the mailbag on the sorting table and asked from her side of the counter, "Could I help you, Mr. Conklin?"

"I've got a leaky water bucket. Rivet and a washer, please. And charge it to the jail."

"Say there, Mr. Conklin. How long you think you can hold Decatur when he ain't even been tried nor found guilty of nothin'?" said Hascal as Billy waved to Libby and let himself out the back door.

"Decatur can't go around stealing horses. Nor throwing his fist in other men's faces," replied Sheriff Conklin.

"Borrowed. As fer fistycuffin', he was provoked," claimed Hascal.

"Is that what you call it?"

Hascal scratched his flat nose. "Politics, that's the name I put to it."

"Hearing's coming up in July. We'll let the judge decide."

The bell on the front door jingled as the lawman shoved his purchases into his pocket. He tipped his hat to Mrs. Brignadello on his way out.

"It's all who ya know in this town. Dad-blamed political chicanery."

Hascal offered no explanation as to why he considered Decatur's detainment "political." Nor did his peers press for clarification. Rather, they dropped their heads as if their ears had suddenly stopped up. It was so quiet, Mrs. Brignadello's wicker basket scraped like a fingernail on slate as she slid it onto the counter.

"You'll have to tell me what it's worth, Libby."

Libby lifted the cloth to find a dozen eggs and three pounds of butter. "I didn't know you had chickens and cows, Mrs. Brignadello."

"I don't. Mrs. Berry and I did some trading."

Libby was glad to get the butter. The Republican Club had bought all she had on hand for the barbecue they were having out at Spring Lake on Independence Day. She counted the going price into Mrs. Brignadello's hand, and spent a moment admiring her picture hat.

Mrs. Bee made a minor adjustment of the two-toned velvet and chiffon wonder, asking, "It's not too much pouf for a luncheon?"

"Oh my no. It's perfect," assured Libby.

"Goin' to Shortfellers Club, is ya, Miz Bee?"

"Why, yes, Minor, I am in a little while."

"And not a feller amongst 'em."

Mrs. Brignadello spared his joke a distracted smile. "We're to answer the roll today with a line from our favorite Longfellow poem. Have you a favorite, Minor?"

"'Hiawatha,'" Minor replied. "Culbertson can say the whole thing, word for word. Ain't it a puzzle what he's got tucked away in his head, and there he is, lost every time he steps foot out of town?"

"It surely is," agreed Mr. Gruben.

"Such a dear gentleman. His daughter's much too free about letting him wander," fretted Mrs. Brignadello.

"We gotta look out for him, sure enuf," said Minor.

The mention of the old war veteran had a unifying effect on the group. Differences momentarily forgotten, they stirred to their feet one by one and drifted for the door.

Mrs. Brignadello seemed in no hurry to go. She was still visiting with Libby when Billy returned, carrying a crate filled with bottled soda pop, which Libby had ordered purely on speculation.

"Beans you ordered for the Republican picnic came in at the station," he said, "along with the rest of your order. Picked up your ice at the icehouse, too. Be better for you if I lugged it in the back way?"

Libby said that it would. She walked Mrs. Brignadello to the back door, which was closer to her Longfellow's Club meeting. "Have a good time."

Two strides on her way, Mrs. Bee turned back. Looking discomfited, she said, "I've a good many hats at home. If you really like this one, I'd be willing to part with it at a greatly reduced rate. But only if you're interested."

"You're wanting to sell it?" asked Libby, surprised.

Color suffused Mrs. Bee's pert face. "Never mind, dear, if you think it's a bad idea."

"No, no. Not at all." Responding to an inner prompting, Libby added, "I'd love a new hat. You go ahead and wear it to your luncheon, though."

"That wouldn't be fair. If it's to be yours, I'll not parade it about town." Mrs. Brignadello removed the jeweled pin, and with one last wistful glance at the adorning ostrich feather, thrust the hat at Libby.

Libby was still standing, hat in hand, when Billy tramped in with a chunk of ice. He carried it into the pantry where the icebox was kept. On his way back through, he indicated the hat with a jab of the ice tongs.

"Wasn't Mrs. Brignadello just wearing that? "

"Yes, well . . . we did some business."

"You old Kentucky horse trader, you." A glint of mischief in his eye, he urged, "Try it on."

"Not now. My hairstyle isn't right for a hat like this."

"Then loose it."

"And have it in my face all day? I don't think so."

Billy dropped the ice tongs. He dusted his hands on his trousers, took the hat from her hands, and thrust it on her head with all the care of a nurseryman planting a shrub. Grinning at her sputtered protest, he cocked his head to one side. "Not bad. Not bad at all. Hold the door for me, would you?"

He strode to the wagon and peeled back the heavy blankets. Libby stood by as he lifted the ice from a bed of straw and carried it inside. He was depositing it in a washtub when Ike Galloway strode in.

Billy greeted him and, with a wink, indicated Libby's hat. "Look what flew in. Makes a handy doorstop, don't you think?"

Ike Galloway peeked under the wide, sloping brim and asked, "Where's the rest of the ostrich?"

Libby smiled at their tomfoolery. "Could I help you, Mr. Galloway?"

"Yes, ma'am. If you see Miss Watson, tell her I came to fix her door."

"She's around here someplace," claimed Billy.

"Yes she is, and she's looking for Billy Young to move some furniture for her," countered Libby.

Billy dived behind the door.

Libby shook her head and tried her best to look downcast. "It occurs to me a good man is hard to find. Particularly when there's furniture to be moved."

"Scarce as hen's teeth," agreed Ike.

Libby pretended to consider him with fresh interest. "How are you at moving furniture?"

"Depends," he countered. "Where are you wantin' it moved to?"

"Over the buggy shed."

Ike scratched his chin. "Down one flight of steps, then up a ladder? Sounds like a good job for an attorney."

Billy peeked from behind the door, grinning in anticipation.

"I guess it does require more than a strong back at that," said Libby.

"Hey! I object!" yelped Billy

"Aw now, don't go and take it personal," soothed Ike. "She wouldn't have said it if she'd known you were lurkin' behind the door. Isn't that right, miss?"

"Whatever you say, Mr. Galloway." Libby smiled at them both and swept up the stairs to find a safe spot for her hat.

Vanity demanded a quick peek in the mirror before she removed the hat. She wrinkled her nose. Her stray wisps and single copper-toned braid were every bit as out of keeping as she'd feared. But it *was* a grand hat. It looked as if it had never been worn. She puzzled over Mrs. Brignadello's willingness to part with it. But only momentarily. She could hear the men downstairs breaking up the ice in the tub. Hoping the same children who had pennies for peanuts could coax a second handout for soda pop, she descended the stairs to put the bottles on ice and met Billy and Ike on their way up.

"If you want to point out those pieces, I've just about gotten over my hurt feelings," said Billy, his back to the stairway wall.

Libby replied with a quick smile, "You're my hero, Mr. Young."

Billy nudged Ike, who stood one step below him. "Hear that?"

"Sounds to me like she's mortal set on gettin' that furniture moved," Ike replied.

Libby laughed. "I'd count it a favor, that's for sure."

Ike took the upstairs door off its hinges, lugged it out back where two wooden horses waited beneath the shade tree, then trudged back up the stairs to help Billy begin moving furniture. The numerous chairs and smaller pieces were handled quite easily. But the larger pieces had to be left on the lower level of the buggy shed.

By the time the bell in the Methodist church tower tolled noon, Ike was hard at work on her broken door. Billy, without prompting, had stayed to fix the broken window upstairs. He called her when he'd finished the job and beamed at her words of praise.

"Who would guess one window could make such a difference? It opens and closes like a dream. And all this light," enthused Libby. "Thank you, Billy. This is wonderful!"

Accepting her gratitude modestly, Billy took a turn around the room, observing, "You've got a lot of open space here."

Libby nodded agreement. There was still plenty of furniture strewn about. But at least she had some options now. "I wonder what it would cost to hire a carpenter to wall off some bedchambers?"

"Have you got some money to spend? This time of year, good carpenters don't come cheap," cautioned Billy.

Libby admitted she didn't. She wandered the room, trying to visualize what she could do to make the open space more homey without sinking a lot of money into it. At length she said, "What about some movable screens?"

"What kind of screens?"

"Something lightweight. Say, nine feet long and maybe six feet tall."

"You mean like the movable walls they use for plays over at the Columbian?"

"Exactly!" said Libby, growing excited. "Movable walls! I could arrange them to my own liking. Where would I get something like that?"

"I don't know. I'll ask around," offered Billy.

"Would you? That would be wonderful!"

Libby led the way downstairs. She paid Billy for the morning's work and thanked him once more for a job well done.

A short while later, Libby stepped out the back door and shaded her eyes from the glare to see how Ike was coming along in his door repairs. Teddy was keeping him company. He stood out of the way, one arm locked behind his back and Sugar at his feet, snapping at a fly.

"Have you gentlemen eaten?"

Ike made a mark on the wood before turning her way. "We were just startin' to talk about it, weren't we, Teddy?"

Teddy's mouth wiggled in his customary noncommittal grin.

"Would you like some cheese and crackers? I could open some canned peaches, too."

Ike dragged his sleeve across his brow. "We'll get a sandwich from the restaurant. Thanks all the same."

Libby went inside, where lunch was further delayed by a customer. By and by, Teddy appeared at the back door. He didn't say a word, just stood looking at her expectantly.

"Did Ike send you in for something, Teddy?"

He considered that for a long moment. "W-e-l-l, you better come see."

Libby followed him out to find Ike crouched down, splashing his hands and face in the granite basin she'd left at the pump. He turned, water trailing down his sunbrowned face and darkening his shirt. "Teddy brought you a ham sandwich."

"How thoughtful. Thank you, Teddy."

Teddy tugged at the bill on his cap, looking everywhere but at her.

"Go ahead and start without me. I'll be right back," she said.

Teddy's eyes lit up when she returned with three sodas. He rose from the upturned bucket and accepted his with a look of keen anticipation and a nod of thanks. Ike had moved the door out of the way and was seated on a board spanning the wooden horses. He indicated her sandwich, wrapped in a cloth napkin, and removed the springed lid from the soda.

Leaving the back door open so she could keep an eye out for customers, Libby shared the improvised bench with Ike. It was a delicious sandwich, a thick slab of ham nestled between two slices of homemade bread. Teddy's stubby lashes came down as Libby complimented his mother's cooking. He made a big business of tossing Sugar a bread crust.

The only root beer Libby had ever tasted had been homemade. Her first swallow of the bottled version made her eyes water. A grin flitted over Ike's strongly built face.

"How's the door coming?" she asked.

"Ready to fit the panel in."

"I appreciate your efforts, Mr. Galloway."

"No more'n neighborly."

When the silence grew cumbersome, Libby asked, "You've mentioned your maple camp from time to time. I confess, I don't know much about it. What is a maple camp, exactly?"

"Just a name for the place maple syrup is made in the spring. The Indians taught the settlers how to gather the sap from the trees. I reckon we've improved on the cookin'-down method some, but basically it's the same principle. Just keep boilin' and boilin'. By and by, you'll get syrup, or sugar, if you cook it even further." Ike paused for another bite of sandwich.

"How did you become interested?" asked Libby.

He finished chewing and took a sip of soda. "Willie taught me when I was a boy."

"I don't remember his ever mentioning having made syrup." Quickly Libby added, "Though I'm learning not to be surprised by anything concerning Uncle Willie."

"Him and Decatur partnered at it for several years. Just a shack with the pan over a furnace pit. He quit camp, once he was married." Galloway flung Sugar a bread crust, then looked Libby in the eyes as he added, "About a year ago he deeded it over to me. I figured if I was going to go at it wholeheartedly, I ought to put up a building. Keep my equipment and myself out of the weather. While I'm boilin' sap, anway."

"So you plan to make a living at this?"

"Supplemental income, at this point. It's seasonal work, in February and March."

"It sounds like a lot of work. Is it worth it?"

Ike grinned. "I reckon it is to me. Anyway, it's step one of a plan. I'm hopin' to buy a piece of farm ground that borders my timber. Comes a time a man wearies of workin' for others and starts thinkin' of ways he can be his own boss. Isn't that right, Teddy?"

Teddy nodded, and in so doing, lost a piece of ham off his sandwich. He toppled his bucket beating Sugar to it. Disappointed, the old beagle sat back on her haunches and whined. Teddy painstakingly dusted fertile McLean County dirt from the piece of ham and restored it to the sandwich.

"Didn't hurt a thing," he said, and took a big bite.

"That's what the farmwife said about the mouse that fell into the cream." Ike grinned at Libby's look of distaste. "Sorry. I'll tell you sometime when ya ain't eatin'."

"Tell *me*," urged Teddy.

He looked disappointed when Ike failed to comply. Doubting Ike's story could be any worse than the word picture Mr. Lamb had painted just a while ago, Libby said, "That's all right, Mr. Galloway. Go ahead and tell it."

"One time this lady come into the store to sell Willie butter, and wantin' to buy butter, too. Willie puzzled over it some. By the by, he says to her, 'Would it be too personal if I was to ask why ye're selling butter and buyin' butter too?'"

"'Why, no,' she says. 'I guess I can tell you.' And with a look over her shoulder to make sure it stayed between jest them two, she says, 'A little mouse fell into the cream. It didn't hurt a thing, mind you. It was just the thought, if you know what I mean.'"

"'Ye're right, lass. Not a wee bit of harm done.'" Mr. Galloway paused to tip up his soda bottle.

"So what'd he do?" urged Libby.

"Why, he didn't do nothin' but march into the pantry, remold her butter, and sell it right back to her."

Libby threw her head back and laughed. Laughter shook Teddy too, his large white teeth shining against his pink gums. Sunlight shone through the leaves, glimmering in Ike's gray eyes and picking out a small scar on one temple.

"Who was she?" Libby asked.

A slow grin spread over his face. "It wouldn't be sportin' of me to say."

"It was her, out there at the dairy," blurted Teddy. "We-l-l-l, it was," he defended, though Ike had not chided him. Nor did he refute Teddy's claim.

"Mrs. Dorrance? And her so proper," exclaimed Libby, surprised. It was clear Teddy had known the story all along. He was humming to himself, still pleased by it.

Ike gestured toward the back door with his empty bottle. "Sounds like you've got a customer."

Libby gave up hoping for the perfect opening, and said in a rush, "If you haven't made plans for the evening, could I hire you to stay and help with the clerking?"

"Might see my way free, once I get the door hung," he agreed.

Libby hopped off the board, taking the empty bottles with her. She was almost to the door when a dark-haired, dark-eyed slip of a boy came hurtling out with a grin as wide as a wedge of pie.

"David! Bless my soul, it really is you!" Libby flung her arms around him, hugging, laughing, holding back tears. "You look so good, I could squeeze the breath right out of you. Where's Father?"

David wiggled free. "He's coming. He said I could run ahead. I got to sit by the window on the train."

"My, now, that was a treat. How's he feeling? Is he coughing still?"

"A little. Guess what, Lib. Adam got married."

"Got married!" yelped Libby. "And I missed it? Why didn't someone wire me?"

"Then it wouldn't have been a surprise." David went silent all at once, his attention arrested by Teddy feeding the last bite of his sandwich to Sugar. "Is that the dog you mentioned in your letter?"

"Yes, and Teddy Baker." Libby introduced her little brother to Teddy and Ike, then hurried inside to get the second surprise of the day.

"Jacob! You came!"

"I had to see for myself Uncle Willie's cast-off. It's still standing, anyway." His dancing gaze swept the store. Stooping to receive her kiss, he indicated with a nod the gentlemen's shopping corner up front. "But you shouldn't have bothered fixing me a room. I'm not staying."

"That isn't your . . . What do you mean, you're not staying? You just got here."

"Yes, and you're laying in to me already." He emptied his arms of luggage and tugged her red braid. "Father's paying our driver. Come along and we'll help unload the hack."

"Why aren't you staying?"

"I have to be back to work on Monday. By then I expect Abigail will have taken over the house." He grimaced good-naturedly and added over his shoulder, "I'll be lucky to get a corner in the washhouse with that lass in charge."

"They're staying at the house, then. That's good," Libby added, not about to betray an unexpected twinge at the thought of Abigail hanging wash and cooking meals and sweeping the floors in the house that had been her own home since she could remember. "How was the wedding?"

"Nothing much to comment on."

Libby sniffed. "Fine. If you don't want to talk about it, I'll ask Father."

"Don't badger him, Lib. It's been a long two weeks since you left."

Libby turned in the door, suddenly uneasy. Jacob's perpetually sunny expression was ragged about the edges.

"What's the matter?"

"Nothing."

A scurry of alarm scuttled along her nerve endings. "The truth, now."

He hesitated, then lifted his broad shoulders and let them fall. "It was a hurry-up wedding, Lib." He searched her face. "You understand?"

Libby's face flushed hot, for she did understand. The trouble between Adam and Abigail. Her anger at his reluctance to set a wedding date. Adam's low queries and Dr. Dillman's tight-lipped response. Hadn't she feared it all along, in the secret depths of her heart?

Doubt suffused Jacob's features. "I'm sorry. Maybe I shouldn't have said anything."

"No, I'm glad you did." Libby swallowed the thick lump in her throat. There'd be shrewd glances, measuring looks. Whispering. A few would even gloat. She drew a deep breath and let it out slowly.

"No point in your brooding over it. Folks'll forget in time."

Libby knew Thistle Down too well for that. She sighed again.

"Adam has wide shoulders." Jacob snaked an arm around Libby's waist and gave her a brisk pat. "You all right?"

She took comfort in the gesture, even forgave him for taking such a man-view of things. Abigail had better develop a tough hide, for she'd bear the brunt of it. Quietly Libby asked, "Did Father tell you? Or Adam?"

"Father." Jacob's mouth tilted in a self-deprecating smile. "I have a feeling it wouldn't have surprised him nearly so much if it had been me."

Heat crept up her neck again. Weakly she protested, "Jacob, that isn't true."

"It's all right, Lib. You don't have to defend me." He took off his straw boater, ran his fingers along the band, and added, "It's kind of nice, actually. Being the *good* brother for a change."

21

Libby's father was still frail, but he couldn't be talked into resting. When the excitement of their arrival had calmed and customers once again claimed Libby's attention, he went out back to renew his acquaintance with Ike Galloway. Later, when the door was ready to hang, Thomas was on hand to help finish the job. Ike, no longer in demand for his clerking skills, packed up his tools and departed, taking the pieces of the chair Decatur had broken along with him.

David poked about the store, then climbed the stairs, only to come down again with a bewildered look and a question as to where the bedchambers were. Wishing she had had time to act on her newest plans before her family arrived, Libby said, "Make believe you're a cowboy. Spread some blankets on the floor by the window where you can look up at the stars."

"On the floor? Can I really?" he asked with such unbridled enthusiasm, Libby laughed. She gave him a broom for a horse, a rag for a six-shooter, and sent him back upstairs with instructions to slay dust wherever he found it.

Evening came and business picked up, just as it had the previous Saturday. Jacob and her father's help made all the difference in service. The soda pop was a hit with adults and children alike, so much so that Libby decided to double her next order.

Sunday passed with services at the Methodist church and a long lazy afternoon. Her father read the Bible while David played out back with Sugar. Jacob oscillated between offering sound business ideas concerning Willie Blue's and teasing Libby about sinking in the "great pot of gold" she'd fallen into. He tired of it eventually, stretched out for a nap, and did not awaken until Thomas went out for a walk. After supper dishes were done, they accompanied Jacob to the depot to catch his train.

"Give my love to Adam and Abigail," said Libby with a parting hug.

Jacob clapped David on the shoulder and shook his father's hand before climbing aboard the train. They waved until he was out of sight, then started home beneath a lavender sky, three astride, Thomas in the middle.

"Ye mother was forever scoldin' me for misplacin' this and misplacin' that. And looky here, if I haven't misplaced two of me own lads."

"They are well-grown men, Father. Both of them."

"Still, 'tis a thorn in me heart to let 'em go." Thomas caught David's hand in his. "Ah well, me Davie's as fine a laddie as ever to ride a broom pony. And Libby, me fair lass, with the freckles afadin' upon her nose."

"At last! I'm overcoming my washerwoman complexion." Libby laughed and slipped her hand over his arm. "I'm glad you're here. I've missed you."

"Hum," said Thomas. "And here I was thinkin' ye so thoroughly the modern lass, runnin' away from ye home and ye family."

Libby chuckled at his gentle teasing.

David raced ahead, galloping up the steps of the bandstand in the park. Libby detoured to Baker's to introduce her father to Mrs. Baker, who was resting out front with Teddy at her side and Sugar at their feet. Libby remembered to thank Mrs. Baker for the sandwich she'd sent by Teddy the previous day.

"Come play in my band, Lib!" cried David from the bandstand where he was directing imaginary musicians.

Libby bid the Bakers good-bye and went to join her

brother on the bandstand. She cocked her elbows as if she held a flute in hand, then whistled merrily to the tune of "Yankee Doodle."

"Faster. Louder!" order David, delighted. "Pretend we're marching."

Sugar came across the street to see what all the noise was about, and Thomas followed.

"'Tis music to send chills fairly dancin' doon a fellow's spine!" he exclaimed, clapping and cheering and stamping a foot to the beat.

David bowed low, then clamored off the stage and raced over the grass, Sugar at his heels.

"Bravo!" called Mrs. Baker from her bench across the street.

Libby turned to see she'd been joined by Minor and Captain Boyd. They both wore broad grins. Laughing, Libby dropped an exaggerated curtsy, waved, and turned away to slip her arm through her father's.

Thomas smiled and said as they walked on. "Uncle Willie's friends have taken a shine to ye, have they?"

"It's mutual," said Libby. There was no need for further explanations. Not to her father, who was ever attuned to the goodness in people.

"That's me bonny lass, so like yer mother." His wistful smile faded, a storm of cares reshaping his expression. At length he murmured, "Be verra cautious when the laddies come a-sweetheartin'."

Libby flushed. She had not expected him to come even that close to mentioning the matter between Adam and Abigail.

He looked off toward the west where the fading sky touched the trees and added softly, "Ye wait for a lad wi' the word of God on his heart. Ye shall save yerself a world of trouble."

"I'm all for saving myself trouble," said Libby with enough pluck to coax a smile from him.

"So tell me," said Thomas. "Have ye a better idea of what manner of woman be Mrs. McClure, now that ye've met her?"

She shot him a quick glance. "Ike Galloway told you I went to her home, I suppose."

"Ye suppose wrong, lass. It was none other than Mr. McClure himself. He'd heard of it through the leddy's father, Mr. Caton."

"You went to see Decatur in jail?"

"Aye, my wee walk took me past." He acknowledged her reproachful look with a gentle smile. "Were ye supposin' ye were the only one could go a-callin', lass?"

"What did he have to say for himself?"

"Aboot what?"

"About trying to wrestle away the store with his tale of a deathbed will. And to blacken his wife's name in the telling."

Thomas flung her a sidelong glance and said quietly, "Be wary of settin' yer affection on things o' earth, for the heart is deceitful above all things."

"Father!" she objected. "It is *our* home, *our* business. Surely you don't think we ought to step aside and let Mr. McClure have it under the guise of claiming it for Frankie? If we were to do so, he'd find his dishonesty a rewarding business, now wouldn't he?"

"He's a dandy-doodle of a fellow, Mr. McClure," mused Thomas. "I'm thinkin' he's his own worst enemy when it comes to soul mendin'."

Torn between impatience with his consideration of Mr. McClure and respect for his unflagging concern for the souls of others, Libby tipped her chin. "I wouldn't expect much from Mr. McClure. Not in the way of repentance, if that's how you're thinking."

"What is to be gained by expectin' too little?"

Libby gave him a pointed glance and tried a new tack. "Did you have a pleasant visit?"

"He has a scaldin' tongue, Mr. McClure. And a fiery-guid temper." Her father gazed at her with a sparkle in his eye and added, "Not unlike me rosy-faced daughter."

Libby knew better than to hope Mr. McClure's personality blemishes would discourage her father from visiting again. In the days that followed, he made frequent treks to the jail. His visits were a great curiosity to Hascal Caton and the rest of the gents who left their assemblage of chairs and crates and kegs and gathered on the bench out front when the conversation veered in that direction. It was in their nature to be cautious of her father's motives. Libby knew that. Knew, too, that it was too soon to worry that they didn't like him.

Anyway, hadn't she better things to concern herself with than the opinions of the local bench brigade? Business was good, the mail steady, and with a home to make livable and a family to care for, she hadn't a second to pen a line in her journal, much less untangle the conjectures of Edgewood's old gents.

With her father's help minding the store, Libby made steady progress cleaning both upstairs and down. Though Billy was unsuccessful at finding the movable screens Libby had hoped to use as room dividers, he graciously offered to try his hand at building them. Her father helped, and together they kept the freestanding screens inexpensive as well as fairly light in weight by constructing them in eight-foot lengths of chicken wire framed in used lumber.

Libby painted one set of screens white. Leaving a space between the identical screens to be used as a doorway, she marked off the end of the room to serve as her kitchen. She positioned a handsome drop-leaf oak table and chairs in front of one screen. A baker's cabinet dominated the other. The cooking stove was against the brick wall overlooking the alley. Libby arranged two spare chairs and a dry sink on either side of the stove, giving the room a needed symmetry. A lantern, some candles, her teapot, and some dishes from home lent a nice touch.

But it wasn't until Catherine came that the room took on a real charm. She brought braided rugs for the floor, and sheer, lacy curtains for the screen that backdropped the kitchen table, then helped Libby arrange dried flowers and grasses in a battered wooden toolbox. They placed it on a low table on the side of the screen facing the parlor and tied the sheer curtains back so that the curtains framed the screen in graceful swags. When one was seated at the table, the arrangement gave the effect of looking out small, octagonal panes of glass into a window box of flowers.

So pleased was Libby with the result that she begged Catherine to return the following day and help with her room. Catherine agreed readily, and came armed with more ideas. At her suggestion, they picked through the wallpaper downstairs and, having settled upon a pastel floral print, covered both sides of the chicken wire in it. It lent the privacy of walls, even though there was no door, and the screens missed meeting the ceiling by at least four feet. It was too flimsy a structure to hang pictures from, but sufficient for hanging hats and scarves and a couple of delicate fans. A few perfume bottles, pompadour combs, and a satin-lined glove box, mixed in with Libby's tablets, pencils, and tiny personal library, lent the room femininity with a faintly bookish flavor. Libby spread her quilt on her narrow bed and felt instantly at home in the room.

On Friday Captain Boyd arrived at work right on time. "Good morning, Miss Willie. Mrs. Payne, Thomas," he added, nodding his silver head to each in turn.

"Guid mornin' to you, Benjamin," said Thomas.

"What's so good about it?" muttered Zerilda, her face a globe of glowering ill humor.

"The sun is shining and the birds are singing and it's a great day in a great country," the captain replied, and promptly began to hum "My Country, 'Tis of Thee."

"Best tone it down and get to sortin'," growled Zerilda with a black glance.

"Don't be a sourpuss, Miss Payne. Nothing like a dose of music to cheer your soul." Captain Boyd winked at Libby and sang in a full-throttle bass voice, "'Our Fathers' God to thee, Arthur of liberty, to Thee we sing! Long may our lambs be bright, with freedom's holy light.' Isn't that right, Miss Willy? Join in! Sing along!"

Giggling, Libby joined him in the last line, singing, "'Protect us by Thy might, Great God our King.'"

"There, there, lass," said Thomas with a faint frown that caused Libby's heart to drop, for she saw on closer scrutiny the sprig of mint caught in the captain's button-hole. His nose was red, his cheeks afire, and his diction, as he sang on without her, was not as clear as it might have been. Good faith! It wasn't natural good humor, he was all but giddy! A wave of heat swept up Libby's high collar.

Seeming unaware that even the innocent among them was wise to his condition, Captain Boyd continued in the same verbose, good-natured manner as he sorted his mail.

Zerilda could not get away fast enough. But Thomas responded quietly to Captain's Boyd lively conversation, and with a look of concern on his lined face, disappeared altogether shortly after the old gentleman had pulled away in his red mail cart.

It seemed unnaturally silent in the store of a sudden. Libby was glad when David came downstairs with a storybook and asked her to read with him. She helped him sound out words until he tired of it and begged for permission to "decorate" the screens enclosing his room. At Libby's hesitant agreement, he helped himself to brown paper off the spindle and climbed the stairs again.

Libby caught up on her work and ventured out to sweep the front walk a short while later. Hascal Caton and his henchmen tucked their feet back and assumed such an air of inscrutability, she supposed they were again diagnosing her father's daily visits to the jail. She finished the chore and walked back inside, only to turn at the window and find them all peering in the general direction of the Columbian. Fingers prodded air. Heads bobbed like ducks on a pond.

"Saw him at the wagon dump."

Startled, Libby swung around to find Teddy had slipped in. "Saw who?"

Teddy's lips flattened out. He jerked his head toward the back of the store. "You know."

"No, Teddy. I don't."

He gave the handle on the coffee grinder a spin and walked out.

Dry-mouthed, pulse pounding, Libby called to David from the foot of the stairs. "I'm going out. Come watch for customers."

"What's wrong?" he asked, hands behind his back as he followed Sugar down the stairs.

"Nothing for you to worry about." Libby flung her apron behind the counter and grabbed her straw hat. "If anyone comes, tell them I'll be right back."

She stepped out the door, trying to reason away a gnawing anxiety for her father. *Wagon dump?* Though Teddy hadn't said where it was, or even what it was, an educated guess would indicate the grain elevator where the farmers dumped their wagonloads of grain.

Hascal Caton and the other gentlemen, gazing eastward where the train tracks cut the town in half, strengthened Libby's confidence that she was headed in the right direction. Waiting at the corner for a horseman to pass, she looked back to find the men stretched so far forward on the rickety bench, it was a wonder it didn't flip them onto the wooden walk. No one called to her. Not a word, reminding her afresh that in their eyes, she was as much an outsider as her father was. Growing apprehension drove her on. She swept past the Columbian and crossed the street where she caught a glimpse of red in the openended wooden structure that leaned against the grain elevator. Her hurried steps slowed as the glimpse of red materialized into Captain Boyd's mail wagon. Why wasn't he on his route?

Down the block, they were still watching. Their interest could not have been more intense had the big top rolled into town. It wasn't Father garnering their interest after all, rather protective instincts for Captain Boyd. A great dread dragged at Libby's feet, but she dared not retreat. Not now.

Eyes hot, throat burning, Libby squared her shoulders and started along the wagon path that shot straight through the structure. Sunshine poured in both ends, but could not dispel the gloom of a steeply pitched roof and a tall thick wall of heavy lumber holding back the grain inside the elevator. She jerked as a bird swooped down from above. It passed so close, the beat of its wings flapped like a sheet in the wind.

"What brings ye here, Elizabeth?"

Libby's heart bumped as Father separated like a shadow from Captain Boyd's red cart. "Are you all right?" she asked.

"Aye, lass."

"And Captain Boyd?"

"There's the sting of it." He drew a deep breath. "Ye take yerself off to the store now. 'Tis no place for a leddy."

Her stomach aflutter, Libby obeyed. Unwilling to face the questioning eyes of Captain Boyd's compatriots, she circled around the block, intending to turn up the alley and in the back door. Self-recrimination dogged her steps. It was not right that her lack of action should shift the burden onto her father's shoulders. She could have stood her ground, accepted the mantle of responsibility that came with the job.

"Miss Watson!"

Libby stopped short, narrowly avoiding a collision with Angus. Had she been watching where she was going instead of racing along trying to outdistance guilty thoughts, she would have seen him exit his law office. "I'm sorry! I was wool-gathering."

He leaned on one crutch and swept off his hat, his hair neatly parted. "And not sparing the horses, either." He smiled and offered with a sweep of his hand, "If a lift would help matters . . ."

"I'm almost there, thank you."

"The store, then?"

She nodded. "I've left my little brother in charge."

"Catherine said your family had joined you."

"Yes, last week." Libby had come three quarters of the way from her starting point. A half block down the alley and she'd be home. She peered down the street toward the elevator. Captain Boyd's mail cart rolled out of the grain dump, his horse plodding along.

Angus straightened his spectacles and followed her gaze. "Who's that at the lines?"

A tremor went through Libby. "Father."

"Captain Boyd under the weather, is he?"

"Good faith," breathed Libby, for Minor and Captain Boyd were emerging from the grain dump on foot. Captain Boyd stumbled and would have gone to his knees, but for Minor. Catherine's laughing words of weeks ago leapt to mind. There was no doubt who was holding up whom today. Heartsick, she averted her face and blurted, "I've made such a mess of things."

Angus shifted onto both crutches and with one fluid shift of his body, was on the wooden walk beside her. "How do you mean?"

"I'm sorry, I've got to get back." Libby stepped off onto the grass, cut across the corner of his office lot, and into the alley.

Angus caught up with her just as she reached the back door of the store. "I'm not sure what the problem is, but I wish you'd let me help."

The genuine concern in his hazel eyes was nearly her undoing. Libby spilled the better part of the matter in the time it took David to respond to her knocking.

"Captain Boyd's drinking? That's what's troubling you?" Angus looked genuinely puzzled.

"A letter to the authorities was no idle threat on Mrs. Dorrance's part. If she follows through, Captain Boyd's certain to be fired." Libby halted her flow of words. David was having trouble releasing the bolt on the other side of the door. "Lift it up and then slide it, that's it, Davie."

The door swung open. David stood with his hands behind his back. His dark eyes flicked from Libby to Angus. He called to Sugar and would have walked on, but Libby delayed him for an introduction.

"Hello, young fellow." Angus reached to shake hands.

Reluctantly David brought a small, paint-smeared hand from behind his back.

"You said I could decorate," he reminded Libby, as if nervous of a scolding.

"What have you done?" she asked.

"I painted brown paper to hang on my screens."

"With your hands?" cried Libby.

David shrugged and dropped his gaze to his toes, murmuring, "I didn't want to pester you for a brush."

"Next time, pester me." Libby reached for his hands, adding, "It isn't going to wash off very easily."

"I know. I tried," he said glumly.

Angus chuckled and clapped David on the shoulder. "Now, now. No need to despair. Take a tin can over to Woodmancy's Livery and ask him for a little of that fuel

he keeps on hand for the automobiles coming through on
their way to the St. Louis fair. It'll take paint right off."

David's face brightened. He accepted the coin Angus
gave him and dashed away, calling back, "Thanks,
mister."

Sugar barked and raced to catch up.

"Thank you, Mr. Cearlock," said Libby, momentarily
distracted from the problem of Captain Boyd. "Come
inside and I'll repay you the coin."

Angus swung in after Libby and leaned his crutches
against the counter. He waved aside the coin she tried to
repay him and said, "Concerning Captain Boyd, he's
been drinking Old Kentucky moonshine for as long as I
can recall. No rational person could expect him to change
at the mere threat of a letter."

"I'm not sure Mrs. Dorrance *is* rational."

A smile tipped his mouth. "Then why are we talking
about her? I've a better idea. Let's talk about the Republican Club's Fourth of July rally out at the lake next week.
Chester invited Governor Yates to speak. His secretary
sent a telegram of acceptance today."

"Mmm."

"The *governor*, Miss Watson."

Amending her lackluster response, she asked, "And
you'll be meeting him, will you?"

"If Chester has his way, I'll not only meet him, I'll be
introducing him."

"That's wonderful." She struggled for the anticipated
enthusiasm. "I'm happy for you, Mr. Cearlock."

"Then make me happy, too, and say you'll come with
me. There will be a barbecue and speeches and music,
then back to town for a torchlight parade and fireworks."
He dropped his voice and added, "You *did* say you'd
forgive me eventually."

"For what?"

Misunderstanding, he beamed. "Ah! Forgiven *and* forgotten."

"Oh, that," said Libby, a beat behind him. She flushed,
reminded of how impatient she'd felt over Angus's
guardian eye, and how he'd distanced himself after she'd
taken him to task for it. He had her full attention now.

"At least consider it. Please, Elizabeth?" he urged.

Though it was rather forward of him, Libby liked the sound of her given name on his tongue. She looked at him for a long moment, trying to recall her reasons for thinking it best to keep their friendship purely on a business level until the whole matter of Uncle Willie's bequest was settled. It was like peering at a cloudless sky—nothing at all to throw up a red flag. Sunshine and heart-glow—he promised it all with a curve of his mouth and a sweep of lashes behind those glasses lenses that gave him such a distinguished air.

"All right, then," she said finally. "I'd be delighted to go."

He flashed a lovely white smile and declared, "Wonderful! And don't you waste another minute worrying about Captain Boyd. He's a tough old soldier. He'll land on his feet, you'll see."

Thinking it sweet of him to try and buoy her spirits, Libby reached for his hand and gave it an impulsive squeeze. "Thank you, Mr. Cearlock. You're a good friend."

His eyes darkened. Before releasing her hand, he brought it to his lips in a courtly gesture that sent a tremor of liquid heat rushing through Libby's body. Even when he had gone, the memory of it wrapped Libby in a haze so mellow, she climbed the stairs and faced with a reluctant smile the screens enclosing David's appointed space.

Patches of brown paper hung at odd angles, not on the inside, but the outside of the screens, which were, in effect, parlor walls. He had decorated the odd-lengthed strips in white handprints from which streaks dribbled like trailing tears. Painstakingly finger-painted over and again were the simple words *DaVIdS rOm*.

Libby covered her face, then looked again, her own dreams for the parlor taking flight as she resolved that David's artwork should stay until he himself tired of it. It was, after all, his home too.

22

Libby's father delivered the mail that day, only a small departure from the regular rhythm of things, yet it threw a cog into the mechanics of Edgewood. For though they did not realize it until the harm was done, word went out that Thomas Watson had fired Captain Boyd. And he, a Civil War veteran, was every bit as revered as Mr. Culbertson.

The rumor caught a strong draft among the town residents. Libby's efforts to dispel it were as useless as one tired rug beater battling a prairie fire. Captain Boyd had not come to work in three days, which threw weight behind the rumble. Nor was Libby's father, who was daily handling the old veteran's route, shedding any public light on the matter.

"What would ye have me do? Stand on the street corner declarin' me innocence of such a deed? Nay, lass. 'Tis always best to be a God-pleaser, for man-pleasin' is a fickle affair."

"I can't think anyone's pleased," muttered Libby, as her father rolled the buggy into the shed across the alley.

Though the rumor didn't seem to affect business at the store, Libby's feelings were tender toward the cool nods and behind-the-hands whispering going on amongst her town customers. The attitude of the old-timers had cooled too. Libby felt the frost in their glances as they came in for their mail, and went out again, their voices as

220

whispery as fans in church. Their kegs and crates and chairs sat vacant about the stove as they convened on her laundry bench, which someone had dragged around to the front.

Loath to admit she missed their gravelly voices and thumping feet, Libby held her hurt inside and kept herself busy clerking and cleaning and cooking and washing and putting the finishing touches on the parlor and her father's room upstairs.

There were exceptions, of course, to the cold shoulder they were receiving. The rural folks, less concerned with town gossip, were cordial. A few on Captain Boyd's route commented upon the improved service, which only deepened Libby's concern over the captain's uncertain future. Mrs. Baker was a faithful heart, a born encourager, unchanged toward them. As was Mrs. Brignadello, though she was preoccupied of late. Catherine, too, was unswervingly loyal. As was Angus, who not only kept Libby posted on the upcoming rally, but delivered payment the very hour Billy loaded into his dray wagon for delivery the mountain of supplies the Republican Club had ordered for the picnic.

Libby's father, however, was amazingly chipper, and busy with plans to keep the store open for Independence Day. What with the slated ball games, band concert, ice cream social, and other festivities taking place across the street in the park, he felt business would warrant it.

"I'm glad I'm going out to the lake for the holiday. I've had about enough of half the town treating me like old Scrooge in Dickens's story," said Libby at the end of a long day.

"Lass, ye're takin' this too much to heart," soothed Father. " 'Trust in the Lord and lean not unto thine own understanding.' " With that, he went downstairs to join David in a game of horseshoes in the back alley.

Later, tired of her own company, Libby went outside looking for David. He was standing in front of the newspaper office next door, sounding out the words lettered in gold leaf on the glass.

"The Ga-ga-gaz-gaz-ut. The Gazutte! Look, Libby! I'm reading," he cried.

Spirits lifting, Libby placed her fingers over David's and helped him trace the last four letters. "Sound out the end again."

"You mean 'ut.'"

"No, not 'ut.' Look at the letters. Try it again."

"Et? Et!" he said with growing confidence. "Gazette!"

Sharing his delight, Libby laughed just as Mr. Gruben came strolling out the door.

"I'm learning to read," David announced.

The editor chuckled. "That's good. I'd go out of business without readers."

Mr. Gruben tipped his hat to Libby, smiled again, and went on his way. Libby's admiring gaze followed him. Someday, when she got her courage up, she was going to ask him just how one went about becoming a writer.

"Come on! Let's read some more windows," said David, tugging at her hand.

"Just one or two more, then I've got to do some ironing," agreed Libby.

A while later, in a much better mood for her time playing with David, Libby dampened her finger to test the iron before putting it to tomorrow's dress. Fashioned of primrose faille, it was her very best frock, and the only one she deemed suitable for the girl on the arm of the legislative candidate who was to introduce the governor of the State of Illinois.

Mr. Gentry had worked tirelessly toward making a success of the Republican Club's rally. He had an army of volunteers and the ear of the newspapermen in their region. Beef was roasting in a pit, to be barbecued and served on buns with beans and new potatoes. That much free food was bound to draw a good crowd. So much so, some were concerned the town's traditional Fourth celebration would suffer for it.

It was anticipated that the crowd would come from forty and fifty, even a hundred miles away, with the C & A providing special service. Angus had purchased tickets for the ten-o'clock train, which would put them on the grounds in time for the ten-thirty exercises. Politics was a man's world. Libby had little interest in it. But a carefree day in the company of Angus Cearlock—now, that piqued her interest!

The Fourth dawned clear and bright. She fixed an early breakfast for Father and David, then had a proper bath. The effort was considerable, for the water had to be pumped out back, hauled up by a pulley Uncle Willie had rigged, and heated on the cookstove. Employing comb and pins, she swept her hair up off her shoulders in a fashionable pompadour, then donned her dress, made from a Butterick pattern. The untwilled silk was skillfully gathered, tucked, and pleated to complement her soft curves. The cinched waist came to a V in front and fell in rich folds to her high-button shoes. Libby poked fan and gloves into her reticule, reached for her parasol, and with hat in hand, descended the stairs.

The front and back doors were propped open to a small breeze. Across the street at the park, the peanut wagon was already at the curb. Ball teams and spectators were gathering in the grass for the morning game. Her father and David were out on the front walk breaking ice into a tub in hopes of wooing soda pop customers.

Libby headed for the full-length mirror in the ladies' corner of the store and donned the two-toned picture hat she'd bought from Mrs. Brignadello. She hummed as she pinned the hat in place, tugged on her gloves, then struck a pose with her parasol, gracefully arched foot, and pointed toe.

The girl in the mirror batted her lashes and declared with a coquettish glance, "Why, Mr. Cearlock, what a gifted introduction!" She held the hand mirror from the nearby dressing table over her shoulder and pivoted for the back view. "I declare, I don't know when I've had such a fine time."

The sound of a boot scuffing over the threshold drew her eyes from the hand mirror. Ike Galloway stood in a shaft of sunlight, mended chair in hand.

"Good faith!" she exclaimed, heat rushing to her face. "Why do you do that?"

A smile hovered beneath his hooded lids as he swept off his billed cap to reveal a tumble of loose curls. "Do what?"

"Sneak up on people."

"Wasn't aware that I did," he said with just enough innocence to keep her guessing as to whether or not he'd overheard her preening. The chair grated across the wooden floor as he nudged it forward with sunbrowned hands. "Here's your chair, good as new."

"So I see. Thank you, Mr. Galloway."

"You like baseball?"

"Baseball?" echoed Libby, her thoughts so far-flung, she was slow to notice the ball glove tucked beneath his arm. She slid one mirror onto the dressing table and edged away from the other. "As well as any sport, I suppose. What position do you play?"

"Wherever I can do the least damage."

"That isn't a very high recommendation, Mr. Galloway."

His mouth tilted. "It's the 'fats' playin' the 'leans'—two good legs and a ball glove will get you in."

"You're not going out to the lake for the Republican barbecue?"

"Somebody gotta stay put to wave the flags and clap at the band. What about you? Got any Republican sympathies?"

"To be honest, Mr. Galloway, I'm content to leave the political haggling to you gentlemen. You seem ever so suited to it."

He chuckled. "If you're going to be around, I'd be pleased if you'd have an ice cream with me. New Hope Church is sellin' it over at Baker's later today."

Having unintentionally misled him, Libby said, "Yes, I know. For their building fund. But I'll be leaving for Spring Lake here shortly."

"Then you *are* going to the rally?"

"Yes."

The tolling of the bell in the park spilled over the stillness that fell between them. Through the window Libby saw a flock of small boys swarming over the bell rope like flies on a strip of gummed paper.

"Game's about to begin." His gray gaze wandered over her face, making her think he had more words on his mind. If he did, they stayed there. He turned his cap in his hands, stirred to the door, and stood there a moment. The light played on his hair like a painter's brush.

"Good luck!" Libby gave him a verbal nudge out the door. "Thank you again for fixing the chair."

He lifted his hand, then stood to one side, trading nods with Angus, who was coming in on one crutch, his summer-weight suit, starched cuffs and collar, and neatly tied cravat a marked contrast to Galloway's gray shirt and denim trousers.

Angus swept off his straw boater with the red, white, and blue band. "Could I interest you in a soda pop, Miss Watson? There's a young fellow out front told me it goes down well with breakfast."

"Don't be taken in. That soda's not been in the ice long enough to chill the sunshine off the bottle."

He laughed. Libby eyed the buttons on his lapel. One was a picture of Theodore Roosevelt. The other endorsed Yates for another term as governor of Illinois. "And me without so much as a flag pin," Libby said.

"We'll soon remedy that." He reached into his pocket and produced a Roosevelt button. "May I?" He put his crutch aside and leaned closer to pin the button to the high collar of her dress.

Libby lifted her gaze just as he lowered his. The light in his eyes and the breadth of his smile tweaked the nerves in her stomach. She tucked in her chin, face hidden by the down-sloping brim of her hat.

"Done. And without sticking you, too."

Not entirely. Her heart, she felt certain, had been pricked. It pounded at a horrendous speed as he shifted onto his single crutch and offered his free arm for the short walk to the station.

A man-made lake used for fishing and boating in the summer and ice harvesting in the winter, Spring Lake seemed a cool and inviting retreat from the July heat, thought Libby as she watched from the train window. Wagons were parked up and down the dirt road that paralleled the railroad tracks. A second dirt path cut through the field from the west. It was littered with more rigs and bicycles. A throng of people meandered about the hayrack that was to provide a platform for the day's speakers. Felled logs and planks supported by short, cross-cut sections of logs served as seating. There were long tents, too, with tables and benches beneath them.

Nearby, men laboring with shovels had succeeded in removing the dirt from the in-ground barbecue pits where the heat of smoldering coals and hot rocks had served overnight to cook the seasoned beeves. New potatoes boiled in huge open kettles. Beans simmered in big black pots. The tantalizing aroma of brewing coffee wafted on the warm breeze.

A uniformed band struck up "The Star-Spangled Banner" just as Libby climbed down off the train and spread her parasol. Angus swung down beside her and crossed his heart with his hat as the crowd joined voices in the national anthem.

Mr. Gentry stepped up to the rostrum as the last strains faded, and called the rally to order. Angus spotted Catherine holding a place for them, and led the way to a plank seat on the first row. Catherine introduced her husband, Charlie Morefield. A large ruddy-faced man somewhat older than Catherine, Mr. Morefield doffed his hat and flashed a broad smile.

"It's a pleasure to meet you, Miss Watson. I was sorry to learn of your uncle's death. He was a friend and a client. Bought one of the first fire policies I ever sold in Edgewood."

Catherine patted his knee and entreated sweetly, "No sales pitches now, Charlie. Angus is about to take the stage."

"If you get the chance, ask the governor what he plans to do for road funding," suggested Mr. Morefield. "Do you know they have over one hundred and fifty different kinds of motorcars down at the fair? Imagine! Why, it would be just the thing for a traveling man like myself, if it weren't for the mud."

"Charlie, don't you even think about it!" cried Catherine. "The dust and the danger and the awful racket—

why, you could hear the wretched things all over the fairgrounds."

"I've seen several come through town." Angus's voice matched Mr. Morefield's for enthusiasm.

"Dreadful, aren't they?" inserted Catherine with a warning gleam in her eye.

"Actually, I find them rather—"

"Dreadful," Catherine prompted, an elbow in her brother's ribs. "Tell him, Angus. Tell him how dreadful they are."

Angus lifted his hand as if to ward off a blow, and said with a wink, "I never disagree with a lady. Particularly when she's brandishing a parasol."

Mr. Morefield laughed. "Next time you're in St. Louis, we'll stroll through the transportation exhibit together, shall we?"

Catherine made a face at them both, then flung a hand in the air. "There's Aunt Sarah Jane and Uncle Kersey. Uncle Melville and Aunt Paulette, too. The whole family has turned out to hear your introduction, Angus."

En route to joining them, Sarah Jane Brignadello spotted Libby's hat. All at once she tugged at her husband's arm and turned so sharply, she nearly bumped heads with the doctor's fashionably attired wife.

"Well, did you ever!" exclaimed Catherine, her face falling. "Now, why would Aunt Sarah Jane come to the rally, then make a point of avoiding us?"

Instinctively Libby knew it was not Catherine Mrs. Bee was avoiding. Wishing to dispel the hurt in Catherine's eyes, she confided in low tones how she'd bought her hat from Mrs. Brignadello, and that perhaps her husband was unaware of the sale.

Incredulous, Catherine exclaimed, "First vegetables, now hats. What has gotten into her?"

If Libby's inkling was correct, Mrs. Bee wouldn't thank her for making the matter plain to Catherine. Fortunately, conjecture on Catherine's part was cut short as Dr. and Mrs. Harding joined them. She was a slim, statuesque woman with a milk white complexion, hair like spun gold, and a faintly aloof manner as introductions were made. A fixed smile in place, she let her gaze roam over the crowd up until the moment Angus mounted the bunting-draped platform to introduce Governor Yates.

Libby promptly forgot all about the doctor's elegant wife, for what an introduction it was! Far more deserving than the giggling homage Libby had paid it in front of the mirror a while ago, his words were met with a storm of cheers from the crowd. Pride swelled within Libby's bosom as Angus shook Governor Yates's hand, then came down off the stage, the applause still ringing.

In those few moments upon the stage, there was about him such ardor, such conviction. And how effectively those spirited words fueled the crowd's enthusiasm!

He spoke of it much later. After the departure of Governor Yates. After the meal, eaten in the company of his family. After more music and more speeches and the awarding of a silk flag to the largest delegation from around the state. After Catherine and her husband had started back to town in their surrey. He stood by Libby's side at the edge of the lake and responded to her compliments with a quiet "I have Chester to thank. Catherine and I have a little fun at his expense now and then, but he's been a good stepfather to me. He's always shared his vision for this country."

"It was he who urged you to run?"

Angus nodded. He picked the petals from a prairie flower and cast them one by one into the water. "Chester taught me that privilege and duty go hand in hand. And that a country is only as strong as its leadership. I want to be a part of the shaping."

His visage shone with ambition, energy, and zeal. For the first time in Libby's life, politics was more than a word. It was a presence. It had a shape and a feel, and could so easily overpower the tender feelings growing between them. Yet there was strength in his smile, as if he sensed her faltering confidence and wished to reassure her that one spark need not diminish another.

He slung his crutch into position and offered her his free arm. "We'd better start back if we're going to catch the train in time for the parade and the fireworks."

As they turned, Libby was aware of men drifting into

the shadows. Angus's gaze flicked toward the trees, too, and back again. "Though it may not be much of a parade, if somebody doesn't dissaude the band from guzzling moonshine."

Libby hazarded a second glance toward the trees where the men had disappeared. "Where are they getting it?"

"That's one of Old Kentucky's better-kept secrets. Poor Chester," lamented Angus. "He will kick himself for not having taken measures to prevent such a turn. He can't abide anything that reflects poorly on the Club. Ah well, it's about what you can expect out here in the woods."

Regretting the intrusion on an otherwise perfect day, Libby murmured, "But what better setting for the day's events? It's beautiful out here." An eye to the waning rays that glazed the trees in luxuriant rose-tinted gold, she added, "No wonder Mr. Galloway speaks so fondly of the place."

Angus nudged his glasses up the bridge of his nose. A frown creased his brows. "I'm puzzled by your continued association with that fellow."

"Mr. Galloway? It was you who recommended I hire him when I needed someone to run the store," Libby reminded him.

"A mistake, I'm afraid. He hasn't proved to be much of a friend."

Libby dropped her hand from his arm. "How is that, Mr. Cearlock?"

"Common decency would dictate he should come forward."

"Come forward?"

"But then, what has he to gain? He's already been granted his heart's wish."

"Heart's wish? I'm sorry, you'll have to speak more plainly."

"The syrup camp." When she ignored his proffered arm, Angus thrust his hand into his pocket and apologized, saying, "I didn't mean to get into this. It's neither the time nor the place."

"Nevertheless, you've piqued my interest." Libby refused to dismiss it. "You aren't under the impression, are you, that I covet his trees for myself? Because if you are, you can dismiss that idea. I think Uncle Willie chose wisely in passing the camp on to someone who knows what to do with it."

"You knew Mr. Blue had given Galloway the camp?"

"Yes. Mr. Galloway told me."

"And did he also tell you he was at your uncle's bedside when he died?"

Libby's steps suddenly stalled. She lifted her face.

Angus nodded in response to her unvoiced surprise. "I went to see Mrs. McClure. She told me Ike was there when Mr. Blue died."

"Naomi told you this? But she didn't tell me . . ." Libby trailed off, realizing suddenly she hadn't told Angus of having visited Naomi McClure. Knowing instinctively this wasn't the time, she amended, "Why would Mr. Galloway keep his presence there a secret?"

"His reasoning is of no importance," Angus said crisply. "The point is, he was there."

Stunned, Libby said, "Then it's no longer a matter of speculation. Ike *knows* whether or not Uncle Willie changed his will."

"Precisely."

"What did Mrs. McClure have to say about it?"

"She claims to know nothing about the will. She'd gone for the doctor, you'll remember, when Mr. Blue passed away." Angus crushed a seeded dandelion beneath his cane, adding, "If Decatur presses his suit, I'll call Galloway to testify."

It struck Libby that he was awfully certain that the will Decatur's attorney had submitted was fraudulent. Confident, too, that Ike would cooperate. Victory seemed in easy reach. The rush of relief that came over her was tainted by a surge of hurt and anger toward Ike. Why hadn't he told her?

As if from a great distance, she heard Angus say, "I'm sorry, Elizabeth. I intended to save this business until tomorrow. But I've come to care about you, and it's all I can do to hold on to my temper when I see you abused in this way."

Abused? The word, oddly enough, seemed to fit her

emotions. Galloway had had countless opportunities. Why *hadn't* he spoken up?

Libby continued to nurse her disillusionment with Ike as they boarded the train and rode back to town. The more she mulled, the greater her indignation became. What sort of friend was he, anyway? Think of it! Uncle Willie, who could scarcely help himself, had helped Ike's family when a blood relative would not. He'd deeded his syrup camp over to Ike. And silence was how Ike repaid him?

23

Some people within the membership of the Republican Club had returned to Edgewood earlier. They were waiting with political buttons, campaign literature, and other free memorabilia to be passed out as the parade made its way around the town square. The men were given torches made of sticks with bottles of kerosene attached.

Angus planned to pass out penny postcards emblazoned with his slogan, *Lock in a Vote for Cearlock.* But when Catherine's husband, Charlie, came along with two lighted torches, it became apparent he couldn't manage the crutch, the torch, and cards all three.

"You don't have enough hands, Angus," said Catherine. "Here, give me the cards. I'll walk along with you and pass them out."

"Don't let Mama catch you at it, or she'll tangle you in your tatting," Angus warned with a grin.

"I'll worry about Mama. Just you take care you don't confuse *torch* and *crutch* and catch yourself on fire. Would you like to help?" Catherine offered Libby half the pile.

Caught up in the excitement, Libby took the cards. She tipped her chin and returned Catherine's audacious smile as the band struck up "America, the Beautiful." A rousing cheer lifted from the marchers. The parade started down the street and over the railroad crossing. Libby and Catherine were swept along in the tide. The deep rumble of men's voices lifted in song, the beat of tramping feet, the glare of torchlight, stirred an answering fervor in the spectators.

Catherine tugged Libby toward the spectators along the walks. The flickering torches lighted the path for the marchers, but the crowds stood in deep shadow. They passed them in a blur, disembodied hands reaching for the cards. Copying Catherine's example, Libby moved briskly along, fitting postcards to hands. She gave out her last one just as she reached the store.

Libby's father and David were on the walk, eyes on the band. She penetrated the line of spectators and slipped up behind them. David spotted her first and broke into a gap toothed grin. She draped an arm over his shoulder and leaned close to be heard above the noise of the parade.

"How are soda sales?"

"All gone!" he cried.

"You're sold out?"

"Thanks to the heap o' lads and lasses pourin' in from the lake picnic!" Father beamed. "Those who didn't wait for connections hiked over from the station and built up a wallopin' guid thirst. Isna God a wonder, tuggin' the ears of the cooks and whisperin' to them to play a bit loose with the salt?"

"Shame on me for doubting you," said Libby, smiling.

"And the ladies wi' ice cream to sell? Sich a business they be doin'." Father rose on tiptoe and peered across the park. "Ech! The crowds be descendin' upon us again, and naebody wi' enough hands. Willna ye help 'em, lass?"

At the same moment Angus was beckoning to her from the street. When she failed to heed him, he passed off his torch to a neighbor and picked his way through the shoulder-to-shoulder crowd lined up in front of the store. "I thought we'd lost you."

"The ladies over at Baker's need a hand with the ice cream. You don't mind, do you?"

"No, of course not. I'll come back after the parade and escort you to the fireworks."

The parade, Libby knew, ended with fireworks at the edge of town. She couldn't ask him to trek back across town for her. Not when he'd been on his injured foot all day. "Oh no, there's no need for all that walking. I don't know how long I'll be. If I can get away, I'll come down with Father and David."

Angus opened his mouth as if to remonstrate, but Catherine and Charlie were calling to him from the street. As his glance traveled to them and back again, his expression reminded her of David, torn between choices.

"Go on!" urged Libby. She smiled and waved as he disappeared into the marchers.

"Seems you've caught the habit of quittin' parades sudden-like."

Libby turned as Ike Galloway materialized out of the shadow of a single porch column. Smiling, he held one of the postcards in hand. Thoughts leaping to his betrayal by silence, she guarded herself against her anger and said with an elevated chin, "If you're talking to me, Mr. Galloway, you needn't bother."

She retreated into the store without a second glance. Leaving her hat, her gloves, and her reticule behind the counter, Libby tied on an apron and retraced her steps to the front walk to find that Ike had gone. She touched Father's arm.

"I'll be at Mrs. Baker's."

"Aye, lass. But before you go shinin' yerself for your guid deed, I canna help but caution ye to be a wee softer wi' Mr. Galloway."

Him, with his tender heart, taking Galloway's part! Libby turned away, all but choking on rising rebellion. She cut through the park and arrived at Baker's just as the parade came around.

Dorene Berry and several other ladies were on the walk, scooping the frozen treat into restaurant dishes, handing out spoons, taking money, making change. Teddy stood nearby, one arm hooked behind his back, watching the line of waiting customers lengthen.

"She's inside," he said, before Libby could ask.

Mrs. Baker was at the sink.

"Where do you need me, Mrs. Baker?"

"It's a race to keep clean dishes. If you don't mind relieving me a minute, I'll help Mother into bed."

"Of course."

Gram Steadman sat in her rocking chair, lost in her voluminous skirts and lacy shawl. Nudging her awake, Mrs. Baker guided the old woman to the doorway, then called back, "You'll have some help drying, as soon as Ike finds the linen."

"Ike Galloway?" Libby swung around.

"He stepped in just a moment ago and offered to help. He's gone upstairs after dry toweling."

Libby bit back a protest. She turned up her sleeves and was elbow-deep in dishes when Ike came along, the grass stains on his torn trouser knee reminding her of his baseball game. He hooked his dusty cap over a chair spindle and washed his hands in a granite basin. "How was the picnic?"

Good faith, didn't he know when he'd been snubbed? Libbby spared him a haughty glance. "It was an informative afternoon. And I'm not referring to the speakers."

"Oh?"

"How is it, Mr. Galloway, that you've never mentioned having been at Uncle Willie's side when he died?"

"So *that's* it." A twinge of remorse flickered in his gray gaze. "I reckon I shoulda told you sooner."

"You didn't tell me at all. Mr. Cearlock told me."

"You got a right to fuss, I guess."

"Don't wear yourself out apologizing. All I want to know is, did Uncle Willie change his will on his deathbed or did he not?"

"No, that's jest somethin' Hascal cooked up."

"Then why have you stood by and let the matter go this far?"

He reached for another dish to dry. "It'd be best if Decatur spoke up himself and said it wasn't true. Better for *him*, anyway," he amended. "It's Hascal's doings in part. He's worked on Decatur, telling him he's got the boy half-raised, that he deserves a little somethin' for his trouble."

Libby's heart thudded like a brick hitting the dirt. "Frankie *is* Uncle Willie's son, then?"

"Yes." The cold blue light directly overhead illuminated Ike's sunburned nose and pewter gaze as he returned her scrutiny with no explanation as to why he'd kept that information from her, too.

"And you've known all along, have you?"

"No. Decatur didn't know it either. Not until Willie lay dyin'. Willie always did have a way with children, even the rascally ones. But there was something special that night, something between Frankie and Willie."

"So he claimed him? With Mr. McClure standing right there?"

"Willie wasn't thinkin' about claimin' or not claiming. Not in so many words, anyway."

"Then what *was* he thinking?"

"Mostly he was just thinking about living. That's what dying men do."

There was a starkness to his words that bespoke experience. Libby's gaze strayed to his tattered ear. Her eyes slid away. "So what is it you expect of me, Mr. Galloway? If I were to hand him the store, would that satisfy you?"

"Frankie's too young and Decatur ain't suited to it," he said, overlooking her stinging tone and taking a literal view. "Can't say any good would come of it fallin' to Hascal's management, which is what the old coot is wantin'."

"Then what is it you expect of me?" she asked again.

"Don't have a right to expect anything. Been thinkin', though, that as long as I keep quiet, it gives Decatur time."

"Time for what?"

"To own up to the truth. Don't do the soul much good to confess, unless it pours out of a changed heart."

"You think Mr. McClure can change?" Libby couldn't contain her astonishment. "That's why you've kept quiet?"

"Ain't nothin' too big for God."

If that wasn't an odd piece of reasoning! Holding her temper, Libby retorted, "Of course He can change him. God can change anyone. But He won't force him against his will."

Ike reached for another dish, but offered no comment.

"Frankly, I don't understand your abiding interest in Mr. McClure's welfare." She tried once more to fathom his long silence.

"We're neighbors," he said simply.

"And who is my neighbor?" The remembered verse from the story of the Good Samaritan, and Christ's response, gave Libby pause. But Mr. McClure wasn't an unfortunate traveler, fallen among thieves. He was a thief himself. Or trying to be. Resenting the need to defend herself, Libby gave one spoon after another a vigorous scrubbing. "Without the store, we have no home, Mr. Galloway. My wages as a postal clerk won't go very far, and Father isn't well. Should he return to the mines, we'll soon be burying him, the doctor said as much." She flung him a sidelong glance and added, "I'm not wanting sympathy. I'm only telling you because your protective manner toward Mr. McClure and his family makes me feel as if you think I'm out to take something that doesn't belong to me."

Ike opened his mouth in protest, but she talked right over him, saying, "No, I'll have my say and be done with it. You speak of God. You should know I prayed for my father's life and He answered over and above what I asked. The store was a gift from Uncle Willie and from God. I won't give it up easily. Not now. Particularly not now."

Even if I ask you to?

It was not Mr. Galloway, rather a voice that spoke to the soul. It struck like a lightning bolt. Libby's breath caught in her throat. Her anger wilted, her spirit crying, *Oh God, you wouldn't ask that of me, would you?*

Tears prickling behind hot eyelids, she escaped with the stack of clean dishes, Ike forgotten. Her footsteps rang hollow through the kitchen and deserted dining room. But once on the walkway, she found that the crowd had vanished. She turned questioning eyes on Dorene Berry.

"We're out of ice cream." The hired girl took the dishes from Libby and carried them back inside.

Libby stole across the town park and over to the store. Her father and David were about to leave for the fireworks display. Declining their invitation to go along, Libby climbed the stairs. The second floor still held the heat of the day. Going to her room, she removed her dress, her corset cover, and her corset, and sat in the dark until the street below had emptied. By and by, she moved to the kitchen and sat at one of the windows overlooking the alley. Through the treetops to the north, she caught the occasional glimpse of colored light bursting upon the sky. Pops and booms and reverberating echoes soon yielded to the thoughts of her troubled heart.

He wouldn't ask her to give up the store, would He? They'd be stranded. No place to live. No prospects in a town where people passed whispering accusations of them treating Captain Boyd unfairly. What possible good could come of such a turn?

Even if I asked you to?

How difficult it was to pray, "Your will be done," with that still, small question echoing in her heart.

David went out on the mail route with Libby's father the next morning. Angus came in for his mail at mid-morning. He told her how much he'd enjoyed her company the previous day, and expressed hope that it was only the first of many such occasions. On the heels of his flattering words, he added that he had bumped into Ike Galloway at the fireworks the previous evening, and taken the opportunity to make it plain he'd be expected to testify at the probate hearing in September.

Libby's breath caught in her throat. "What did he say?"

"That he'd figured as much." Angus drew a hand over his smooth chin and frowned. "Agreed so readily, in fact, I asked him to tell me about that night. He said he'd already told you, and he didn't see much need in repeating himself."

Libby nodded. She tried to put her embarrassment to one side as she relayed the news that according to Ike, Uncle Willie was indeed Frankie's father.

"Nonetheless, Mr. Blue made his wishes clear," Angus said, showing little surprise. Smoothly he added, "His relationship to Frankie is a moot point."

His analytical position came as no surprise to Libby. She found herself envying the simplicity of it.

"Though I would be interested in hearing how Galloway explained why he'd waited so long to tell you," said Angus, his lip curling.

"Something about confession being good for the soul. Decatur's soul, that is." Irritably Libby added, "He wouldn't have told me at all had I not confronted him about being at Uncle Willie's side when he died and asked him point-blank about the alleged change in will."

"And he said?"

"That there was no deathbed will. He assumed that was Hascal Caton's concoction. That Hascal! He's some father, isn't he?" said Libby, sidetracking herself. "Instead of trying to protect his daughter, he jumps at the first opportunity to drag her name through the mud. And for what? Choice pick of the nail kegs at the store? I tell you, if he was my father, I'd have put myself up for adoption years ago!"

"Hascal's one of a kind, that's for sure. And a little shortsighted, too, I'm thinking."

"You mean the toll it's taking on Frankie? Exactly! Judging by the way he's been behaving, I wouldn't be surprised if he isn't emotionally scarred for life!" said Libby heatedly. "Hascal is sadly misguided if he expects the boy to thank him for all this pain."

"Actually, when I said Hascal was shortsighted, I meant concerning the store. Even if he and Decatur could have pulled this off, neither one of them stands to profit from the store. Any profit realized would have been held in trust for Frankie when he came of age. Anyway, Galloway could have it all wrong," Angus pointed out. "Decatur may have cooked up the whole plan by himself."

"Maybe," said Libby. But privately she doubted it. These people were Ike's neighbors. He seemed to know instinctively what made them tick. Thinking back, she added, "Ike never did say exactly how he knew Frankie belonged to Uncle Willie. Just that he hadn't known himself until my uncle lay dying."

"It doesn't matter, really. Galloway's testimony will remove all doubt." An anticipatory smile twitched at Angus's lips. "In fact, a word to Decatur's attorney should facilitate this whole matter. We may not even need Mr. Galloway."

"Decatur will drop his suit?"

"If I were his attorney, I'd strongly advise him to, yes."

"We've won, then?"

"It certainly looks that way." A tiny frown flickered. "Though no one would guess it by looking at you. What's wrong, Elizabeth?"

What could she say? That that still, small voice had spoken, indicating God might ask her to give up the store anyway? Mr. Cearlock would think she'd lost her mind. She averted her gaze. "I'll be glad when the hearing's over and done with, that's all."

He had no time to question her further. A wagon had pulled up out front, a familiar occupant spilling over the side. Chloe Berry burst through the door, her plain features flushed and shiny with the heat. The threshing crew had arrived that morning at Charlie Morefield's aunt Maudie's farm to thresh oats. Mr. Berry tenant-farmed for the elderly Miss Maudie, which meant Mrs. Berry was in charge of the threshing dinner. With no menfolk to spare, Chloe had come to town for tea and ice and a few other neglected necessities.

"If you talk to your mama," Chloe called to Angus as he left by the back door, "be sure and tell her I'll be back out to Erstwood first thing in the morning. If Mother's feeling better, that is."

She pushed a lock of hair beneath her straw hat and added for Libby's benefit, "Mother's got a stomach ailment, and twenty-four men to feed. We've been baking for two days, and up since three, getting ready. Miss Maudie came over wantin' to help. So far she's knocked a chunk out of the kraut crock, spilled the pickles, and caught the cat in the door. Mother's about to fly apart, she's makin' her so nervous. I promised her I wouldn't be long."

Libby was relieved to learn that Chloe wasn't in it alone. Her married sisters had come home to help.

Dorene, who'd been all week at Baker's, was to ride back with her. She came in just as Libby tucked a package of tea into Chloe's basket.

"'Morning, Libby. Did you tell Chloe what a bang-up success the ice cream was?"

Chloe looked up from the short column of numbers Libby was tallying. "Mother was worried, what with the rally out at the lake, whether there'd be a soul left in town."

"I can set her mind at ease, then. Ladies Aid is having a meeting over at Mrs. Shaw's house tomorrow evening. Should know by then how much we made after expenses. You ready to go, Chloe?" asked Dorene.

"Soon as I sign the charge slip."

"You've nothing to trade?" asked Libby.

"No. Mama still owes Mrs. Bee a pound of butter on that crystal vinegar cruet she traded. We used the rest of it getting ready for today's dinner. The eggs, too."

"Vinegar cruet?" echoed Libby.

"Pretty thing," Dorene said. "You probably saw it at the last meeting. Mama nearly knocked it off, sliding her Bible onto Mrs. Bee's lamp table."

"I remember now," said Libby. "She had a lovely collection."

"She didn't say why she was willing to part with it," said Chloe. "But Mother thinks she's got herself in a bind, volunteering to pay for the lodging of whoever wins the trip to the fair."

Bristling, Dorene inserted, "Thanks to her sister for backing her into a corner. Mrs. Gentry ought to be ashamed."

"It wasn't Mrs. Gentry's intention at all!" came Chloe's spirited defense of her employer. "She was appealing to Mrs. Dorrance, not Mrs. Brignadello."

"She had no business appealing to anyone," said Dorene.

"Why not? Mrs. Dorrance owns a dairy. She's got plenty of money."

"Yes, but if it isn't about temperance, it doesn't interest her. Everyone knows that," countered Dorene.

"Bosh! Mrs. Bee tripped over her own pride."

The sisters were still arguing the point as the door closed behind them.

Taking Fels Naphtha soap from the shelf, Libby calculated the weeks remaining until mid-September, the date set for the prize trip. Mrs. Bee was no sluggard. She'd raise the funds. If her hats and crystal held out. But it seemed to Libby there must be a less painful way.

Libby left a sign on the counter, propped the back door open, and went out to the woodshed. Her father had done a bit of trading himself, securing an old rusty two-holed laundry stove and installing it in the woodshed. Libby stacked what was left of the wood along an outside wall of the shed, swept the debris off the earthen floor, and heated water in a copper wash boiler. By the time Billy dropped the noon mail, she'd dragged the front bench around back, parked three galvanized tubs on it, and was bending over the washboard.

Mercy, it was hot! She dragged the back of her forearm across her perspiring brow. And yet, even as she stood melting down in her shoes and waving away a persistent fly, there was something soul-satisfying about washing. Berry stains and newspaper print and dirt ground into the knees of knickers—those were problems she could solve. Unlike some others she could mention.

24

🔀 Zerilda pitched her battered hat aside. Her pitted face was lined with heat and fatigue, her hair as rumpled as a haystack after a needle search.

"Threshers poundin' away at the oats crop. Some fool team ran me clean off the road." She pulled the band off the letters she'd gathered on her route and thrust them at Libby. "Caught a shoelace in my bicycle chain and like to never get loose."

Libby murmured her sympathies and leafed through the letters, getting the daily count. The address on the bottom envelope brought her head up with a snap.

Zerilda's eyes glittered. "It ain't my business to notice —but if it was, that'n there'd give me a queer start, too."

Libby walked to the yawning back door and held the letter up to the light.

"That's agin' the rules. Ain't you read the book yet?"

"But she's written to the postal authorities!"

"You shoulda knowed she would. Ain't nothin' Miz Dorrance hates like strong drink."

"But Captain Boyd . . ."

"She's gonna spray that bottle with buckshot, don't matter who's holdin' it."

Her head pounding, Libby entreated, "So what do I do?"

"You drop the durn thing in the mail pouch and send it out, that's what you do."

"I mean what do I do to save Captain Boyd?"

"Day after day, he come in here smellin' like he crawled out of a moonshine jug. You ain't give him the devil once, and now you wanna save him?"

Libby had no defense. The small bit of peace she'd found while scrubbing clothes evaporated as Zerilda slapped and banged through her remaining tasks. Bringing her workday to completion, she turned at the door.

"Iffen it was me, I'd drop his bottle down the privy, catch him by the scruff of the neck, and tell him his vacation is over."

"Vacation?" Libby swung around.

"He's been on vacation, ain't he? Leastwise, that's what I'd be tellin' Miz Dorrance iffen I was you. Which I'm durn glad I ain't." Zerilda smashed her hat on her head, kicked the prop aside, and slammed the back door hard enough to ring the bell on the front one.

Vacation? It was a straw to cling to, anyway. But she'd have to act fast. The week was nearly spent. If Captain Boyd wasn't back in the traces by Monday . . . She'd go see him. Or should she send Father? No, it was her place, not Father's.

Libby tied on a clean apron, dished up a bowl of the soup she'd been cooking on the wash stove, donned her straw hat, and left a note on the door before locking up the store.

She strode along, training her footsteps to the rhythm of her pounding heart. Why was she so fearful? Not of Captain Boyd himself. Then what? Confrontation? Rejection? Anger? Hurting his feelings? *Oh, God. I can't even name it.*

The front door of the old veteran's cottage sat nearly on the sidewalk on the east side of the railroad tracks. Libby stopped before it, clinging to her bowl of soup. The blacksmith's hammer from a block away rang louder than her knock. A train rumbled through town, deadening her second attempt. Knees shaking, a prayer in her heart, she raised her fist a third time.

"He's out back."

Libby swung around to find Teddy watching her from the street. Sugar trotted over and jumped on her skirt, tail wagging, damp nose quivering.

Teddy came after her. "Aw-w-e-l-l. You come on, you old dog you. Leave her be, she's got folks to see."

Sugar whined in protest, but Teddy kept a good grip on her, freeing Libby to walk around the side of the house. Half of the backyard was fenced in chicken wire. Chickens scratched in the sand strewn beneath the fruit trees. A grape arbor thrived on the unfenced side. Hollyhocks grew between the privy and the cobhouse. There was a pump just feet from the back door, and a clothesline running from the corner of the house to a post at the edge of the alley.

"Captain Boyd?"

Getting no reply, Libby walked around the arbor of vines and found him sitting on a stump in the sun. Back turned. Bareheaded. Dirty shirt untucked from crumpled trousers.

Libby called his name again, then sucked in her breath as he turned. Pockets of pallid flesh drooped beneath slitted eyes. His fine silver hair was matted and dull, his waxen jowls creased and peppered with gray stubble. He lifted his hand in a shooing motion, and faced away again.

Poised between pity and revulsion, Libby felt her stomach tighten as he dropped his face between his knees. He shuddered and heaved as if to retch up his very lungs. God have mercy! She set the bowl of soup on the slab by the well, grabbed the basin beneath the pump, and rushed to his aid. He kept heaving, but nothing came.

"You're ill, Captain. You need to get out of the sun."

When the dry heaves stopped, Captain Boyd lifted his head with a groan. Traces of earlier sickness stained his shirt. He tried to get to his feet. But the great convulsive waves of sickness had left him weak and trembling.

Libby got an arm around his waist. "Lean on me, I'll help you inside."

"Privy."

Libby feared it was already too late, but she got a shoulder under his arm and inched gingerly along the beaten path. Captain Boyd moaned with each jarring step.

"No place for a lady." His fine velvet voice was as rough as a rasp.

Libby caught the privy door with her foot and nudged it open. The summer breeze fluttered through the pages of yellowed catalog hanging by a string.

"Lift your foot, that's it," she murmured, and when he was in, pushed the door closed again.

"You go on home now, miss," he called from inside.

A curtain stirred next door as Libby crossed to the stump and picked up the soup. She let herself in by the back door, but the odor nearly drove her out again. Had he been sick all week? Libby slid the soup onto the stove, and hesitated. He had told her to go. And yet . . .

There was no sense so strong for stirring memories as odors. Even foul ones. For an instant Libby was transported in time to their home in Thistle Down. Uncle Willie staggering past the lilac bush and up the path. Unwashed, unshaven, ragged, and pitiable. Father and Mother always there to greet him with generous hearts and gentle hands.

Libby walked out into the sunshine, came back with a bucket of corncobs, and fell to the task. She soon had a fire licking on the stove grate, adding to the heat of the July day, and water warming in the reservoir. She stripped the place of soiled sheets and clothing. It would be easier to wash them at home. She put fresh linen on the bed, then found lye soap and rags and a bucket and started scrubbing the place down.

Captain Boyd was a long time coming back to the house. His startled expression at finding her there turned quickly to dismay. His face contorted as he came on unsteady limbs, moaning in a thick voice, "You shouldn't. Oh, please don't. Please, miss. You shouldn't be here."

He stooped over as if to pull her to her feet and nearly fell into the table. A shuddering sob shook loose. He gripped the table, sank down into a chair, and buried his face in his arms. Libby laid a hand on his shoulder.

"I've brought you some soup. Can you eat?"

He didn't answer. Nor would he lift his head. Quietly

Libby finished her cleaning, emptied the water, washed her hands, and set the bowl of reheated soup before him.

"I'm leaving now," she called from the door. "But I'll be back this evening to check on you."

Still he did not answer. Libby picked up the basket of laundry and started home. David was sitting by the pump, watching for her. He leaped to his feet and came running.

Libby's heart bolted at the sight of his torn knickers and a web of scratches on his cheek. *Now what?* She dropped the basket and reached for him. "What happened? Are you hurt?"

"Not me, it's Father. Proctor spooked. Father thought we were going to tip over. We jumped."

"From the buggy? Where is he?"

David lifted thin shoulders. "We never found him."

"Not Proctor. Father!"

"Oh. He's at Doc Harding's." David blinked and said in a calmer voice, "He sent for you."

"Then he's walking and talking and . . ."

"We both walked. Ouch, you're pinching."

Libby loosened her grip on his thin arms. "I'm sorry, I didn't mean to. You walked back to town?"

"Till Doc came along. Father said he was an angel of mercy. He said God sent him." David examined a scraped knuckle. "Doc's helper might be an angel, but I don't think the doctor is, do you, Lib?"

"That's just an expression Father used. Lift your face. Ach! Look at you." Libby dampened the corner of her apron at the well and washed the muddied traces of sweat and dust from his freckled cheeks.

"Maybe she wasn't an angel. Cause if she'd been an angel, she would have known what the doctor needed before he asked for it."

"Mrs. Brignadello? That's his sister, and quite often she *does* know before he asks."

"She didn't today. She cried."

Libby's hand went still. "Forevermore! Why?"

David rolled his lower lip up over his top one, thinking. "Maybe it was the doctor. He said, 'Where the devil is Sarah Jane when I need her?' That's when she cried."

"You mean it wasn't Mrs. Bee? Then who?"

David shrugged.

Relieved she hadn't dumped her tubs of water earlier,
Libby retraced her steps to the basket of laundry, "Just let
me put these clothes in to soak, then we'll go see about
Father."

The doctor had wrapped Libby's father's ribs and
tended a twisted ankle. His wife, Paulette, came into the
back office as Libby was helping her father into his boots.
Libby could see how David might mistake her for an
angel. Just as she had yesterday, she thought that Mrs.
Harding had the ethereal look of a Gibson girl straight off
a magazine advertisement, though with none of Mrs.
Bee's reassuring influence or lively interest in injuries and
ailments. Paulette sat on the doctor's stool looking detached as Libby questioned her concerning her father's
injuries.

"Doctor didn't say," came her pat reply to every
question.

"Could you ask him?" Libby said finally.

"I'm sorry. He's with another patient." Oblivious to the
rumpled room, she crossed one knee over the other and
continued flipping through the file of sheet music in her
lap.

"Then we'll wait," said Libby, growing annoyed.

"'Tis all right, lass," Thomas said later, wincing as he
edged off the doctor's table, bracing his rib cage. "I canna
think but that me own twisted stump and battered ribs be
the best judge of what I can and canna do."

They made the short walk home at a painstaking pace.
The last mail drop of the day lay on the back step. With
the store locked, Billy had been unable to pick up the
outgoing mail. Libby made a mental note to take it to
the station herself, but a failed attempt to get her father up
the stairs drove the chore from her mind. She made him
as comfortable as she could downstairs and went outside
again.

Coupled with her concern for her father's discomfort
was a new dilemma. Who would handle Captain Boyd's
route tomorrow? She had told Captain Boyd she'd be

back later to check on him. Perhaps when he became
aware of present circumstances, duty would win over the
bottle.

The woodshed was as hot as an oven. With a few hours
of daylight remaining, Libby refueled the stove for heating more water, then carried the soup inside and served
supper downstairs.

While they were eating, Teddy came into the store with
Sugar at his heels. He took up his place on a nail keg, but
declined Libby's offer of a bowl of soup. There was the air
of the messenger about him.

"We-l-l-l, if you was to look over at Woodmancy's, ya
might find him."

Thomas looked up. "What is it ye're sayin', lad? Find
who?"

"You know." Teddy gave the coffee grinder a spin.
"And not a scratch on him."

Thomas brightened. "'Tis Proctor ye're speakin' of,
laddie? What of the buggy?"

"W-e-l-l, it came home, too."

Father thanked him warmly for bringing word.

"Proctor didn't mean to run," said David. "It was the
boy in the tree. He hit him with a stone."

"A stone?" echoed Libby, for this was the first mention
of it. "Were you up at Old Kentucky?"

"Aye, south end," said her father. "Near the lake."

"Did the boy have red hair?"

"Redder'n yours." David sopped up soup with a slice of
bread.

"We-e-l-l-l, that would be him, then," said Teddy,
inspecting a jagged fingernail.

Temper rising, Libby muttered, "That's twice he's
pulled the same dangerous prank."

David cocked back his head. "Do you know him?"

"Do ye, lass?"

"Frankie McClure," said Libby, as certain as she'd ever
been of anything.

The sun was dappling the sky in deep pinks and grays
when Libby returned to Captain Boyd's cottage with his
wet washing. He didn't respond to her knock, nor was he
in the backyard. Libby found clothespins in a rusty can

beneath the line. Hoping it wouldn't rain in the night, she began stringing his clothes to the line.

A chorus of voices came from the house next door. It was the New Hope Ladies Aid meeting Dorene had mentioned that morning. Their voices came wafting on the evening air as they united in a familair song. Softly Libby hummed along.

It wasn't long before she heard the ladies dispersing on the walk in front. A stillness settled over the neighborhood as the skies shifted to purple. Libby's quiet humming grew into a song as she hung the last few pieces.

"Good evening, Miss Willy. I heard you singing," called Captain Boyd as he stepped out on the back stoop. "It made me think of my wife. She always sang when she hung the wash."

"It goes hand in hand," said Libby, returning his smile.

"Carry on! I was enjoying it."

"I'll have to write and tell the smithy who lived next door to us in Thistle Down. He called my singing caterwauling." Seeing the captain's lips twitch, she added, "I don't mind saying he was a meddlesome old critic."

"Ah, well. There are worse things than meddling." Freshly shaven and clad in clean clothes, the captain crossed to the stump and sat down. He asked, "You feeling lonesome for home, Miss Willy?"

"If I was, it wouldn't be Mr. Rhodes I'd be missing." Libby dropped the empty basket on the back stoop and sat down beside it.

"Who, then?"

"My brothers. Our friends. The lilac bush in the yard."

"No sweetheart?"

"No."

"Forgive me, miss. I didn't intend to be meddlesome like your smithy neigbor. But I heard an ache in your song."

"There's an ache in you, too, Captain Boyd." Libby's words surprised herself as much as him.

"In all of us." His voice rumbled low.

"We don't have to carry it alone."

"You've a good heart, miss. Like Willie. But you're

young." He sighed, his way of saying she didn't understand.

He was right. She didn't. She was tired. Tired and dull,
with no idea of how to say all that needed saying.
Somewhere in the neighborhood a cow lowed a plaintive
lament. Reminded once more of Mr. Rhodes, Libby drew
in the dust with a stick and recounted how the old smithy
used to turn his cow loose after dark, and let it graze in
the neighborhood. She told how she'd rebounded off its
flanks in the darkness one time while taking out the slop
jar.

"The jar went flying. Milk and table scraps and everything else came down on me, and the cow as well. And if
Mr. Rhodes didn't tell me the next day I owed his cow a
laundering."

"'Long may our lambs be bright,'" sang the captain.
"Er, make that cows."

Libby chuckled, enjoying the sound of the captain's
velvet laughter mingling with the sleepy chirping of birds
and the ring of the hammer and the plea of the cow.

"I should be going," she said at length, and pitched the
stick over the fence.

"Yes, miss. Your father must be wondering about you."

Libby stirred to her feet. She crossed to the stump and
laid a hand on his shoulder. "Your friends miss you,
Captain Boyd. The folks on your route, too."

"It's fallen into capable hands."

It was the perfect opening to tell him of her father's
accident. And yet, at the last moment, Libby changed her
mind. She bent her knees, bending until their eyes met in
the deep shadows.

"I came here to tell you that your job is waiting and that
I was worried over certain ones who may make trouble
and that you'd be making it a whole lot easier on yourself
and on me, too, if we called it a vacation. But it isn't a
vacation. It isn't even about the job. It's about you,
Captain Boyd, and wanting things to be better for you."

Wordlessly he stretched out a trembling hand and laid
it against her cheek. A tear slid free and spilled over his
hand before she could wipe it away.

"Aw, Miss Willy, don't you go and do that. On your

feet now, and home with you. I'll see you in the morning."

He said it like he meant it. And maybe he did. And yet, somehow, she walked home feeling doubtful, for even as he promised, she'd caught the tangy scent of whiskey on his breath.

David, bless his heart, had dragged the cot down the stairs and was padding it with blankets to make it more comfortable for their father.

"You can sleep down here, too, if you want to, David. It's cooler." Libby stepped over Sugar to help her father off with his shoes.

"You had company," said David.

Heart tripping, Libby raised hopeful eyes.

A twinkle glimmered in her father's eyes. "Nay, Lib. Not the lad. 'Twas a raven-haired leddy with dark eyes and a firm chin."

"She didn't give her name?" Mystified, Libby asked, "What did she want?"

"'Twas a letter she was claimin' to hae mailed in haste."

"Did you tell her the mail had already gone out?"

"Ye're forgettin', lass. It hadn't. See it there on the counter yet?"

"You're right!" Wearily Libby rose to her feet. "So did she find her letter?"

"Aye, she found it. And away she went withoot another word."

"I wouldn't mention it to Zerilda. There's sure to be something in the book about folks retrieving things from the mailbag."

"Ach, lass. What guid be there in complainin' of poor Zerilda?" Thomas beckoned to David. "Go with yer sister, that's a guid laddie."

Libby tightened the strap on the mailbag. With David at her side chanting to himself, she set off for the station to see that the mail got on the next train.

"Door . . . door ants. Door-ants." David pressed closer to her in the darkness. "That was it."

Libby shouldered the bag and took his hand. "What is it you're saying, Davie?"

"Door-ants. I watched her pick out the letter."

Gooseflesh rose on Libby's arms. "Dorrance? David! Was that the return address? Are you sure?"

He nodded, certainty growing. "Door-ants. I sounded it out."

"Dark hair, dark eyes, straight as a table leg? Well, bless my soul." Libby dropped the mailbag and flung her arms around David, then laughed out loud at his startled protest. "You're brilliant, Davie. You really are."

He didn't have to understand her delight to appreciate such high praise. "I'm strong, too. See?" He slung the mailbag over his shoulder and puffed out his chest.

Libby laughed and would have hugged him again, had he not been trying to be so manly.

25

🌹 Libby looked up from sorting mail to exchange greetings with Zerilda as she came in the back door the next morning.

The mail carrier's dour gaze cut across the counter to Thomas. "What's ailin' you, Mr. Watson?"

"Would ye believe I leapt oot o' my buggy wi' Proctor a-thunderin' along? Wasn't that a daffy trick?" Thomas sat forward in his rocking chair and reached for the cane Libby had found upstairs.

"Frankie McClure and his stones again," Libby explained. "Father sprained his ankle and bruised some ribs."

Zerilda's hands stilled. "Who's carryin' mail today?"

"Captain Boyd's coming back today." Libby avoided meeting the dark doubt on Zerilda's face, saying, "Sit still, Father. What is it you need? David, fill Father's cup, that's a good fellow."

Libby kept busy, sorting mail and keeping her father off his feet. But not so busy that she couldn't feel the tension grow as the minutes stacked one upon another with no sign of Captain Boyd. Zerilda cased her mail, bundled it, and rolled her bicycle in the back door. And still he had not come.

"I thought you talked to him," Zerilda said at length.

Heat swept up Libby's collar. "I did. He said he'd be here."

"So what're you gonna do?"

Certain she'd disapprove, Libby shot her a cagey glance. "You've read the book. What am I supposed to do?"

"In an emergency, you're to get yer clerk to work the counter, and run the mail yerself."

"Then that's what I'll do."

Sensing she'd been outmaneuvered, Zerilda said with narrowed eye, "You ain't got a clerk. And not much chance of gettin' one, when half the town's got their back up."

Mr. Gruben, who'd come for his mail and a stamp, said, "There's an opening, is there? It won't be of much help today, but I could post notice in the next edition."

"Thank ye, Mr. Gruben, but let's let it drift for noo, shall we?" said Thomas. "I'll do the clerkin' while the lass runs the roote."

Libby had considered as much, but had hesitated to suggest it out of concern for her father's strength. It wasn't the postal work that concerned her. It was the store. It took a lot of stamina to tend it single-handedly, and today was Saturday. The farm families would pour in all day long. She asked, "Are you sure it won't be too much, Father?"

"Ach! Dinna worry ye head aboot it. Me Davie will help, won't ye, laddie?"

Looking pleased, David thrust back his shoulders and nodded.

"You'll hold the fort, then? That-a-boy." Smiling at her brother, Libby added, "I'll be back before you know it."

Mr. Gruben, assessing Thomas's bindings, suggested, "Take a lesson from the storekeep out at Old Kentucky and tell folks to come back when you're standing up."

Thomas chuckled. "Would that be the tumbledown hatch by the bridge ye're speakin' o'? I canna believe the gloom o' the place. And ye say 'tis open for business?"

"Yes. Mother and son run the place, though you don't see much of the old woman. I told Skiff business would likely pick up if he'd advertise in the paper. 'What?' he said. 'And have folks in here botherin' me all the time?'

Which reminds me," said the editor, when Thomas's laughter faded. "You might benefit by placing an ad yourself."

"Aye, 'tis a sound idea," said Thomas. "But ye shall have to speak to Elizabeth. The lass can put a bloom on the page like no other."

Mr. Gruben turned Libby's way. "Would you like to write the ad yourself, Miss Watson? You did a good job on the short notice regarding the mail job Billy Young filled."

Such words from a seasoned writer pleased Libby beyond measure. Heart thumping, she said, "I've never written an advertisement before. But I'd love to try."

Mr. Gruben quoted his rates for space, then plucked his pencil from his stiff patch of white hair, drew a narrow tablet from his pocket, and offered both to her.

"Oh no, not now. I like to mull before I put pencil to paper."

Her earnest response made him smile. "What have we here? A writer in the making?"

Flushing, Libby screwed up her courage and admitted, "I hope so. I've dreamed of being a writer since almost before I could read."

"Is that so?" Mr. Gruben tapped the tablet against his leg and regarded her with fresh interest. "What sort of writing would you like to do?"

"I'd like to write of adventure and mystery and romance. The sort of stories that people don't have to think too hard to enjoy," she added.

The editor chuckled. "I see. At least you're honest about it."

Worried she'd given him the wrong impression, Libby flushed, adding, "Not that there's anything wrong with thinking. Just that I believe a story should be fun to read."

"You don't think the writer has an obligation to present thought-provoking ideas to the reader?"

"In the newspaper, yes. But I'd like to write things that give people . . . well . . . a vacation." Doubtfully Libby asked, "Is there something wrong with that?"

Mr. Gruben smiled at her sudden misgivings. "No, of course not. Though I contend that with a little effort, a good writer can accomplish both objectives." Poking his pencil behind his ear again, he added, "Would you be interested in attempting a piece for the paper?"

Libby tempered her rising excitement and countered, "On what subject?"

"Why don't you report on the progress of threshing locally? That's a subject of much interest to my readers, and one that shouldn't cause them to think too hard," he quipped, still smiling.

Wishing again she hadn't been quite so brash in airing her opinions, Libby swept a stray tendril away from her hot face and said with all the dignity she could muster, "I'd like that very much."

"Very well, then. If it's good enough to use, I'll print your ad for free. Fair enough?"

"That would be more than fair," Libby agreed.

The editor tipped his hat and started away, only to turn back again. "By the way, Miss Watson. Would you care to come to my house for dinner on Sunday? My wife would enjoy meeting you and exchanging ideas on books."

"She's a writer, too?" asked Libby.

"No," said Mr. Gruben. "A reader. Between the two of us, we have quite a library."

The word "library" was icing on the cake. Barely able to contain her excitment, Libby cried, "I'd love to come."

"Would six o'clock be convenient?"

Libby assured him it would.

"I'll look forward to it, then." Mr. Gruben smiled and tipped his hat and went on his way.

"Father! Dinner with a *real* writer!" breathed Libby in wonder. "And a chance to write for the paper! I can scarcely believe it!"

Thomas beamed. "He's a God o' surprises, thunderin' in on a white horse. I winna dampen' your joy by askin' what is it ye know of threshin' runs."

"Nothing. But I can learn."

"Aye, and swiftly, too," said Father with a twinkle. "Best take oot yer tablet with ye, lass, and see what ye can glean while ye're trottin' old Proctor aboot the countryside."

"I won't have much time. I can't leave you stranded all afternoon."

"It will be my penance for landin' ye in such a caboodle o' trouble with me flyin' off the buggy."

"I'd like to thrash that Frankie McClure! If I spot him today, I'll have that slingshot of his." She brightened, and flung her arms around her father's neck, her heart brimming with thanksgiving for the wonderful opportunities before her. "I've got to hurry. Pray I bump into someone who can take time for my questions, would you, Father?"

Because of the length of miles to be covered, the route was divided into three stretches, enabling each patron to receive delivery twice a week. Today's section, stretching to the northern end of Old Kentucky, would be different from yesterday's, and Monday's different from today's. Libby's trip to Mrs. McClure's was her only experience on the rural roads. Teddy must have judged himself more reliable than the map with which Libby had armed herself, for he was waiting in the buggy when she came out the back door.

"Teddy! You're riding with me?"

He muttered, "Ah-h-h, well. I got nothin' better to do."

Libby loaded the mail, then hurried back inside for her sandwich, a jug of water wrapped in burlap, and her writing tablet. She donned her flat straw hat with the navy grosgrain ribbon and headed straight north out of town past fields of green corn, shocked oats, and golden wheat. The sun burned from a cobalt blue sky. The road was bone-dry, the flies a nuisance. But her first real writing assignment was all the tonic she needed.

Libby wasn't long in spotting a threshing crew. She guided Proctor to the side of the road at Erstwood and flipped to a blank page in her Memorandum book. Teddy tumbled out of the buggy and ambled across the field without looking back. But Libby stayed where she was, words taking shape as she viewed the shocks of oats strewn across the field. *Miniature peaks, shimmering in the sun.*

The threshing operation was centered just south of the barn. A cloud of black smoke shot from the stack of the engine, softening as it rose, then curling away in billowing wisps. Libby scribbled a few notes and lifted her head.

A surrey was approaching from the direction she'd just come. Recognizing both the horse and the driver, Libby patted her beaded brow dry and straightened her hat.

Angus was almost upon her before his expression changed. His shirtwaist gleamed white in the late morning sun as he stopped the surrey alongside her buggy and reached into his vest pocket for his spectacles. "Elizabeth! Now, here's a pleasant surprise. Have you come for the threshing dinner?"

"No, no, nothing like that. Father bruised some ribs yesterday, so I'm delivering Captain Boyd's route."

Angus brushed the dust from his neatly creased trousers and indicated her open notebook. "Is the mail so slow, you feel called upon to invent some letters along the way?"

Libby smiled and explained the notebook and pencil.

"Another hidden talent. Why doesn't that surprise me?"

She flushed at his flattery, confessed her ignorance of the threshing procedure, and offered only token resistance when he invited her for a closer look.

"Park up the lane and we'll walk up behind the barn," he invited.

Libby left her buggy amidst a host of conveyances. Angus sprang over the rutted ground on his crutch, leading her to within a dozen yards of the core of activity. She could see that Teddy had crept even closer.

Chaff and cinders and the scent of coal smoke lingered in the air as the great hulking engine hissed and popped off steam. A wide whirring belt ran from the engine to the pulley on a red machine Angus called a "separator." As they looked on, a loaded wagon lumbered abreast of the rig. A wiry fellow climbed up on the stack and began pitching bundles into the separator. The bundles ran through the machine. A spout spit straw in one direction, the stack growing twin peaks as the spout was turned from side to side. A second spout emptied grain into the wagon at the other end.

Angus raised his voice above the noise of workmen and machine. "The oats are threshing out at about sixty bushels."

"An acre?" asked Libby, and he nodded. "How many men are here working?"

"Chester was counting on eighteen. Five for the machinery. They feed coal to the engine, keep water in the tank, watch the gauges, grease and oil, and such as that. Five more to pitch, and eight haulers."

Libby listened as Angus further described the responsibilities of each man on the threshing crew. Leather creaked and whiffletree chains jingled as a team of horses pulled a hay wagon past them on its return to the field.

Libby shaded her eyes as hard-muscled men in sweat-soaked shirts and slouch hats walked alongside, pitching the bundled oats onto the wagons. The fuller the wagon, the harder the work, the bundles heaped five, six, maybe seven feet high.

Angus began his explanation of the procedure with the binding of the oats, then went on to relate how the field hands stood the bundles in shocks. He called it "shocking the oats" and said that it was done several days in advance of the threshing crews' arrival so that the bundles dried adequately. He talked her through the threshing and the transporting of the grain to the elevator, then gestured toward the shady side of the house where long tables waited in readiness for dinner.

"Catherine and Chloe are helping Mother. Aunt Sarah Jane, too, and a couple of cousins. Are you sure you can't stay and eat with us?"

"I wish I could," said Libby with regret. "I'd love to be a part of it. What a lot of work it must be."

"Mother dreads it more each year," he confided. "She was too tired last evening to drive in for the New Hope Ladies Aid meeting." He nudged aside a clod of dirt with his crutch and added with a hint of intrigue, "I've a report to pass on to her. Would you like a briefing?"

Libby darted him a glance from beneath the brim of her hat. "Me?"

"As long as you're taking notes for The Gazette, why not a bit of news on the New Hope Ladies Aid?"

Mystified, she crooked one eyebrow. "Since when have you such an interest in the organization, Mr. Cearlock?"

"Actually, that isn't where my interest lies."

His hazel gaze warmed her face like sunlight. Shading herself from the directness of it, Libby flipped her notebook open and poked her pencil in the general direction of the threshing rig. "It's quite a piece of machinery, isn't it?"

He murmured agreement. But his focus had not shifted to the steam engine or the separator. Or the straw stack or the wagon of grain or the men, laboring in the heat and soot and cinders and sweat. He inclined his head to be heard over the commotion of man and machinery. "If Captain Boyd weren't such a grand old chap, I'd be jealous."

Libby's heart bumped. "What did you hear?"

"Ah, I've got your attention now, have I?" He beamed with boyish delight.

"You're a dreadful tease, Mr. Cearlock. Worse than Jacob, Adam, and David all rolled together." Libby sniffed and slid him an injured glance.

He laughed and said, "You've found an unlikely champion in Zerilda. I overheard her having a run-in with the old-timers this morning. Told them if they had a backbone to share between them, they'd quit jawing and get over to Captain Boyd's and lend Miss Watson a hand drying him out."

"My!" Libby breathed in wonder.

"Though, in the interest of a balanced report, you should know that when I commended her for her defense of you, obscure though it was, she said to take my 'politicking' on down the road, she'd no use for gold-standard men."

"That sounds more like it." Libby's laughter mingled with his. "And speaking of getting on down the road . . . You've been a big help, Mr. Cearlock. I can't thank you enough."

"I wish you'd make that 'Angus.'"

"All right, then," said Libby, though she couldn't quite bring herself to say it.

His smile was a wordless entreaty, bunching up clean-shaven cheeks and rounding his face as he waited so expectantly. She flushed and amended, "All right, then, *Angus*."

Libby called to Teddy. He looked her way, then turned back to the threshing again.

Angus chuckled. "You may as well go. He likes watching the fellows work. You won't be able to pry him away now."

Libby remembered something Ike Galloway had once said about not trying to tie Teddy down. He hadn't meant it unkindly. Only that Teddy had his limitations, and a person would do well to understand them. It was a lesson well taken.

"Is it all right to leave him?" she asked.

"Certainly. He'll walk or catch a ride back with one of the men."

Angus accompanied Libby to the buggy and was handing her up when Mrs. Brignadello came up the lane, sleeves turned up, red-faced and perspiring.

"Aunt Sarah Jane!" exclaimed Angus. "Are you just arriving? You didn't walk out from town in this heat, surely?"

"Kersey was going to drop me by, but he left too early, and I didn't want to be in the way. Your mother said there was no need of my coming before noon." She fanned herself with her hat. "Ida always did complain I've too free a hand with the spices."

"And for that she put you on cleanup detail? By thunder, you're a saint, Aunt Sarah Jane." Angus stooped to kiss her cheek.

Somewhat mollified, Mrs. Brignadello turned her attention to Libby. "You aren't leaving before lunch, are you, Libby?"

"I've tried to talk her into staying, but she's filling in for her father, who's filling in for Captain Boyd. Neither snow nor heat nor threshing dinner stays this courier from the swift completion of her appointed rounds."

"I think you tangled that, Angus."

He laughed. "Fair enough, Auntie. I'll leave the quotations to Mr. Culbertson."

"The old dear." Mrs. Bee patted her nephew's hand. Abruptly her attention shifted to Libby. "I've been so busy, I've seen almost nothing of you this week. Perhaps I could ride to the end of the lane?"

"Of course." Libby made room on the seat and lifted her hand to Angus as his aunt settled beside her. She turned the buggy in a wide circle and headed Proctor down the lane.

"I didn't want you to think I was avoiding you out at the lake Thursday," Mrs. Brignadello set right in explaining. "I hadn't told Kersey of our bargain over the hat, and was uncertain how he'd react, should he recognize it."

"I thought as much." Libby stole a quick glance and risked overstepping her bounds. "Though I would think he'd appreciate the sacrifice you're making. Or haven't you told him yet of his generous funding of St. Louis accommodations?"

"Then you knew?"

"Why you're parting with everything from garden produce to vinegar cruets? I had an idea." Libby snapped at a fly with her buggy whip. "It occurs to me that if it's a financial burden, you might explain to the women and—"

Mrs. Brignadello shook her head. "No, no, I can't go back on my word."

"Then you plan to tell Mr. Brignadello?"

"I already have."

It was Libby's turn to be surprised. "What did he say?"

"He'll make good on it. He'd be embarrassed not to, and so would I."

"True friends would release you from the obligation, Mrs. Brignadello," Libby insisted.

"You don't understand. How could you? Brothers are different than sisters. There's no . . ."

"Competition?" Libby supplied the word, guessing the woman's secret dread of being diminished in the eyes of her sister.

Her flushed cheeks took on a darker stain.

"I'm sorry," Libby said. "I wasn't being critical. I just don't like seeing you so upset over . . ."

"Kersey's already chided me for my foolish pride." Eyes swimming, Mrs. Bee reached up her sleeve for a handkerchief.

Libby stopped at the end of the lane and laid a gentle hand on her arm. "Was he angry?"

"No, he was sweet."

Misunderstanding, Libby said, "Then it's all right?"

"He wanted to go to the fair himself." Mrs. Bee's chin quivered. "He's been saving for months. It was to be a surprise . . . a surprise . . . for my . . . birthday."

Libby slid a sympathetic arm around Mrs. Bee's slender waist. Waiting as she gathered her composure, she asked, "How are you and Mr. Brignadello at memorizing?"

Mrs. Bee questioned her from watery eyes.

"I was just thinking if you were to win the contest . . ."

"Oh!" Her face brightened, but only for a moment. "No, that would never do. It wouldn't be sporting. Kersey wouldn't hear of it, I know he wouldn't."

"Then what are you going to do?"

"Nip and tuck and save every penny I can get my hands on. My husband is going to St. Louis. Even if I can't, Kersey must see the fair. I couldn't forgive myself if I cheated him of it." She brushed a burr from her skirt, drew a deep breath, and squared her trim shoulders. "I'm sorry I broke down, but it's so miserably hot! I got in the nettles. And the mosquitoes about carried me off."

Libby spared her disheveled hair a second glance. A twig was caught in the distinctive white streak of hair that fell away from her brow like a dove's wing. There was a grass stain on her skirt and mud on her shoes. "Where did you get into nettles?"

Reticent all at once, she replied, "Along the roadside."

"And the mud on your shoes?"

"Oh, all right, then. I was out at the lake looking for ginseng, if you must know. But don't you breathe a word of it. Kersey dropped me here at the gate at six o'clock this morning, and as far as he's to know, I've been here ever since."

"Ginseng?" echoed Libby, trying to puzzle it out.

"Yes. It's a woodland plant. There's a good medicinal market for the root."

"I know what it is, but I thought it was harvested in the autumn."

"It is. But it's very hard to find. I thought if I began looking now, I'd have a head start."

It was a valid point, Libby supposed. And if she could

find it, selling ginseng was a good plan. Better than selling her treasures, anyway.

"I didn't mean to keep you," said Mrs. Bee, climbing down. "I just didn't want you to be thinking poorly of me for deliberately dodging you at the picnic."

"The hat's just between us. Your trek into the woods, too," Libby promised.

Mrs. Bee smiled and, on impulse, stepped closer to the wheel. "There is one more thing you could do for me. I found a dozen canning jars in an abandoned cabin in the woods. I tugged them along in a gunnysack until they got heavy. They're by a fence post up the road a piece. Would you mind . . ."

"Hauling them back to town for you? No, not at all."

"Thank you, Libby." Mrs. Bee started away, then turned back. She ventured, "Kersey once mentioned that Mr. Skiff up at Old Kentucky will pay a penny a jar. Will your route take you past there today?"

"Skiff's Store? Here it is, marked on the map." Anxious to get going, Libby nodded agreement and shook the reins over Proctor's back.

The gunnysack, fastened with a stout piece of wire, was just where Mrs. Brignadello had said it would be. Libby tucked the dirty sack in the space behind the seat and was on her way again.

26

🌹 Traveling north, then east, Libby consulted the map as she matched the mail to unmarked boxes. She'd nearly emptied her water jar by the time she passed the cemetery, church, and school. The mailboxes were few, most at the mouth of wagon tracks leading deeper into the woods.

She followed the north bend in the road, turned east, and crossed the same creek again. If not for the map, Libby might have missed the little store, so hedged in by trees was it. Beyond the screen of greenery sat a lanky fellow, boots propped up on the porch railing as he whittled away at a piece of wood. He had a crust of dirt upon his clothes, and hair like matted sheep's wool. It escaped the confines of his black felt hat and skulked across his face, masquerading as whiskers.

"Is this Skiff's Store?" Libby called from the buggy.

The fellow lifted his head, his gaze piercing the undergrowth to light on her face. He nodded, wood shavings falling away like carrot peelings.

"Is Mr. Skiff around?"

"Yer lookin' at him."

"Are you still buying Mason jars?"

A stream of tobacco cleared the fellow's boots as he continued to measure her. "Depends on who's askin'."

"I'm asking. I've some stowed behind the seat."

266

He folded his knife away and rolled to his feet. "How many ya got?"

"Twelve."

"Let's have a look-see. Ain't payin' fer no busted 'uns." He picked his way through the undergrowth and out to the road as Libby reached for the sack of jars and untwisted the wire. She pulled them out one by one.

Satisfied, he said, "I'll give ya six cents."

"I was told a penny apiece."

"Fer clean ones, maybe. Them-air 'uns is dirty."

The shrewd gleam in his muddy eyes stiffened Libby's neck. She'd dealt with fellows like him, wanting their laundry for a song. "I can't let them go for less than twelve cents."

"Nine, then," he bartered.

"Twelve." Libby held firm.

"Ten."

"Twelve."

"Eleven. And you take 'em around to the pump and splash the dirt out of 'em."

Libby returned the jars to the bag, stashed them behind the seat, and gathered the reins. "Good day, Mr. Skiff."

Surprise skipped like a stone in his rain-puddle eyes. "By jing! Ain't we gonna do business?"

"I've mail to deliver and no time for washing jars nor quarreling for a fair price."

"Whoa there, gal. Did I say eleven? Twelve, then, though jest betwixt you, me, and the shadders, they's mighty pricey jars yer totin'," he added with a sniff.

Libby could scarcely keep from grinning. "All right then, twelve it is."

The man paid her, retrieved the jars, then circled around and patted Proctor's neck. "It's a mortal pity, old hoss, if she drives you like she drives a bargain."

Wasn't *he* a fine one to talk!

Libby continued on, and soon reached the line of boxes just short of the C & A crossing and depot. Hearing the sound of a saw chewing wood, she glanced toward the cabin she'd noticed on her previous trip, and in so doing, allowed Proctor to swing too wide for the row of mail-boxes.

Hopping down, Libby was tucking the mail into the boxes when a rock came out of nowhere, striking her arm. Yelping, dropping the mail and gripping her arm, she swung around just as Frankie McClure's red head bobbed up amidst the trees. His mouth spread in a fiendish grin. He stretched back his arm, drew a bead between the forks of his slingshot, and let fly again. Libby leaped to one side just as a second projectile whizzed past. It thumped against the buggy and fell to the ground. A buckeye, the little demon!

Temper flaring, Libby tore into the woods after him, feet pounding as fast as her blood. He had legs like a rabbit, zigzagging through the undergrowth, over a dead log, into a cloud of mosquitoes, and right through the nettles. The hairy-stemmed weeds stung Libby's legs as she ran, saplings biting her face.

Frankie, king of his green domain, crowed at her from atop a stump. "You run like a girl. You'll never catch me!"

He soared from the stump to the ground with the grace of a bounding deer, then tripped over a root and went sprawling. Libby lunged and caught a piece of his shirt. He kicked, flailing arms and legs, fighting to free himself.

"Ha! Who runs like a girl now?" Libby planted a knee in his back and snatched the slingshot from his pocket.

"Hey, that's mine!"

"Spoils of war," panted Libby, holding it overhead.

"Give it back or I'm tellin' my grampa!"

"You'll be lucky if I don't feed it to you, you little monkey! You could have killed my father and my little brother yesterday! How would you like it if I took target practice on *you*?"

Frankie took advantage of her loosened grip. He was instantly up and away, shouting back curses as he raced toward the break in the trees. Proctor whinnied as the boy burst upon the road, Libby in hot pursuit. The horse whinnied again. Libby looked back to see her humble white steed at her heels, caught up in the spirit of things. He seemed to be laughing as he came along, ears forward, air sifting his mane. Side aching, lungs fair to exploding, Libby came to her senses. She wrapped her hand around a piece of harness strap and stopped to get her breath.

Knees, calves, and shins stinging like fire, she climbed into the buggy, flung the slingshot behind the seat, and reached under her skirt and thin petticoat. Her stretched-out stockings had puddled over her shoe tops and down around her ankles. Digging at her bare legs only worsened the itching. Wretched nettles. Wretched boy.

Red curls fraying loose of her braid, and with no idea where she'd lost her straw hat, Libby turned Proctor around and went back to pick up the mail she'd dropped. She matched the letters to the names on the boxes, and wondered about the people as she did so, for out of the half dozen boxes, she only knew one family, and that was the McClures. She reasoned that one box must belong to the cabin across the road. The other families no doubt lived up the lane past the McClures' boxcar home. It was a beautiful, serene setting, though awfully isolated. Small wonder Naomi had welcomed her the day she'd gone calling. Or that she seemed lonely. Who wouldn't be, in such an out-of-the-way place?

The syrup camp was next on the route. Libby crossed the tracks, rattled over the creek for the third time, and turned south at the T in the road. There was nothing to mark the camp as such, just a clearing in the trees, a frame of raw lumber and rafters, and a roof in progress. Libby's interest quickened as she thought of Uncle Willie making syrup here. With the help of Decatur McClure. And Ike, though he would have been just a boy at the time.

Though Ike was nowhere to be seen in the green shadows, the ring of a hammer gave away his presence on the roof. Libby hadn't seen him since the Fourth of July at Baker's. She hadn't forgotten him withholding the information he knew. He'd just the same as sided with McClure. It made the hair rise on her neck, thinking about it. But she tried to shake off her ill feelings, for today, in this mail buggy, she represented the United States Postal Department, and the man had a registered letter. Which meant she must collect his signature.

There was a ladder against the west side of the building. Opal's cat was stretched out at the base of it, wearing a doll bonnet. As Libby prepared to step out of the buggy, a pair of blue eyes peeked over the roof ridge. A pale blond head popped up beside Frankie. The glance the pair exchanged was plainly conspiratorial before they slid out of view.

The seizing of Frankie's slingshot seemed suddenly a hollow victory. He'd only make another. So what had she achieved? *Rid yeself o' enemies by befriendin' 'em*, so her father would say. He had a hard veneer, this one. Could Frankie be befriended? Should she be so bold to try? There'd be no better time. He was a captive audience, up there on the partially planked roof with nowhere to run, except down the ladder.

Libby fixed that by laying the ladder on the ground before circling to the back of the building. Ike had his back to her, nailing planks to the rafters on the north end. Frankie watched from the south end of the roof as she passed below. Knees tucked beneath his chin, thin arms hugging his legs. Coiled like a spring. Wary, and yet silently brazen, a catalog of contradiction, which Libby attributed to Ike's close proximity. This boy was nobody's fool. He knew the man was in his corner.

Opal lay on her back beside Frankie, arms spread, hair a waterfall of white gold against weathered planks as she lifted her chin and peeked over her dusty toes.

"Good afternoon, Mr. Galloway," Libby called. "I've a registered letter."

He revealed no sign of surprise as he stilled his hammer and came to the edge of the roof. "You'll be needin' a signature then."

Libby nodded.

"How's things at the store?" He made conversation as he drove a nail through a strip of wood and hung it over the side.

"Fine."

"Sugar shanty's coming right along. Frankie's got where he can hit a nail square on the head. Ain't ya, Frankie?"

Frankie didn't respond.

"Just poke your paper on the nail and I'll sign for ya," said Ike, hanging the strip of wood down to her.

Libby could feel Frankie watching her as she fitted the paper over the nail. Ike signed her paper with his carpenter's pencil, then stretched the wood strip down again. She retrieved her paper containing his signature, passed the registered letter up in the same manner, and still had not found an opening for what she wished to say to the boy.

Galloway took off his hat and wiped his glistening brow on his shirtsleeve. He hunkered down there on the roof, resting his forearms on his knees. "Thought Thomas was deliverin' the mail."

"He bruised some ribs and twisted an ankle yesterday."

Concern flickered along Ike's sunbrowned face and softened his mouth. "How'd that happen?"

"Someone threw a stone and scared Proctor while Father was delivering mail south of Old Kentucky." Libby cast a glance in Frankie's direction and found herself studiously ignored.

"Frankie, you know anything about that?" prompted Ike.

"It was just a little ole buckeye."

"No call for folks treatin' other folks that way."

"Didn't mean no harm."

"It seems Mr. Watson's feelin' some."

Casting Libby a look as hard as Ike's hammer, the boy rocked forward on the balls of his feet and spit over the side of the roof.

"Come here, son." Ike spoke quietly, but his sun-chapped lips flattened and his gray eyes took on a deeper hue.

"I ain't sayin' I'm sorry, if that's what yer thinkin'. Pa's in jail on account of them folks."

"Mama said that wasn't true," inserted Opal. "She says he's in jail on account he drank too much corn liquor and acted like a fool."

"Yer a sissy-girl, what do you know?" Frankie reached over and gave her toes a twist.

Ike came to his feet in one fluid motion. Frankie sprang away like a cat, over the ridge and down the other side. The swift slap of his feet drew a shout of alarm from Libby.

"Stop! The ladder's down!"

The warning came too late. His startled screech grabbed at her stomach like a hard fist as she flew around the building. He lay flat on his back in the green shine of all that leaf-filtered light. Not moving. Libby shot a heart-in-the-throat entreaty to Ike as she ran. He gripped a ceiling joist and swung down, closing the distance on quick strides. She threw herself down beside the boy and reached for his wrist.

Opal, still on the roof, burst into tears. "You've kilt him!"

"Oh, no, honey." Libby tried to calm the child and her own runaway panic. "He's got a strong pulse. See there, his eyes are open."

"So were Mr. Blue's," sobbed Opal.

Libby felt the reproach of Opal's sniffles echoed in Ike's silence. Guilt-stricken, breath caught, she waited as he checked the boy's limbs, peered into his eyes, patted his hand. Even Mother Cat's eyes glittered with censure as she padded up to Frankie on soundless paws, her bonnet coming loose and dragging the ground.

"I didn't mean to hurt him!" Libby blurted.

"He got the wind knocked out of him," said Ike. "See there? He's coming around. Frankie? Can you hear me?"

Opal hung over the roof, sobbing. "Get me down, I want down. I want my brother."

Libby rushed over and righted the ladder. She climbed up to help the child down. Once on firm soil, the girl squirmed away and flew to her brother's side.

"I thought you was dead. You ain't, air ya, Frankie?"

He coughed once, sat up, and rubbed his eyes. His dazed expression faded as he spotted Libby.

"I'm sorry, Frankie. I wanted to talk to you, that was all."

He recoiled at her outstretched hand, scooting back on his bony backside.

Opal flung Libby a vengeful glance. "Get up, Frankie. We'll go tell Mama what she done."

"Yes, and while you're at it, you ought to mention what Frankie done to Miss Libby's father," said Ike evenly.

His words had a quelling effect on the boy. Opal screwed up her thin face, looking from her brother to Ike and back again.

Frankie climbed to his feet. He crossed his arms over his chest and glowered at Libby. "Reckon we're even now. Come on, Opal."

The little girl picked up her cat and hurried after him. They'd gone but a short distance when their young voices turned quarrelsome. Libby leaned against the ladder and expelled the residue of spent panic. "I guess he's all right. He's found enough wind to fight with his sister."

"Sure sign he's a-curin'," said Ike.

Libby's gaze lingered after the children as they hurried along the dirt road toward the bridge. Opal's knee buckled. She put the cat down, stood in the road and cradled one foot, wailing, "Wait up, Frankie! I stepped on somethin'."

Several yards ahead, her brother turned with a sigh and came back. After a brief parley, he stooped, let her crawl up on his back, and over the bridge they went.

Ike's mouth tipped. "Ain't they a pair?"

"She's the better half of it."

He picked up a nail off the ground and tossed it in his hand, a slight frown on his brow. "Frankie's all knots and nerves these days. Seems like the only pain he feels is his own."

Libby said nothing. The droopy eyelid lent a deceptively lazy grace to Ike's anticipatory expression as his gaze skipped over her face.

"He's out of hand, and that's a fact," he added. When Libby still offered nothing, he picked up another nail and came toward the ladder, asking, "What's the matter? Did you just remember you're still mad at me?"

Libby flushed at having it put so directly, but didn't back away from the question. "I don't like being betrayed by a friend."

The beginnings of a grin stole over his face. "Now, there's a revelation. Didn't know you counted me as one."

"I don't. Not anymore."

"What about Cearlock? Still friends with him, are ya?"

"Leave Angus out of it." Her face heated at his probing gaze. "It's none of your concern, anyway."

"Jest trying to ketch up on the news."

"Then get yourself a copy of *The Gazette*," she retorted.

He chuckled, pleased, Libby supposed, at having struck a nerve. She backed away as he gripped the ladder with one hand. "Wouldn't have time to read it, anyways. Reckon I best get back to work if I want this place under cover before the next rain."

Libby was on her way back to the buggy when he called to her from the roof. She turned to see him looking over the bridge in the direction from which she'd come.

"You know, as quick as you are, you ought to leave old Proctor at home and deliver the mail on foot. Why, I wouldn't be a bit surprised if you couldn't shave an hour or two off the route." His mouth curled, confirming her sudden suspicions of his bird's-eye view. "It was a purty good game of tag, Miss Libby. Though I couldn't tell from here who won."

Her withering glance only broadened his smile. Libby retreated to the buggy and started away, her thoughts in a tangle. For as his mouth tilted, and his eyes twinkled, she had for one fleeting moment thought of that night in the store. Remembered the rain-soaked scent of him and his hand gentle on tearstained Frankie. And felt a stir in the pit of her stomach, as exquisite as it was disturbing.

Libby returned to town to the rush of a typical Saturday at the store. Though her father didn't complain, it was clear the crowded day had left him exhausted. He leaned a hand on David's shoulder and climbed the stairs a little before nine, leaving her to close up for the night.

Libby was glad for the time alone. She thought of her dream for more schooling as she counted the receipts for the day. If business continued as it was, the money to further her education would cease to be an obstacle. Her father's health was still a grave concern, but she refused to dwell on what *might* stand in her way, and praised God instead for the store and the little miracles of opportunity shining on her horizon.

Throughout the long, busy day, she had been thinking about the notes she'd taken, and was anxious to begin work on the threshing piece so that she could take it with her tomorrow night when she went to Mr. Gruben's home for dinner. She hadn't yet met Mrs. Gruben, as Mr. Gruben habitually picked up the mail and did the shopping, so there was that to look forward to, too.

Libby settled into the rocking chair by the cold stove and, with the light burning overhead, opened her Memorandum book and reread her notes, beginning with: *Miniature peaks, shimmering in the sun.* The biblical account of Joseph's dream in which he and his brothers were binding sheaves in the field sprang to mind. Those sheaves of grain must have looked much the same as the shocks of oats standing in the fields around Edgewood. Struck by the timelessness of planting and growing and harvest, Libby wrote:

The oat fields have ripened, and in a seasonal ritual as ancient as the Bible itself, the cutting, the binding of sheaves, and the gathering in shocks has begun on the farms surrounding Edgewood.

Libby closed her eyes in an effort to recapture the sights and sounds and smells, even the taste of dust in the air and the feel of sun and coal ash and breeze drying her skin. The weariness of the day forgotten, she picked up her pencil again and poured onto the page a vivid description of the fields and the men and horses and the fire-breathing steam engine powering the threshing machine.

Night deepened. The windmill in the park creaked, an owl hooted, and a train rumbled through town as she erased and rewrote and rearranged her words until the descriptive passages flowed smoothly. Consulting her notes intermittently, Libby concluded with what Angus had told her concerning the condition of the crop.

"The straw is in fine condition, the grain is good. The lowest known yield among area farmers is thirty bushels to an acre. The twenty acres Chester Gentry sowed in 'Big Four' oats has yielded almost sixty bushels, a fine crop indeed!"

Libby's shoulders were throbbing by the time she reached the closing paragraph. Tired from sitting so long, she wandered to the front of the store and peeked from behind the shade just as the night watchman passed on his rounds. Retreating, she paced a bit, thinking the piece ended too abruptly. How could she give it a more satisfying finish? She sat down in the rocking chair by the stove, reread what she had written, and hit on an idea that seemed to neatly tie the end to the beginning.

And so it is that seed sown in expectation, watered and warmed by God's own hand, brings another season's harvest to local farmers. It must have been this cycle of nature that inspired the hymn writer to pen the joyous lines "Bringing in the sheaves, bringing in the sheaves, we shall come rejoicing, bringing in the sheaves." Also rejoicing is the farmer's wife, relieved that the hard labor of yet another threshing dinner is behind her.

Libby lit a candle, then put out the light with the wick stick and climbed the stairs. Bone-tired, yet proud of what she'd accomplished, she undressed and prepared for bed, thanking God all the while for being a benevolent Father who delighted in preparing His children in expectation of that sudden open door. She fell asleep looking forward to dinner at Mr. Gruben's home, and praying he would be pleased with what she'd written.

27

🌺 Sunday seemed to drag along, so keen was Libby's anticipation for her evening at the editor's home. She took great pains making her toilet, arranging her hair in a neatly braided coil at the nape of her neck, and donning the stylish hat she'd bought from Mrs. Bee. With moments to spare, she plucked yellow roses from the bush that grew behind the buggy shed, pinned one to the lapel of her black serge suit, and poked the rest in a small cream pitcher she'd found upstairs.

Nerves fluttering like butterflies, Libby set off on foot past the Columbian and the jail, then crossed the railroad tracks and turned left at the end of the block. Mr. Gruben's home, a white bungalow with a wide veranda, was three doors down. Two cats and an assortment of kittens sat with their backs to Libby, staring through the screen door as she stepped up to knock.

A large-framed woman on a single crutch came to the door. She cocked her gray head to one side in frank appraisal.

"You must be Miss Watson."

"Mrs. Gruben? I can't tell you how much I've been looking forward to meeting you. I hope you like roses," said Libby.

A faint relaxing of the mouth relieved the woman's network of wrinkles as she took the pitcher of rosebuds in her free hand. "That was thoughtful, Miss Watson. Let's find a spot for them, shall we?" She pushed the screen door open with her foot, warning, "Don't trip over the cats."

"Supper smells delicious," ventured Libby.

"Lucius is cooking tonight." Taking care not to catch any feline paws in the door as it closed, Mrs. Gruben added, "Just go on through to the kitchen. Lucius? Miss Watson is here."

Libby stepped to one side to let Mrs. Gruben lead the way, and in so doing, saw that the woman was missing a leg. She lumbered along on the crutch, the hand holding the flowers moving in a repetitive balancing motion that reminded Libby of a weaver throwing the shuttle. Libby was debating whether she should offer to carry the flowers when Mrs. Gruben relieved her of the decision by placing them on a well-used sideboard. She took a moment to turn the pitcher just so, then resumed her laborious pace through the crowded dining room where a centerpiece of garden flowers adorned a table set for three.

Libby's own small offering paled so by comparison to the lovely arrangement, she wished she'd left the roses on the bush. Had she been a bit more sure of Mrs. Gruben's welcome, she might have said so. Was she merely reserved? Or was this a chore she was enduring out of duty to her husband? Striving to find an inroad, Libby ventured, "I hope you will let me reciprocate your hospitality by joining us for dinner sometime soon."

"That's kind of you, Miss Watson, but I doubt I could make it up the stairs to your apartment," Mrs. Gruben called over her shoulder.

Libby winced at having overlooked such an obvious obstacle, and quickly amended, "Dinner at Baker's would do just as well."

"Perhaps. Though as a rule, I don't get out much." Mrs. Gruben nudged a door open with her crutch. "Watch your step," she warned, indicating the drop in elevation just beyond the threshold leading into the kitchen.

A blast of heat hit Libby in the face as she followed Mrs. Gruben down one step and into the kitchen where Mr. Gruben stood before the range, forking chicken from a pan onto a platter. "Good evening, Mr. Gruben. Dinner smells wonderful!"

Mr. Gruben turned from the stove and greeted her with a smile. "I hope you like fried chicken, Elizabeth."

Libby assured him it was a favorite meal of hers. She asked, "Is there something I could do to help?"

"No, no. That isn't necessary," said Mr. Gruben. "We'll eat just as soon as the gravy is ready."

"I'll finish up here," said his wife. "Why don't you show Elizabeth into the parlor where it's cooler?"

"Very well. Elizabeth? Right this way."

A wave of shyness swept over Libby as Mr. Gruben ushered her through the dining room and into the parlor. He was quick to notice the notebook she'd brought along.

"What's this? Your advertisement for the store?" he asked.

The ad! She'd forgotten all about it in her eagerness to write the threshing article. Flushing, Libby admitted, "I haven't written that yet. But I did bring along my article about the oats being harvested."

He crooked a brow. "I see. Could I read it while we're waiting for dinner?"

"Yes, of course." Libby's nerves leapt as she turned to the correct page in the notebook and passed it to him.

Mr. Gruben took a chair near a window where the light was strong, and settled back to read her article. His gaze moved swiftly down the page.

Why is he smiling? He shouldn't be smiling! Libby's heart dropped, her agony such that she couldn't bear to watch him read any longer. Turning her head, she occupied herself drawing general impressions of a comfortable room dominated by large light-giving windows and an extravagance of books. She tried to read the title of the novel lying facedown on the nearby table, then snapped to attention as Mr. Gruben cleared his throat.

"You did your research," he said, as he passed the notebook back to her.

Libby nodded, her hands perspiring as she held his gaze. "They were threshing oats at Mr. Gentry's yesterday. Mr. Cearlock explained the whole procedure. What do you think? Is it something you can use?"

Mr. Gruben stroked his chin, looking for all the world like a man about to be tactful.

"Don't think you have to spare my feelings," she added quickly.

"All right, then. You've done a thorough job of describing what you saw. But you must remember this is farm country. These folks know all about the sights and sounds and hard labor of threshing."

Libby's rising hopes promptly plummeted. "You can't use it, then?"

"What my rural readers expect is an accurate account of the quality of grain being harvested, the yields, if the crop is poor, average, or excellent," he explained. "You cover that near the end. If you could expand on that portion a bit, I'd be willing to look at it again."

Only one paragraph! She'd been up half the night, and all he could use was one paragraph?

Recognizing her unspoken disappointment, Mr. Gruben replied, "I was remiss. I should have explained my expectations."

In other words, he'd credited her with knowing more than she knew. What *did* she know about writing for publication? Nothing! Hiding her discouragement, Libby lifted her chin. "I appreciate the chance to try again."

He nodded approval. "I was hoping you'd take that view. Before you leave tonight, I'll give you some past issues of the paper. Notice as you read how reporting news differs from telling a story." He rolled down his sleeves and buttoned his cuffs, adding, "Who, when, what, where, how—those are the questions you must strive to answer."

Now that he pointed it out, her mistake seemed an obvious one. She fanned her flushed face with her notebook and said, "I guess I was looking at it more from the viewpoint of telling a harvest story."

"Newspaper writing doesn't interest you?"

"No! I didn't mean that at all!" she cried. "I'm thrilled to write anything!"

"Very well. Treat this as lesson one, Elizabeth. The key to good writing is rewriting." He folded his spectacles into his pocket, adding, "You might like to try your hand at reporting some social news, too. Such as the Ladies Aid meeting."

Before he could expand on the subject, Mrs. Gruben called him into the kitchen, asking for help in carrying the food to the table.

Over dinner, the conversation turned once more to writing. Libby didn't admit how little formal schooling she'd had for fear of diminishing herself in Mr. Gruben's eyes. Nevertheless, the aging editor asked insightful questions and offered suggestions as to how one went about submitting short stories, even novels, for publication. Libby found the simple act of visiting at length with someone whose career hinged on the written word—someone who knew the obstacles and encouraged her anyway—a tremendous morale booster.

It was over dessert that Mrs. Gruben offered, "I don't pretend to be a writer, Elizabeth, but I've lived with one long enough to offer one piece of advice—write the sort of things you personally enjoy reading."

Libby was as surprised by the suggestion as she was pleased. She considered her personal tastes. "I like adventure in a story. Intrigue, even tragedy when courage triumphs."

Mrs. Gruben nodded vigorously. More animated than she had been all evening, she prompted, "And romance? What about romance?"

"Oh, yes! I like that too. I loved *Little Women.*"

"Have you read *Jane Eyre? Pride and Prejudice?* What about *Wuthering Heights?*" Looking more disappointed each time Libby shook her head, Mrs. Gruben cried, "Lucius! We have to loan this girl some books!"

Flushing, Libby admitted, "I've been reared on my brothers' hand-me-downs. *The Adventures of Tom Sawyer, Huckleberry Finn, Treasure Island.* And some of my father's books, like *The Life and Opinions of Tristram Shandy, Gentleman,* by Laurence Sterne."

"An interesting work," said Mr. Gruben. "Ideas and dialogue carry the book rather than plot. I wouldn't recommend trying such a technique as a beginner."

"I have all of those books. Wonderful books!" enthused Mrs. Gruben.

Her inroad! And right under her nose, too. Libby turned the question, asking, "What are your favorites, Mrs. Gruben?"

Her hostess gave quite a list, adding as she did so that books had long been her best friends. From that point on, all constraints disappeared.

They soon retired to the veranda where the air was cooler and Mr. Gruben could smoke a cigar. Sharing story lines and memorable characters and techniques used by various authors, Mr. Gruben challenged Libby to think why some techniques worked in some novels more successfully than in others. He suggested she learn to read, not for entertainment or knowledge alone, but as a writer, studying the craft, thinking how she might have told the story, had she been the author.

And so it was, as twilight deepened upon romping kittens and chorusing birds and dusty streets, Libby found herself lugging home several dozen past issues of *The Gazette* as well as the novel *Jane Eyre*.

Homework, Mr. Gruben called it. All those books seemed more like Christmas presents to Libby. She couldn't wait to get started.

Captain Boyd arrived well ahead of Zerilda the next morning. But Libby's relief was short-lived, for he'd come to tender his resignation. The euphoria of the previous evening faded as Libby tried her best to dissuade him. But he was firm in his resolve to make this his final week. He didn't mention her coming to his home, nor did she. And yet he had traded his easy manner for a formal politeness. In trying to help, had she destroyed his pride beyond repair?

Billy Young interrupted Libby's anxious pondering with the first mail drop. He didn't stay long. As she was dumping the mail on the table, Captain Boyd wandered to the other side of the counter and joined Libby's father by the cold stove.

"Ye've a fine reputation for yer past soldierin', Captain Boyd," she heard her father say as she began presorting mail. "What drew ye to it?"

"A reluctance toward disappointing my father," he said

with a smile. "He was a military man. Very disciplined. Very exacting."

"Twenty-five years ye were in uniform?"

Captain Boyd conceded it with a modest nod and reciprocated her father's interest, saying, "I understand you made your living in the coal mines."

"Aye, me own faether was a miner back in Scotland. Like ye with yer faether, I grew my way into it."

"A hard way to make a living, I've heard."

"The risks are common known. I willna go into 'em except to mention the menace of gas seepin' in." Thomas gestured toward a small wire cage high upon a corner shelf. "We kept a bird with us as we went aboot our pick-and-shovelin'. Canaries are sich ones for singin', when their music stops, 'tis soon noticed."

"And time to clear out," guessed the captain.

"Aye." Thomas supported his wounded ankle on a crate. "There was one wee bird the lass and her brithers named Dickie. The scamps slipped him treats as they cleaned his cage, and were forever misheedin' me warnin's not to wrap their hearts around him."

"You took him home with you?"

Thomas nodded. "He was me own bird. One day gas seeped into the shaft. Dickie's silence saved us. Ech! How me bairns cried when I came through the door, Dickie's cage swingin' empty in me hand. 'Twas his own life he'd given, sparin' ours." Thomas held Captain Boyd's gaze a long moment, then made the transition, saying quietly, "Poison seeps into ever' man's life, Captain. But we dinna haf to be hopelessly doomed."

The old soldier turned an empty enamel cup in his hands, his gaze swiftly falling from Thomas's face.

"Would ye hear more?"

Libby ceased her shuffle of letters and paper, and listened, breath caught, for Captain Boyd's reply. He sighed into the early morning stillness of the store. "I don't mind saying things are looking pretty dark right now, Thomas."

"Then will ye come upstairs wi' me, lad? The lass left coffee on the stove. 'Twould be a small matter to warm it a bit and fill yer cup while we talk."

Libby's heart twisted at the defeat curving the old soldier's shoulders as he followed her father up the stairs. Back in Thistle Down, her father had a reputation for being fair and honest, even wise. What often went unrecognized was how deeply he cared, how earnestly he prayed, and how faithfully he served as a channel through which God's love flowed. Occasionally, when some fellow was knocked to his knees by life's blows, he would come to her father as if guided by some internal instinct. *Work through him, Lord*, Libby prayed. *Help Captain Boyd understand how eagerly You wait, wanting to be his tower of refuge.*

The men were still upstairs when Zerilda came in the back door with a dark mood stamped across her face. It got even darker when Libby told her that Mr. Boyd had given his notice and would retire when he had finished out the week.

At eight, when she unlocked the doors, the captain came back downstairs to his sorting case. He greeted Zerilda and went to work, seeming lost in thought of a gentler hue.

Mr. Lamb came in to buy nails for coffin building. His relief at seeing the captain was echoed by the stationmaster's cheerful greeting. Hascal Caton wandered in a few minutes later, with Major Minor close behind. Teddy Baker came in, much to the joy of Sugar.

Seeing the old men gathered about the cold stove, Teddy lingered at the fringe of the group with the old beagle at his feet, whining to go out. By and by, Teddy inserted into a lull in the conversation, "We-l-l-l, it's nice to have things back to normal."

"What're ya gettin' at?" asked Hascal gruffly.

"You know," came Teddy's customary reply. Lacking the social skills to be tactful, he added when pressed, "Sitting inside instead of out front."

Hascal shuffled his feet. Mr. Lamb cleared his throat and made a grand production of studying the telegram he was waiting to deliver to Mr. Gentry should he come in. The other old gents who'd filed in looked equally sheepish.

"Gettin' kind of warm in here, Miss Libby? Or is it jest me?" asked Minor with a wink.

Libby figured that was as close to an apology as she was going to receive from the bench brigade for the cold shoulder they'd been giving her after believing the unfounded rumor that her father had fired the captain. Ready to mend broken fences, she cleared the air, saying, "You came in from the country, Mr. Caton. Tell me, how's the oat threshing progressing out in your neighborhood?"

It got the conversation flowing in a useful direction. Libby tore off a piece of brown paper and scribbled down their general observations concerning how much of the oat harvest had been completed and how the yield and quality varied from farm to farm.

Mrs. Brignadello came in midmorning. She'd heard that Captain Boyd was quitting, and thought a retirement party was in order. Libby jumped at the idea, and welcomed Mrs. Bee's help in planning it. With that on her mind as well as the regular business of the store, it was midafternoon before Libby had revised her threshing article to her own satisfaction and written her advertisement.

28

🌹 Printer's ink and molten lead and cigar smoke hung in the air at the newspaper office. Seeing Libby in the door, Mr. Gruben ceased typing and beckoned to her, saying, "Come in, come in! Have a seat."

"I won't keep you. I just wanted to give you the revised article and the advertisement for the store," said Libby, perching on the edge of the chair.

"Let's have a look."

The cigar smoldering in an ashtray made Libby's eyes burn. Beyond the editor's desk, the hulking shape of the Linotype dominated the room. A young apprentice turned from setting type in the trays. His apron was ink-stained, as were his hands and printer's hat of folded newspaper.

Libby's gaze came to rest on Mr. Gruben. Her heart skipped a beat as he lifted his eyes from the page and combed his fingers through his white hair, searching for the pencil that lay on his desk.

"Much better," he said at length. "I'll run it. And the store advertisement too, per terms of our agreement."

Trying to be adultlike, Libby hid her elation and folded her hands in her lap. "You mentioned a piece on the Ladies Aid Society. When would you like to have it turned in?"

"Tomorrow, if possible." Mr. Gruben reached for his cigar. Squinting at her through a screen of smoke, he

286

remarked, "I heard Captain Boyd is retiring. Mrs. Bee says a party is being planned. A piece on that would be nice."

"But that's supposed to be a secret!"

"Exposing secrets is the journalist's bread and butter, Elizabeth. But if you don't have the disposition for it . . ."

His expression was so serious, it took Libby a moment to realize she was being teased—he had no intention of running the piece prior to Captain Boyd's party. Rather, what he intended her to write was a report of the party itself. She smiled and said, "I'd be pleased to record the event."

"How's your reading coming?" he asked.

"I hope to get to it tonight."

He returned the cigar to the ashtray and said, "You were good medicine for my wife. There's nothing she likes better than talking about books."

Pleased, Libby asked, "Does she belong to Longfellow's Club?"

He shook his head. "Florence isn't a joiner. Besides books, flowers and cats are her passion."

"Mrs. Bee invited me to Longfellow's Club. She says they discuss different poems and books and even theatrical groups that come to the Columbian. As much as Mrs. Gruben knows about books, she'd be an asset, I'm sure. I plan to go myself, if I ever have the time."

Mr. Gruben smiled. "An inquiring mind should be fed. Have you thought about college, Elizabeth?"

"I think about it all the time!" she confessed. "I've saved a little money. Though with my father in poor health and David to care for, I can't in good conscience get away right now."

"You're the best judge of your own circumstances," he said, then added kindly, "Anyway, life itself is a pretty good educator for the one who is willing to read and look and listen and learn."

"That's what my father says! But I thought he was just trying to make me feel better," said Libby, rising to go.

Mr. Gruben laughed and came around his desk to hold the door for her. "Let me know what you think of *Jane Eyre*. Florence is eager to hear."

Much later, after the store closed and the supper was

eaten and the table cleared, Libby slipped the novel in the oversized pocket of her apron and went outside in search of David. Failing to find him out front, she circled half the block and came up the alley.

"Davie?"

When she heard a faint stirring overhead, Libby looked from the empty crate to the upended laundry bench propped against the trunk of the tree at the rear of Willie Blue's. She dropped her head back and shaded her eyes, peering into the leafy branches. "David? What're you doing up there?"

At length his small voice called back, "It isn't me, it's somebody else."

"I see. And what is 'Somebody Else' doing way up in that tree?"

"Nothing. Honest," he said so quickly, Libby's curiosity was aroused.

Checking to make sure she was alone, she gathered her skirt in one hand, clambered up on the crate, and stretched until she had a precarious foothold on the upended laundry bench. She wrapped her hands around a branch, and dangled there kicking, building momentum, swinging one foot into the fork of the tree, then pulling herself up. David was perched on a branch several feet above her, his hands behind his back in an unsuccessful attempt to hide Frankie McClure's slingshot.

"So what're you doing?"

He shot her a guarded glance, then ventured, "I'm pretending I'm a shepherd."

"A shepherd?"

He nodded. "Yep. I'm watching for giants."

"Oh! Like Goliath, you mean?" Libby pulled herself up beside him and asked, "Have you seen any?"

He pointed toward Angus's law office. "There's one hiding in there."

"Oh really!"

"Yep. Sometimes he comes to the window. Watch."

"If you hit a window, Father will tan your hide," Libby warned.

"I won't. I've been practicing. Watch," he said again.

Against her better judgment, Libby sat by as her little

brother fitted a rock into the sling, found an opening between branches, and took aim on the roof of Angus's law office. A second attempt brought Angus to the window.

"See! There's the giant."

Angus looked out on the alley and scratched his head a moment before retreating from the window. "Such a kindly-looking giant, too," murmured Libby. Grinning, she added, "That's a pretty good trick, Davie."

It was so good, in fact, she found it hard to resist trying it herself just for the joy of seeing Angus's face in the window. She snipped a leaf off the tree instead, tore it along the vein, and breathed deeply of the fresh green scent while David fitted another rock into the sling and aimed for the buggy shed. In a while she'd see that he returned the slingshot to the buggy. But for the time being, she wanted only to sit in the tree with her brother and be a part of his world of pretend, where shepherds took on giants and won.

As the week progressed, there was a marked improvement in the captain. He came to work smelling only of soap, and it was a Bible, not a bottle, he slipped into his pocket when he didn't think anyone was looking. The change in him was an answered prayer.

As for the nail keggers, they gathered around the stove each morning and smoked and chewed and spat and quarreled and spun their yarns as before. With one notable difference, and that was their acceptance of Libby's father.

Libby took her share of teasing, particularly in regard to her marching in the Republican parade. Though she had yet to decipher what they meant by asking her if that was Spring Lake mud a-dryin' on her shoes. Sometimes there was just no understanding their curious brand of humor.

As for Zerilda, she tramped in each day, dark of visage, slamming and banging her way through the mail, with nary a word for anyone. Libby counseled David, who wasn't accustomed to such antics from grown-ups, to stay out from underfoot.

Meanwhile, Mr. Lamb was commissioned to craft a rocking chair for Captain Boyd to symbolize the ease his friends wished him now that he was retiring. The wood was funded by the donations of well-wishers within the community. The party would be a brief gathering prior to the captain's final mail run. Teddy was entrusted to spread the word without ruining the surprise.

And surprised, Captain Boyd was when, at eight-thirty on Friday morning, a host of well-wishers flooded behind the counter to shake his hand and eat Mrs. Brignadello's cake and anticipate the moment when Mr. Lamb would pull the quilt off the chair.

Libby was sorry Angus couldn't be there. Circuit court was in session over at the Columbian today, and he'd warned her that it would be early evening before he'd be free. Decatur McClure would go before the circuit judge on charges Angus had filed, accusing him of assault and horse theft. It was talked of in whispers at the party, for Hascal Caton was prickly on the subject, having all along maintained that his son-in-law's incarceration was "dirty politics." Whatever the outcome, Libby would learn of it that evening if not sooner, for Angus had invited her to accompany him to the Thespian Club's performance of *The Poor Mr. Rich*. Paulette Harding, Angus's aunt, was involved in bringing the production to Edgewood, and eager for a good showing from the community.

Dr. Harding stopped by to wish Captain Boyd well. He didn't stay long, but Libby took advantage of the opportunity; she got him off to one side and mentioned, in a tactful way, how folks were missing his sister's efficient, sympathetic presence at his office.

"No more than me," he said. "I don't know what's got into her lately. She doesn't come by at all unless I send for her. And even then, I can't seem to keep her long enough to bandage a skinned knee."

Libby pretended to consider the problem for a moment. "I can't really say about Mrs. Bee, but if it were me, an increase in salary might induce me to find a hole in my schedule."

"An increase?" he echoed. "Sarah Jane never would take anything. I know. I've tried."

"Try again," Libby whispered, and cut him a large slice of cake.

Mr. Gruben was next in line for cake. He smiled and passed a newspaper over the counter, saying, "It seems like a good trade to me, a piece of that fine-looking cake for a copy of today's *Gazette.*"

"Hot off the press?" Libby laid the paper flat on the counter and quickly scanned the front page.

"Page two, top left-hand column," the editor said, then strode off to congratulate the captain.

Libby moved past the byline, which was most satisfying in itself, and read the short article. He'd printed it almost word for word! It gave her such a feeling of exultation, she felt like tossing her hat into the air and cheering. Instead, she grinned at Teddy Baker and cut him a generous slice of cake. He promptly dropped to his knees and fed a corner of it to Sugar.

"Teddy, cut that out!" scolded Mrs. Bee.

"Aw, now," he said with a loose grin. "She's a good old girl, she likes cake, too."

The refreshments were going fast when Libby noticed Zerilda stamping toward the back door. Supposing all the milling and hand-pumping behind the counter was "against the book," Libby left Spike Culbertson making the old ones smile and the young ones jump at his rendition of *Little Orphant Annie.* She cut another slice of cake, and tried to coax Zerilda into the spirit of the occasion.

"Got no time for cake an' nonsense." She would have strode back outside, but Libby got between her and the door.

"Please don't go, Mrs. Payne. At least wait until they've presented the chair. If you go, Captain Boyd will think he has to too."

"Girl, you got your mind everywhere but where it needs to be. Now, step out of my way, I got mail to deliver."

Was there no softness in the woman at all? Libby let her through, then followed, temper sparking. "I wish you'd reconsider. Perhaps it seems trifling to you, but I can't help thinking how tenuously he clings to sobriety, and it makes me feel so . . . so . . . careful of him," she said for lack of a better word.

Zerilda swung around and popped off like a steam valve. "Careful? I cain't believe my ears. You sold out for twelve cents. Why, yer mopping up after him with one hand and passin' the bottle with the other!"

"Sold out?" echoed Libby, so benumbed by her hissing fury, she could get no further than the twelve cents.

"I said it plain enough. When ya sell the glass right back to Mr. Skiff, ya got a hand in it, girl."

"A hand in *what*?"

"In the Old Kentucky moonshine jug line. What do you think them men in there've been sawin' away at all week?"

Libby's heart constricted. "Are you saying Mr. Skiff is making . . . I sold jars to a *moonshiner?*"

"If he ain't, he's in cahoots with whoever is. What'd ya think they's doing with them jars—cannin' vegetables?"

Libby had been so focused on not letting Mrs. Bee be taken, on driving a hard bargain. She'd been so prideful in her victory, when all the while the truth had been staring her in the face. She squeezed her eyes shut, struck by her own stupidity.

"I didn't think . . . I didn't question . . . Good faith!"

Zerilda softened just a fraction before rocking back on her heels, arms crossed. "If that ain't trouble enough, ya wait until Miz Dorrance hears of it. Or ain't Angus told ya how he called her off Captain Boyd with his slick politicking?"

"He told you that?"

Zerilda snorted. "He ain't in the habit of consulting me. But I know what I know, and there you are, addle-headed as poor Teddy ever thought of bein'. Thunderation! Don't know when I seen a gal so wet behind the ears."

Zerilda flung the mail in the basket, mounted her bicycle, and pushed off without another word. Head humming, Libby watched her pedal away. She had thought it was God's work, Mrs. Dorrance retrieving that letter. And maybe it was, through human hands. Bless those hands, for they had spared Captain Boyd certain humiliation and enabled his honorable retirement.

Does Angus know about the jars? No, he would have mentioned them. Between his law practice and planning his election campaign, he had no time for cracker-barrel repartee. Nor was his father one for mixing with the old fellows. Perhaps he wouldn't hear of it at all. She prayed he would not, for beyond the humiliation of her blunder was her pledge of silence. Mrs. Brignadello's pride, it would seem, had landed them both in a "kaboodle o' mischief," as her father would say.

Libby let herself back in just as Captain Boyd cut the bow on his chair. "My, what a beauty." He eased into it and rested his silver head against the gently curved oaken back. "A good fit, too. And here I thought you were measuring me for a coffin, Mr. Lamb."

"Wouldn't be no point in that," said Hascal brusquely. "You'll likely bury us all."

"Oh?" asked Captain Boyd in his velvet voice.

"Why, ain't ya heard only the good die young?"

"Yessir, Benjamin, and yer already too blamed old for that," chimed Minor.

The old men laughed and slapped their knees and took their turn at trying out the chair. Libby's father was right in the midst of them, commending Mr. Lamb on his craftsmanship. The mortician stood by, left eye twitching as he took pleasure in the compliment.

It wasn't long before Captain Boyd remembered the country folk waiting for their mail. "That was fine cake, Mrs. Bee. The finest I ever tasted," he said, while the well-wishers were dispersing.

Libby was the last to shake his hand. "We're going to miss you."

He beckoned toward the rocker. "It looks so good there by the stove, I may make it my outpost, if that's all right with you."

"I was hoping as much," she said.

His fine old chin trembled as he smiled and nodded and shook her hand again.

Libby waited until everyone had gone before getting Mrs. Bee aside. Her surprise turned swiftly to dismay when she learned the purpose of Mr. Skiff's jar buying.

"Moonshine? Land sakes! What are we to do?"

"It's done. What can we do?"

"But it was in innocence! Though who's going to believe that? If Ida catches wind of this . . . Or Chester. Or Angus!" Mrs. Brignadello flung open hands to her scarlet cheeks and went on wavering between self-defense and self-deprecation. "Kersey never gave a hint that the jars were used for such a thing. It was him who told me that Teddy catches a ride out to Skiff's now and again, taking his jars. That's what gave me the idea. Of course, no one in Mrs. Baker's family is running for the state legislature. On a prohibition platform, at that."

Premonition siphoned the air from Libby's lungs. Of a sudden she saw Zerilda's words concerning Mrs. Dorrance in a new light.

"I'll give the old rascal his twelve cents and retrieve the jars, that's all I can do. But how?" Mrs. Bee's loaded glance landed squarely on Libby.

"I'll be carrying the mail there tomorrow, if you'd like me to do it for you," said Libby, feeling an urgent need to see the blunder swiftly rectified.

"I thought your father was taking Captain Boyd's job."

"He is, once his ribs are healed."

"So you're filling in?" At Libby's nod, Mrs. Bee added, "I'll ride along, then, if that's all right."

"You don't have to," said Libby.

"Yes, I do. It's only right, after all. None of this is your doing."

Then why, oh why, did the burden of it fall so squarely on her shoulders, stealing even the joy of her first published piece of writing?

29

🌸 The mason jar folly in mind, it was with a mixture of anticipation and trepidation that Libby dressed for her evening with Angus. She bathed and donned her blue silk dress and an old hat she had brightened with fresh ribbons, then went downstairs to wait. David was in the park playing with a new friend. It was just she and her father when the knock came at the back door. He closed the accounts book and reached for the cane he'd been using.

"Sit still, Father, I'll get it."

"Na, na. If it's the yoong man come a-sweetheartin', ye dinna wish to rush the door all adither."

"Father!" protested Libby, laughter mixing with reproof. But she let him answer the knock, and was mortally glad she had. For it was Decatur McClure at the door. The shock of it rocked her back a step.

"Mr. McClure! Ye be oot, then. A free man?"

"Yessir. Judge booted out the horse-thievin' charge, and ordered me to pay fer the use of it, instead."

"And what aboot the other?" Thomas asked quietly.

"Give me a warnin', made me pay the doctorin', and set me loose. Mr. Sparks says he went easy on account of Cearlock provokin' me, speakin' of Naomi thataway."

"Come in, lad. Sit doon," Thomas invited with a sweep of his hand.

Mr. McClure wagged his dark head. "Obliged fer yer visits, Mr. Watson, and fer somethin' ta read. But like I told ya b'fore, it don't change nothin'."

Gently Thomas said, "It isna for me to change ye, or fer ye to change yerself. Nae, but for ye to put yerself whaur God can reach doon inside and do His work upon ye heart."

The big man remained silent, respectful, and all the while it was evident that Thomas's words were falling off him like rain off oiled leather. He reached inside his shirt and pulled out a Bible. "Returnin' what's yers."

"Keep it, lad," said Thomas.

"No, take it," said Mr. McClure, pressing the Bible upon him. "I got no need of it." He turned out the door and was gone.

Libby released her held breath, Mr. McClure's short, terse phrases lingering in her mind. "What was it Angus said about Naomi?"

"Nae guid comes of stirrin' a scorched pot."

"If I'm to go sweetheartin' with the fellow, don't you suppose I should know?"

Mildly her father admonished, "Dinna be saucy wi' yer old faether, lass."

She turned away, sensitive to the rebuke, not for her own sake, but because his refusal to discuss it impeded her urge to defend Angus. For how could she, when she knew so little of the matter? Libby climbed the stairs to grab her forgotten reticule.

Upon her return, she found Angus had come. He and her father were chatting amicably. Her anxiety lessened, for her father's manner was in every way accepting of the young man in the frock coat and silk hat.

It was a warm, sunny evening. The short stroll to the Columbian couldn't have been more pleasant. The production was a well-executed comedy. Light and playful, seasoned throughout with farce and fun and frolic. Every bit as enjoyable was the reaction of the audience, who were thoroughly caught up in the production. Angus's aunt Paulette, stationed at the door with her husband at her side, was fairly staggering beneath the load of compliments as the audience made its way past.

"A smashing success, Auntie." Angus stooped to kiss her cheek.

"Thank you, Angus. What a lovely dress, Miss Watson. So glad you could come."

Heartened by the first show of warmth from the woman, Libby returned her smile, exclaiming, "It was a wonderful production!"

"How's the ankle, Angus?" asked Dr. Harding.

"Healing nicely," he replied, shaking hands with his uncle before the swell of the crowd propelled them out the door.

Libby took Angus's proffered arm as they started home on foot along the lamplit street. He swung along with a token limp, scarcely needing the cane.

A sigh of pure satisfaction escaped Libby. "That was first-rate entertainment. I don't know when I've laughed so hard."

"Yes, and if ever I needed a laugh, it was today."

It was the first he had alluded to his day in court. Sobering, Libby ventured with a careful glance, "I heard it didn't go quite as you had hoped."

"So it's made the rounds, has it?" The streetlamp picked out the fatigue upon his face. But the hard set of his jaw softened at Libby's murmured "I'm sorry."

"Ah well, I'll take it on the chin. Again."

His dry quip freshened her reminder of his face, battered but a month ago by the hand of Decatur McClure. "What of his family? Does his temper put them in danger?"

Angus guided her around a wheelbarrow left on the wooden walk, a slight frown forming. "I'd have no idea about that."

Sensing a change of subject was in order, Libby said, "That was a kind thing you did for Captain Boyd. Just what did you say, anyway, to change Mrs. Dorrance's mind?"

"My stand on prohibition pleases Mrs. Dorrance immensely, as you can imagine," said Angus, his smile a little weary. "She stopped by my office on behalf of the Women's Christian Temperance League with assurances concerning their endorsement for my candidacy. And she assured me she would work tirelessly right here at home, seeing that the laws on the books against alcohol use were vigorously enforced."

"Even if it meant launching a one-woman crusade against Captain Boyd?"

Angus nodded. "I pointed out the danger of splitting the community if my campaign platform was somehow linked in the minds of local voters with Captain Boyd being fired because of his drinking. I don't mean to imply I'm wishy-washy on the issue," he added quickly. "But at the same time I don't want every man who has a bottle hidden out in the barn to get the idea the law is going to come haul him off to jail if prohibition is passed. I could see that concept wasn't altogether unappealing to Mrs. Dorrance. So I pointed out the broader application."

"Which is?" asked Libby.

"That she was hurting the girl with the strawberry curls, and I just wouldn't stand for it."

Flushing, laughing at being taken in, Libby insisted, "No, really. How did you sway her?"

"I just kept stressing the point that it takes a grassroots effort for an unknown candidate such as myself to be elected to public office. And the importance of beginning here at home with a solid core of supporters."

"She finally agreed?"

"Let's just say she weighed the gains and losses and decided to go along."

Libby mulled that over for a moment. "I'm not sure I'd be comfortable with her on my team."

"It's a balancing act, that's for certain." Angus held the door for her, and dismissed Mrs. Dorrance altogether, saying, "Enough politics for one night. Could I drive you home from services on Sunday?"

"I'd like that," said Libby.

"New Hope or Methodist?" he asked.

"Methodist," replied Libby, in fear once again of colliding with Mrs. Dorrance. Angus had made no mention of mason jars or Skiff's Store. She could only hope that if her blunder came to his attention, it would be after she'd done all she could to rectify the matter.

"Fine! Catherine will be home by then."

"She's out of town, is she?"

"She took the train to St. Louis early in the week."

"So that's why she wasn't at Captain Boyd's party."

"Yes, well, there was a house Charlie wanted her to see. He's gotten a promotion and a nice raise. He's grown weary of traveling."

"Catherine mentioned as much."

"Did she also mention we've a standing invitation for dinner at her house?"

"We couldn't impose on her that way," Libby said quickly. "Not when she's been away all week."

"Of course we could," he said, and grinned.

There was a light burning inside the store. Her father and David continued to sleep downstairs, due more to the heat than her father's injuries. Libby wondered, as she reached into her reticule for her key, if the light had been left on for her, or if father was sitting up reading.

Angus unlocked the door for her, but seemed in no hurry to say good night. Silver-headed cane hooked over one wrist, he returned the key to her palm, and folded her fingers over it. It was a feeling to relish, the touch of his hand through her gloves as he lifted her fingers and pressed them to his lips. She lifted her gaze to find a tender expression on his face.

"'Who can find a virtuous woman, for her price is far above rubies,'" he recited in a soft voice.

"You're embarrassing me."

He chuckled at her frankness, and countered, "I can't help it. You inspire me."

The shift in his mood freed her to say what she'd been wanting to say all evening. Lifting her gaze to his face again, she murmured, "I'm sorry you lost the case against Mr. McClure."

"Funny, I don't feel it so acutely now." He smiled into her eyes for a long moment, and squeezed her hand before making his departure.

The next morning Mrs. Brignadello sent Teddy with twelve pennies wrapped in a handkerchief and word that Dr. Harding had summoned her for a medical emergency. She couldn't ride along today. The return negotiations, it would seem, were up to Libby. She departed beneath overcast skies.

The heat was oppressive, no breath of a breeze. By noon, thunderheads were brewing. They churned as dark as coal smoke over wheat shocks and hay fields and thriving green corn. Distant lightning splintered the heavens. Heaving clouds, like skilled jugglers, shifted their burdens end over end without losing a drop.

Clouds without rain skipped to mind. Libby fervently hoped so, for she had Old Kentucky yet to deliver. Thunder cracked just as she started into the green sheen. The sullen skies had given the flies a hearty appetite. Proctor's hide flickered in syncopation with his swishing tail.

"Step it up, that's a good fellow." She urged him into a swifter gait.

The air stirred, lifting the leaves and cooling Libby's steaming back. For a moment she enjoyed the reprieve. But thunder soon struck a deeper, more ominous chord. It was a foregone conclusion, as they passed the cemetery, the school, and the church, that she wasn't going to beat the storm.

The covered bridge on the approach to Skiff's Store was in view when lightning ripped the bottom out of the clouds. The rain came with a freshening wind behind it. Blinding, battering blankets of rain beat on the buggy top and swept through the uncurtained windows. Proctor required no urging. The bridge represented shelter, and he wasn't long in getting there.

Sore from sitting so long, Libby climbed out to stretch her legs while she waited for the storm to pass. It was an old bridge. The gaps between boards were generous. It would be easy to catch a heel. Libby was watching where she put her feet when she found herself looking through a knothole into Naomi McClure's upturned face.

"Good faith! What're you doing in the water?" In the intervening seconds between recognition and reply was the race of visual messages. Naomi's tear-swollen eyes. Her glistening nose. Her unnatural stillness as the heavens shook, the rains pounded, and the swiftening creek crashed against her thighs. She had not meant to be seen. What now?

"My line's snagged. I was wading acrost ta free it," Naomi shouted back.

Belatedly Libby saw the sapling pole. *Fishing, in a thunderstorm?* The air left her lungs. She filled them again, mentally writhing. Should she pretend that nothing in this scene struck her as unusual? Or should she . . .

"I reckon I'll jest cut bait and come up," Naomi said, relieving her of the decision.

Sodden skirt clinging, bare feet scrabbling for a hold, she climbed the mud-slickened creekbank and joined Libby beneath the sheltering timbers of the bridge.

"Decatur's home," Naomi said, dropping her chin, avoiding Libby's scrutiny.

Embarrassed, not knowing what to say, Libby looked away, then back again, thinking of the Sunday afternoon she'd called on Naomi at her boxcar home deep in the woods. Of her children and her garden and the flower buds she'd pinched back for the strengthening of those that remained. Hesitantly she asked, "Are the children all right?"

Naomi nodded. "Frankie ketched a ride in town with Ike. Opal's home. He ain't no danger to her, not even when he's drinkin'," she added. "Though it hurt me somethin' mortal ta have ta walk out the door and leave her behind."

Libby wasn't sure of Naomi's meaning, but timidity and a reluctance to further intrude kept her from asking. Seeing her tremble, she said, "You're wet to the skin. We could wait this out in the buggy."

Naomi climbed up, skirt dripping, teeth chattering. "I worked hard at makin' Opal understand what she's worth so she wouldn't ever hurt herself lookin' to be loved. But when I hugged her, she pulled away like she wasn't loved at all."

Her eyes welled as the words came with passion and pain. "Different words had ought to be used for the different kinds of love. Or spelt different, anyways. Like flower and flour. The one makes life awful sweet, curlin' yer toes and meltin' ya like butter. But the other's a staple you cain't live without. You go confusin' the two, and there's more hurt than a body can shake a stick at. I reckon it don't matter much anymore. Not about me, leastways."

Libby found herself remembering the poem Naomi had read that Sunday. What was that first line? Something about the world's need for a love built upon forgiveness. She was struck suddenly by the realization that such a love did exist. Gently she said, "You left a love out. The third love, and it *is* spelled differently. It's spelled G-o-d."

Shamefaced, Naomi murmured, "I know. I *do* know. A preacher come through here years ago and told me all about it. That it was the best love of all. Decatur was courtin' me then. He was so jealous of that preacher, I had to fight hard at gettin' anything out of the evangelist's words, for worryin' Decatur'd come bustin' into that tent, sayin' something crazy, and I'd die right there of embarrassment."

"Father'd say that was the devil in him, workin' distraction," said Libby.

"Destruction?"

"Well, yes. That, too. Telling you you don't need that third love."

"I need somethin'. Something to stop this hurtin'."

Libby wasn't sure what she meant. Was it something Decatur had done? Something he'd said? Or was it the past reaching into the present that was causing her such anguish?

Distraught, Naomi climbed down again and paced from one end of the bridge and back again, wet skirts clinging. "I don't know what to do. I was hopin', with all that time to think, he'd of measured the cost and decided it wasn't worth it, keepin' this thing goin'."

"Your marriage?" asked Libby.

"No. Gettin' revenge on a dead man who was the best friend he had right up to the day he died." Yards from the buggy, she was shouting to be heard above the storm.

"I'm sorry," Libby said, then winced at the ineptness of her words.

"No, *I'm* sorry. This ain't about you, and it ain't about

the store. It's about me standing up in court and namin' Frankie's father."

Then Decatur intended to go on with this lawsuit? Why? He must know he couldn't win. Not if Ike testified that he had been there, and Willie hadn't changed his will. Libby climbed out of the buggy. Waiting, wondering, hesitant to ask.

The wind sang through the bridge, buffeting the hard curves and sharp planes of Naomi's body. She wiped her nose with the back of her hand and sighed from deep inside. "Forever and always, Decatur's wanted me to name the man. Even when it looked like things might work out between us, he wanted to know. I wouldn't say because it was before him and nothin' to do with him. He knew when he married me I was carryin' a child and it wasn't him who'd laid with me."

"You don't have to tell me any of this," Libby inserted quickly.

"Ye're gonna hear it one way or another. Ye're caught in the middle, havin' to go to court fer what Willie already made yers."

"Maybe not. Maybe your husband won't go through with it. Angus says he can't possibly win."

"It ain't about winnin'." Naomi huddled against the bridge wall, hugging her arms across her chest. "Decatur has known the truth about Willie since the funeral. He's got a hankerin' to hear me put words to it, that's the thing."

"It's just words," said Libby, baffled that she would face the indignity of a hearing rather than tell her husband what he already knew.

Naomi peeled a matted plait of rain-soaked hair away from her throat. "Jest words. I said 'em to Mr. Cearlock, thinking they'd get back to Decatur, and that ort to be enough. But it wasn't. And somehow or another, I can't tuck my chin and say them same words to him." Her green gaze lifted. Shamefaced, she added, "You must be thinkin' mighty poorly of me."

"No," said Libby, too quickly, too vehemently.

"I was a fool-headed girl. I ain't complainin'. I'm jest sick for my young 'uns, and wonderin' what's next."

Her eyes made Libby think of the enduring patience of a cat, backed into a dark corner. Hungry and cold and wet, the discomfort so familiar, it didn't occur to her to seek help.

"Can't you go to your father?"

"Fer what?"

There was no self-pity in her, rather an acceptance of folks as they were and a raw, plodding courage. *How does she keep her balance in such a teetering existence?* Libby's eyes misted as she relinquished her own narrow, preconceived notions. Quite without meaning to, she blurted, "Uncle Willie must have loved you very much."

Naomi's face broke. Tears spilled over careworn creases and crevices.

"I don't think he ever did. It wasn't like that," she said. "Only happened once and it wouldna then, except he was drinkin' and I went to him cryin' over Pa takin' me out of school."

School. The yearning for an education, something Libby understood all too well, melted away her awkward inhibitions. The kinship she had felt that Sunday afternoon when Naomi had read from the book of poems and spoken with soft regret of her interrupted education stole over her again. She put her arms around Naomi as naturally as if she were David, come with a skinned knee or a disappointed heart. As the rains lashed and the wind blew and the creek rushed below, Naomi's halting words painted a much more dismal picture, a picture of a father so different from her own. Well intentioned at times. Plainly misguided at others. True to his friends, and yet unwilling or unable to love his daughter as his daughter needed loving. Silently Libby derided Hascal Caton for being so lacking. So set on sons that he couldn't appreciate daughters. So stiff and unyielding and narrow.

"Ain't it a wonderment, the tender picture a gal ken get in her head?" said Naomi. "But it wasn't like that. Nothin' purty about it. Jest bodies clashing and me sick with shame afterwards and lonelier than ever. And Willie . . . For weeks and weeks, I wasn't even sure he knew what he'd done." She sniffed and wiped her eyes with trembling fingers and shot Libby a glimmering glance. "Ya want me to shet up?"

"I'm listening," murmured Libby, keeping hold of Naomi's work-worn hand.

"Not knowin'—that's what kept me from goin' to him when I missed my monthlies. That and havin' played the fool. Fer once I opened my eyes, it was plain enough he was in love with somebody else."

"Ike Galloway's mother," said Libby, knowing that much of the story. Naomi nodded. Gently Libby asked, "You never spoke up?"

She shook her head. "Preacher Jericho married Mrs. Galloway. Willie married Addie for her strength, I reckon, and there was Decatur, champing at the bit to wed me. It was him or stay with Pa." She wiped a tear from her chin. "I'll allow it was weak of me, but the thought of Pa railing the truth out of me was more'n I could bear."

The storm was passing. Thunder and lightning had traveled on. The rain had slackened to a drizzle and Naomi was talked out. She looked through a crack between the boards and murmured something about her sapling pole.

"I'm going to have to finish the mail route. Can I drop you somewhere?" offered Libby.

"I reckon I'll go to the shop. Fish ain't bitin' anyway."

"Skiff's Store, you mean?" asked Libby, for it was just beyond the bridge.

"No. The cabin there by the train crossing."

Remembering the cabin, Libby wondered once again who lived there. But Naomi was already on her way down the bank, going after her fishing pole.

Libby brought her father's round pail out from the space behind the seat while she waited for Naomi. Moments later, as Proctor plodded past Skiff's Store, Libby was sharing her lunch and musing over all Naomi had and hadn't said. She forgot all about the twelve pennies she was to return for pondering how mistakes so far in the past could rear their heads and so violently disrupt the present.

When they reached the cabin, Naomi invited her in, and though Libby had already lost a good deal of time, she couldn't refuse her. The place proved to be a carpenter's workshop. There was a chair under construction. A cabinet. And several other pieces. Libby stopped short at the sight of them.

"Whose shop is this?" she asked, for the craftsmanship was strikingly familiar.

"Mine." Naomi picked up a wood gouge and sat down at the lathe. She rocked the pedal with the same ease Libby had at her treadle sewing machine. Chips flew from the spindle she was shaping.

"You made these things? They look just like the pieces over the store." Sudden comprehension drove the breath from her lungs. "It was *you?*"

Naomi blew away the wood curls spilling over her hand. "Willie taught me. He had a true eye and a good, steady hand when he wasn't drinking."

"You remained friends even after . . ." Libby flushed, and finished quickly, "After he married and moved to town?"

"Him and Decatur were the best of friends. He didn't aim to teach me furniture-makin'. It was Decatur who was supposed to be learnin'. Jest newly wed and livin' in a old boxcar, with nary a stick of furniture. But he went at it like he was killin' snakes." She smiled the faintest of smiles. "Willie'd tease him and say there was tokens— that's what he called spirits, 'tokens'—in the wood and that they was hangin' on to every splinter, hidin' themselves, they was jest that scairt when they saw Decatur comin'. But that they'd come trottin' out fer me on account I could pick up a tool without turnin' the air blue."

Libby sensed that the pleasant times in the early years of Naomi's marriage made the present difficulties all the more painful. She said, "It's your work upstairs, then? At the store?"

Naomi nodded and blinked tear-washed eyes. "I thought Willie was selling the pieces. Decatur thought so too, right up to the day of his funeral. Why, he hepped him load most of it onto the train here at the switch. A little time'd go by, and here'd come Willie, sayin' the money'd come in the mail."

"But he hadn't really sold them? I don't understand."

"I didn't either," said Naomi. "But Decatur did, eventually. He went lookin' for some kind of proof for what he'd seen between Willie and Frankie as Willie lay dying. First he tried abusin' it out of young Mr. Cearlock, on account he was Willie's attorney."

"What did Angus say?"

Naomi flushed. "Cain't say I hold a little coarseness agin' him. Giner'ly speakin', a feller don't like bein' ketched up and wallered about in the mud."

"What *did* he say?" Libby asked again.

Her color deepened. "Nothin' Decatur ain't said himself a dozen times since."

Libby did not ask again. Naomi went on to say that Decatur had found his proof of paternity in the furniture.

"How do you mean?" asked Libby, failing to understand.

She sighed deeply. "The closest I can figure, Wille was looking to shoulder his responsibility with Frankie, onct he realized it was his boy. But he knew if he up and claimed him, it'd like to kill Decatur on account of them bein' sech good friends. I reckon he worked it out in his own mind that he'd be payin' somethin' toward supportin' Frankie if he was to buy the furniture hisself."

"But not to resell it?"

"If he'd resold it, he wouldn't of been payin' fer Frankie's keep, he'd of been in the furniture business. That wasn't his intention," reasoned Naomi. "Course, I didn't guess sech a thing at the time. It's now, looking back on it, trying to see it through Willie's eyes, that it come to me. Willie always did have his own way of lookin' at things," she added.

"So Decatur pieced it together because of the furniture?" said Libby, still trying to understand.

Naomi nodded. Color swept up her cheeks. Dropping her gaze, she said, "Decatur's figurin' don't exactly square with mine. He got it in his head maybe Willie's holdin' on to all them pieces was his way of holdin' on to what had been between us."

Like a shrine? Or could it be Decatur was now suspicious it had been an ongoing affair? If that was the case, Naomi didn't say. She fell silent, powering the lathe with her foot. The whirring music of the lathe was almost soothing in its monotony.

Libby pulled up a stool and watched, all the while thinking of Uncle Willie. All those years ago, when they thought he was no good for himself, much less anyone else, he was paying for his son's keep the best way he knew how. To salve his own conscience? Maybe. But give him his due, he did what he thought needed doing, and did it so cleverly that Decatur, who knew him better than any of them, couldn't see the forest for the trees.

Layers to the man. Ike Galloway's phrasing all those weeks ago came drifting to her mind. What a puzzle was Uncle Willie. Trying to mend what he'd broken. Libby looked into Naomi's face, and knew that he had failed. For suffering had outlived Willie Blue. In Naomi. In Decatur. In Frankie and Opal. Would there be no end to the pain?

30

🐚 The sun was out by the time Libby made it back to town. But Naomi's story had fostered a growing uneasiness in her. She kept thinking how Naomi had said it had hurt her to walk out the door and leave Opal behind. If she was only going fishing, why would she feel hurt at leaving Opal? *When I hugged her, she pulled away like she wasn't loved at all.* It sounded eerily like a good-bye. Yet Naomi had seemed puzzled at Libby's suggestion that she seek help from her father. So where would she go? Throughout the busy Saturday night, Libby thought of her out there in the green grove. And wondered. And prayed. And waited like one watching the sky as a storm assembled.

Later, when the doors were locked and David was asleep on his cot, Libby told Father of Naomi's dilemma and how the purchase of all those pieces of furniture had been Uncle Willie's surreptitious way of contributing to the support of his son.

"Poor lass. Poor laddie," said Father in such a tender voice that Libby was unsure whether he was thinking of Frankie or of her mother's dead uncle.

Under the circumstances, it was difficult to sustain an opinion of Uncle Willie. He'd played a key role in the trouble unfolding in Naomi's life today. At the same time, there was something touching about his attempts to provide for a son he could not openly claim.

And what of Frankie? Libby found it curious that it was Opal's name on Naomi's lips as she talked of the dangers of a child growing up feeling unloved. Was she so consumed with sparing her daughter a fate similar to her own that she was blind to the holes in Frankie? How much of the story did he know? If Decatur really had done right by him up to the present time, what were Frankie's feelings toward him? Toward Uncle Willie? Toward Naomi herself? Libby closed her eyes, wishing she could erase from her memory the traces of tears on the boy's face. Where had his toughness been then?

"It comes to me, lass, that in namin' ye as his beneficiary, Willie was entrustin' more than a store," mused Libby's father at length.

Libby considered her father's words. Jacob's simple explanation of favoritism as the basis for Uncle Willie's bequest was a lot easier to live with. It was easy, too, to dismiss the McClures as a tragic case of reaping what had been sowed. Except for the innocents. And except for that still, small voice forewarning that something more might be required.

Libby awoke the next morning with Naomi on her mind. She dressed for church in the pale yellow gown she'd worn to the Republican Rally at the lake and the hat she'd bought from Mrs. Bee. But when she looked in the mirror, the very hair on her head reminded her of Frankie and his sister. *How are they faring? Naomi wouldn't leave them. Surely she wouldn't leave them, no matter how difficult things have become with Decatur.*

"Lib? Are you ready?" David's voice came drifting up the stairs.

"Be right down."

Father and David accompanied Libby to services at the Methodist church. Angus was waiting for her in the churchyard when the last notes of the closing song faded. He shook Libby's father's hand and David's too, and offered, in view of Thomas's wrapped ankle, to drive them home.

"That's kind of ye, lad, but we've a dinner invitation to keep."

"Dinner?" echoed Libby, surprised.

"Aye, Mrs. Baker's invited the lad and me for a bite. She sent word last evenin' by Teddy when he was seein' Sugar home. By the look of ye, lass, ye'd think this was the first ye'd heard of it."

His innocent tone might have fooled Libby, but for the spot of color high on his cheeks. It was a curious sight, seeing him blush. She hadn't but a heartbeat to ponder the possibilities, for he'd no more than walked away when Catherine came along, all aglow in white silk and chiffon with her husband at her side, little Tess on his arm.

"Angus! Libby! Wonderful news!" she cried.

"Charlie's bought an automobile?" asked Angus, grinning.

"Bite your tongue. I wouldn't have one of those vile, coughing monsters. Now, guess again."

"I can tell by the look in your eye that you've been shopping. Now, if I could only figure out *what*," teased Angus. He gripped Charlie's hand. "How's the insurance business faring?"

"It's going just grand," Catherine answered for him.

"She hopes," said Charlie.

"Found a house, eh? A nice one, is it?"

"It's a roof over our heads," claimed Charlie modestly.

"Yes, and four bedchambers, a huge dining hall, a library, a lovely, sunny parlor, and a kitchen with all the modern conveniences. There's gas lighting throughout. City water. And our own telephone, of course."

"Of course," quipped Angus, winking at Charlie.

"You'll just have to come see it when we get moved," Catherine said, ignoring her brother's playful goading. "It has a big yard where Tess can play. And huge old trees shading the veranda."

"It sounds wonderful. But oh, how I'm going to miss you!" said Libby, feeling a twinge of regret even as she shared Catherine's excitement.

"We're not going right away. It'll be the first of August." Catherine paused all at once. She gripped Angus's arm, turning him around. "Is that . . . It is! It's Maddie Dorrance!"

Libby turned as a tall, raven-haired young woman approached. She was dressed all in black, the lines of her costume accentuating her graceful curves, elegant carriage, and flawless skin.

Catherine embraced her old friend. "I can't believe my eyes! Your mother never mentioned a word about your coming."

"I surprised her." Maddie straightened the hat that Catherine's hug had bumped.

"When did you arrive?"

"Just yesterday."

"Is Dr. Daniels with you?" Struck silent by Maddie's expression, Catherine stopped short and with an intake of breath surveyed Maddie's black garb. "Oh no, Maddie. Don't tell me you've lost him."

"Six months ago," said Maddie, putting on a brave face. "Mother never told you?"

Catherine's flush conceded that and more. Maddie's chin hardened. She pursed her lips and said with a haughty air, "Ah, well. I knew when she didn't answer my telegram that nothing was forgiven or forgotten."

"I'm so sorry," said Catherine.

"It's her way," said Maddie.

At the young widow's clipped words, Libby remembered the account Catherine had given her of her childhood friend's elopement with a handsome silver-tongued fellow by the name of Dr. Daniels. The man had come to Edgewood with his medicine show, and swept Maddie Dorrance off her feet. Mrs. Dorrance thought the man was a fraud, selling liquor under the guise of a cure-all elixir. The incident had caused a rift between mother and daughter that apparently had yet to heal.

Maddie stretched a finger to Tess. "She's got your coloring, Catherine. Your dimples, too."

"You think so?" Catherine took her little daughter from her husband's arms. "This is Mama's good friend, Aunt Maddie. Can you say hello, precious?"

Tess hid a shy face against Catherine's shoulder.

"At least one of us has found happiness," said Maddie, though there was no self-pity in her voice.

Catherine put an arm around her, and when they had talked a moment longer, introduced her to Libby.

"This is my friend, and Angus's too—Miss Elizabeth Watson."

"Miss Watson." Maddie's throaty voice hovered over the name, as if it struck a familiar note. All at once a smile flickered in her dark eyes. "Yes, of course. Mother mentioned you last evening. Mr. Skiff and the Mason jars?"

Libby flung Angus an anxious glance.

Quick to notice, Maddie added, "I haven't embarrassed you, have I? Don't be! I was inspired by your pluckiness. My father used to do some trading with Mr. Skiff. He'd take me along sometimes. As young as I was, I remember how that man hated being outbargained."

"What's this, Libby?" asked Angus.

Cornered, she murmured, "A misunderstanding. It's a long, tedious story. That's a lovely dress, Mrs. Daniels."

She was admiring the rich lace and exquisite embroidery bedecking the gown when an awkward pause gave her second thoughts on the social correctness of complimenting widow weeds.

Catherine, bless her, bridged the moment by conveying, once again, her tender sympathies for Maddie's loss. Maddie, when questioned, revealed that a hunting accident had claimed her husband's life. She had spent the past months supporting herself as a teacher at an Indiana finishing school for young ladies, but she'd grown lonesome for home and family.

The fact that she had worshiped here, and not with her mother and the New Hope congregation, was an indication that all was not well. It was wicked of her, Libby supposed, to feel less sympathetic than she might have had Maddie not mentioned the Mason jars. She felt flushed, and timid of lifting her face to Angus. Meanwhile, Catherine was urging her old friend to join them for dinner, an invitation Maddie accepted.

"Charlie and I walked, but I'm sure Angus would give you a lift."

"I'd count it a privilege," Angus agreed.

"I've got Mother's trap. I'll have to take it by the

Columbian and tell her I won't be there for dinner. You can pick me up if you'd like," said Maddie.

"New Hope's meeting there?" asked Catherine.

Maddie nodded and, with a hand on her skirts, started toward the street where a collection of rigs waited.

"I'll swing around to the curb," Angus called to Libby, then lengthened his stride, falling in step with Maddie.

Libby heard her say, "Mother tells me you're making a run for the legislature."

"Widowed!" exclaimed Catherine, her countenance shadowed. "And not a word from her mother. Can you imagine!" Fussing with her daughter's small bonnet, she lowered her voice to a whisper, adding, "I've never seen her look lovelier, though. Whatever was in Dr. Daniel's elixir, it surely did clear her complexion!"

Catherine's home was small, but cozy and well kept. The meal, much of it fresh from the garden, was prepared in advance and served on a beautifully set table. The conversation was spontaneous, flitting from bringing Maddie up-to-date on all that had transpired in Edgewood in her absence to the world exposition in St. Louis to Libby's short piece in *The Gazette*.

It was Catherine who mentioned it, saying, "I saw your byline in the paper, Libby. I was so surprised!"

"It came about rather suddenly."

"It was a fine piece," said Angus, his words bringing a flush of pleasure to Libby's cheeks.

"So you're a journalist?" said Maddie, regarding Libby with fresh interest.

"Actually, my true ambition is to write fiction. But Mr. Gruben was kind enough to give me a start in his paper."

"I see," said Maddie. "Where did you go to school?"

"Thistle Down," replied Libby.

"Thistle Down?" Maddie's brow puckered. "I don't believe I've heard of it. Is it an institution for training teachers?"

"No. Thistle Down is my hometown in southern Illinois."

"I see," said Maddie.

Cheeks warming again, Libby added, "I hope to enroll

in college sometime in the near future. In the meantime, I plan to learn all I can from Mr. Gruben."

"He puts out a good paper. Though in my opinion his views are a little conservative," said Maddie.

"By necessity," said Charlie. "Edgewood is a conservative community."

"If everyone is finished, why don't we go out on the porch?" Catherine ended the discussion. She excused herself to put Tess down for a nap before joining the rest of them on the porch.

Libby sat with Maddie on the top step while the men settled in chairs behind them to smoke and talk of the fair and automobiles and the fall election.

"Mother's thrilled with your platform, Angus," Maddie said, smiling over her shoulder at Angus as she made room on the top step for Catherine to sit between her and Libby. "I understand she's approached Dr. Harding's wife about putting together a singing group to go campaigning with you."

"It's the sort of idea that appeals to Aunt Paulette," said Catherine. "What about you, Maddie? You've always had a nice voice."

Maddie arched her slim white neck, glancing once more at Angus. "The truth is, Angus, I'd be pleased to see you take a bolder stripe, if you don't mind my saying so."

"I'm always open to suggestions."

"All right then, if you mean it. A fellow with enough courage to stand up and fight for the women's vote would interest me tremendously."

"Women have no vote," said Catherine.

"That's just my point."

"The woman in our house does," claimed Charlie. "She tells me who's clever enough to keep this country out of mischief, and that's who I vote for."

"That's very democratic of you, Mr. Morefield. Ladies such as Miss Watson and myself should be so fortunate."

Angus chuckled. "You've given me food for thought, Maddie."

"Then chew it later," said Catherine, rolling her eyes. "I'm sorry, Maddie, I get a steady diet of this at Mama's.

Politics is all Chester ever talks about. And here lately, Angus has become almost as annoying."

"I object!" protested Angus, laughing.

"Overruled!" exclaimed Catherine, brandishing a stick. She giggled at her brother's feigned retreat and moved to the bottom step. "See here, while I sketch our house in the dust. Nothing fancy, just a rough idea of the room arrangement."

Maddie and Libby joined her. But Maddie's interest strayed when Angus mentioned playing golf in college. She spoke up, saying that she had learned the game from her late husband. They fell to discussing swings and clubs and tees and terms the like of which Libby had never heard. All the while, Catherine was musing about curtains and carpets. In lending an ear to both conversations at the same time, Libby managed to miss the better part of each. Maddie had been Catherine's classmate, which made her younger than Angus by two years. Catherine had never hinted that there'd been any sparks of interest between Maddie and her brother. And yet, she couldn't help feeling a twitch of her heart at Angus's attention to the young widow. Or was it the Mason-jar explanations looming over her that accounted for her prickly feeling?

By and by, Charlie fell asleep with his feet on the porch railing. Catherine smiled and touched a finger to her lips. "Poor fellow. He's put in a rough week." She got to her feet and pulled Maddie up, too, saying, "Come around back and look at my roses. You too, Libby."

"Libby's seen them. You two go ahead." Angus countered Catherine's baiting smile with an obtuse flick of an ash off the end of his cigar. But when their backs were turned, his eye lingered upon his sister and her friend. "They were inseparable as children. Like two little ducks, one fair as the other was dark."

Grown into beautiful swans, thought Libby, their loveliness enhanced by shining curls and sleek gowns and a natural grace. She felt dowdy of a sudden, in her homemade primrose faille.

"What is this about you and Mr. Skiff?" Angus unwittingly prodded her bruised spirit.

There was nothing to do but tell him. Conscious of her

promise to Mrs. Brignadello, Libby abbreviated the tale, leaving his aunt out of it altogether. "I'm taking his money back and retrieving the jars. I planned to do it yesterday, but between the storm and Naomi McClure—"

"Naomi?" he interrupted. "What's she have to do with this?"

"Nothing. She was fishing under the bridge when the storm hit. We waited it out together. I have a feeling it hasn't been easy for her since her husband came home. Frankly, I'm worried."

There was no mistaking but that Angus had an altogether different concern as he said, "If you'd like a little advice from your attorney, stay away from the McClures."

"If you mean Decatur, I can put your mind at ease."

"I mean all of them, including Naomi. She's a talker, like her father. A likable person, but she's Decatur's wife, and Old Kentucky to the bone."

"What's that supposed to mean?" said Libby, growing defensive.

"You're an intelligent woman, Libby. I don't have to explain to you, surely, that your sympathies can't go both ways. You're fighting for your inheritance against these people, you'll remember."

Libby tipped her chin and retorted, "I have every intention of claiming what's mine. Our livelihood depends upon it, as well as my plan to return to school. But that doesn't mean I have to be cold and unfeeling about it."

He wagged his head, as if he were clinging to his patience by a thread. "If you can't keep your sympathies from spilling over your good common sense, then you might want to consider turning the mail route over to your father and staying away from Old Kentucky altogether."

Bristling, Libby replied, "The only reason I'm delivering it now is to give Father's injuries time to heal properly."

"I'm sorry. It was a poor choice of words," he conceded. "I'm trying to offer you some legal advice, that's all."

"Well, it's Sunday. In my family, we don't talk business on Sunday." She stood up abruptly.

He could not have looked more pained if she'd kicked his tender ankle. "Libby, be sensible. Sit down a moment, and let me explain . . ."

"What is there to explain? You made yourself perfectly clear. I'm going home. Excuse me while I thank Catherine for her hospitality."

"If you really want to go, I'll bring the surrey around and drive you home."

"No, thank you, Mr. Cearlock. I relish the exercise." She flushed at the realization they'd awakened Charlie with their quarrel, and turned across the lawn in haste.

"What'd I miss?" she heard Charlie ask.

"Hot pepper and Mason jars," muttered Angus.

It galled her that he was so quick to see it was the jars, as much as anything, that had spawned the quarrel. But pride prevented her from retracing her steps.

Maddie was asking Catherine about Ike Galloway when Libby rounded the house. She intruded long enough to thank her hostess and convey her pleasure, however dubious, at making Mrs. Daniels's acquaintance, then turned her feet homeward.

No one answered Libby's knock when she arrived home. She used her key and let herself in to find the place deserted, upstairs and down. Guessing Father and David were still at Mrs. Baker's, she changed her clothes, collected her journal, and settled on an old quilt beneath the shade of the tree at the back of the building. She wrote a few lines, airing her frustrations, but they didn't give her the release she'd hoped for. Or the peace of mind. Finding it hard to focus, she put the pencil aside and flipped back through the pages. Her gaze fell on the words she'd written en route to Edgewood for the very first time:

Dearest Mother:

I saw mama robin nudge her baby from the nest in the lilac bush this morning. His squawking and clumsy

*hopping and flapping were painful to watch, and still I
envied him.*

*I was so sure the other day on the bluff that the time
had nearly come for me to pursue my education, for what
is my ambition to write without an education? Now, after
Father's brush with death, I feel all the more bound to
him. He is so fragile.*

She lay back on the quilt, arm shading her eyes, taking
the long view of where she'd been and how she'd come
along. Despite his recent injuries, Father's overall health
had improved dramatically. He was winning the respect
and affection of folks in Edgewood. And of Mrs. Baker,
apparently. Libby couldn't remember his ever having
accepted a widow woman's invitation for lunch. But that
was all right. In fact, it was more than all right, it was
good. They didn't come any finer than Mrs. Baker.

Libby reread the entry. The goal she'd thought the
hardest to achieve had come so easily. She could only
think that God must still be smiling over her surprise at
seeing her first published works, if only in a small-town
newspaper. Her spirits lifted, then leveled again as she
thought of Maddie Daniels questioning her about her
education. In all fairness, Maddie's manner hadn't been
disparaging. Libby knew that her defensive reaction to
the question was spawned by her deep desire to learn and
the obstacles in her path. The simple act of writing a short
piece for Mr. Gruben had taught her how much she had
to learn before she could hope for a successful career in
writing.

With Adam married, Jacob on his own, and David
growing more independent each day, she should cease to
think of higher education as a dream and begin planning
to make it a reality. There was a teacher's college in
Bloomington. She could board at the school during the
week, come home on Saturday mornings to help her
father with the most hectic day at the store, and return to
school in time for classes on Monday.

*But could she achieve her dreams, and give her heart away
too?* The thought came out of nowhere. The honesty of it
startled her, but she refused to let her emotions beguile

her into brushing it aside. Their quarrel didn't change
what she felt for Angus or blind her to his good qualities.
Not only was he handsome and witty and fun, he was
intelligent, hardworking, thoughtful most of the time,
and yes, politically ambitious. If their courtship continued, would his law practice and political hopes so con-
sume her that there would be nothing left for herself?
And if so, could she be content with sharing his life at the
expense of her dreams?

More confused than ever, Libby closed her journal and
her eyes and listened for that still, small voice.

Nothing came.

31

Libby carried the mail beneath a sweltering sun on Monday and came back to town, hoping to see Angus. She wanted to apologize for losing her temper and to try to explain her conflicting emotions concerning the McClures. But to shed light on her empathy for Naomi, she might have to disclose how very little formal education she herself had received. How else was Angus to understand her special bond with Naomi, who had had a much more difficult experience than she? But what if such a revelation lowered his opinion of her capabilities? There was also her blood relationship with Frankie to sort through. A sticky problem, by anyone's definition. And easily postponed, for Angus was not at his office, nor did he come to the store.

Tuesday came and went with still no sign of Angus. Libby's hope of clearing things up with him before Wednesday's mail route took her past Naomi's workshop dimmed. *Is he angry? Or just busy?*

Welcoming the distraction of a good book, Libby read *Jane Eyre* as she rode about the countryside delivering mail. It stirred a familiar hunger that took her beyond the characters of the novel to wondering about the author herself. What was her education? Was the story drawn on personal experience or was it pure fantasy? How did she so skillfully weave plot and character and pour it forth in mere human words? Would she ever . . . could she ever . . . Was she deluding herself, harboring such a dream?

Libby was eager to share her impressions of the book with Mr. Gruben and his wife, but felt shy of calling on them without an invitation. Contenting herself with waiting until Mr. Gruben came into the store, Libby turned her thoughts once more to entering college.

She was thinking how she might bring up the matter as they were eating supper on Tuesday when Father puzzled over a letter he'd received from the postal agent, Mr. Albert Tyson, offering him the position of postmaster at Edgewood.

"Noo, what do ye suppose gie the fellow the notion I'd be wantin' sich a job?" He cast the letter and a suspicious glance Libby's way, adding, "See here, lass, if he isna under the impression I filled oot a form, puttin' me bid in for the job. Why, see here if the old scalawaggin' colonel himself didn't give me a glowin' recommendation. Hum! If I didna know better, I'd come to suspect there's a plot afoot to hae ye old faether earnin' his keep."

"Oh, Father! When have you not earned your keep, and the rest of ours, too?" Libby burst out. "As for the application, you know very well I did it, and with the best of intentions."

"Whist! Shame on me for thinkin' I might hae heard of it from ye instead of Agent Tyson and the United States Postal Department." He expelled a sigh. "What other fine, fine plans have ye made for me, lass, if ye dinna mind me askin'?"

She apologized with his favorite dessert, bought that afternoon at the bakery, and only when he had devoured his second helping, dared to ask, "So will you take the position, Father?"

"Ye willna be offended if I seek Higher Advisement, will ye, lass?"

"While you're seeking, I have a concern, too." Libby stopped short of mentioning it with David in the room.

Discerning it was a matter requiring more privacy, Father rose to help clear the table. The dishes waiting to be washed were enough to send David scampering away with table scraps for the dog.

"What is it ye hae on ye mind, Lib?" asked her father, when they were alone.

"Writing for *The Gazette* has me thinking about further schooling." Libby was encouraged by his faint look of relief. "I've saved most of my washing money. I'm hoping the business here at the store is profitable enough that the teacher's college in Bloomington would be within my means."

"I see."

Anxious he not think she was trying to escape her duties to home and family, she added, "There's David to consider, too. I know you don't have your strength back altogether, and that the work here is taxing. Doubly so if you should accept the position of postmaster. But I could come home on the train and help out on Saturdays."

"Ye needn't worry yer head about that. I'm growin' stronger each day, lass."

"It wouldn't be for a while, and not just because of the money. I don't think I can go until this legal business is settled. What do you think, Father?"

"It is for ye to decide." He leveled her a gentle look. "Though I canna help me wonderin'—is this sudden wish to hae mair education mixed up somehow with yer young attorney friend, Mr. Cearlock?"

"It isn't sudden at all," she said, avoiding the question. At his knowing look, she added, "Though I do believe Mr. Cearlock's feeling cross with me."

"If ye go, go for yerself, lass. Dinna let yerself be blown by the winds of sweetheartin' gone hiltie-skiltie."

"I know, Father. I know. Anyway, our disagreement had nothing to do with my wish for more schooling."

Father didn't ask any question, nor did she volunteer further information. Rather, she climbed the stairs and sat down at the small writing table in her cubicle of a room and polished her piece on Captain Boyd's retirement party. Her words seemed painfully clumsy in comparison to the language of *Jane Eyre*. But it was writing. *Her* writing, and she took infinite pleasure in the process itself.

On Wednesday Mrs. Brignadello came along just as Libby finished casing the mail. She had prearranged to ride along to Old Kentucky and put to rest her business with Mr. Skiff.

"Can I help you with something?" asked Mrs. Bee, as Libby bundled and strapped the mail.

"Grab the water jar and the lunch bucket, and I'll bring the mail." Sparing Mrs. Bee a second glance, she added, "That's a very pretty dress. Much too fashionable for delivering mail."

"I made it," said Mrs. Bee, smoothing the full pale pink skirt of summer-weight fabric. "Ida's got a dress very similar to this, only she paid the earth for it."

"You're quite accomplished, Mrs. Bee," said Libby admiringly.

Mrs. Bee smiled. "I haven't always been. Mama tried to teach me when I was a girl, but I wasn't interested then. In fact, my poor sewing skills were something of a family joke. Then a friend taught me while I was with the circus."

"I should say she did," agreed Libby, sparing the lovely gown a lingering glance as they crossed the alley to the buggy shed.

She had loaded the mail and their lunch by the time David came from Woodmancy's Livery with Proctor. Teddy was with him. Proctor was a steady horse with a good disposition and generally no trouble at all. But this morning he tossed his head and danced when David tried to lead him into the shed. In a hurry to be on her way, Libby took over, but had no better luck.

"Ye-s-s-s, well, there's your problem. Looky there," said Teddy.

Libby followed his pointing finger and jumped back, suddenly appreciating Proctor's antics. "It's a snake! See there, around the buggy shaft."

Mrs. Bee bolted out of the shed. David did too.

Only Teddy ventured closer. He picked up a stick, soothing, "Looky, looky, Mister Bull Snake."

Libby shuddered as the snake slithered to the ground at his gentle prodding.

"Lawsy-daisy, look at the size of it. Must be six feet

long!" exclaimed Mrs. Brignadello. "Get a shovel, Teddy, and kill it."

"A-w-w, now. You've scared the poor fellow," said Teddy.

The *poor fellow* escaped into the shadows along the earthen floor of the shed. They pulled the buggy out into the sunshine, and Proctor became his usual docile self. Libby and Mrs. Bee were soon under way.

It was a pretty morning, tufted clouds hanging in an azure sky and a breeze stirring. Libby enjoyed having a companion along for the ride. Mrs. Bee had lost her preoccupied air, and was once again bright-eyed and in tune with the heartbeat of Edgewood. When Libby commented upon it, she confided her brother had taken a load off her mind by asking if he might hire her as his office assistant.

"I thought you'd always helped him," said Libby, playing the innocent.

"Yes, well, he needed help. He's a good doctor, but he'd soon bury himself beneath the clutter of office keeping. I never expected any pay. It was enough to know I was helping. Though sometimes I got to feeling . . ."

"Unappreciated?" Libby suggested.

Mrs. Bee arched a wry smile. "That's the word. But we had an earnest talk, and from what I could make of it, a few days of Paulette filling in for me had him looking at things a little differently."

"He figured out your value, did he?"

"He's ready to concede, anyway, that some people are better equipped to serve sick and hurt folks while others serve cake. Paulette's not without talent," she added in all fairness. Libby's brow climbed. Shamefaced, Mrs. Bee added, "I know, I know, I haven't always been tolerant of her differences. I'm going to work on that."

"I trust he's paying you enough that you won't have to sell jars."

Mrs. Bee took the gentle ribbing in stride. "I'm fairly confident that there will be enough for both Kersey and me to go to the fair, come September."

"That's good, Mrs. Bee. I'm glad it's worked out for you."

"Don't think I don't appreciate what you've done to help. I hope it hasn't caused you too much grief."

"Not really," said Libby, averting her face.

Shrewdly her friend prodded, "Catherine had an idea you and Angus might have quarreled Sunday."

Libby flicked the whip, chasing the flies off Proctor, and studiously avoided her scrutiny.

"Not over the jars, I hope," Mrs. Bee persisted. "You told him, didn't you, that you were just helping me out?"

"Not exactly."

"Well, for goodness' sake! Why not?"

"I promised you I wouldn't mention it to anyone."

"But I certainly didn't intend . . . Are you still at odds?"

Embarrassed, Libby said, "It's difficult to say. I haven't seen him."

"That's right. He's out of town for a few days."

"He is?"

"Yes. He's arguing a case in Bloomington." She darted a quick glance at Libby, adding, "You leave it to me, dear. I'll straighten things out."

Libby didn't know how to explain that it wasn't about the jars. Not without bringing Naomi McClure into it, and she was reluctant to do that. She changed the subject altogether, saying, "I understand Mrs. Harding and Mrs. Dorrance are trying to put together a singing group to accompany Angus on some of his campaign stops this fall."

"You know about that?"

"Maddie Dorrance—Daniels, rather—mentioned it Sunday."

"Catherine said she was in town."

An approaching horseman spared Libby further mention of Maddie. It was Sheriff Conklin on his way into town. He stopped in the road.

"You ladies will want to keep an eye out for Mr. Culbertson," he said as they drew even with his horse. "Mrs. Robins came by my house early this morning. Seems he never came home last night."

"Dear me! I knew this was going to happen," exclaimed Mrs. Bee. "When did Cordelia see him last?"

"Yesterday morning. I've got a handful of men spread over the countryside looking. Could be somebody's found him by now. I'm heading into town to see if there's been any word." He tipped his hat and trotted his horse up the road.

They plodded steadily along, spreading the alarm to others as they drew ever closer to Old Kentucky. But no one they encountered had seen the old fellow.

It was approaching noon when Proctor drew them past the church, the cemetery, and the school. Then east and north and east again, over the covered bridge and on to Skiff's Store. If they'd been a minute later, they'd have missed Mr. Skiff. He came out the door, long-barreled gun in hand. Hounds spilled out from under the porch, wiggling and barking and tripping over themselves in their eagerness to be off.

"Must be going hunting. This shouldn't take long." Mrs. Bee climbed down and waded through the dogs.

Libby couldn't hear a word of what was spoken for the racket the dogs were making. She drank the last of the water and waited as Mrs. Bee gestured. Planted her hands on her hips. Shook a finger under the man's nose, and finally tramped around the side of the house. She returned in short order with six jars, and tucked them behind the seat with their lunch, Frankie's slingshot, and the remaining mail.

"Aren't you going back for the others?"

"That old fox charged me two cents a jar to buy them back. I'll be hanged if he's going to profit off of my ignorance," she seethed.

Libby said, "You did the best you could."

"The other six are washed and lined up along the well, just as sweet as you please. I could horsewhip the fellow, I declare I could!" Mrs. Bee sat down so hard, she rocked the buggy.

A dismal silence prevailed for the next hundred yards or so. "What you need is a little lunch to cheer you up. Reach under the seat there," said Libby.

Mrs. Brignadello reached under the seat, all right, but what she drew into her lap was not lunch. Rather, it was

Frankie's slingshot, which David had returned to the buggy at Libby's insistence.

Mrs. Bee looked back toward Skiff's Store and ordered, "Pull over right here."

Revenge wasn't an altogether unpleasant idea, but Libby's common sense demanded she ask, "What if he hears the glass breaking?"

"With those hounds howling and pulling on his arm?"

Libby cocked her head to one side and listened. The dogs were covering ground fast. She could scarcely hear them at all now. Still, she felt an obligation as representative of the postal department not to run afoul of the law while delivering the mail. She said as much.

"Land sakes, you're just stopping to eat your lunch. There's surely no law against that," declared Mrs. Brignadello. She climbed down and marched back up the road and slipped into the woods.

Libby hadn't long to listen for breaking glass jars. Nor for Mrs. Bee's return. She sailed into the buggy and motioned for Libby to continue on. Their smiles grew into nervous giggles. And giggles to laughter to side-splitting howls.

"Someday I'll tell you about my time with the circus," said Mrs. Bee, wiping her eyes.

"You must have been a marksman!" declared LIbby.

"I did a rope act. A little comic opera. And in the aftershow, a knife-throwing demonstration." Mouth wiggling, Mrs. Bee added, "Knife or rock—it's all in the eye. I declare, Libby, I didn't know the sound of splintering glass could be so downright satisfying!"

32

❧ Libby pulled up to the line of mailboxes at the mouth of the wagon track across from Naomi's wood shop. Thoughts of Naomi's difficulties surfaced as she dismounted to fit the papers and letters into the proper boxes. There was a letter in one mailbox, and two cents for the stamp to send it. She poked the letter into the canvas mailbag behind the seat, then crossed the road, calling back to Mrs. Brignadello, "I'm going to say hello to Naomi. Climb down if you'd like."

But Naomi didn't answer her knock. Nor was there any sound of life coming from within. Libby put her face to the window and found the shop dark and deserted.

"Let's check around back."

Mrs. Bee followed, but it was quiet there too.

"I guess she's not working today. We may as well fill the water jar while we're here." Libby returned to the buggy for the jar, her concern for Naomi mounting.

They washed the dust from their hands and faces and filled the jar. Libby stopped at the front window on her way by and peered through the glass one last time.

"What's the matter? You seem anxious," said Mrs. Bee, watching her.

"I guess I am."

"Decatur's not such a bad sort when he isn't drinking," offered Mrs. Bee.

329

"Do you think he'd hurt her?" asked Libby, her apprehension fermenting in the pit of her stomach.

"I don't know, Libby. I guess . . ."

"What?"

"Well, that it's not our business to know what goes on between a man and his wife."

"Even if she needs help?" Libby asked, lowering her voice to a whisper.

"Did she ask you for help?"

Libby conceded that she hadn't.

"Then she probably doesn't want it."

"I guess you're right. We may as well go."

There was a train sidetracked, taking on wheat at the Old Kentucky crossing. The trees parted enough to let the sun through as they crossed the bridge that spanned Timber Creek and turned right. Libby had no mail for the syrup camp, her last box on this leg of the route. Proctor was eager now, a feed bag and the comfort of the livery stall serving as incentive.

Libby lapsed into silence, trying to assuage her mounting trepidation.

They'd had the top down since leaving town. The warm sun, a full stomach, and the rocking motion of the buggy were taking their toll on Mrs. Brignadello. Libby could see she was fighting to keep her eyes open. She slapped at a fly when something pinched her leg. With the snake incident of that morning hovering just below the surface of conscious thought, the pinch all but propelled her off the cracked leather. Mrs. Bee let out a simultaneous yell, and whirled around in the seat.

"Opal McClure! By jing, you scared the bewilikers out of me! What do you mean, startling us like that?"

"Sorry, Missus Bee." Opal threw off the canvas mail-pouch covering she'd curled beneath and tried to stand in the cramped space behind the seat. "Jest wanted you to know I was comin' along to town with ya."

"Do your folks know you're were catching a ride?"

Opal's downcast eyes was answer enough.

Libby stopped the buggy and beckoned. "Climb over, Opal."

The girl tugged a wispy white-gold curl to the corner of

her mouth, her guarded glance darting from Libby to Mrs. Bee and back again.

Libby's heart turned at the child's pinched expression. "It's all right, we're not going to scold."

It was all the encouragement the girl needed. Opal tumbled over the seat. Mrs. Bee, recovering from her scare, pulled the child onto her lap. "Now then. Tell us what this is all about." She spoke to her as if Opal were a patient come into Dr. Harding's office for treatment.

"Mama came home whilst Daddy was hitchin' the team to the wagon."

"Came home? What do you mean 'came home.' Where had she been?" asked Libby.

Opal blinked at the sharpness of her words. "She'd been stayin' at the shop."

"Overnight, you mean? But why?" asked Mrs. Bee.

Opal shrugged. "All I know is she come home and she says fer me to go on over to Ike's whilst she and Daddy talk. But when I got there, there weren't nobody there. I was headin' back when Mr. Culbertson come along . . ."

"Mr. Culbertson?" chimed Libby and Mrs. Brignadello. They exchanged startled glances.

"You're sure, honey?" asked Mrs. Bee.

Opal nodded. "It was him, sure enuf. He was pickin' up wood, sayin' it was chillish out, and recitin' the queerest words about bitin' snow and sech. I got scairt and lit out for home. But I was rememberin' Mama sayin' not to come back till she came for me, and thinkin' maybe she and Daddy was quarrelin' again, and I didn't want to listen at that. So I figured I'd jest ride into town and see if Frankie and Ike was there."

Quarrelin'. The word rang in Libby's head like a gandy dancer's hammer. She was careful not to betray her alarm. But with Naomi's tears for Opal, her words about love, and her own growing intuition of trouble in the offing, she knew Naomi hadn't sent the child away without good reason.

"Maybe it would be better if you went to your grandpa's. Your mama could find you there," said Mrs. Bee.

"Paw-Paw ain't there. He was gonna meet up with Mr. Skiff fer some huntin'. Leastwise, that's what he said when he came by the house with his dogs, jest before Mama come along."

"We'll go back then, and tell your mama you're going with us." Libby turned the buggy around.

"I reckon if *you* was to tell her, she couldn't fault me none for not minding," Opal ventured.

"Yes, of course. I'll tell her." Ignoring the misgivings in Mrs. Bee's eyes, Libby added, "You can wait in the buggy with Mrs. Bee."

Satisfied, Opal nodded. But cares beyond what was fitting for a child so young carved shadows beneath her eyes and drew her mouth down.

"Was it here you saw Mr. Culbertson?" Libby asked, looking into the woods as they passed the syrup camp.

"No. The other side of the bridge," said Opal. "He ain't ridin' back to town with us, is he?"

"As short as we are on space, I don't think he'd fit," Mrs. Bee said, soothing her fears.

Libby stopped the buggy right on the bridge. They looked through the trees and called his name, but without result. Mrs. Bee wondered aloud if the men loading grain onto the train car might have seen Mr. Culbertson. Agreeing to meet at the shop when Libby had returned from delivering word of Opal, she climbed down.

She gave Libby a worried look over the top of Opal's head and said, "Take care, you hear?"

Libby nodded, then waved as Mrs. Bee set off up the tracks with Opal clinging to her hand. Alone now, she turned the buggy up the wagon track leading into heavy timber. The green glaze wrapped around her like a shroud. A mosquito whined, and another sucked at her hand, leaving blood as she slapped it away. Branches tangled overhead, muting sound, screening light. The air was close, damp, musky. Bony-fingered undergrowth scraped at the bottom side of the buggy. Her nerves leaped as she peered through undergrowth and shadow, watching for the boxcar home. A rabbit jumped across the track. Leather creaked.

Libby hummed to fill the unnerving silence, her voice tapering to a low, tuneless monotone. Abruptly she stopped, hearing in the distance wheels rattling over the ground. The sound grew louder, replete with pounding hooves and cracking whip. The trees distorted the direction from which it was coming.

Libby stopped and looked back. No one behind her. Nothing coming toward her. She urged Proctor on, only to stop him again and stare in disbelief as a wagon thundered across the McClures' front yard. It passed within a few feet of her buggy, careening over the ground between the trees, circling the clearing and passing a second time. And still she had not collected her wits enough to scramble out of the buggy.

Decatur McClure drove the team of grays with the ferocity of an embattled charioteer. Legs planted like oak trees. Feet spread. Hair trailing. Lines gripped in one knotted fist, cracking whip in the other.

Libby scrambled down and ducked behind a tree as he came full circle again. Nostrils flared, eyes burning out of control. The horses foamed and strained at the traces as the whip hissed over their glistening backs. They pounded across the pasture, hooves spitting sod. Into the cornfield, slashing young blades. Over the garden, where Naomi shrank against a faceless scarecrow. Through the flowers. Moving at breakneck speed. Making another pass. And another.

"Stop it, Decatur! Stop it, you hear? Ain't gonna be a bean or a blade of corn left, and then what'll we do?" Naomi pleaded.

The wagon slowed. The horses stood blowing, and for a moment it seemed the world would right itself. But no. His eyes! Dear God, they were boiling. He started the wagon with a crack of the whip. Over the pasture and corn. Angling toward Naomi as she stood with her hands in her hair, trying to tap some vein of reason.

"Isn't that what ya wanted, fer me to say it? Well, I've said, and jest look how yer carryin' on," she cried.

One pain-drenched word of condemnation was torn from his lungs. He stretched out his arm. The whip danced over the glistening horses. Cold fingers walked down Libby's spine as the heaving grays gathered their legs beneath them, moving again. Picking up speed.

"Stop! You'll kill her!" screamed Libby, her leaden

limbs moving. The distance was too great. She could not reach her in time. And even if she did . . . Libby opened her mouth to scream at him again. But the words were lost in the nightmarish netherworld to a younger voice and an incongruous warning.

"Fire! Fire! Fire!"

Frankie burst out of the trees from the other side of the clearing, just feet from the garden. Trousers torn, face streaked with dirt and sweat. He raced over the trampled field toward the wagon bearing down on his mother.

"Fire! Fire!" He threw himself into the path of the horses, screaming, "Fire! The woods is on fire!"

Decatur's distorted features shattered like glass at the sight of the boy flinging himself headlong toward destruction. He swore in a vicious stream and sawed on the lines. Sawed so hard at the horses' tender mouths that they panicked and turned. Frankie jumped clear just as the wagon went over in a splintering, screaming, cursing melee of wood and horseflesh and man. The wagon tongue snapped and the horses, lathered and heaving, were off across the garden and into the timber, lines, singletrees, and doubletree dragging.

Thrown clear of the broken wagon, Decatur rolled onto his back. Eyes glazed, nose oozing blood. He shook his head like a sleeper suspended between dreams and reality.

Frankie ran to Naomi.

"Frankie. Dear God, Frankie! What have we done to you!" Naomi held him, crying like a woman bereft of her child, only to stop and with a fear-filled look beyond him, cry, "Where's the woods burnin', son? Is it comin' this-away?"

"There ain't no fire, Mama. I jest said it."

Libby's eyes filled. Loving him for his cleverness, for his raw courage, she forgave Frankie every prank. She picked her way past the matchstick wagon. Decatur rolled onto his side and stretched out a blood-smeared hand. She looked down where he lay and saw Opal's eyes. Such a feeling came over her. Confusion, sweeping sadness, aversion, cold fury, all tangled together.

He struggled up on one elbow. "You tell Cearlock there ain't no need in goin' to court. Weren't but one will."

"You made it up." Just as Frankie had made up the fire. Evening the odds the only way he knew how. "Why, Mr. McClure? Why?"

Pain streaked across McClure's bloodied features as he struggled to sit up. "Ain't none of yer business. Git off my place and take them with ya. Go on! Don't want none of Willie's castoffs. Not the store, nor the woman. Nor the boy neither."

The words were like the crushing heel of a boot on a weed. How like a weed was Frankie! Springing from fallen seed. Thrusting his way between stones. Fighting to survive. He'd saved his mother. But who would save him? Ike had implied there was decency in this man. Naomi had said he'd never taken his feelings out on Frankie. Clinging to that hope, she stretched a hand toward him, hoping he would relent, just for the boy's sake.

"Mr. McClure . . ."

"I'm goin' after my team. Don't want to find nobody here when I get back." He came slowly to his feet, picked up his hat, and limped into the woods.

Naomi gave no notice of Decatur's retreat, nor Libby's approach. She spoke to her son.

"Thought I told you, when ya come by the shop, to stay with Ike today."

"I know. But when him and me come back from cutting wood, there was Mr. Culbertson, trying to make a fire in the sugarhouse. That's what gived me the idea to say . . ." Seeing no explanation was needed, he continued. "Ike reckoned he'd better see him back to town b'fore he got himself into real trouble. So I went to the shop. When ya wasn't there, I figurt—"

"Where's Opal?" asked Naomi, her alarm freshening.

"She's with Mrs. Bee. They're waitin' for Miss Libby." He turned, hearing Libby behind him, and fell silent.

"Go fetch her home. It's gonna be all right now." Naomi's gaze followed her son as he started away. It was as if she couldn't bring herself to meet Libby's eyes.

Softly Libby said, "Last Saturday, when you were under the bridge—had he put you out of the house?"

Shamefaced, Naomi dried her tears on a tattered apron and said, "Said for me not to come back until I could name Frankie's father. A few days hardly seein' the young 'uns and I was thinkin' maybe I could say those words after all. Maybe there'd even be healin' in 'em." There was no bitterness in her short laugh. Just sorrow finding no easy expression.

"So you told him and this is what happened."

"It was the liquor in him. Man cain't tolerate liquor any better'n him hadn't ought to try."

It wasn't the sorry excuse so much as Naomi's need to place the blame for his actions anywhere but on him that brought tears to Libby's eyes. Should she tell her it was all for naught? That he wanted her out and Frankie out too? Gently she said, "Pack a few things and come back to town. We'll make room over the store."

"I cain't."

"You have to, Naomi."

"I reckon he'll get over . . ." Naomi flinched and hung her head. "Would ya listun at me? He ain't got over it in all these years."

Libby tried to stop shaking and couldn't. It wasn't all fear and it wasn't all anger. There was helplessness mixed in and the soul-sick realization the hurting was far from over. Naomi had feelings for this man. She caught her trembling hand in hers and held it tight. "You can't save him, Naomi."

Looking surprised, as if she'd exposed some unseemly part, Naomi tugged at her wrinkled and faded dress and murmured, "Hard fer you to understand, I reckon, but he's always took care of us. He don't take it out on Frankie."

"There's a better way," said Libby, knowing enough not to dispute her word. "There's people in town to help. The sheriff, if you need him. My father and Mrs. Baker and Mrs. Bee. And the old ones at the store," she said, knowing it was true.

Fresh tears glittered in Naomi's eyes. "I come betwixt him and Willie in a way there jest ain't no healin'. How can I take Opal from him and turn Pa agin' him and have the townfolk talkin'? . . . I don't know, I jest don't know."

She was crying in earnest now. Libby put her arms around her, patting, soothing, talking low. "Remember what you told me about Uncle Willie saying there were tokens in the wood? There's someone inside you wanting out, too. But you're clinging to the splinters, Naomi."

She drew a shuddering sigh. A tremor in her voice, she allowed, "Makin' slow work for the carpenter. But when shavings is all ye've got, it ain't so easy, lettin' go."

Tears stung Libby's eyes as she nodded, for the words were true of her too. God had been chiseling away at her pride, her temper, her earthbound fears, her indecision about Angus and more schooling and oh, so many things she'd been trying to reason out. Talking to her in that quiet way, saying she could relax her grip and trust Him. That He had never meant for her to have the store. That He'd only put it in her keeping for a little while.

Even if I asked you to?

He'd asked. And she knew, as she helped Naomi gather a few things to take with them, that there was only one answer.

Mrs. Brignadello took swift stock of the number of people who needed to get to town and the size of the buggy. She offered to take the train back to town. Frankie set off with her, lightening the load Proctor would have to pull. Libby watched him stride along, hair waving like a flag in the breeze, thin shoulders swinging. He was as agile as a cat. Boarding the Down and Out. Just as Uncle Willie used to do.

33

The train had beaten Proctor back to town. As they came over the crossing and turned north on the square, Libby saw the bench brigade gathered in front of the store. There was Minor with a wad in his jaw. Mr. Lamb, Billy Young, and her father. Mr. Noonan in his green eyeshade. Captain Boyd and Hascal Caton's friend, Squire Palmer. Mr. Gruben with a pencil stuck in his hair. And Teddy Baker, an arm locked behind his back, looking on as the rest of the men clustered around Mr. Culberston. *Keepers of the town*, thought Libby, touched by the men's welcoming home of their timeworn comrade.

Mr. Culbertson's daughter, Cordelia Robins, was hurrying up the walk toward Willie Blue's. The sheriff was with her. Teddy saw her approaching and alerted the others. Their heads all turned in that direction.

Libby was sorry for Mr. Culbertson, but the distraction spared Naomi from being the center of attention as they crossed Morgan Street and continued half a block to turn up the alley, past Angus's law office. Ike's wagon blocked the alley. He was pumping water into a bucket for his horses. Frankie was holding his team. The boy spotted them first and motioned to Ike as Libby stopped the mail buggy.

Ike's head swung in their direction. The sun slanted across his face as he pushed his hat back, his gray gaze skipping from Libby to Naomi and Opal. His expression

338

was grave, though not surprised. Frankie must have told him what had happened. *What are his thoughts about his friend Decatur now?*

"This is close enough, go ahead and water them," Libby called as Ike started to move his team and wagon out of the way of her mail buggy.

Subdued by her mother's uncharacteristic silence, Opal crawled out of the buggy, slipped past Ike as he came down the alley to meet them, and went to help her brother with the horses.

Libby was sore from sitting so long. But Naomi sat unmoving, her eyes downcast, her hands knotted in her lap.

"Why don't you let yourself in the back door and go on upstairs? It would do you good to clean up and stretch out on my bed awhile," Libby said quietly.

"Reckon Miss Libby won't mind if I show you the way," said Ike, stopping beside the buggy.

"Would you, while I unhitch Proctor and walk him over to Woodmancy's?"

"Leave it go, the young 'uns and me will see to it here in a minute," Ike offered as he helped Naomi down with work-roughened hands.

Grateful for the unobstrusive manner in which he took charge, Libby nodded agreement and stepped out of the buggy unassisted. Hearing the leaves stir in the nearby tree, she tipped her head back and searched the thick branches for her little brother. "Davie? Are you up there?"

Wordlessly he dropped down out of the tree and scuffed across the dusty backyard to whisper with a note of censure, "You gave away my hiding place."

It was apparent by his narrowed eyes and turned-down mouth that he recognized Frankie as the culprit of the slingshot incident that had frightened Proctor and caused the accident the day he'd gone on the mail route with Father. Postponing introductions, Libby nudged David toward the back door.

"Tell Father I need to talk to him, would you please? He's out front."

With one last guarded glance at Frankie, David darted up the path to cut through the store.

Libby drew a deep breath, sensing the children's unspoken apprehensions. Frankie looked up from shifting the bucket from the reach of one mare to the other as she approached. He darted another glance toward the door where his mother had disappeared with Ike. Something in his face sent Libby's thoughts reeling back across the years to the night her mother lay dying. Heart twisting, she knelt before the children, her thought-prayer a plea that she not trivialize their fears with pat reassurances. Taking each by the hand, hoping that God's love for these little ones would flow through her, she said, "You are fine, brave children. This trouble is not your fault."

Frankie's fingers twitched. His lashes swept down. Libby moved her hand up his arm and would have hugged him, but he stood tense and unyielding. Gently she added, "I'll fix some supper in a while, and maybe after she's eaten, your mama will feel rested and more like talking."

Frankie didn't respond, but Opal's chin quivered. She crowded closer and took the hug Libby wanted so much to give Frankie.

Eyes burning, Libby brushed Opal's pale hair away from her face. She kissed her sun-warmed cheek and held her until the thin arms about her neck loosened their grip. At the sound of approaching footsteps, Libby wiped away the tears that had gathered and swung around to greet her father. Ike, who was with him, had seen her furtive gesture. Averting his gaze while she collected her composure, he thanked the children for watering his team and returned the empty bucket to the pump.

"Keep hold of 'em, will ya, Frankie, while Opal and me unhitch Miss Libby's buggy?" he called back. "Then how about ya two takin' Proctor over ta the livery? I've got some wood-cuttin' tools there in the wagon I'm gonna drop by the blacksmith shop for sharpening. I'll come by soon as I drop 'em off, and we'll get us a bite to eat over at Baker's." Ike came back to drape an arm over Opal's thin shoulder. "Don't know about you, but Frankie and me missed lunch."

"I was just saying I'd fix them something in a bit," said Libby.

"Ain't no need in ya goin' to the trouble. Mrs. Baker won't mind the business."

Libby's father chimed agreement. "'Tis a guid plan, lass."

Noting how Opal brightened at the anticipated treat, Libby capitulated with a shrug.

Wanting to talk without risk of being overheard, Libby slipped her arm through her father's and turned up the hard dirt path to the store. David was on the floor on the other side of the counter, helping Teddy pick cockleburs out of Sugar's tail.

"W-e-e-l-l, she's been huntin'," Teddy said by way of explanation, then bent his head once more to the task.

Privacy at a minimum, Libby followed her father out the front door. The *clackety-clack* of Mr. Gruben's typewriter and a distant cough drifted through the screen door of the newspaper office next door. But at least the bench in front of Willie Blue's was empty and the walk momentarily deserted.

"So dinna keep me in suspense. 'Tis somethin' amiss with the McClures?"

"Quite a lot." Hardly knowing where to begin, Libby paced a few feet and back. "I've felt uneasy over Naomi ever since I saw her at the bridge on Saturday. And with good reason. Though she didn't tell me at the time, Decatur had kicked her out that very day."

The crevices in her father's face deepened. "'Kicked her oot?'"

Libby nodded. "He made her leave the house and told her not to come back until she was willing to name Frankie's father."

Her father sighed heavily. "Sich a fellow, our Mr. McClure! Could it be he has been tippin' the bottle again?"

"Oh, he's been drinking, all right. Enough to turn him into a madman!" Unable to erase from her mind the dark fury boiling in the depths of McClure's eyes, Libby tersely related how he had destroyed his field and garden and turned the team and wagon on Naomi when Frankie's courage spared her.

"'Tis small wonder the leddy comes seekin' refuge."

"I invited her, Father. Decatur doesn't want her anymore. Or Frankie. Or the store either," said Libby, her voice brittle to her own ears.

Her father winced as she repeated Decatur's words concerning Uncle Willie's castoffs. "Ach! He's got the devil in 'im, all right. Ye did well, bringin' the leddy and her bairns to town, lass. 'Twould be wrong not to offer friendship and shelter. The laddie and I hae been sleepin' doonstairs anyway."

"I want Frankie to have the store, Father."

Thomas's eyes grew round. "Do me ears deceive me, lass, or did ye not jest tell me tha' Mr. McClure isna wantin' the store any longer?"

"It isn't Decatur's place to say. Frankie is Willie's rightful heir. The store should go to him."

"But 'tis such an astoundin' aboot-face ye be doin', if ye dinna mind me sayin' so, lass!"

"I know, I know." The drone of the typewriter next door slowed to an intermittent *clack* between long pauses as Libby struggled to explain. "I was so hoping . . ." She stopped and started again, blurting in a rush, "But what else is there for Frankie? Uncle Willie couldn't be a father to him. Decatur doesn't want him any longer, and Naomi has no way of providing for him or Opal, either one."

Her father, so seldom surprised by anything, seemed unable to believe his ears. "Do ye know what ye're saying, lass? Why, seems only a moment ago ye bubbled over wi' plans fer more schoolin' so that ye might fulfill yer dreams of writin' wee stories and great books. What of that?"

Libby ducked her head, fighting the tears that burned her throat at the difficulty of the decision. It wasn't too late. She could change her mind. Save her future. And yet it was so rare a thing, the clarity of that still, small voice. How could she disregard it? She drew a steadying breath and admitted weakly, "I don't think God ever intended me to have it."

"Ye're placin' yer dreams in His safekeepin'?" asked Thomas, his voice dropping.

"And our next meal."

A slow smile tugged at her father's mouth. "Ye've forgotten so soon, hae ye, how yer meddlin' in yer old faether's affairs hae netted him a fine, fine offer from the United States Postal Department?"

"Then you're going to take it?"

"Aye, lass, 'twould seem God was preparin' the way for sich circumstances as these."

"We'll have to move. If we can *find* a place." Libby paused, faintly aware that the typing had stopped. Hearing a chair scrape the floor, she drew her father closer to their own door.

"Dinna worry, lass, 'tis a small thing to God." Father put his arm around her. "'Tis a proud moment. A fine proud moment indeed. My wee bairn has grown a great trustin' heart." He kissed her cheek and with a hand on the small of her back, ushered her through the door. "Run upstairs wi' ye noo, and see to Mrs. McClure's comfort."

Libby returned to the buggy first to collect belongings Naomi had hurriedly gathered before leaving her boxcar home in the woods. She lugged the heavy sack up the stairs, wondering how to introduce the subject of the store with Naomi. It was, after all, her life. Her son. Their future. It could be that she had no interest in living over the store and acting as a proprietor until Frankie was old enough to tend the place himself. *What then, Lord?*

She knocked before entering. Naomi was at the window overlooking the square. She hadn't washed her tear-streaked face nor smoothed her hair, but it looked as if she'd been reading.

Libby was struck at first by the incongruity of her holding a book when her whole world was falling apart. And yet, on closer thought, she conceded that she, too, had found refuge in books when life was hard-fisted. She dropped the gunnysack on the floor.

"I brought your things. If there's something I could do to make you more comfortable . . ."

Naomi waved aside the offer. She pushed a strand of hair away from her face and asked, "Is it true, Decatur talkin' thataway? That he didn't want me or Frankie comin' back?"

Libby's gaze flew to the open window. She and father had been standing one story below! Her jaw dropped, a flash of heat sweeping to her cheeks as she remembered how Hascal Caton's gossip concerning her had carried so clearly to her that first night in Edgewood as she sat in the window, and he with the squire on the walk below. "You heard?"

"I was lookin' fer stronger light." Naomi's rough, square-tipped fingers gripped the book. Struggling to keep her composure, she added, "I don't want it wrapped gentle, miss. What was his words?"

"All right, then," Libby said, letting her breath go slowly, and repeated Decatur's words as best she could recall them.

Naomi's mouth thinned to a hard line. "Sayin' it about me is one thing. But he's got no call to take his anger out on the boy. Ain't none of this Frankie's fault. It was my doin'. Mine and Willie's. Not his."

Libby said nothing. Her heart was beating hard, her breath short as if she'd been running. "Could I talk to you about the store?"

"I heard that too." Naomi's green gaze met Libby's. Though her tone of voice didn't change, her chin came up and her shoulders went back, just as Frankie's had in the alley a short while ago when Libby had wanted to comfort him. "I ain't aimin' to sound ungrateful, but we don't take charity."

"But it isn't charity, it's Frankie's birthright," said Libby.

"Willie didn't leave it to him."

"He couldn't. He was afraid to for fear of what your husband would read into it. And with good cause, it seems. But I think somehow . . ." Libby paused, seeing in Naomi's closed expression that much rested upon her finding the right words. It grew so quiet, she heard a perambulator rolling along the wooden walkway below, a mother's footsteps, the tired whimper of a baby, and a child's bright voice claiming, "I can push, Mama. I'm a big girl. Let me push."

Swing me, Uncle Willie. Watch me stand on my head. Listen, Uncle Willie, I know all the words to the song. Tears gathered in her throat.

"I think when he left it to me, he was hoping I wouldn't focus so on the store that I'd miss the true gift. I never really knew Uncle Willie. But maybe, if you'll let me, I can find a little of him in Frankie."

Naomi was quiet for a long moment. At length she shifted her weight and asked with a searching look, "Ya want that?"

"Yes, very much."

"If ye're shore, I reckon we can stay for a spell, anyways. See how it works out," said Naomi. She blinked, but failed at holding her tears at bay. In a broken whisper she added, "I'm obliged fer yer k-kindness, miss."

Libby opened her arms, comforting, being comforted. When the tears were spent, she found the book had changed hands. Leafing through it, she murmured, "I was going to return this to Mr. Gruben. But if you'd like to read it, I don't think he'd mind if I kept it awhile longer."

"Iffen I was gonna read, I wouldn't read that," interrupted Naomi.

Surprised, Libby said, "But it's a wonderful story."

"About an orphan woman learnin' an orphan child, and a man with a madwoman for a wife, and a fire that leaves him blinded. I reckon I got enough grief without fillin' my head with plain Jane and her poor dark Rochester."

"You've read it!"

"Back in school. It's books like that make a gal think she can change a feller's natural bent." Naomi swept her hair away from her careworn face and retrieved a dress out of the gunnysack. Her voice full of hard, sad wisdom, she added, "Well, I'm here ta tell ya, ya cain't."

"What are you going to do about Frankie?" Libby asked softly.

"I'm going to tell him about his father. I reckon he's got a right to know how it happened, and why. And most of all that it ain't his fault, and he don't need to feel ashamed." Naomi's sigh shook her whole frame. "Could be Decatur was right about one thing—I shoulda owned up to it a long time ago."

34

ℒ Belatedly remembering this was her deadline for Friday's newspaper article, Libby retrieved it from the writing table in her room. Taking *Jane Eyre* along with her, she went next door to Mr. Gruben's office.

"I thought maybe in all the activity, you'd forgotten," said the editor, as Libby turned in the piece about Captain Boyd's retirement party.

"Activity? You mean Mr. Culbertson?"

"Mr. I-Once-Was-Lost-But-Now-Am-Found."

It wasn't Mr. Gruben who had spoken, rather a young man swathed in a long apron with a smudge of printer's ink on his clean-shaven cheek. He stepped away from the hulking Linotype machine and flashed Libby a friendly smile. Certain it wasn't the same boy who had been working at the machine the last time she'd come in, Libby asked, "What happened to the other fellow?"

"Burned himself, pouring lead. I'm not having much luck with printer's devils," added Mr. Gruben at Libby's murmured concern. "Earl here is a quick study, but he can't keep his eyes on lining letters when a pretty girl walks in."

"Earl Morefield, miss." The young man introduced himself with a courtly bow and a broad grin.

Thinking of her friend Catherine's husband, Libby asked, "Are you Charles Morefield's brother?"

"Cousin," he said. "You won't hold that against me, will you?"

"Get back to work, young man, before you scare off my promising new journalist," said Mr. Gruben with mock severity. He extinguished his cigar in the ashtray and grabbed his suit jacket off the back of his chair. "I'll be back shortly, if anyone should ask."

"Yessir," said his apprentice.

Mr. Gruben held the door for Libby. "I'm going over to Baker's. Walk along with me, and we'll talk about the book. You did finish it, didn't you?"

"Yes," said Libby, falling in step at his side. "I enjoyed it very much, though there are some people who think it's a little misleading."

"Oh? How is that?"

Briefly Libby paraphrased Naomi's comments.

The editor grinned. "Most folks are too intimidated by a classic to criticize."

"Actually, those were Naomi McClure's words, not mine," Libby admitted.

"I was going to suggest you write a book review for the paper. Perhaps I should ask Mrs. McClure instead." At Libby's fallen expression, he gave a short laugh and prompted, "Well? Don't keep me in suspense. What was your opinion?"

Libby took a moment to sort her thoughts as they started across the park. "I admired Jane's strength of character. There was no one to care what she did. No one she needed to worry about disappointing. Yet she remained true to the standard she'd set for herself."

"And why was that?"

Noticing that Ike's wagon was in front of Baker's, Libby said, "Because she cared for her own opinion."

"Anything else?"

Libby ventured with a sidelong glance, "How would it be if I were to put it in writing?"

He chuckled. "I'd be willing to look at it. By the way, I understand your family may be looking for a place to rent. There's an empty house three lots north of us on Fisher Street, should you be interested."

Libby missed a step, lurched off the curb of the park,

and nearly went down before Mr. Gruben caught her elbow. "How could you possibly know we're looking for a house?"

"A good newsman keeps his ears open." He smiled. "It never hurts having your door propped open to voices on the street."

Abashed at having been so reckless as to be overhead not only by Naomi, but by the editor too, Libby said, "Your apprentice—he didn't . . ."

"No, he was in the back. Angus, on the other hand . . ."

"Angus Cearlock?" Libby's nerves reeled.

"He was waiting on a printing order. Campaign sheets to pass out as he goes on the stump."

Remembering having heard a cough and a chair scrape the floor, Libby winced. "What did he hear?"

"That would depend upon the keenness of his ears." Mr. Gruben stopped abruptly, peered over her head, and nodded toward the street. Angus had just crossed the railroad tracks in his surrey. "Here he comes now. Why don't you ask him?"

"Rest assured, I will," Libby said, then stopped, suddenly suspicious of Mr. Gruben's motives in suggesting she confront Angus.

Noting her narrowed expression, he answered her unvoiced question with a mirthless grin. "There's a lot of tough issues to be negotiated in Springfield. Before I vote for a man, I like to test his mettle, see if he can keep his head in the heat of battle."

Finding his sense of humor baffling, Libby sniffed and lifted her chin. There wasn't going to be a battle. She was capable of holding her own without losing her temper. She *was!*

Mr. Gruben tipped his hat with an enigmatic smile and changed the subject. "I'm looking forward to that book review. Now, if you'll excuse me, I'll see what kind of pie Mrs. Baker is serving today."

Libby looked after the retreating editor, and in so doing, caught a glimpse of Ike and the children at a table on the other side of Baker's wide glass window. Mr. Gruben joined them, and peered out the glass with lively

interest as Angus turned at the corner and came toward
the restaurant. Shrinking from such a public confrontation, Libby changed her mind about questioning Angus
and turned to retreat across the park. But he had already
seen her. Quickly he pulled up alongside the walk and
blocked her path with his surrey.

Tone clipped, he said without preamble, "I'd like a
word with you, Elizabeth. Get in."

"I beg your pardon?"

"I said get in."

"If this concerns a legal matter, I'll meet you at your
office in five minutes, Mr. Cearlock," Libby replied.

"It doesn't." He stretched out his hand as if to pull her
up beside him.

Indignation stirred by his imperious manner, Libby
retreated another step and set her trim shoulders. "If it
has to do with your overhearing conversations not meant
for your ears, then again, I suggest we talk in private."

"Gruben told you? Ye Gad, this town is a fishbowl!" he
declared, hazel eyes snapping behind his lenses.

"Indeed!" Libby cut around his surrey and lifted her
skirts as she stepped down off the walk and into the dusty
street.

"Wait a minute, Libby." Angus leaped to the ground
and bolted after her. "You have a heart the size of Texas
and absolutely no business sense!"

"We have an audience in the window of Baker's,"
warned Libby.

"I don't care who's watching! I only care what happens
to you, which is more than you seem to be considering.
Don't say anything," he forestalled her with an uplifted
hand. "Just listen."

"How democratic!"

"One minute, Libby. Then I'll shut up, and you can
speak," he promised as he fell in step with her. "You said
yourself you needed the store. Your father isn't well. You
have a little brother to think about. And what's this about
more schooling?"

Annoyed he was pressing the conversation in spite of
her attempts to postpone it, Libby loosened the guard on
her tongue. "I suppose you don't approve of that either?"

"Yes, I approve. I approve heartily. What I don't approve is your giving away the means of achieving your dreams!"

"You don't have to approve. Quite frankly, it doesn't concern you."

His face fell. He thrust his hands in his pockets. "Is that the way it is? You really feel that way?" Into her stony silence he inserted, "I'm sorry, Libby. I guess I misunderstood. I thought we . . ."

A train whistle drowned out the rest of his words. Angus stopped suddenly and looked back toward the south side of the square.

"Thought we *what*?"

He didn't reply.

Heart in her throat, Libby swung around to see him dashing across the park. His horse, startled by the train whistle, was galloping past the Columbian, the empty surrey rocking precariously as it made the corner.

She darted a glance back over her shoulder and saw Mr. Gruben in the doorway of Baker's. There were more faces at the glass. Men looked on from in front of the grain elevator, too, as Angus tried to catch his runaway horse. Heat crept up Libby's collar. But *good faith!* She'd tried her best to warn him, and still, he'd not only pressed the conversation, but carelessly left his horse and surrey unattended to do so.

And you lost your temper, came a quiet reminder that her conduct hadn't been flawless, either.

It was a long evening, with no further word from Angus. Ike returned the McClure children to the store, and left them in Libby's care as he climbed the stairs to check on Naomi. He was gone long enough for Opal to break the ice with David, though Frankie, Libby noted, held himself aloof. Libby found small tasks for the boy to do, and was finding him surprisingly cooperative when Ike came back downstairs and suggested Frankie fetch a fresh bucket of water for his mother, that she'd like to help out by starting supper for Libby and her father and David, if Libby didn't mind. Libby quickly agreed, and Frankie went out back to get the water. When he didn't come back downstairs, Libby assumed Naomi was talking with him about Uncle Willie. She prayed he wouldn't be further injured by the truth, which had been withheld from him for so long.

Ike went on his way shortly thereafter, saying he planned to stop by the blacksmith shop to pick up his tools before he started home. It was nearly closing time. With no customers to serve, Libby went out back where Opal was teaching David how to skip rope. She'd tied one end of the rope to a nail in the clothesline post and held the other end, turning it as David tried to match his steps to the rhythm of the swinging rope and Opal's singsong chant.

Libby darted a glance toward Angus's law office at the end of the alley and saw that the window was dark. Hoping he'd caught his horse without damage to the rig, she stood watching the children.

"Play with us, Lib," called David.

"You kin turn the other end," chimed Opal.

At the children's insistence, she joined in the fun. She was skipping rope as they turned it when Sugar trotted up the alley with Teddy close behind. The old dog pricked up his ears, barked, and ran at the swinging rope. Rope and dog tangling beneath her feet, Libby tripped and fell in the grass. Out of breath, flushed and laughing, she ruffled Sugar's ears and tried to hold on to her as the children resumed their play without her.

Teddy stood off to one side with his arm behind his back, looking on. "W-w-e-l l, looks like she's staying," he said, and loped on down the alley.

"Lib, make her stop!" David complained, when the dog broke free of Libby's arms and tried once again to catch the rope.

"Come on, Sugar. Let's go for a walk." Libby darted another glance toward Angus's office window as she strode past, but there was still no sign of life inside.

Curious about the house Mr. Gruben had mentioned being available, Libby turned up the street, past the Columbian, the jail, over the railroad tracks, and down Fisher Street. Delicious smells of supper cooking wafted on the evening air as she walked along, Sugar beside her.

She stopped near the edge of town in front of a small, deserted-looking yellow house. The paint was peeling from the clapboards, weeds had overtaken the lawn, and the backyard looked out on the railroad tracks. But it appeared to be weather-tight and was well shaded by lovely old trees. Thinking a coat of paint and some attention to the lawn would do wonders, Libby was about to head back to the store when Sugar startled a rabbit out of the tall weeds and tore after it.

Paying no heed to Libby's call, the old beagle bayed at full pitch as she followed the rabbit's zigzagging path over the neighbor's yard, around the next house, and into the grass skirting the familiar road Libby took into town after delivering the mail each day. She debated a moment whether to follow. It was the thought of having to make an explanation to Teddy should some mishap befall Sugar that sent her down the road after the dog.

She hurried along, charting the beagle's progress by keeping an eye on her brown-tipped tail moving through the roadside grasses. Slowly losing ground to the swifter rabbit, Sugar came out of the shallow ditch, up over the road, down into the ditch on the other side, and back again. At length she lost track of the rabbit altogether and dropped to the ground beside a fallen tree. The dog was still panting from her exertions when Libby caught up.

"Poor Sugar! You're too old for these games,"

Libby perched on the decaying log, watching the sun spill shades of deep reds and violets across the horizon as she waited for the aging beagle to catch her second wind. The subtle softening and muting of breathtaking hues turned her thoughts inward. Much like the sky, her life was ever shifting, ever changing. A day could be crowded, or deceptively lazy, and yet when it was finished and gone forever, she was further along in this business of life. Sometimes it took a month of days before she could see variation. Sometimes change struck with the drama of a thunderstorm rolling across the heavens. So it had been today.

Giving away what she was never meant to keep was not easy, for she had poured herself into the store. Not just in the arrangement of the place, but in overcoming obstacles on the path to enduring friendships. Yet with the bitter-sweet loss came an unexpected sense of completion at having made a hard choice. Completion and peace, and yes, even joy. Could she make Angus understand?

Libby fondled the beagle's ears and practiced words in her head. *The store was the channel God used to bring me here. It was a tool. If I were to hang on when He said to let go, I would be putting my faith in the tool instead of the Carpenter.*

Sugar whined and pricked her ears and looked down the road. Libby followed the old dog's gaze and saw a wagon leave town and come their way. It was too far away to make out the occupant. She sank once more into her reverie, thinking of the Carpenter and His endless supply of tools with which to shape His children. He knew her dream. If life was a lathe, then He knew best what lay inside her, and what chisels to use in the turning.

The sun was down, the sky the color of new wine by the time the wagon drew close enough for Libby to recognize the driver as Ike. He stopped the team as he drew even with her.

"So it's you." Curls tumbled over Ike's brow as he tipped his hat back. "From the edge of town, you looked like a prairie rose."

Libby returned his smile. "Very poetic. So tell me, what exactly *is* a prairie rose? A flower? Or a fungus that grows on a dead log?"

Ike chuckled, but left her question unanswered. "What brings ya out this way?"

"Sugar, on a rabbit chase. She's worn herself out."

Holding the lines loosely in his brown hand, he offered, "Want a lift back to town?"

"You're going the wrong way," Libby hedged, remembering the only other time she'd ridden with him and how, at the end of that day, he'd responded to Billy's teasing by saying he'd hire a buggy someday and show her he wasn't such a bad fellow with horses.

The hint of a smile lingering about his eyes made Libby think his thoughts might be running the same course. He proved her right, saying, "I reckon if I was to try real hard, I could keep this 'un right side up."

"That's kind of you, but I think we'll just walk."

"You been pretty kind yerself today, Lib. Naomi told me 'bout ya givin' up the store fer Frankie. She don't quite know what to make of it."

Ike's approval conjured another memory, this one of him kneeling beside her, his face shadowed by candlelight, the scent of rain clinging to his skin, on the night they'd found Frankie asleep under the counter. Libby's gaze flitted from his hands as they held the lines, to the shadowed indentations in his cheeks, to the softening of his mouth.

"Sure you don't want a ride?" His smile broadened as he added, "I'd say, 'Get in,' but the last feller who tried that is still picking off the ice slivers."

She flushed at the reminder of Angus. "Folks who stand in the window spying on other folks often misread what they see."

The shift in his smile was almost imperceptible. But like the sky, it had changed even as she looked on. "So what yer sayin' is Angus ain't altogether fallen from favor?"

Not wanting to mislead him, she said gently, "We need to come to an understanding, that's all."

"I reckon we jest did." He tipped his hat again, and averted his gaze, saying, "Good night, Libby. Don't keep that old dog out too late, now."

Though she'd been speaking of coming to an understanding with Angus, not Ike, Libby lifted her hand and replied, "We're heading back right now."

The sound of Ike's wagon rumbling away in the opposite direction awakened a lonesomeness within her. Libby quickened her steps, relieved when the creaking of wood and leather and plodding hooves grew too faint for her ears.

She thought once more of Angus, but gave up mapping out words, choosing instead to trust her feelings for him to God, to let Him paint in the brush strokes, if it was meant to be. You couldn't rush a sunset. You just let it unfold.

Hungry, Libby hurried toward the lights that glimmered from the windows of town. Her heart quickened as she passed Mr. Gruben's home, feeling the pleasure of that association and the fresh page it had presented for her writing ambitions. Getting to know him might prove to be an education in itself. She thought of Mrs. Gruben, too, and her love for books, and wondered if she'd be willing to share them with Naomi when she realized her quiet hunger for beautiful words. If her dream of more schooling was a while in materializing, maybe the three of them could get together from time to time. Like Mrs. Bee's Longfellow Club, discussing what they liked and what they learned. What was that Proverb? *"As Iron sharpens iron, so one man sharpens another."*

Women, too.

A light step carried Libby across the train tracks, past the jail and the Columbian, and on toward Willie Blue's. She was almost to the door when a dark shape separated from the shadows and called her name.

"Angus? Good faith! You startled me."

He gripped his hat in his hands. "David said you'd gone for a walk."

"I hope you haven't been waiting long," said Libby, testing the waters.

Shamefaced, he quipped, "A sentiment far too kind to be spent on an impatient fool. I'm sorry about this afternoon."

"I'm sorry, too."

He sighed, sounding tired all of a sudden. "Too much politics and no play has turned me into a bore. And it's still a long road to November, I'm afraid."

"You're anything but boring, Angus, and I'm in no hurry," said Libby.

His hand found hers in the shadows. "There'll be skating at the Columbian tomorrow night. Would you like to go?"

Libby tipped up her face and asked, "Are you their piano man?"

"Ladies' choice," he said, and asked with a smile, "Any requests?"

Time, she thought. Time to be who God meant her to be. Gently she asked, "Are you still upset about my passing the store along to Frankie?"

He searched her face for a long moment, and said, "You

were right, Libby. I overstepped my boundaries. Mr. Blue left it to you. It's yours to give away if you choose."

"You mean it?"

He nodded, his mouth tilting. "Give away your store, your home, all that you own. I won't say another word about it as long as you promise me one thing." At her questioning glance, he brought her hand to his lips. "Hold your heart in trust for me."